Millicent DeGroenfeld Rice

RICHARD SANDERS POLIN

 FriesenPress

One Printers Way
Altona, MB R0G 0B0
Canada

www.friesenpress.com

Copyright © 2025 by Richard Sanders Polin
First Edition — 2025

All rights reserved.

No part of this publication may be reproduced in any form, or by any means, electronic or mechanical, including photocopying, recording, or any information browsing, storage, or retrieval system, without permission in writing from FriesenPress.

ISBN
978-1-03-831312-6 (Hardcover)
978-1-03-831311-9 (Paperback)
978-1-03-831313-3 (eBook)

1. FICTION, NOIR

Distributed to the trade by The Ingram Book Company

To my children, SBP and EGP—my joy and my meaning
To JCS, found lost found lost

Table of Contents

Chapter 1: Writer's Block ... 1

Chapter 2: A) Libel B) Slander C) Both D) Neither ... 13

Chapter 3: Ginnifer Goodwin or Natalie Dormer ... 21

Chapter 4: Loser ... 35

Chapter 5: Le Petit Prince ... 45

Chapter 6: You Can't Say That on the Air ... 57

Chapter 7: Hipster Santa ... 69

Chapter 8: Lenny Bruce of Grunge ... 85

Chapter 9: The Etiquette of the Mosh ... 101

Chapter 10: Get Back ... 119

Chapter 11: You May Be Right, I May Be Crazy ... 129

Chapter 12: Sasquatch ... 141

Chapter 13: I Wanna Be Sedated ... 155

Chapter 14: The Addictive Lure of Infinitesimal Danger ... 163

Chapter 15: The Dutch Golden Age of Hallucinogenesis ... 175

Chapter 16: Don't Look Back in Anger ... 185

Chapter 17: Take the D Train ... 197

Chapter 18: Ruh Roh ... 209

Chapter 19: Backlash ... 229

Chapter 20: Subreddit/Horgan ... 241

Chapter 21: Our American Cousin ... 251

Chapter 22: Joey Ramone's Shorter Brother ... 259

Chapter 23: I Want It Now ... 267

Chapter 24: That Magic Feeling ... 277

Acknowledgments ... 281

Chapter 1:
Writer's Block

It was a throwaway song, what used to be known as a B-side. It was the tenth and final track for the last CD of a three-disc deal for an overmatched band hitched to an uninterested label. Not that his contractual obligations mattered much to Melvin "the Troll" Horgan. For Melvin, the completion of the composition signified not a vanquishing of crippling writers block but an opportunity to abandon his dingy flophouse for the familiar spoils of a six-month tour returning to a some-expenses-paid proper period of debauchery. Melvin spent his days asleep and his nights drunk or stoned when he could afford it, with strewn papers of discarded lyrics meandering in coffee cake cinnamon swirl patterns around his desk. There had been some semblance of order at one point. The promising candidates for the finale of the trilogy, created for Infinity Records by the creative genius behind Billy Goat's Gruff, loitered in a choice spot to the left of the remaining blue, black, and green ninety-nine-cent back-to-school Target notepads. Whereas the dead ends were haphazardly discarded amongst the PBR and Bud cans intermixed with pizza boxes and the occasional Old Granddad bottle. The sheer volume of the rejects now blended into the keeper pile like drippings of red paint absorbing into a bucket of white.

Weeks turned to months in the Ellington Motel, named graciously and respectfully after that dignified jazz icon by an admirer in segregated D.C. now morphed into an amalgam of probationers, castoffs, hideaways, and schizophrenics with sufficient income to stay off the streets for at least a week at a time. Melvin had landed here after he'd run out of money from his last tour, with just enough to manage the $140 weekly rent. To maximize vice spending, breakfast came from a big bag of bulk dry-roasted peanuts. Lunch was Top Ramen—chicken, pork, or beef in rotation. Dinner would consist of peanuts and ramen unless there were a few coins left over for Ledo's or Magruder's.

The Ellington entertained an itinerant clientele in a series of identical rooms only slightly larger than office cubicles. The largest inanimate was a souped-up cot pilfered from a Naval Yards military auction. The desk was only slightly bigger than a bedside table, wooden with one drawer only a shade or two off from the chafing wood floor meant to be covered by a rug. The chair was bingo parlor surplus and could have folded were it not for a kink in the collapsing mechanism. A sink provided free mixers when needed and occasionally oral hygiene until the complementary toothpaste samples from the last real hotel could no longer be coaxed to provide product. If there was a trash can, it was long past overwhelmed by the refuse, as the Ellington's rudimentary cleaning staff only handled turnovers.

This third CD was an act of futility. No fucking chance Infinity Records would extend. They had an obligation to release and promote one more tour, after which presumably Melvin and Billy Markwell would fade back into the underbelly of Portland or Seattle and try to survive on a percentage of the gross like they had back in the day. If any one of the suits knew his name or could pick his ugly face out of a mugshot, it was only because of the formal complaint by the DJ in Cleveland who had objected to Melvin's homophobic rhetoric when he was just having some fun, or the rumpus from the hotel manager after the tour finale at the Mayflower here in D.C., when they sicked the cops on the boys and Billy and Melvin spent the night in the joint and had to be bailed out the next day. That thing, he told the company lawyer, was just a misunderstanding with a hired escort. But even if he did produce his masterpiece in song number ten, the industry had shifted. Music that meant anything, or the replicas of said music that Melvin formulated, had surrendered to the dreck that was *American Idol* or *The Voice*. "Pretty people with pretty voices singing pretty little songs. Fucking meaningless," he would often mutter.

Melvin Horgan and Billy Markwell had started Billy Goat's Gruff as a garage band in High School in Sacramento. Billy and Melvin, friends since middle school, each from their own brand of dysfunctional home (two drunks, one disability scammer, and one deadbeat between the four putative parents), had a love of punk, and then grunge transformed them from a Plinko path tumbling towards options of service station attendant, petty crime tweaker, crooked security guard, or carny. To be fair, Billy fancied the music more than Melvin, but Melvin had ulterior motivation. Five-foot-five with craggy features and a bald spot already visible in late puberty, "the Troll" was such an accurate nickname that Melvin never seemed offended by it. No matter the negative connotation, he wore it. It was not like he was likely to be "Smiley" or "Mad Dog" or some cutesy reworking of his name, like "Melsie" or "Horgs." He was "the Troll," and as "the Troll," he reasoned that virginity was his calling without lowering his measly physical or moral standards or getting a real high-paying job and becoming a "solid citizen," which seemed even less appealing. Melvin's instincts suggested his simplest road to fornication involved the subconscious disinhibition of the groupie.

About halfway through their senior year at Luther Burbank High, Melvin and Billy, already both self-imposed and community-driven social exiles, formulated a rock-paper-scissors election to "borrow" an ancient El Camino owned by Billy's cousin Lester, doing a stretch for check fraud, and headed north to Seattle, where Nirvana had already popped. They ran out of gas money outside of Portland and settled in Old Town, making a buck here and there bussing tables or washing dishes while working on their craft. Billy toiled harder, bartering his services at the Star Theater in exchange for the occasional guitar lesson with the owner and consequential sub-minimum-wage earnings. Try as he might, Melvin could never gain proficiency on any instrument north of the tambourine, severely limiting the range of their offerings as a duo.

They acquired a drummer unconventionally on a rainy April evening when they went outside to take a drag and found a mixed-race brute with a Mohawk pulling the hubcaps off the El Camino with his bare hands. The scoundrel turned out to be a simple-minded VOC school truant who likely would have hospitalized them both on the public dime had Melvin not demonstrated the great sense to offer the giant a seat in the band.

Lloyd Atlas, who went by "Tiny," had only the most rudimentary musical sense or drumming skills, but that seemed to match the deconstructed tunes Melvin was writing, with their clever, belligerent lyrics and gaunt rhythms.

The first drums they acquired for Tiny, used Pearl kits appropriated from backstage at Dante's and cobbled together, shattered under Tiny's fury. They bought a used Roland kit, which proved impenetrable, and started playing free shows in small Eastside bars on Wednesday and Thursday nights.

Small free shows morphed into regular gigs at bigger venues, five dollars a head and a percentage of the gross. Ramen noodles upgraded to Kraft Dinner, Totino's to Red Baron. Billy Goat's Gruff got a following; it was hardly a musically sophisticated one. They covered some punk tunes and butchered Nirvana, while Melvin introduced new material, mostly knocking off the Ramones with a slower cadence and more self-defeating, mad-at-the-world lyrics.

The boys apprenticed like this for about two years, scratching out enough for a shared one-bedroom flat within walking distance of about a half dozen clubs with a Ranier keg and a reasonably priced dealer named Texas Jim, who knew when to push the pure stuff and when to unload the trimming crap for a song.

Talent is discovered organically. Mistakes occur uniquely via some combination of serendipity, ignorance, incompetence, and nepotism. On a Wednesday night in April of 2004, the boys were the second of four bands appearing at the Doug Fir Lounge in Portland, a local landmark with a four-hundred-patron retro venue populated by local bands during the week and independent acts on budget tours on the weekends. On this Wednesday evening, Musty Snodgrass was in Portland, to check out a local band called Tekken batting cleanup in the show. Musty's background was folk and bluegrass with passing competence in adult contemporary. In the '60s, he'd haunted Tin Pan Alley and the Village clubs, with seven or eight competitors thick as thieves all hunting the next Dylan, but more or less gabbing critiques too loud for politesse during the performances of strained, self-important, anti-war anthems. Like every shlock purports to be writing the Great American Novel to rival Finn, every open-mike performance offered a laughable sequel to "Blowing in the Wind." But protest folk died with the withdrawal, and bluegrass was never commercial. Infinity was hardly positioned for disco or heavy metal, but they were able to pivot slightly, looking for an Andrew Gold or Leo Sayer clone who could occasionally grasp at the Top 40.

But times changed, and with a new boss, the label shifted towards hip hop and grunge without the ground game to compete with the major labels. On this Wednesday, sixty-year-old Musty, in a Native American beaded jacket and a Portuguese fisherman's cap, was a talent scout for the new grunge/alternative division of Infinity Records, a lesser "major label" looking to expand into modern music.

Musty meandered in and out of the venue, taking notes and acclimating himself to what he considered a lesser art form than what he was accustomed to. As it turned out, he was in the back of the auditorium when Billy Goat's Gruff played their finest work to date, a Melvin Horgan original called "Dusty Heaves," written about a mongrel who occasionally crashed in their apartment and downed about half a batch of hash brownies and spent the rest of the night either flatulent or regurgitating and eating the vomitus.

By this time, the band had a steady loyal following of regulars who knew the setlists and were prepared for the only song in rock and roll history to start with "This fucking mutt."

> *This fucking mutt lives out in the alley*
> *Goat lets him in whenever it rains*
> *Who the hell knew he could jump on the counter*
> *Eat up my stash and fry his brains*

> *Dusty spins and heaves some more*
> *Don't eat the chunks up off the floor*

The crowd was thoroughly engaged, hands in the air and singing along with the refrain, which impressed the hell out of Musty Snodgrass. The next song was a rudimentary reworking of Alice in Chains' "Angry Chair," which the audience also appreciated, but Musty incorrectly thought it was an original. He made a few phone calls, and that night, he signed Billy Goat's Gruff to a three-CD deal under the Infinity label. Infinity added a session bass player named Bebe Mustang to the sessions and then included him on tour both to mellow the sound (and Bebe could mellow Steven Wright) and give the label eyes on the band.

The first CD got modest play and recognition on college stations, and Billy Goat's Gruff went on a national tour supporting Interpol initially with a secondary tour headlining smaller venues. The second CD had one minor hit—"Froggy Went a Snortin'"—and bought them an appearance on *Letterman* and a middling *Rolling Stone* review, but the ensuing tour as a headliner was truncated and downsized due to sagging attendance and download rates, which were frankly disappointing.

So, after their tour ended, Melvin was resigned to the fact that one more Infinity rodeo would be their last, unless he could conjure some magic. He disappeared into D.C., keeping email contact with Billy only to avoid ire from their manager, agent, and handlers and formulate at his own pace. Only problem was, six months in, there was no magic, just a collection of tripe guaranteeing an anticlimactic fail.

Song number one was "Tiger Drag," as every Billy Goat's Gruff CD was highlighted by a song teaming animals and drugs. It was their calling card. It wasn't going to get anyone on *Letterman,* even if Jimi Hendrix emerged from his crypt to front it. "Money Grab" was a diss on other NW bands who had gone corporate and mainstream. "Claudette Wants Flowers" was a failed attempt to go corporate and mainstream. "Claudette" was the closest thing Melvin had ever written to a love ballad. "Lola's Room" was an homage to a Portland hall where they had played their first real gig. "Thumbsucker" was interesting but so honestly self-loathing that Melvin knew he could never play it live. "Fuck Charles Goren" was pulled from the reject pile under a pizza box when the writer's block took hold to feign a little progress. The last three writer's block songs—"Russian Roulette," "Fire in the Hole," and "Bumbershoot 2008"—were seven to nine, with "Bumbershoot 2008" just consisting of Melvin yelling over and over again some iteration of "Who will give a BJ for a three-day pass." And then number ten and nothing, literally nothing, came to mind as if Melvin didn't really want to finish the damned thing.

The eventual inspiration for song number ten, if you could call disinterestedly glancing at page three of the Metro Section of a three-day-old copy of the *Washington Post* while squatting in the bathroom of a Popeye's in Suitland the morning after a bender an inspiration, was an eight-line article/obituary about a thirty-three-year-old stripper who had been found dead by a Girl Scout on an outing with her troop. She'd slit her wrists in the outhouse adjacent to the pachyderm enclosure at the National Zoo. It was neither the circumstances of the victim nor the conveyance of her death plot that triggered song number ten. It was, instead, the name of the dead girl. Her name was Millicent DeGroenfeld Rice, which seemed so incongruous with her station of life and details of death that Melvin wrote the name down on his arm and hurried back to his room to conceive a post-punk anthem/biopic that he called "Millicent DeGroenfeld Rice."

Before "Millicent," song number ten had gone through any number of aborted formulations. As the writer's block festered, the number of abominations increased, and the number of lines written until futility ensued decreased logarithmically. Songs about beautiful women who sneered at him on the street, songs about Russian mobsters at strip clubs in Seattle, songs about the guy selling bootlegged Madonna CDs in Chinatown, songs about masturbating in the alley behind a laundromat in Cincinnati on tour—all wound up crumpled on the pizza box/beer can side of the room.

But "Millicent DeGroenfeld Rice" emerged rather quickly. Like most of Melvin's work, it was derivative: Jim Carroll Band, "People Who Died." Twelve people who died. Twelve reasons why a stripper with a librarian name would slice her wrists in the bathroom of a zoo. Somehow, the writer's block just evaporated, melted away. The refrain came first:

> *Millicent DeGroenfeld Rice, come on and make another slice*
> *Friday night pole dance, Saturday found with your blood coagulating*
> *by a Girl Scout in an outhouse at the zoo*

The stanzas came a bit slower, but the whole process lasted barely six hours.

> *Did your four-year-old die of juvenile sarcoma?*
> *Did Crohn's disease find you shitting through a stoma?*
> *Did your high school sweetheart find you dancing in the pit?*
> *Were you down ten grand on smack and threatened by a syndicate?*

> *Did your stepdad fuck you in the ass while mama's brains were fried on Xanax?*
> *Did a senator finger you in the VIP and then deny it with a grin?*
> *Was your fourth application to Starbucks returned in the mail?*
> *Or did the pimply-faced manager demand a blow*
> *job which he spuged on lips and chin?*

Richard Sanders Polin

Did your psycho cop boyfriend smack you for talking to the postman?
Did your club combat declining sales by forcing you to screw a horse?
Off your meds, did visions dare you to burn down the national zoo
or did the voices finally convince you the world was better off without you?

Melvin phoned Billy after finishing whatever he had created. It was a short conversation; it had to be on a pay-by-the-minute plan with four minutes remaining on his contract. "Goat, I'm finished. Send money. I need to come home."

Billy met him at the airport, wearing his Doug Christie T-shirt. As freshmen, Melvin had snuck them into a Kings game and lifted the shirt from the stadium store when he said he was heading to the john at halftime.

Melvin, in response, was plastered. He had gotten a fifty-dollar security deposit back from the Ellington and spent most of it on little bottles of Jack. They finally cut him off over the Rockies, but he was still staggering when the plane landed and kept trying to wander through the orderly disembarkation line, trying to shove past businessmen and fathers before getting butt-blocked by a distinguished bald man wearing a bright-green sports coat. From there, he sat back down and fell asleep again until awakened by 26A wanting to get off the plane.

Billy tried to hug his partner as he emerged from security. Hordes of happy passengers with pastel signs welcomed Ali back from France or Merle home from an overseas tour or brave hairless mee-maw from cancer treatments at the NIH. Melvin waved his friend away but handed over an overstuffed backpack. Melvin's stench was horrific, with different competing odors from every orifice. Urea from a bladder accident over Montana overwhelmed fecal methane until he opened his mouth and crusted tomato sauce emesis from the night before emerged. Melvin was holding his pants up from the pockets, and his face was gaunt. He may have been the only adult in the airport with a single-digit BMI. Once they arrived at the El Camino, Melvin finally looked up at Billy and whispered, "I know, Goat. I will eat tomorrow. But I just need to get some sleep, man."

They'd kept the same shithole apartment decorated with trash and paraphernalia. When Melvin woke up the next afternoon, it was in the same partitioned corner of the one bedroom he'd left fifteen months before, when tour two had begun. Same vinyl EP of Dusty Heaves next to the Fading Terry

Nunn "Metro" era poster, with the black tips of her straight blond hair, huge black eyes staring out in spunk-promoting wistful longing, next to a Roseland poster for a Nirvana show Melvin had pocketed after opening for Hockey opening for Modest Mouse (the venue had wanted a second intermission to push booze sales). Isaac Brock wouldn't come onstage until ten thirty earliest. Now that's a rockstar.

Melvin rummaged the kitchen for four-o'clock breakfast and settled on WinCo brand corn pops with two-days-expired chocolate milk served in what appeared to be a Toys "R" Us giveaway Ninja Turtles big-boy bowl. He downed one serving in the kitchen and refilled before joining Billy in the common area, which was really just a TV nook with a sofa. Billy was examining the lyrics for Melvin's ten chosen compositions. He was tapping his pen in rhythm, making notes, when Melvin announced his presence with loud cereal smacking.

Billy Markwell wasn't a troll. In fact, if not for what could best be explained psychologically as sympathy hygienic devaluation, he might have been an attractive man. Instead, with oil-slicked hair born of neglect rather than sculpting, shaggier than Shaggy's beard, adult acne from lack of cleansing, and a single tattoo of a sea monster, which highlighted rather than concealed an incipient leatherneck, he seemed to be deliberately drifting down into the proximity of his partner's 1.5.

"Oh hey, Troll. Just getting a head start while you slept it off. Sing me a song or two. It's damn good to be back working again." Billy had a Rainier can on the table and a third of a bag of Smart Pop. There was a little white residue subtly visible on the beer can.

Melvin went back to the kitchen and searched for another can but came back to the table empty-handed and sore. "You hate everything? I pretty much hate everything."

"I like 'Tiger Drag.' 'Claudette Wants Flowers' might play. It's different for us, I'll give you that. I can't wait to see you sing 'Bumbershoot.' Oh yeah, who the fuck is Charles Goren?"

"Bridge, dude. Don't you read the fucking paper?"

"Guess not. Final question. What's a 'Millicent DeGroenfeld Rice'?"

"Dead stripper. Killed herself. Saw her name in the paper. You got another beer, Goat?"

"No more beer. Wait a second. So, a girl kills herself. A real person who killed herself? And we're gonna record a song about her?"

"Got any cash? Anyway, why the fuck you care? What's it to you?"

"It's a motherfucking human being, Melvin. Brother, sister, parents, boyfriend."

"So? It's just a goddamned name. I don't give a fuck. Rice rhymed with 'slice.' Fuck if I care. Look, it ain't as if anyone's gonna understand the lyrics when I sing 'em. I mean, maybe some of the refrain, but the girl's name? Fuck no. The verses? Fuck no. You think we're gonna publish the lyrics? Fuck no. No one is going to know we wrote a song about a dead stripper. You remember our last tour. Dozens of friends and relations, and that's about it. Nobody protests ghosts. No one knows who the fuck we are, so there's no reason for a bunch of shrill bitches with signs outside the arena. Last thing I need. Look, took me months just to get enough material to finish this bitch. Let's just get back in the fucking studio, back on the fucking road."

"We're all going to hell."

"I've been well on my way since I met you, brother. Not really sure a dead stripper's gonna have much influence on my trajectory."

"My God, Melvin. This is our last shot. This disc don't pop, no more contract. I don't wanna go back on the streets."

"Us, pop? Good goddamned luck. We're not gonna pop. I suck, you suck, Tiny sucks. Bebe, Bebe's not one of us, and he half sucks. We got fucking lucky. These bastards didn't know dick about our scene. They signed us because they didn't have Nirvana or Pearl Jam or Nine Inch or Alice or STP. They scattershot and fucked up, landed us and a bunch of other dead ends. We're a dead end. We could come up with *Nevermind* Two. They wouldn't promote it, wouldn't understand it, wouldn't appreciate it. As it is, you've read the stuff I wrote. It's crap. There's nothing redeeming or memorable about even one of the ten. It's a load of dreck."

"It's not that bad, Troll. I like 'Claudette' a lot. It's different for us. 'Tiger Drag' will be okay. I even have a thought or two for arranging the dead stripper song. It's not that bad."

Melvin looked away from his friend, right at the Rainier can. He ran his fingers through his knotted morning hair, trying to force the mat down on his bald spot. "You just have a five? Could really use a beer. Expectations aren't healthy, Goat. Let's just get back out there. Maybe savor it. We'll be back home for good soon enough. I really think we can do better. Tiny's been taking lessons. I talked to the A&R man. They think they can get us some play. They also already have a name for the CD. Hope you didn't have your heart set on anything else."

"They fucking named our CD before we started recording or know the music? That's the most corporate shit I've ever heard. Already named the damn album?"

"*Space Needle Pricks!*"

Melvin had borrowed one of Billy's shirts as every one of his required fumigation. It was two sizes too big, such that when Melvin raised his arms to produce an air of exasperation, all you could see were the sleeves as he replied, "*Space Needle Pricks*? What kind of bullshit name is *Space Needle Pricks*."

"I think they want the world to think we're from Seattle."

"Jesus Christ. Any of those idiots know we're not from Seattle." Melvin furrowed his brow and circled twice around the room, contemplating the alternatives of a complaint to management or an adult temper tantrum, which would generally involve slashing the tires of a random Lexus or Mercedes.

"Whatever. *Space Needle Pricks*. Let the cunts call it what they want. Do we get to tour? Do we get a festival? Do we get our per fucking per diem?" Melvin looked down at borrowed pajama pants with the frayed strings tightened as much as he could muster. Still he had to pull them up once a minute.

"I haven't weighed this little since I was twelve. It'll be okay, Goat. Tour ends and we come back to Portland with Tiny. Get back to what we do." Billy looked down on Melvin with pleading eyes, connoting a hope Melvin had long since abandoned.

"Goat, you're worried because you got a taste on the road for that fucking five-dollar coffee. So here's what I'm gonna do. I'll get you a Starbucks gift card. Twenty a week, rest of our lives, if I have to suck dick to get it. Or even better, what about I take it in the ass, trick a Benjamin. Go buy yourself one of those home machines, roaster or whatever, and you can avoid having to go into those bourgeois shitholes and listen to their fucking Kenny G and Carly Simon. That work for you?" Billy Markwell realized this was a brotherhood forged in negativity, and his modest goals represented a divergence from their implied covenant.

"Fuck you, Troll. I'll pay for my own fucking coffee. Just take the motherfucking tour seriously. Practice this time. When Tiny has the opportunity to work with us, he can play a little. We aren't half bad."

"Seriously. Don't I take everything seriously. Stick with me, kid. We're gonna be big stars."

* * *

Melvin conjured up $4.50 from seat cushions and pants pockets with the final two bills retrieved from the inner lining of a red Lincoln High hoody he had swiped and wore through the left pocket. There was a pen in there as well from a State Farm Insurance agent, probably the mom of the prior owner. He swore as he realized it had splotched his hand with bleeding ink and threw it outside into the alley, wiping his hand on some wet leaves as a washcloth. There was a drizzly haze at midday, small puddles situated like land mines along ruts in the neglected alley. A kick-starter pilgrimage to the Plaid Pantry comprised three blocks and two hacking spells with one car alarm triggered. You took your life in your hands in Southeast D.C., just going to the 7-Eleven for a PBR. It was good to be home.

Chapter 2:
A) Libel B) Slander C) Both D) Neither

Infinity Records' corporate offices started out in the Brill Building, like so many other labels, and moved into swankier and larger space as their stable branched into rock and roll and R&B in the '80s and alternative and grunge in the '90s. The current offices were situated in two floors of the 560 Broadway Building in Lower Manhattan.

Chief Legal Counsel Roger Smith stroked his Princeton Ring and gazed around at the one Warhol Double Elvis behind the CEO's desk and the ten nobodies placed in orderly procession around the impressive office. A glass obelisk sparkled on the desk next to ebony figurines of a piano player in overalls and a tribesman riding a rhinoceros. Roger Smith had joined the company before the expansion and was a leftover from the old guard. Roger was in his early fifties and dressed as a Manhattan businessman should dress. His hair was thinning but well kept, and he had the look of someone who played tennis on Saturdays but not too seriously, and golf on Sundays with a cart and without scruples. It was a one-day-a-week exercise physique.

After a few minutes and a few answered emails, the boss walked in. Tee Nash had been brought in as CEO/chairman of Infinity in 2002. Tee was better known as Mysterious T from a moderately successful rap career and subsequently for a litany of failed relationships with initially B- and now C-level starlets, as well as an ongoing feud with Bam Bam Bowser, his former manager and now CEO of rival Dreadlocks Records.

Tee Nash emerged from the side door, followed by Vanity and Apollonia or whatever the hell they were known by in this hip hop multiverse. Roger Smith knew the dance. There would be some small talk, perhaps post-coital, perhaps not with the girls, and Nash would look at some sales and download data. Smith would be ignored at this juncture. Then he would go through and address each of twenty to thirty sign-me tabs and make a joke about suits, addressed to the girls. "Girls, how many suits does it take to polish a floor? Only one if you can convince him it's somebody's ass." "Girls, how many suits does it take to change a tire? Thirteen. Twelve to issue statements of plausible deniability and lack of causation and shit, and the one with a brain to calling the fucking AAA."

And so, Roger would laugh. Not too loud. A laugh of contempt but well-disguised contempt. Then the girls would produce a laugh of well-disguised ennui. Then Tee Nash would laugh, a fake laugh but recognizable: Axel Foley "banana-in-the-tailpipe" laugh one day, Vincent Price laughing in Thriller the next, a high-pitched nervous Michael Jackson on a Japanese talk show asked about "Never-rand," a Barney Rubble staccato cackle punctuated by a Fred Flintstone "Oh, boy." Just so you knew who was in charge, when Tee's laugh ended, the girls' laugh ended, and Roger Smith's laugh ended, then you got to work.

This was a cloudy Thursday in November in New York, the last Thursday before Thanksgiving, when attention spans were already fading in anticipation of six of nine days off come the weekend. With the holiday approaching and sales slow but corporate nerves prepared for the holiday rush, Tee Nash wanted to sail though his morning huddle and lose track of time. Roger Smith was used to short attention spans. Marvin Woodover, the founder's son, had a short attention span. His successor, Blaine McCormick, who steered the company into alternative and grunge for long enough to acquire dead weight like Billy Goat's Gruff, had limited attention. And with Tee Nash, he had about twenty seconds and/or four questions, whichever came first, to grab Tee Nash or lose him into Vanity's tits for the remainder of their session.

"Sir, I have only one line item for discussion this morning, listed on your schedule as a meeting with Melvin 'the Troll' Horgan of Billy Goat's Gruff. Sir, Billy Goat's Gruff is part of our small alternative/grunge effort, and Mr. Horgan wrote a song called 'Millicent DeGroenfeld Rice,' about a stripper who commits suicide. Legal felt there was potential exposure. A&R thought they could just change the lyric, but the writer appealed, and consensus was best for you to talk to Mr. Horgan and have final say. He's—how do you put it—a bit socially awkward and defiant of authority. We thought coming from a fellow artist might be more conducive to a resolution."

"Song about a dead hoe? What's the problem with that? Half my songs about hoes. Dead hoes, live hoes, cheating hoes, messed-up hoes. You know why, Mr. Smith? Because hoes sell. Every dumbass suburban, gangsta wannabe wants to hear songs about hoes. Dumbass hoes, too. Write a song about fucking hoes, it's gonna sell."

"Technically, sir, the dead woman was a stripper, as opposed to a prostitute."

"I heard you, suit." Here, his boss switched momentarily to his condescending Axel Foley "banana-in-the-tailpipe" affectation. "I know the difference between a stripper and a prostitute. On the street, sir. Stripper, prostitute, junkie, they's all hoes, and all hoes sell. Can't blame this Troll for trying to sell."

"Sir, with all due respect. There's a difference. Maybe a subtle one, but the difference between a generic, unnamed 'hoe' and a specific, named non-celebrity individual thoroughly denigrated is significant and potentially actionable if the family is offended."

"Let me see the lyric sheet. Well, first of all, this is bullshit. Stripper named Millicent? No stripper I ever known named Millicent."

"Understood, sir, but apparently that was the young lady's real name as well as her stage name, at least at some establishments. She worked at several clubs in D.C. and killed herself last fall, just as the song reports."

Tee Nash took some time and peered over the lyrics and seemed to re-read them several times with alternate expressions of pain and confusion. "Good Lord, there are some awful technical terms in this motherfuck. Some crazy-ass lyrics. Makes you nostalgic for 'Love, Love Me Do.'"

"That being said, sir, the lyrics will get out, and if there is a song speculating about the young woman being a victim of incest or committing bestiality, an angry relative may come after the label. The second we copyright, it's entirely our responsibility."

"Is this Billy Goat's Gruff an asset? I've never heard of them."

"No, sir. One tour as an opening act, shortened tour as a headliner with poor attendance. Two songs on the college charts, one at twenty-eight, another peaked at seventeen. CD sales and download rates rather pedestrian.

Essentially, revenue neutral. They signed a low-guarantee, three-disc deal, which ends with this disc, and between the fact that we're phasing out their division, and the fact that frankly they represent a corporate misinterpretation of the market, they will be released after we fulfill our contractual obligation to produce and promote."

"Well, let's get this over with. I have other matters to attend to." He gazed off in the general direction of his harem. "But do me a favor, Brother Smith, and provide me an explanation of why a stripper name in a song by a bunch of loser nobodies should occupy my time."

"Well, frankly, sir, legal was prepared simply to give a blanket disapproval, but contractually, there is an appeals process, and all grievances technically can be arbitrated internally up to the CEO. It's just that this never happens. Give him a minute, throw him out, and feel free to move onto your"—here, Roger paused for affect—"more pressing issues."

The main office door opened, and a wee crag of a man was shown in by a more traditional secretary than the two personal assistants. Melvin "the Troll" Horgan might have been the only man in New York City on a late November morning—who did not live under a bridge—who was wearing flip-flops. This isn't to say Melvin could not have been easily taken for a man living under a bridge, or a rock or in a cave for that matter. Tattered jeans can be tattered jeans or can be strategically and fashionably altered for artistic or stylistic purposes. Melvin's remnants had no designer affectations. They were midway between cutoffs and pants, as if they had been discarded by a younger even more destitute tramp and then worn on a two-week hike down the Appalachian trail during the rainy season. His T-shirt was a faded red/pink—which had bled, perhaps, in its first and only sad trip through the washer on an inappropriate warm setting—and said in big born-white-now-slightly-pink letters "I Abrams Scrap Metal." There were microscopic rips in the back of the shirt. Years of accumulated sweat had created a precipitated crust in the cotton under the armpits so dense, you could hear it crackle if you rubbed it between your fingers, one of Melvin's nervous habits. He completed the ensemble with a royal-blue hoody with a busted zipper and one torn sleeve.

Melvin Horgan shuffled in, head down, displaying his considerable bald spot. Melvin glanced around the room once or twice during his procession to the inquisitor's chair with a look that his minimal capacity for expression could have represented awe or angst. One of the girls may have laughed or coughed or something. It was hard to predict what effect his craggy mug would have on normals. Melvin had tried to beautify himself once. He'd tried to grow long, flowing glam hair but only succeeded in creating a more secluded habitat for the heartiest of his lice. His best feature was his eyes, which were a steely blue and expressive but counterbalanced by a touch of hypotelorism. A prominent brow shielded them, which was a useful trait if only for an antisocial.

Melvin took his seat and glanced up at the double Elvis, before looking back down.

"Brother Horgan. Tee Nash, sir. Welcome to corporate. You like that Elvis/Elvis. Predates me here, Brother Horgan. This here record label's been here a good, long time. You and I both weren't welcome here first forty years. Americana label. Folk, jazz, American modern classical. Nothing avant-garde, brother. No lyrical freedom, like what's in this song of yours. Moon in June, peace and love. Wholesome white boys in matching turtlenecks. May I ask you why they call you 'the Troll?'"

Heretofore, Melvin had been head-down in his large red leather chair. Upon this question, Melvin looked up and stared for about a second at Tee Nash, and then at Roger Smith, and just barely at the women, and gave a shrug of the head and a hand gesture and resumed looking down at about a sixty-degree angle, which appeared to be his comfort zone.

"Well, I can see it. I can see it but a bit disparaging all the same. Brother Horgan, tell me about why you're here. This song about the Rice girl. Interesting. Broad diction. Words I ain't ever heard in a song, sir."

"Whaddya mean?"

"Crohn's disease. Awful technical, Brother Horgan. You have a medical background? Something you did before your musical career?"

"Nah. Just the internet. Can find all kinds of shit on your phone."

"'Spuged.' Not sure I know that term."

"Sure you can figure it out. You're smart."

"You know who I am, Brother Horgan."

"Yeah. Suit in charge."

"Brother Horgan, I do indeed wear a suit, but I certainly do not consider myself a suit. This gentleman's a suit." Tee Nash pointed at Roger Smith, who took the jab squarely on the jaw but didn't flinch. "I am a performer like you, elevated into an administrative position but more a performer than an executive."

"Yeah, sure."

"Tell me about the girl. What do you know about her?"

"Just what I told the suits. Hung over in a john and saw this in a paper. Girl offed herself. Name struck me. Wrote a song. Just the name, really."

"Don't know her?"

"Met plenty of strippers. Never met a fucking Millicent."

"True that, Brother Horgan. Never met one either. Suits think this song is insensitive. Might get Infinity Records sued. Can you see that?"

"Yeah. Look, that's how I wrote it, and that's how I think it's best. If I need to, just let me know how much I have to change the name for you suits, and I'll change the fucking name. Doesn't really matter, just like it how it is."

"Brother Horgan, didn't you listen to me, sir? I'm not a suit. Ever hear the song 'Ram Bam'?"

"No."

"Well, that's a shame. Some of my best work, Brother Horgan. Let me preface: You aware of a cat named Bam Bam Bowser?"

"Maybe heard the name."

"Colleague of mine. Not particularly close. Had a girl named Lulu, delicious she was. Here's a bit of a song I wrote." Tee Nash loosened his tie.

Roger Smith dipped his head and looked out the window. His boss was about to adjudicate based upon rap lyrics again. He tried to tune out and formulate believable resume embellishments, but Tee was too damned loud.

> *"Ride a cock horse named Mysterious Tee*
> *I fucked this bitch Lulu and I worry 'bout her sanity*
> *Twelve years a slave with a faggot in her bed*
> *Bam Bam don't want Pebbles, but he'll suck off Fred."*

"You like that, Brother Horgan?"

"It's okay."

"Yes, okay indeed. My label called me in for a meeting like this. Insisted I change the girl's name . . . the dick licker's name. Worried about slander and shit. You know what I said?"

"Nah."

"First Amendment, motherfuckers. That's what I said, and that shit went out, convinced them wouldn't be no lawsuits, and you know what happened?"

"What happened?"

Tee Nash pulled up his silk shirt to show a scar in his lower abdomen. "This shit happened. Bam Bam didn't much like being called a fag or me insinuating I rammed his woman. In my world, weren't no libel or slander. Now in this case, some old auntie or ex. Might even have beat her, like you insinuating. Might take offense at this young girl's name being made light of. You see the dilemma. I'm all for First Amendment, freedom of speech, Brother Horgan. I'm on your side, spiritually. But if they come, they ain't coming after you. They coming to the bank, and I'm the bank. They coming to get paid."

"I just want to get my shit recorded, preferably the way I wrote it, and get back on tour, back to making money."

"Exactly. Okay, Brother Horgan. You have my word I will treat this matter seriously. You go into the studio and finish your other lovely pieces of genius and let me worry about Millicent here. Not a suit. Have to think like a suit sometimes but not a suit."

Melvin rose and turned to leave, avoiding eye contact, but about two steps away, he turned halfway back towards Tee Nash and, head still down, said, "Hey, you actually fuck this Lulu."

"Nah. Met her just the once. Nice eyes."

Melvin paused again and once more hesitated. Roger internally smoldered, calculating regrets. There was the rejection by Geffen. There was his chickenshit cowardice when he should have gotten on a plane and cold called every studio in LA after graduating Phi Delta Phi at Columbia.

"Distinction. Your song is actually a lie. You ain't been with Lulu, and this Bam Bam may actually not eat cock. My song's not a lie. Millicent did die. Unless the newspaper fucked up, girl did kill herself. And I offer theories. Never said she got fucked by a horse. Bring it up as a possibility. You done

19

slander, to be true. My only refrain is truth; rest is hypothesis, possibility, not accusation."

"Not sure that discrepancy is exculpatory. You know what that means, Brother Horgan?"

"Yeah, I ain't stupid. Pass it by Dick Chaney over there. After all, he's the suit."

"Thank you, Brother Horgan. I told you I would."

And with that, Melvin put his hands in pocket and flip-flopped out into the hall and perhaps down under a bridge, or if not under a bridge, into some Lower East Side dive if the label gave him a per diem for this trip.

Roger Smith had purposely avoided the interplay between this insignificant speck of the Infinity universe and what he considered his insignificant boss. In fact, he had kept his chair slightly tilted towards Tee Nash to avoid any eye contact with Horgan, although there was no real reason to have done so. Once the Troll had left the room, Smith turned to Tee Nash. "Sir, can I send this up to A&R requesting a rewrite? I suggest Millicent is off limits, DeGroenfeld or any name anywhere similar also needs changing, and Rice can have a homonym. Or do you just want the entire song deleted?"

"Thinking, suit. We got a PI, right. Maybe's nothing to worry about. Investigate this Millicent. Identify the liability. Then we make a decision. Don't like censorship, suit. Actually prefer I got cut and sang my song the way I wanted to. Make it happen."

Roger Smith sighed and, seeing Vanity and Apollonia engulf the boss, walked down the hall to his office to start the inane and meaningless process of investigating a dead stripper.

Chapter 3:
Ginnifer Goodwin or Natalie Dormer

Like every corporate lawyer for a studio or record label, Roger Smith had two private investigators on speed dial. There is the bulldog you call when you need to get your major talent exonerated. When you need to discredit an accuser or figure out a method to provide reasonable doubt to exonerate one of your cash cows, you call your fixer. When you want obvious, fast, and cheap investigations without agenda or artifice, you've got your workhorse.

Dane Griffin was his workhorse who would work quickly, answer the questions posed to a reasonable degree of certainty, and move on to his next assignment, staking out some Manhattanite and their personal secretary.

Dane Griffin's report on "Millicent DeGroenfeld Rice" was to be fair, spot-on, accurate, and concise. It was perfect for the short attention span of Tee Nash. Roger Smith was satisfied. Happy clients begat more business. The report read:

> *Millicent DeGroenfeld Rice*
>
> *Born 9/7/77, Died 4/21/11*
>
> *Mother Susan DeGroenfeld Rice born 1956, died 2006*
>
> *Father Rusty Mueller Born 1953, died 1992*
>
> *No siblings or half-siblings*
>
> *All four grandparents diseased*
>
> *Both Susan Rice and Rusty Mueller only children*

> *Millicent DeGroenfeld Rice lived Dublin, Ohio, 1978–1997, New Orleans, Louisiana, 1997–2000, Washington, D.C., 2000–2010. No dependents, no progeny, never married, no evidence of co-signing on dwellings. Sole beneficiary of mother's will. Died interstate with no tangible assets. No parties claimed or sought any such assets.*
>
> *Conclusion: No reason to believe or presume any first-degree relative or romantic interest would have an actionable claim against Infinity Records.*

Now, Dane Griffin's report would almost certainly have resulted in permission for Billy Goat's Gruff to proceed and record "Millicent DeGroenfeld Rice" as the final track on *Space Needle Pricks*. If his investigative mind wondered for a second as Melvin Horgan's did that morning in a bathroom in Suitland as to why a stripper was named Millicent DeGroenfeld Rice, he dismissed the notion as tangential. While neither Dane nor Melvin had any way of knowing how Millicent came to be a peeler, only Melvin pondered further the mechanism of her demise.

Most strippers have names equivalent in scope and syllables to a Brazilian footballer. Coming out on the Lollipop stage is "Angel!"—"Angel," not Angel Monica Suarez—"Princess," "Lelanee," "Velvet." We don't expect Millicents. We barely expect Sarahs or Julies. Even if we strip away the fake pole names, the actual given names of strippers should be Mary Jo Murtaugh or Emily Sue Johnson or Angie Ellis or something eminently brown-bag suggesting—if only in a mainstream media, stereotypical kind of way—an upbringing involving the trappings of a poor, white rearing by poor but strict, Bible-fearing but abusive parents in small town Missouri or West Virginia.

But let us assume for a second that in the movie version of *Millicent DeGroenfeld Rice*, there would be no need for Amy Adams or Brie Larson. Such talent would be wasted in such a minor role. Millicent was the stuff of a Natalie Dormer or a Ginnifer Goodwin—a solid professional actress, beautiful but not Hollywood beautiful, and willing and able to tackle pivotal, small, supporting roles. Even Natalie or Ginnifer would need a backstory, a psychological reason for her character's actions and motivation, or in this case, not only why she had become a stripper but also why she insisted on

Millicent DeGroenfeld Rice

retaining an incredulous, proud, and incongruous name likely to restrain rather than augment her professional career.

* * *

Millicent DeGroenfeld Rice was born at the Dublin Methodist Hospital on September 7th, 1977. The birth certificate listed her mother as Susan DeGroenfeld Rice and the father was listed as Rusty Klaus Mueller. The two never married.

Rusty Mueller was born to Heinz and Lucinda Mueller, and the roots of the Mueller family go back to the initial settlers in the German village of Columbus before the Civil War. The Muellers were cobblers—a tradition handed down father to son. Heinz was an only child and defied family tradition and went to work as a typesetter at the Columbus Citizen in 1935 and worked there until his retirement in 1969. Heinz was apparently a chronic smoker and died of lung cancer in 1980.

Lucinda's family emigrated after WWI and settled in Dublin, and Lucinda was an only child. They likely met through Trinity Evangelical Lutheran Church around 1933 when he was just out of high school, she a young girl, and married soon after Heinz was promoted to a foreman in 1942, before he went off to the Pacific. She was still quite young at the time, and after the war, they moved to Dublin Heights into a modest, three-bedroom rambler. Lucinda never worked outside the home and died of complications of pneumonia in a chronic care facility in 1990.

Rusty was their only son, born when Lucinda was twenty-eight, in 1953. She stayed at home, and other than PTA registrars from elementary school, she barely made a blip in the social register. Primary care notes suggest some mental health issues, likely depression and/or alcoholism.

The maternal line consisted of Vincent Rice, a postman in Columbus for many years who married Millicent DeGroenfeld in 1947 after he returned from the war. Millicent's parents were landowners in Mecklenburg, distant relations to General von Blücher with a historical seat in Rostock. In 1929, when she was twelve, Millicent absconded with about ten thousand dollars' worth of Deutsche Marks and booked passage on the Hamburg American Line eventually arriving in New York Harbor. She moved to Columbus and lived with the family of a schoolmate who had emigrated three years prior.

Richard Sanders Polin

During the Depression, the family reconnected with her. Her father ran a munitions factory outside of Rostock and was a party member and never spoke to her or of her, but her mother apparently found ways to smuggle her funds, and by 1939, she bought a boardinghouse in Dublin, which she ran with the assistance of a staff made up entirely of African American women. She was only twenty-two and, by the time the war broke out, had made the place quite elegant. Vincent Rice was actually the postman on her route, and they corresponded throughout the war and married soon after he returned from active duty in 1946. There was one stillborn child in 1948, and another who died of rheumatic fever as a baby in 1951. Susan DeGroenfeld Rice was born in 1956. Vincent was paralyzed when hit by a drunk driver while delivering the mail in 1962 and lived until his death in 1970 in a back room of the boardinghouse.

Millicent DeGroenfeld never remarried and ran the establishment as best she could through changing trends and markets. Her middle-class neighborhood lost its luster, and the clientele trended towards what she considered undesirables. When Vincent passed and his pension faded, she was forced to lay off many of the staff, counting on Susan to pick up the slack. Susan's father was a nonentity, and her mother was strict. Simultaneously fueled by pop influences such as "Born to be Wild" and *Bonnie and Clyde*, Susan gravitated towards elements at school which represented freedom. At Dublin High School in 1972, Susan pursued Rusty. The poor sap just wanted to fuck, and she wanted an adventure.

The story of Susan and Rusty is boring, a bad after-school special. Good girl exploring her dark side. Irredeemable but adequately charming mook. Rebellion meets rancor. The girl with the proverbial angel and devil deliberating teenage angst in a three-round, Olympic-style free-for-all. The boy without the benefit of the angel with little psychic dissidence and scant chance of anything more than a gutter-ball ending.

Whether through intermittent use of protection, vacillation of intention by Susan, with guilt drawing her back home to Millicent and intermittent boredom forcing relapse or just dumb luck, it took a full five years for Rusty to knock Susan up. By that time, she was at Columbus State Community College well into a Hospitality Management Program at the request of her mother, who assumed her dalliance with "the hoodlum," as she called him, was truncated.

In the winter of 1977, Rusty had just returned from Franklin County after being caught in a sting jacking of all idiotic things, a 1973 AMC Javelin that may not have netted him enough to spend a week in the DeGroenfeld flophouse. He was released for Christmas 1976, and this two-month romance resulted in the conception of Millicent DeGroenfeld Rice. By the time Millicent was born the following September, Rusty was back in Franklin County.

Vegas is too highbrow, but Ladbrokes might have taken this action. With prescient knowledge of the state of infectious disease in America in the '70s and '80s—Rusty Mueller: 3:1 AIDS, 4:1 Hep C, 5:1 OD, 7:1 Shivved in prison, 10:1 DUI, 15:1 death by cop, 100:1 hepatic carcinoma. If you had Hep C with a side of portal hypertension and varices, you would have cashed in. Before Rusty started coughing up most of his cardiac output during an argument over cigarettes in the low-security wing of the Franklin County Jail in 1984, doing a six- to ten-year stretch for GTA with vehicular assault, he knew that he was a dad but had expressed little interest in the trappings of parenthood.

Parenthetically, Susan had a positive test result in March but waited until May to tell Rusty, who had faded back into a tenement in a Columbus neighborhood even Susan's trapezial Beelzebub cowered from. Susan had no interest in corralling Rusty and, in fact, likely wanted to steer him as far away from the child as possible. She wasn't a fool and had maternal instincts. On the other hand, a lifetime of cartoons taught her that a little bit of reverse psychology worked better on Yosemite Sam than it did on Bugs Bunny. A teasing of feigned picket-fence nostalgia resulted in a criminal equivalent of a Freudian slip landing Dada in the Delaware County Jail well prior to delivery for a short stint for B&E at a baseball card shop in Upper Arlington, caught red-handed with a complete 1973 Topps set, a George Foster rookie card, a 1969 autographed Johnny Bench, and an Archie Griffin jersey—which took the combined value, including the busted window from misdemeanor to felony.

Millicent DeGroenfeld Rice started life as a glitch. An intentional mistake. A volitional transgression followed by a compensatory transgression that wiped the slate clean.

The three females ran the boarding house, reborn in the '80s as a B&B with pluck.

Millicent the elder handled the money and hosting. Susan took over day-to-day operations after gaining her two-year degree. Millicent the younger's role was to defuse any arguments between her mother and grandmother and to form the crux of an advertising campaign designed to invoke nostalgia but was more likely to lure the Chris Hansen crowd to Dublin. The lack of grandfathers, fathers, and brothers, much less uncles or second cousins once removed, must have influenced Millicent the younger. She was devoted to the grandmother who doted on her as grandmothers do, and clashed with her mother as daughters do.

Rusty had passed through Millicent's life for the final time before tangible memories imprinted, and inquiries of him to her grandmother were deferred to her mother with a barely detectible "arschloch." Her mother would answer honestly even when the girl was five or six. Not just the standard "Your father has made some mistakes" bullshit but literal "Your father is a mediocre thief doing three to five years because he forgot that the cloth he used to wipe off fingerprints itself actually retains fingerprints."

In his presentation to the American Academy of Child Psychiatry, eminent behavioralist Gerald Mortenson presented work interviewing thousands of children in families of divorce and other single-family households. The crux of the paper was that all a child needed to survive a troubled upbringing was to have the influence of "one sane parent or parental figure." If only Millicent the older had not persisted in the vices of her old-world heritage. She was gracious, charming, and ageless in 1981 when the first-imprinted memories in her namesake were formed but deteriorated rapidly from 1986 through 1988 from a combination of chesterfields and almost daily consumption of multiple bratwurst (18 percent increase in colorectal cancer for every daily fifty-gram portion of processed pork found in bacon and sausage according to the World Health Organization). Emphysema, colon cancer with lung metastases, diabetes, heart failure, and osteoarthritis turned her rather quickly from a sixty-five-year-old who looked fifty-five into a seventy-year-old who looked eighty. Ageing did mellow Millicent, and the intransigent dogmatic raising of Susan morphed into a quiet and patient sweetness with her granddaughter. The sane parental figure Millicent needed died when she was nine.

Susan could never quite figure out the conundrum of whether Millicent was wanted or unwanted. Her mother's death spurred a realization that her daughter was far more tethered to her mother than she had ever anticipated or desired. She quickly surmised that even the child's name was a subverting ploy engineered by her mother, whose luster of metastatic suffering quickly faded in the realization of the fucking mess she had left behind. Susan felt herself a prisoner once more but this time—especially with Rusty now permanently unavailable and a delusional belief that his taint rendered her undesirable—without escape. Millicent became increasingly a totem of the elder and consequently emotionally marooned.

Had Susan Rice brought her daughter to the posh Silver Spring offices of Gerald Mortenson, he would have given the mom a preliminary diagnosis of schizoid personality disorder. No strong relationships, her one sexual encounter cursory and distinctly not intimate, indifferent to the social niceties of central Ohio, dismissively cold especially to her daughter, and finally enmeshed initially in her Bonnie and Clyde fantasy involving Rusty and now in a strange double life of the B&B, which became her Greenbriar on a semi-sane day, Fantasy Island on the more delusional ones. The strange baseball scout from the Expos organization—staying for a week to evaluate Columbus Clippers prospects in a proposed Andre Dawson deal for Yankees farmhands—was secretly Mickey Mantle disguised as a bespeckled, round nebbish to avoid recognition. The itinerant poet who scribbled couplets and discarded them around his room was Alan Ginsberg prepared to howl against whatever the hell Allen Ginsberg wanted to howl about in 1982—probably the smug cultural hegemony of the Reagan years, notwithstanding the fact that this Allen Ginsberg lacked both a Bell's palsy and a predilection for men.

One can debate whether the lyrics in "The End" by the Beatles are the most profound or the tritest (or both) that Lennon and McCartney ever fashioned. But in the context of the Rice family, that either simplistic or profound statement comparing emotion to the first law of thermodynamics applies splendidly. Let's accept that a normal child craves emotional warmth and also—except perhaps as a teenager—provides the same. There is a steady state achieved between parents and parental figures and children. One sane parental figure is sufficient, and for a time, the elder Millicent nurtured her granddaughter sufficiently and, in turn, received the bulk of young Millicent's affection. The mother gave and received a percentage, according to her capabilities. Then when the old woman passed, there was a resulting imbalance between the mother, who neither emitted nor absorbed warmth, and the daughter, who had normal but unfulfilled requirements. The death of the old woman placed the family balance into disarray.

So, the nine-year-old tried to derive emotional support from an incapable source and wound up frustrated and hollow. She tried for a few years to turn off/calm down and became a withdrawn mirror of her mother, but that was dissonant.

A rich girl would ride horses, bond to a golden retriever or a Labrador, and find a special friend. She could even the equation through external means while Mommy dulls herself with Midazolam and Merlot. A poor girl has no such outlets. Fifteen percent residual mom plus 10 percent equestrian bonus, 30 percent canine, 25 percent with Muffy, with early weed use dulling down needs from 100 percent to 80 percent. That works. A poor kid—no horses, no dogs, friends but 10 percent are more acquaintances really because what interest do eleven-year-old girls have in exploring a dingy flophouse? Eventually, the other girls get tired of Millicent coming over all the time. No Mrs. Cleavers or Mrs. Bradys around to understand and take her in, accounting for an unexpected bonus. Instead, just frustration after frustration and a gradual withdrawal to equate to the mother. But you can't really equate to the mother while you care what others think, care about trying to fit in, try to matter.

And then Millicent was fifteen, old enough for Natalie or Ginnifer with a little makeup and some hair creativity to join the action. And inevitably they get actress braces as well, which conveys tenth grade but is entirely incongruous because Mrs. Rice would never have noticed or cared about an overbite or underbite.

Scene thirteen, take two, fifteen-year-old Millicent at school: A brave, tough-girl loner meets graduate teaching assistant who is the first one to see the vulnerability and beauty. He's a twenty-three or twenty-four-year-old, not too good-looking but convincingly influential or captivating, though not necessarily authentic. Can Tom Felton shed his accent? He would be perfect, notable, but not someone who would expect major billing, not like the they're beating down the doors for the typecast wizarding-world players. Let's contact his agent. Filmography: Draco, Draco, Draco, Draco, Draco, Draco, Draco, Draco, Sly Dobbins. Sly Dobbins comes to Dublin High as part of his Buckeye graduate teaching program to intern in Mrs. Stonewall's sophomore European literature class. He notices the reticent maiden in the third row who barely makes eye contact, doesn't participate in class, but writes beautiful short essays with a really unique view of Ophelia as the true protagonist in *Hamlet* and, later in the semester, provides a cogent argument on why Eustacia Vye committed suicide. He starts spending time with her at first platonically, as he has a lovely (but ultimately fictitious) girlfriend. He becomes her warmth, securing himself to her with small gifts, which augment her appearance (asexual stuff-socks and Buckeye caps) and intellect (self-congratulatory graduate school flotsam—*The Crying of Lot 49*, *The End of the Road*, *Tropic of Whichever*) and little events the fake girlfriend can't attend—Doug Etzler and the Buckeye Hoopsters take on Wisconsin, the Gin Blossoms in concert at St. John Arena, a Radiohead release party at Spoonful. How could Millicent not fall for Sly?

After Sly's internship is completed, he takes a spot as a substitute at a middle school in Westerville and keeps up correspondence with Millicent. She, in turn, eschews the attention of her classmates as she lets her strawberry-blond hair grow long, and her features mature into a mellow brilliance she cannot perceive. The imperfections, a pound here, a splotch there, haunt her, and she is unable to process that she has become radiant. In sexual utilitarian terms, she is a nine and Sly a six, but if you asked Millicent, you'd hear the reverse. He finally allows himself to have sex with her in her senior year ("Colorblind" by Counting Crows—no, that was already used in some other film . . . so how 'bout "Tender" by Blur) after going to see *Sense and Sensibility* and telling her that the girlfriend was a ruse he'd made up to prevent her from falling in love with him and to remind him not to act on impulse since he's loved her since he'd first [blech/yadda yadda/tommyrot]. It's technically stat rape, but by this time, he's completely convinced she wouldn't tell anyone, and her mom wouldn't care to prosecute if he had her gang-raped by a carful of clowns. Still, for reasons perhaps not immediately clear, in June 1995, after she has graduated from Dublin High as a straight-B student with plans to start OSU in a nursing program, Sly asks her to move with him to New Orleans.

Now unpredictable tales can wallow in predictable puddles, and perhaps this was such a predicament. The story of Melvin "the Troll" Horgan was anything but a Lifetime movie, but the next few pages could be plagiarized from Jennie Garth and Gregory Harrison in the 1994 Lifetime made-for-TV movie *Lies of the Heart: The Story of Laurie Kellogg*, co-starring Sharon Spelman as Mom. Millicent's first eighteen months in New Orleans are a joy as she feels loved and nurtured and gains confidence. But every time she expresses the desire to start taking classes to be a nurse, a teacher, a counselor, an accountant, a social worker, Sly calmly but firmly tells her she will have to wait until he gets a permanent teaching job while he subs in Slidell Parish. She, of course, capitulates because even if things aren't perfect, they're so much better than they were back home, as she's reminded whenever she calls Susan out of duty and gets the distinct idea that *Judge Judy* is imminently more impactful to her mother than her daughter's life. She contributes as a hotel front desk attendant in a Holiday Inn Express and helps prep classes.

The year 1998 begins with good fortune as Sly gets a permanent gig teaching English Lit at Salmen High School in Slidell. He gets three sessions of tenth-grade American Lit, and one senior elective in World Literature between the wars. With the steady income, they move into a bigger place in Bonfouca and talk about pets, school for Millicent, even marriage. But there's no fruition, and by the end of the year, there are more and more parent teacher nights and field trips.

The summer of '99 is a blur as Sly teaches summer school, and the two take a brief vacation back to Columbus and peep in on the B&B, which is aging and fading from neglect.

As the '99 to 2000 school year starts, we're starting to worry whether the career lifeline we handed to Tom Felton will sabotage the credibility of the production. Clearly, any reader/viewer of middling intelligence knowing the future of Millicent can predict that Sly is not a sweet, loving partner, although perhaps a grizzly random death could provide the identical outcome. The question is whether Tom could possibly deliver a convincing performance as the sensitive savior before turning heel. After all, given a generation weaned on the Potter narrative, would this be a Reeves in *Here to Eternity* moment at the screening, with a mirthful test audience yelling "Mudblood" at the screen as he slaps Millicent, who caught him in Beignet Au Lait with Emily Kinney and had the audacity to question his faithfulness? Maybe if his hair is dyed brown or red and sneers are avoided at all costs. The inevitable New Year's party for the millennium would be the final straw, as Emily would show up unannounced and there would be direct evidence of Sly's infidelity. Sly is apologetic in public, but later, when he and Millicent are alone, he cracks a couple of ribs, a zygoma, and orbital bone, eventually resulting in Millicent fleeing New Orleans with four hundred stolen dollars and winding up in the nation's capital, which she had visited once on a school field trip under the name Millicent Mueller.

There are few places in the world where a lack of formal education is more limiting for a white girl than Washington, D.C. Maybe San Francisco would have been a more challenging locale, but the combination of cost of living and lack of opportunity is stifling. Millicent takes a job waitressing at Pizzeria Paradiso off Dupont Circle, using her father's last name, but she can't afford her rent in a six-hundred-square-foot apartment off Mass Avenue just south of American University. She switches to slinging drinks at the Zebra Lounge on Wisconsin near the cathedral, but the Zebra is slow, and although she can make rent, the hope of making enough to afford school remains a pipe dream.

So, the last named actor absolutely necessary for this biopic is the incredible, the stupendous Joe Pantoliano. If Joe is busy with *The Fugitive 3*, Dan Hedaya will suffice as Archibald, owner of the predictably named Archibald's, a high-end strip club with a lobbyist ceiling and a convention center floor. You are likely to see a dry cleaner from Chattanooga side by side with an undersecretary of Commerce, one being treated by a representative from Monsanto and the other being treated by a representative of Monsanto.

Archibald encounters Millicent in the Zebra in June of 2001 on a day when Millicent is sporting a busty blouse that accentuates her pale blue eyes, and she has her hair cut medium-length with bangs like a little girl. Archibald recognizes talent and offers her a bartending job for a 30 percent raise, on the spot. Millicent is vulnerable to flattery—the more direct and obvious, the more effective—and Archibald never minces words. Millicent does some math and quickly accepts, not knowing the nature of her employer.

If the strip club and the obligatory propositions, groping, and pinching ever bother Millicent, she never complains. Her employment at Archibald's replicates her relationship with Sly. The old man starts as a mentor, teaching her about savings, using her sexuality to enhance tips, and learning to differentiate drunks who could be exploited from drunks who should be bounced. He accompanies her to the kinds of events minor-level celebrities in the nation's capital attend—the Christmas Tree lighting (in the public section). United playoff games, a production of *The Iceman Cometh* at Ford's Theater, starring some actor who had played a bad guy on the trifecta of *Law and Order*, *Law and Order SVU*, and *Law and Order Criminal Intent*, and a traveling version of Cirque du Soleil Zumanity playing in a tent outside Tysons Corner.

But ultimately, Archibald's becomes untenable due to a combination of the transition of Archibald's attentions from fatherly to amorous and perhaps more importantly his refusal to let her ride the pole, which becomes her overriding obsession, eclipsing returning to school.

Her desire to do so is both monetary and psychological. Quite frankly, she see less motivated, less attractive, dumb girls taking home twice her salary working half her hours. Furthermore, she postulates that any of her latent body image issues would be vanquished with strangers throwing money at her feet. She takes classes at Pole Pressure and the P Spot and repeatedly declares herself ready to have a hybrid position, and after repeated abject refusals, she concludes that this represents old man jealousy and decides to move on.

Now, being in final negotiations with Ginnifer and Natalie, we have reached a snag. It should have been quite clear since this is the role of a stripper that full frontal would be expected. To be honest, Ginnifer is our preference. We know Natalie can lose the accent, but Ginnifer is perfect for innocence corrupted, for restrained sexuality, for vulnerability and fragility. But she doesn't appear to do full frontal. We know that's not a problem for Natalie—*The Tudors* and *Game of Thrones* prove that conclusively—but Ginnifer's only been seen from behind. We have to figure out quickly whether it's philosophical or situational. Call her agent.

It's 2003, and Millicent contemplates reclaiming her real name, no longer looking over her shoulder for Sly, and starts a position dancing three nights a week and bartending two at the Good Guys Club in D.C. She remains distant from the other girls, an order of magnitude more mature and intellectual. She reads voraciously in her days off, visits the National Gallery, takes up photography, and has a Cherry Blossom Kenwood photo published in the *Washingtonian*. She may be the only peeler in Christendom to read *Anna Karenina* for pleasure in the breakroom (we're not counting the college girls doing classwork) and disrobing to Radiohead's "High and Dry" (the manager gives her one free-form song a week) or Modest Mouse's "Gravity Rides Everything."

Millicent sheds her pseudonym and takes back her given name in 2004, having stopped worrying entirely about Sly coming back to claim her and feeling confident she could kick his ass physically and emotionally. She defies every attempt her Goomba manager makes to change her name, rejecting Veronica, (Queen) Victoria, Venus, Vanessa, and Valentina (the manager was Vince the Wop and felt all "V" names exuded sexuality, and his "V" name for her, Vassar, never made it to the emcee). Consistency in attendance, an underrated trait in her field, and dollar-per-dance productivity gave her leverage to maintain an unusual degree of autonomy.

In seven years, she makes a consistent living of between sixty and eighty thousand dollars a year, much of it under the table. She never takes to drugs, occasionally volunteers for more lucrative private parties and VIP exclusive experiences, and takes only one lover (a lovestruck urologist who comes to the club for meals after tough cases and eventually convinces her to accompany him, more with meekness and self-deprecation than bravado, but he eventually fades from favor, as she realizes that the self-deprecation is not an act, and it becomes tiresome).

Over the years, she communicates with her mother less and less frequently, and the two play a game of miscommunication in which the occupation of the daughter is guarded with the same degree of assiduousness as the illness of the mother. Susan is brought into Dublin Methodist after a seizure and is found to have widely metastatic disease from breast cancer, which even a cursory degree of self-awareness or surveillance would have diagnosed years before. Susan dies in hospice care in 2008, never informing her only living immediate family member of her plight. Millicent comes back to Columbus for the funeral and sells the property to Susan's site manager for a pittance to complete her emancipation.

No one really understands why, in 2010, Millicent's exemplary and reliable attendance falters, and eventually she just stops coming to work. She has no close friends among the girls and refuses to reply to Vince's initial sincere and subsequent half-hearted attempts to corral her back to the club. In April of 2011, she is found dead with explicit instructions in a three-line note to cremate the body without ceremony or celebration and donate her estate to a battered women's charity.

Now this may or may not be the last appearance in the narrative for Ginnifer (we really hope her scruples concerning disrobing can be circumvented) or Natalie, but the screenwriter may want a last montage at the Washington Zoo, if the Smithsonian authorities would allow it. Considering this is a far more serious piece of work than that *Night at the Museum* travesty, how could they refuse. On the other hand, given the lack of violence, this is likely to be an indie, and the cost may be prohibitive. It may be necessary to use some lesser, cheaper zoo as an alternative. But the National Zoo would be the best place for a zoo montage. All filmmakers love a good zoo montage with the suicidal Millicent roaming for one last look at her beloved animals (perhaps they can interject a scene with her grandmother at the Columbus Zoo for some subtle foreshadowing). If the production crew is patient, a panda shot would be epic, but the damned things sleep twenty-three hours a day. What montage song? "At the Zoo" is too obvious. How about "No Distance Left to Run." It doesn't exactly pertain, but it is somber and beautiful and not overly familiar to an American audience. We will make it a Blur monopoly. Morose, gaunt, anorexic Ginnifer or Natalie hangs out with the elephants, then quietly slinks into a bathroom stall with a razor blade and a tourniquet, empties her blood into the toilet, and slumps down into unconsciousness.

Chapter 4:
Loser

The break room at the Revolution Concert House in Boise, Idaho, had intentionally been kept as a rock and roll time capsule. The same sofa and chairs where Cream had waited in the '60s and Three Dog Night in the '70s, Duran Duran in the '80s, and Pearl Jam before they went over the top in the '90s would have witnessed the same layout as Billy Goat's Gruff for the initial show of their *Space Needle Pricks* tour in support of a new Infinity act called He Got the Giggler.

In the far corner of the room, mounted on a metal shelf, was a twenty-five-inch RCA with perhaps the last set of rabbit ears in Boise. The right ear was perked up, and the left was detached and disheveled as befitted a thirty-year-old piece of metal. The set was turned on with the volume down, and the screen showing a mixture of 30 percent static and 70 percent Jerry Springer or some facsimile. When the volume was turned up, the percentage of static and Springer was reversed such that the sound never stayed on for long.

The two chairs and one sofa were aimed at the TV and were in proximity to the entrance door. At the far side of the room, the TV was on the left, the exit to backstage in the center, and the mini kitchen on the right. Really the only change since the last time Billy Goat's Gruff passed through almost two years before was that some management buffoon had decided to save a few bucks by exchanging the six-ounce mini Cokes, Diet Cokes, and Sprites with their Kirkland budget alternatives, likely to save pennies a soda on the one perk provided in this Kmart of venues.

The chairs were really the highlight of the place. Sturdy oak frame survivors, which were decades past any warrantee, with yellow leather cushions and arm rests never re-upholstered since their creation with consequent pressure tears where elbows were liable to loiter. The cushions detached and could be reversed at will although there was little benefit of doing so. The yellow was a buffer for the various accumulated liquids over the years. The yellow had absorbed every fluid imaginable, from foodstuffs to saliva to semen to blood both menstrual and corporal. Each painted a distinct residual pattern and shade on either side of the chair as to create a Rorschach image from the debauchery—each side a distinct psychological imprint to be interpreted diversely by the adult contemporary, by the hip hop, by the heavy metal, by the grunge.

Melvin Horgan slumped down in the one chair to the left of the door, apart from the sofa and the other chair. Beside the hidden left arm of the chair was what remained of a six-pack of Stroh's. Under the right arm were half of the initial contents of the six-pack. At his feet was a wrapper from an Egg McMuffin, and he concentrated on a Game Boy Advance, playing *Resident Evil* in a particularly gruesome zombie nullifying sequence.

Billy Markwell and Tiny Atlas walked in from the outside, having just returned from lunch. Although this was the first show of the tour, the ritual was unquestioned. There was no reason to ask Melvin about rehearsal. Rehearsal was for Billy and Tiny. God knew where Bebe hid from arrival to show, but he'd be there on stage, on time, on cue. Melvin would use his per diem to get just loose enough to make it on stage but not sloppy enough to flounder. Billy would lead Tiny through the cues well enough to stay on point. Simple. It was a ten-song set they had settled on. Headlining, they had needed sixteen and a two-song encore, one of which was a cover.

Headlining and warming up had different structures. Warming up was a sprint. Get your good stuff played, start out strong, and no matter what crap you finished with, the crowd would be so psyched when you told them it was your last song and the headliner would be up soon; they would clap for anything. Boise should have some fans from the old days. The boys had come to smaller venues here a half dozen times on the Northwest circuit, so most likely there would be some Billy Goat fans in addition to the crowd to see He Got the Giggler, whatever that was. "Dusty Heaves" would lead it off. Hit 'em hard. Everyone loved "Dusty Heaves." Then "Lola's Room," which was a decent track from the new CD. Then they'd go back to "Gut Shrieker," which was the second single from the second CD. "Tiger Drag" would be fourth. The hardcore fans would appreciate the new song, which was their bread-and-butter formula. Then "Claudette Wants Flowers" and one from the first CD, "Hovercraft." "Froggy Went a Snortin'" would go seventh to try to hook in any latecomers, followed by "Millicent DeGroenfeld Rice," "Money Grab," and finally "Bumbershoot," which would serve as both conclusion and invitation.

Billy had asked Melvin, "Why the Millicent song?" The response was "'Froggy' is hard on my voice. Millicent' is easy. Just screech everything but the refrain. Then you and Tiny have a good ninety-second drum/guitar solo, and I get my voice back for the end. Gotta connect on 'Bumbershoot.'"

So, while Billy worked with Tiny, Melvin lounged in a chair ambivalent to the blood and semen and urine stains, getting prepared in his way for the show with a slow, steady drunk. Just before three thirty, after ninety minutes of silent reflection, button mashing and drinking, Melvin saw his first visitor. The entry door opened and in walked a tall, fresh-faced kid, really high cheekbones, pretty/handsome with wavy, black hair, long but not scraggly, and naturally feminine eyelashes. The newcomer came up to Melvin, who was staring intently at his Game Boy during a mini-boss battle.

"Are you Mitch Ferrell? We were supposed to check in with Mitch Ferrell."

Melvin gave no response.

"I'm sorry. Don't mean to bother you, but we're playing tonight, and we're supposed to check in with Mitch Ferrell. I think he's the stage manager. We have a ton of equipment out there and need to—"

Melvin spoke but remained fixated on his five-inch screen. "You mean Toad? I don't know no fuckin' Mitch Ferrell, but I know Toad. He's in his office, most likely. Down the hall to the left."

"Thanks, man. Marc Bauer. Lead singer for He Got the Giggler."

"So you're the Giggler. Holy Fuck." Melvin still hadn't glanced up from his Game Boy.

"And who do I have the pleasure?"

"I ain't no pleasure, boy. Melvin Horgan."

"Troll Horgan? Big fan, big fan. Remember seeing you on *Letterman*. Lenny Bruce of Grunge. The Melvin 'the Troll' Horgan. It's an honor, sir."

"Cut the crap, kid. Save the honor bullshit for Bono."

"Really, an honor. We've never played outside of SoCal. To be paired with pros, an honor." Melvin tapped the pause button and took a quick glance and saw a "just add water" metal boyband lead singer. He coughed and went back to his game.

"Won't be an honor for long. Roadies unload in back. You don't have any, do it your fucking self. We have the stage until four. You have it four to six if you need rehearsing. Doors open seven, we're on eight to eight fifty, and not a minute longer. You're on nine fifteen to whenever before eleven you want to stop. My guess is you've got about fifty minutes of play, and you plan to 'jam' every song to reach ninety minutes and add in a cover of some kind, by the looks of you, 'Wanted Dead or Alive' in the encore to stretch it out to ninety-five, which fulfills your contract and gets us all the hell out of here by midnight so we can reach wherever the hell we are playing tomorrow. I get some of that right?"

"Stretch out, no need, man. We're cool. Been at this game five years. First commercial CD but lots of material. Joe Griffin and I started playing together early sophomore year. Other guys joined over the years, so we've been together awhile."

"High School?"

"No, man. UCLA film school. We're all Bruins, Sons of Westwood."

"What the fuck is a Bruin."

"A bruin is a brown bear. It's a Dutch word used by the British in folk."

"Okay, okay," Melvin interrupted. "I get it, it's a fucking bear. And what in the name of God is a Giggler?"

"You'll love this." Just then Billy Markwell entered by the stage door, droplets of sweat beading on his temples. "At UCLA, one of our friends was this Orthodox Jewish guy. From Israel. Back home, sheltered family, no television, no movies, certainly had never watched any sex or violence. Was at school two months and hooked on television, up all night watching old movies. One night, he watched one of those Bronson *Death Wish* movies and was spellbound. He bought 'em all on disc, but his favorite was *Death Wish 3*. We would watch it at night with this guy Alan Agronin. Now, the rest of us would play this drinking game, one Stoli shot for every poor bastard Bronson wasted. Alan was Orthodox—didn't drink but just would get so overheated, you know, whenever one of the dirtbags was shot. His favorite

Millicent DeGroenfeld Rice

was this tall, swarthy-looking white guy in a black doo-rag with a porn-stache and a leather biker's vest who'd laugh as he committed petty theft, and his buddies called him 'The Giggler.' So there is this classic scene where Bronson carries out a camera, and some citizen asks him what it's for, and he says 'Bait,' and then the Giggler snatches it, and Bronson nails him with one in the back and the other bad guys lament it, and every time we'd watch it, this guy Alan in a yarmulke would dance around the room screaming, 'He got the Giggler,' even though the real line was something else. And that's how we got our name."

"You got your name from a drinking game and some fucking kike? At college?"

"And your name. Always loved it. Favorite story as a kid?"

"Are you blind, Giggler. I'm a fucking troll. And this here is the Billy Goat. Come on over here, Billy, and meet the Giggler."

Billy came over and extended a hand. "Billy Markwell."

"Marc Bauer, pleasure to meet you."

"Don't mind Melvin. He's a bit nervous about the tour."

"Now, Billy, you know that's a damned lie. I'm nervous not being on tour. No, I was just remembering that drinking game we played back at Princeton, Goat. You know the one where we used to watch that movie you loved, what was it called, *Schindler's List*. And every time someone got offed, we took a shot of Schnapps. Man, we'd get good and toasted by the end of that piece of art. Tiny Atlas—that's our drummer, Giggler, and the brains of the operation—would run around the fraternity at Princeton—that's where we all met—and yell, 'He Got the Rabbi. He got the Rabbi.' Good times. Thank goodness for your sake we didn't use that as our name. The whole Giggler thing would seem pretty stale considering we would have done it first."

"Shut the fuck up, Melvin."

"It's okay. I know he's just kidding,"

Melvin started to respond, but Billy rushed over to put up his hand over Melvin's mouth. "Melvin is only half kidding. His old man was a Jew and left."

Melvin shot in, "Enough, Goat. Off limits. That bastard's no more my father than the next seven assholes Mom brought home. Yeah, Giggler. I don't really hate Jews. I'm just envious. If we had a Jew manager instead

39

of Billy's dumbshit cousin maybe we'd be headlining Bonnaroo instead of warming up bumfuck Idaho for some no-talent posers."

"For fuck's sake, Melvin. I thought you wanted back on the road. Kid has nothing to do with this. Leave him alone."

"Yeah, you're right, Goat. Sorry, Giggler. Didn't mean to offend you. Thing is, we have a forty-city tour with ya, and there's nothing to look forward to. No Austin City, no Bonnaroo, no Sasquatch, not even a fucking Project Pabst. You want us to be friends, get your Jew—or at least I assume he's a Jew—manager to get us a festival."

"A festival?"

Melvin looked up and stared at Marc Bauer with a twisted grin. He pointed a Stroh's bottle at him. "Yes, for Christ's sake. Don't you know anything yet? A festival. These one-night stands in shithole towns. We come in, set our shit up, play a quick set, pack up, and go. Half the time, sleep on the road. By the time you're off stage, we're on the bus. There's literally two hours after our set to find some groupie, fuck her, and get on the bus, even less if they have some strange desire to survive until the end of your encore. Festival, that's two, maybe three days. Hotel room, couple days we're supposed to be collaborating, schmoozing, networking. So the label fucking lets us linger a bit. Now for a festival, you'll also get five or six all-access passes. That's gold. Let's say you have five. You take two and get laid. Drunk bitch at a festival'll do anything for a backstage pass. One a day, get your rocks off. Another two, get you high. At a proper festival, there's smack, snow, MJ, X, Molly. Whatever the hell you want is there for the asking from your 'fans.' And finally use the last for random shit. Sasquatch in 2010, Billy, what's that shit you got?"

"I got a Segway, from this drunk moron I convinced Anthony Kiedis was playing a private show for the bands backstage."

"That's right, the Segway. What happened to that piece of shit?"

"Tiny tried to ride it. It had a weight limit."

"And me, I got this here delightful palm-of-my-hand video game console, and this here zombie-killing game from a fourteen-year-old I convinced could meet Jack White with a backstage pass at Firefly in 2011. That paranoid fuck is on and off stage quicker than we are, and I've been killing zombies in prep rooms for years. Get us a festival or two, Giggler, and we'll be the best of friends."

"And how are we supposed to get a festival?"

"Call your fucking manager. Call the fucking label. Use big boy words like cross-pollination or harmonic fraternization. So, let's forget about the shit I just said. Maybe it's our truth, not your truth. Maybe you're still about the music. We're on tour together for a shit-long time. We might get some local talent opening up here or there, but they suck balls. We are godawful. You know Nirvana—we are to Nirvana what Stroh's"—as he holds up a bottle—"is to Dom-fucking-Pérignon. And looks of you, chances are you the Stroh's version of Guns N' Roses. Festival—you get blues, rap, soul, grunge, hip-hop, adult contemporary, alt, folk under one roof. Go ahead, don't waste your shit like we do. Learn something that you couldn't derive from *American Idol* or *American Bandstand*. I fucking dare you. Then maybe next tour, you won't get stuck with no-talent hacks like us."

"You haven't even heard—"

"Yeah, I haven't even heard you. Chances are I'll try very hard to spend as much time as possible pushing merch when you're onstage, and if I have a typical tour, at least every other show, make it backstage with some slut while you're playing 'All that Glitters' and trying not to chuckle onstage when Goat here tells the people how excited they should be for your set because that's what we're contractually obligated to do, but I've seen you little cocksuckers a million times with your classical training, your fucking musical theory classes, your goddamned Flock of Seagulls haircuts, your Twisted Sister wardrobe, your synthesizer vocals, and your motherfucking all new Johnny Bravo looks. You fit the suit, man. You fit the suit. You can tell the ones with talent who don't fit the suit. Dylan didn't fit the suit. Cobain didn't fit the suit. Hell, Michael Jackson weird-ass motherfucker didn't fit the suit. We don't fit the suit, but whatever talent we have is Bebe's, and we're just renting it. You, on the other hand, fit the fucking suit, and the last original thought you had was to name your band after an obscure line in an obscure movie."

At this point, Melvin turned back down to look at his lap and commenced once more pushing buttons on his Game Boy, representing both shotgun and machete kills of viral induced super-zombies. If residual malevolence persisted, it was channeled into the zombie apocalypse as if the inquisition and deconstruction of Marc Bauer was intended as motivation to a more effective and efficient level of button mashing.

Goat took a stunned Marc Bauer backstage off in search of the manager with an obvious intention to obfuscate the meaning of the Troll's lashing.

Melvin Horgan played on, accompanied only by the staccato interruptions of the Springer guests and audience. After about five minutes, when a level was completed, triggering a cut scene, he closed the device and stood up and turned off the TV. He sat back in his fluid-stained chair displaying the pattern of four nearly symmetrical praying mantises or copulating eagles, depending on your orientation or neurosis, and started very softly to sing.

Fragments emerged of Gruff songs old and new. Key elements, all songs from the act. Some verses, some refrains, sung as a secret, barely above a whisper. Words and cadence often repeated several times with a steady, methodical toe tap. Not much time on "Dusty" and "Froggy." Those were internalized, the kind of automatic recollections liable to compete for a last moment of ultimate consciousness as the most meaningful tidbit this diseased brain produced. But there was the tricky second verse of "Millicent" when the rhyme structure breaks down. He went through that one twice. "Bumbershoot" was a breeze. "Tiger Drag" needed a complete walkthrough. Finally, he went through "Claudette Wants Flowers" more as a prayer than a song.

"Four dates, this girl don't hate me
Walk in the park and second-run showing of Twilight Saga: New Moon
Ten dollars from homeless, ten percent of a human
Fifth date inconceivable for a goddamned buffoon.

"Claudette wants flowers
Hell, she deserves 'em
Don't have forty bucks for the FTD
Claudette wants flowers
I can steal 'em or pick 'em
from the park at the back of the church cemetery."

Melvin finished his medley and went through a half dozen cues and looked back around the room to ensure he remained alone, and then continued in his somber library voice:

"Jeremy Spokane, Spokane. Jeremy Spokane, Spokane. Jeremy Spokane class today. Time to take her home, her daisy head is conscience fading. For my next assault, everything's my fault. I'll take all the blame, I can see folks' shame." And now two clicks louder. "Those are people who died, died. Fucking Douchebags who died, died. Those are people who died, died. Those are people who died, died. I have no friends, they all died." And now a little louder but still essentially private, unless there were spooks at the door. "In the time of chimpanzees, I was a honkey. Butane in my veins, so I'm out to spank the monkey. And my crime is a piece of wax fallin' on a termite who's chokin' on a splinter. Fuck it. I'm ready," he finished, and opened back to the cut scene, snapped open another Stroh's, and continued mutilating the infected.

Chapter 5:
Le Petit Prince

The Revolution Hall was built in the '20s as a big-band dance palace. Swing bands would play, and the town's population would swell the joint to the fire marshal's limit. It was constructed in an era when the pursuit of acoustic perfection was an art. Consequently, the acoustics were both perfect and demanding. In a lesser hall, foibles in voice would be drowned out in the instruments and ambient noise, and missed notes would be submerged in unintended reverb. It was a double-edged sword, especially to less-gifted musicians. Conversely, when a band was truly tight and on pitch, there was almost a barbershop quartet effect, voice guitar, bass, and drum merging together in synchrony like CSNY, and it was a thing of beauty.

It was also one of the bigger venues this tour would visit and, consequently, potentially embarrassing. Doors seven, show eight was pretty standard, but it was also pretty standard for the rail to be occupied by rushing superfans by 7:05 and at least a ten-deep mosh by seven thirty.

Tonight, at seven forty-five, there was what could best be described as milling around of staff and a few patrons who were more interested in four-dollar pizza and six-dollar beer than lining up for a choice view of Billy Goat's Gruff. Revolution was a twenty-one-and-older club, but it's not like Billy Goat's Gruff catered to teeny-bopper fans, who would be excluded by age restrictions.

Another downside of being an opening act was having to do a fair percentage of the roadie work oneself. Tiny was valuable for the manual labor aspects, but Melvin hadn't done a sound check for himself in four years, and it was more than a little deflating to be standing in front of an empty auditorium speaking, "La-la-la, ka-ka-ka, check, check, pa-pa-pa."

The band had a logo on a silk screen behind Tiny's drums and another on the drum kit itself. Backstage after check and ten minutes before eight, there wasn't any chatter between the band members. Bebe never had more than two words per tour. He wore the same outfit he arrived with, and it was seemingly the only one he had: skinny jeans, white T-shirt, red, gray, and black flannel shirt, leather jacket, red/brown boots, and brown-tinted shades. Tiny wore what might have been the wife beater wife beaters were named for—stretched and tattered with its own Rorschach pattern solely of tendrils of blood dating back, who knew—ten to fifteen years—with jeans with more subtle but no less definable blood stains. Billy brought, by tradition, four pairs of jeans per tour and majored in attire pandering. He had a cheap T-shirt from whatever sports team the city of record harbored. In this case, a well-worn blue-and-orange tee with the number five and lettering on the back, which suggested a Zam opening and a Polish ending.

Melvin was even more Spartan in his tour packing. He had two pairs of jeans at any one time, a holy sagging Lee option for most concerts, and a newer pair of Diesels he found for twenty-four dollars at the Nordstrom Rack and kept for situations in which he was trying to impress. Seventy-five loiterers in Boise didn't rate. Melvin's tour T-shirt collection was a combination of their own merch, free T-shirts from various festivals, and the occasional fan gift. Today, he wore a US Navy recruiting promotional T-shirt he'd "won" by turning a wheel at Sasquatch in 2007. Flip-flops were a Horgan staple.

Melvin's flip-flops had lost some tension in the rubber, and they doubled under, causing him to lurch forward into Tiny as they marched onstage in Boise. If anyone noticed in the audience, there was no audible evidence. *We might as well be playing in the fucking garage,* Melvin thought when he saw the meager gathering around the stage, with vast emptiness until the bar in back, which was plenty busy. Billy Goat's Gruff broke one cardinal rule of rock and roll bands. The lead singer is virtually always the frontman. Guitar player is musically intense, the bassist is chill, the drummer insane, but the lead singer is the frontman. But talking to an audience, more exactly engaging an audience, was not a Melvin Horgan attribute, and Billy Markwell was adequate, meaning at least he didn't alienate or enrage the audience, even if he came off banal.

There had been nights back in Portland in the independent days when Billy could whip a partisan crowd up into a frenzy.

"You motherfuckers ready to rock?"

"How the fuck are you, Portland?"

"Put your goddamned hands in the air for Billy Goat's Gruff."

But in a large hall with half the souls who used to pack the Doug Fir, a hale and hearty "Hello, Boise" greeting would have been ludicrous. Instead, with the lights down and all four in position, Billy laid down a subdued, "We're Billy Goat's Gruff," and immediately commenced the sampled guitar riff that led into "Dusty Heaves."

It was a mistake starting with "Dusty Heaves." It was a point of arrogance, assuming that there was a following, a loyal cadre of troupers who would be pressed up to the rail, pinballing in the mosh, crowd-surfing, and slam-dancing. To waste the best of their presentation on the lightest of the crowd was an egregious fault, and while it was true that the familiar strains of the refrain, as close to a hook as Melvin had ever written, conjured a thicker crowd, the auditorium remained essentially an abyss.

Toad Ferrell had indicated two-thirds capacity in the advance, with another hundred or so typical in walk-up. It was fucking conceited to assume even a paltry sampling of the crowd was here to see Billy Goat, which was apparently well farther down the career arc than Melvin had even surmised. The majority of the two-thirds plus a hundred were here because of some fucking payola Giggler crap they had heard on the radio that reminded them of some slightly less putrid fucking payola crap, and that was why they were coming to Revolution Hall on this particular Wednesday: to put their hands in the air and take videos of that song getting radio play. Sheep knowing one Giggler song but willing to screech at each opening riff, as if they knew the secondary shit. Nobody bought Radiohead albums anymore, much less He Got the Giggler or *Space Needle Pricks*, for that matter.

This show dragged. Try as he might, Melvin's attempts to connect with the audience failed as the background din of conversations and transactions trumped the elements of musical subtleties. Sure, the songs could still be heard, but the hidden albeit sampled riffs and voice play were stilted in the din of background sounds, which only intensified as more patrons entered the halls but congregated in the back, waiting for the annoyance of the opening act to conclude. Six songs in, things were only fading. It was time for "Froggy," which was either going to make or break the show. "Froggy" had the advantage of a built-in, familiar melody as well as airtime and, if anyone was interested, YouTube fame (with some PG lyrics substituted for radio and TV). If "Froggy" didn't work, Melvin would prefer to cut out "Millicent" and "Money Grab" and go straight for "Bumbershoot," try to hook some pussy.

"Froggy Went a Snortin'" was the song Billy Goat's Gruff had sung on *Letterman* and the song that prompted the following three-star review in *Rolling Stone*:

> *Billy Goat's Gruff will never be mistaken for commanding the technical artistry or musical inventiveness of the White Stripes or Nirvana, but if the tracks from their first two offerings are an indication, it is just that lack of polish that makes them interesting. On "Froggy Went a Snortin'," Melvin Horgan's lyrics infuse the familiar folk tune with counterculture themes of defiance and cynicism. His sarcastic and eventually nihilistic world view cements his role as the emerging Lenny Bruce of grunge. Troll Horgan has the courage not just to reject the peace and love folk culture of the '60s as a simpleminded Utopian fantasy, but to openly mock it.*

In truth, on shrooms, watching *Reality Bites* for the twelfth time while Billy played "Nevermind" in the other room for the 112th time, Melvin got the idea for "Froggy" based upon a revenge fantasy against a Plaid Pantry owner who chased him out of the store for bothering some high school girls. He stole the tune and cadence from the folk song and stole the voice and attitude from Cobain's opening riff from "Territorial Pissings" mocking the Youngbloods. Only Melvin maintained that tone throughout the song.

Billy hadn't addressed the audience since the opening, but the crowd, paying attention now, took up close to a quarter of the arena, and an equivalent number milled around at the back.

"Hey there, Boise. Hope you're having a good time. We've got a couple more"—there was slight applause—"and then you're gonna hear a fantastic band, He Got the Giggler." More applause. "First we're gonna play you a little song was a hit for us a couple years back. Troll, take it away."

"Froggy" was a two-and-a-half man show—not much of a drum piece, and Bebe really just laid a simple backbeat. Billy played two introductory chords, and Melvin started in:

> *"Froggy went a snortin', he did ride, mhmm*
> *Froggy went a snortin', he did ride, mhmm*
> *Froggy went a snortin', he did ride*
> *Rolled a drunk by the riverside, mhmm.*
>
> *"Knocked at dealer Mouse's door, mhmm*
> *Knocked at dealer Mouse's door, mhmm*
> *Knocked at dealer Mouse's door*
> *Said I got forty dollars and I want to score, mhmm.*
>
> *"You get one gram for forty brah, mhmm*
> *You get one gram for forty brah, mhmm*
> *You get one gram for forty brah*
> *Six lines easy, I throw in the straw, mhmm.*
>
> *"Got a key, you want it all? Mhmm*
> *Got a key, you want it all? Mhmm*
> *Got a key, you want it all?*
> *I'll set you up for a slip and fall, mhmm.*
>
> *"Weasel works at the Mighty Quik, mhmm*
> *Weasel works at the Mighty Quik, mhmm*
> *Weasel works at the Mighty Quik*
> *He'll polish the floors and make them slick, mhmm.*
>
> *"I'll send you to attorney snake, mhmm*
> *I'll send you to attorney snake, mhmm*
> *I'll send you to attorney snake*
> *He says embellish never fake, mhmm.*

Richard Sanders Polin

"Next see chiropractor Quack, mhmm
Next see chiropractor Quack, mhmm
Next see chiropractor Quack
He'll swear to God you fucked your back, mhmm.

"Froggy limped up to the witness stand, mhmm
Froggy limped up to the witness stand, mhmm
Froggy limped up to the witness stand
Collar on his neck, cane in his hand, mhmm.

"I can't work, can't hardly hop, mhmm
I can't work, can't hardly hop, mhmm
I can't work, can't hardly hop
Damn sciatica just won't stop, mhmm.

"Froggy cleared five thousand and his key, mhmm
Froggy cleared five thousand and his key, mhmm
Froggy cleared five thousand and his key
celebrated with Ms. Bee, mhmm.

"Fucked her in a bathroom stall, mhmm
Fucked her in a bathroom stall, mhmm
Fucked her in a bathroom stall
Pig detective filmed it all, mhmm.

"Froggy, you're gonna have to sing, mhmm
Froggy, you're gonna have to sing, mhmm
Froggy, you're gonna have to sing
Don't care 'bout you, we want your ring, mhmm.

"Froggy got shivved in a holding cell, mhmm
Froggy got shivved in a holding cell, mhmm
Froggy got shivved in a holding cell
Mouse says he'll see you in hell, mhmm.

Millicent DeGroenfeld Rice

"Now here's the biggest tragedy, mhmm
Here's the biggest tragedy, mhmm
Here's the biggest tragedy
Pig detective sniffed the key, mhmm, mhmm."

And amazingly, as if the show was in 2010, the entire crowd erupted in spontaneous singalong with "Pig detective sniffed the key" and finished the song with both flourish and applause, and if for only the moment, Melvin "the Troll" Horgan was a headliner again. The loiterers in the back seemed to have been compelled towards the front, and the arena only recently populated like a remote Greenland fishing outpost had transformed into an actual concert scene—amazing what one familiar tune could accomplish.

"Thank you very much, Boise. Love being back here," started Billy Markwell.

And then Melvin ad-libbed, "It's about fucking time, Boise. Fucking pig detective, I know. Here's another for you potato-eating bastards."

And then they started into "Millicent."

Most hits are carefully crafted, written formulaically with researched themes and predictable hooks refined by A&R men to a target demographic. Occasionally, however, there is an unexpected outlier, an anomaly. A single abnormally firing neuron can trigger a grand mal seizure. One renegade neuron can trigger other adjacent and morphogenetically normal neurons to fire, and the next thing you know, the whole damned brain is asynchronously firing and the organism has dropped on the floor randomly shaking in a frenzy, bladder expelled and tongue lacerated as convulsions proceed until stopped by medication, by resumption of neural control over the renegade, or by death. Such is the kindling at times of a hit song. Something about that song touches one fan, and then another, until the momentum of the chaos is unstoppable.

"Millicent" started in anonymity, the crowd drawn in by "Froggy" lingered as if anticipating, and then the refrain came, the only intelligible words somehow electric in minds and consciousness.

"Friday night pole dance, Saturday found . . ."

And there was an effect of enchantment, and the audience swelled but contracted simultaneously as the packing became denser. There wasn't much the performers could see in the dark hall except shadows, but those shadows looked like bizarre blobs tying to synchronize or internalize the undiscernible second-stanza lyrics, but when the refrain returned, a subpopulation seemed to have remembered them and attempted a quizzical harmony.

By the third stanza, there was a universal engagement, and Melvin decided to deviate from plan and clearly and distinctly enunciate the final phrase—"life is meaningless"—which produced a mild roar leading into the third refrain, by which time the apparently deceptively catchy tune and lyrics had become imprinted as if by programming into the impressionable, fertile souls, and the accompanying harmony to Melvin's lyrics equaled the singers' in volume and intensity.

After the major vocal component ended, Melvin and Billy had plotted about ninety seconds of guitar solo with an accompanying crescendo drumbeat. The guitar solo was a bit of a Meat Puppets rip-off, with alternating D-major and A-minor riffs with superimposed staccato phrases intended to mimic pole music with intermixed strife and conflict. The bass part was simple and complementary only to the riffs. The drumbeat started slow and took advantage of Tiny's only reliable skills: timing and intensity. Tiny had been asked to start the tempo with moderate intensity at sixty beats per minute and escalate over the course of the minute to 150 bpm, with ever increasing power per stroke. Melvin looked over the hall as he stepped away from center stage and allowed Billy to meet the spotlight. The audience now seemed to occupy much of the hall, save some crannies near the exits and around the bars.

During the instrumental jam, Melvin carried a tambourine more as a prop than an instrument. It was a glorified metronome to keep his focus until the cue to interrupt Billy and Tiny with one more full refrain and then a truncated final "Millicent DeGroenfeld Rice" before fadeout. As he slapped the world's lamest instrument, the sorry canvas even kindergarten orchestras restrict to their most hapless mandatory participants, he scanned the audience as if the recent reversal of fortunes might provide an opportunity for transient companionship.

With only about ten seconds left before he cued back in, Melvin saw a crevasse form in the crowd towards the front right center of the mosh, about ten feet in front of the stage. As the patrons stepped away, there was a lone figure prone and convulsing on the ground, a young man clutching with one hand towards his left chest, the other one shaking at his side. His T-shirt was purple-blue and stained with vomit, and it bore the design of a white-cratered planet with a lone green figure and some words in French above the planet. A frumpy goth girl was on her knees, appearing to fret over the body with dire hysterics. Someone else was suddenly astride him, checking for a pulse and then initiating CPR.

The house lights came on, and the stage lights and sound system were killed as the focus of the theater shifted to the young man on the ground. Tiny and Bebe stopped playing, Tiny tethered to his kit and Bebe disappearing backstage to find a smoke. Billy put down his guitar, and he and Melvin veered to the front of the stage to view the proceedings.

"Dibs on the T-shirt. Is that fucking French? Never had a French fucking T-shirt."

"Melvin, kid's OD'ing. Who the fuck cares about a T-shirt."

They had sat him up to get the vomit out of his mouth and throat. The goth girl was hugging him. They twisted and turned him around such that the boys got a panoramic view before they laid him down once more.

"Look at that dick. He has the goddamned Family Feud of douchey haircuts. One guy. We asked one hundred people what kind of haircut a douchebag gets and came up with the top four answers. Number one: ponytail."

"You know you'd have a ponytail if you could grow one, you fucking troll."

"Yes, Goat, I am a douche. That's not news. Number two answer: man bun. Number three answer: monk cut. Number four answer: little girl braids. All four on just one guy. It's the fucking Mount Rushmore of douchiest haircuts on one dude. And here he is OD'ing just as we were fucking slaying it."

"We were getting over."

"Sure as hell were getting over. 'Millicent DeGroenfeld Rice.' And you said—"

"Yeah, I know what I said. Not sure I understand it."

"No need. Who the fuck would get 'Closing Time.' Who the fuck would listen to anything by Sugar Ray much less 'Fly,' but that shit sold."

"Sugar Ray sucked."

"Of course, Sugar Ray sucked, but these same fucks. Not these fucks, but the ten-years-ago Boise dumbfucks made Sugar Ray rich. He was a no-talent prick like Giggler, but he was a face, and next thing you know, he's the musical interlude in Scooby Doo. Maybe this was to be our fucking 'Fly,' and then this dumbshit with a man bun and a ponytail—maybe it's more of a fucking rattail, which is even douchier—and a monk cut in front, and those little fucking girl braids is going to fuck it up forever, and yes, I want that damned French T-shirt as reparations."

The EMTs burst into the room in a squad of three, with one handling crowd control and two others continuing the resuscitation, taking over from the drunk patrons who had initiated bystander CPR. Almost immediately, a large set of scissors was deployed and cut right through the cloth, separating the Little Prince's planet in half and cleaving between the cursive "P" and "r" of "Prince" and then again between the "n" and "t" in smaller block letters of "Saint."

"Oh shit. My goddamned T-shirt, you malevolent fucks."

For a good ten minutes, they alternated CPR, adding in four or five electrical shocks but only succeeded in eliciting more vomitus from above and relaxed sphincter tone from below before wheeling him out, still pounding on his chest, presumably towards the hospital.

The house lights stayed on, and the band congregated backstage and waited until about five minutes later when Mitch Ferrell emerged from his office and gave a throat slash. "Ladies and gentlemen, due to circumstances beyond our control, management regrets to inform you that out of respect, the rest of the show has been postponed. We are not yet sure of the return date. Revolution Hall sincerely apologizes for any inconvenience but, given the circumstances, feels it would be inappropriate and disrespectful to continue."

Melvin Horgan hustled his tambourine back to the van. He passed Marc Bauer in the hall, who was staring aimlessly on the static on the TV screen concealing an episode of *Law and Order SVU*. "We killed tonight, kid. Literally killed 'em. Saved you some embarrassment, most likely. You should thank us."

"Man, some kid in the audience died tonight. Is that normal? It can't be, right? Not cool, not cool."

"I know. That douchebag was probably one two-hundredth of your fan base in Boise. Unbelievable. Come on. You don't have to thank us. You still get paid, get to come back, probably without us, and you don't have to experience the angst of losing the crowd from your lead-in. Only downside, I don't think any of us is getting laid tonight. Nothing ruins the mood like—"

"Ruins the mood? What mood? Some guy just died! And you hadn't even finished your set."

"No, a junkie OD'd. Boo-fucking-hoo, Giggler. You have the big comfy bus. You enjoy the ride to Ogden. We'll see you there tomorrow, and maybe, just maybe, you'll get to start on the pathway to being a rockstar."

And with that, Melvin "the Troll" Horgan feigned a stroke of his dick, turned around, and exited Revolution Hall and retreated back to the motel for a solid five hours of sleep before the van started off in the morning.

Chapter 6:
You Can't Say That on the Air

The drive between Boise, Idaho, and Ogden, Utah, took about four-and-a-half hours, representing a straight shot on Interstate 84 East. It might have taken a little less if Tiny had not insisted on stopping for food every time he spotted he saw a Taco Bell decal on the "Food Next Exit" signs.

Before he'd become a rock-and-roll drummer, Tiny Atlas had been a Taco Bell addict through a form of coercive panhandling, in which he would stand outside the Rose Garden after Blazers games, collecting the coupons the team gave out when they hit a century. The promotion policy was changed to prevent Tiny from redeeming eight at a time by limiting the number available to one per customer, but Tiny would then roust up neighborhood derelicts (which eventually included Melvin and Billy) to augment his haul.

A stopover in Twin Falls was necessary to load up on booze before hitting a dry state, and while Tiny's per diem went for chalupas and cokes, and Billy's was earmarked for a Weber State jersey, Melvin spent all but a pizza slice worth on Coors Lights and one bottle of Old Granddad. The beer served as cheap Xanax for the bus ride and maintained slumber until arrival in Ogden with six hours to kill before the show. As a headliner, there were responsibilities, not necessarily pleasurable ones, but there was a nostalgia for the annoyance of promotional obligations.

For a headliner, these dead intervals were usurped by promotional appearances at record stores and radio stations. Both were necessary and entertaining in their own way. Record store promotional experiences were a double-edged sword. On the one hand, the sycophantic cretins habituating the greeting lines were in general a quicksand pit of boredom and banality.

Sitting with Billy signing CDs and pretending to banter with sixteen-year-old walking Propionobacterium incubators was harmless, but no more or less interesting than sitting in a hotel room watching *Alf* reruns buzzed.

On the other, it was an opportunity to meet groupies and hand out cards to get backstage access, which would occasionally hit for a post-concert fuck. Groupies could be corralled either at the show or pre-show. The advantages of the show were impairments of vision and judgment, while the advantage of the record store was less noise. Either way, each AA burg was a better play if some assistance at finding post-show companionship was included in the itinerary.

The radio interviews were of no such assistance unless there was a willing intern, but at least they provided an avenue for harmless fun. The goal for Melvin was to get run before the scheduled end of the interview for content inappropriate but not profane. Depending on the station and the part of the country, radio interviews could be divided into three genres: the aging hippie elitist, the shock jock, and the militant. The hippies (occasionally increasingly supplanted by hipsters) were graying old fools with ponytails and bald spots. They wore Velvet Underground T-shirts and sandals and asked inane, unanswerable questions, like your fucking musical influences. Billy would always go first: "Well, certainly the Kirkwood brothers, and then not just Cobain, but I've always emulated Buzz Osborne, you know, from the Melvins. Best friend a Melvin . . . favorite band a Melvin, ha-ha."

"Yeah, Billy, the Melvins are great, but you can't deny how much of Skillet there is in our sound. Dig those cats, dig them. And you're gonna laugh, but I would stand at the mirror for hours and just Air Supply out. Full-frontal Air Supply. If I can bring half what those dudes can bring, fireworks, brother, fireworks."

And then the inevitable dinner-party question. As if Melvin "the Troll" Horgan had ever had a dinner party, attended a dinner party, been invited to a dinner party. "Well, we grew up as musicians in the Northwest, and it would be a Northwest dinner party. I never met Elliott Smith, man, but he was a genius. Like to capture some of that and, of course, Hendrix. Maybe if I ask him nice, he would give a lesson or two."

"Billy Goat, nice answers, nice answers, but Elliott Smith and Hendrix would be pretty damn boring, you ask me. Let's face it, Elliott was a bit mopey, dolorous really. Not much fun, and Hendrix would be tripping and some old junkie at Pike's Market told me the mofo didn't share. I would invite Karen Carpenter. I know what you're thinking, double standard, but she just starved herself to death, and I hear she was a freak—might let me in her ass while she sang 'Close to you.' And then"—and here he paused in contemplation—"I think Bubbles the Chimp."

The jocks would throw their hands up incredulously while Billy chuckled having heard this thread before.

"You know, Michael Jackson's pet chimp. But, how would you say, mutated or something like a *Planet of the Apes* chimp who could tell us what the hell went on with that whack job and all those little kids. Did Bubbles have to watch or maybe participate? That's who I would invite."

One of the jocks would snort. "You would invite a genetically enhanced ape and an anorexic adult contemporary act? I know you're joking, Melvin."

"Not joking, bro. Look, I don't know dinner parties, but I can just boil a couple of bananas for Bubbles, and she's the world's cheapest date, right? And it's probably not good to admit, but I'm a troll, see, not a big guy. I generally have trouble reaching the bung—can I say 'bung'? But she's so damned emaciated, no cheek impediments. I'm down for brown."

"Billy Goat's Gruff, ladies and gentlemen."

Then there were the shock jocks. The local Howard Stern wannabes with one-tenth the talent and one-fiftieth the imagination. "We're here this morning with Infinity Records artists Melvin "the Troll" Horgan and Billy "the Goat" Markwell, leading Billy Goat's Gruff at the City Theatre tonight. Melvin, your hits 'Dusty Heaves' and 'Froggy Went a Snortin'' are both about drugs. So, tell me you about the most wasted you've ever been onstage."

"Great question, Tiny Tim and Mushmouth. We did a show in Richmond in oh-seven, backing up John Mayer, standing in for AFI, and this prick roofies us about an hour before we are set to go onstage. I was already lit up a bit, but he slips this shit in our pre-concert beer so he can ass-love us—can I say that?"

"Ass-love you?"

"Well, I would say [bleeped out], but it's live radio, Mushmouth. Now, fortunately, Tiny doesn't drink, and he is not the brightest soul, but he's protective like a rottweiler or an Irishman, and he beat the living crap out of Mayer, and that's when Jessica Simpson dumped his ass. It was Tiny plus the fact that he actually likes [bleeped out] either way. Goat and me were still roofied but made it through an eight-song set we topped off with a cover of 'White Rabbit.'"

Or another time in Terre Haute, when the DJs said, "Melvin and Billy. We are obsessed with groupies. We want to know about your groupies. First of all, do you get groupies?"

"Not sure exactly what you mean by that, Broadway Barnicle. Groupies. We have fans, of course. But . . ."

"Come on, Goat. Of course, we have groupies. Highest form of flattery. Sure, you guys get them too, Barnicle, and especially you, Meltdown Milton. The rage, the rage, they love it."

"Well, we get the occasional reject, but what I want to hear is the fugliest groupie you've ever banged."

"Great question, Milton. I have to admit that even though I'm an international superstar and the greatest gift to grunge since Cobain himself, I'm humbly a bit of a troll in appearance, so any sex for me is good sex. And I'm appreciative of each and every young lady who is willing to show their appreciation for my genius carnally, so to speak. But having been rejected and rejected and rejected before my talent was recognized, I never say no. So, let's say in Knoxville one time, there was a young lady with some form of birth defect so that when the light shone right through, I think they call it a harelip, you could see up into her cranium, which is frankly disconcerting when you're trying to . . ."

"Uh, Billy Goat's Gruff, ladies and gentlemen."

The final type of interview was the political hegemony insistence. This was generally a leftist ideologue who had interpreted a song about a dog getting into a stash of pot to signify a presumed shared belief in a national minimum wage or closing Gitmo. The least you might expect is that they'd bring up legalized pot.

"Well, Symone, I sure as hell hope they don't close that place. I'm actually in negotiations to be an executive producer about a reality show at Gitmo. Dick Chaney greenlit it and loves the idea. We're gonna take a civilian who could pass for Arab and place him at Gitmo within a five prisoner pod, and see if the guards can tell the difference. It's on pay cable, so you have leeway in terms of any interrogation techniques."

"You're going to torture? Civilians?"

"So, they get ten thousand dollars for showing up, and they will win a hundred thousand if the guards think one of the real terrorists is the citizen. Even the terrorists get five K, so it's win-win. Torture? Whatever you want. They'll sign a waiver. Let them do waterboarding, the German chair—that's when they get tied backwards to a metal chair that gets tipped backwards. We've got a hot actress trained as a guard who will play good cop and get them blue balls, then have this crazy bastard who comes in as bad cop and takes their blue balls and puts this Syrian clamp on it and dials up the pressure until they pass out—it goes so much faster and more intense with blue balls. So, close Gitmo and ruin the best American TV since *The Wire*—I think not."

"We have here Infinity Recording artists Melvin Horgan and Billy Markwell of Billy Goat's Gruff, playing tonight at the University Pavilion. Melvin, here in Delaware, we have an item up before the state supreme court regarding the legality of gay marriage. Your lyrics have generally applauded American counterculture. What would you say to those who try to restrict the rights of the LGBTQ community?"

"What would I say? I would say nothing to them. They're imbeciles. Wait, I'd tell them to mind their damned business. What do they know about LGXZ's, or whatever."

"LGBTQ, Melvin. I quite agree."

"But then I'd find whatever moron is trying to promote gay marriage and try to knock some sense into them. I mean that's the dumbest idea in the history of dumb ideas, unless you're a divorce lawyer—then it's an outstanding idea."

"I'm not sure I understand."

"Look, I've got nothing but love for the LGTU, but you've got to realize that the superiority of your thing, your movement. The thing us feature-challenged, small-pricked straights wrestle with is our bloody holier-than-thou morality and inhibitions. Yeah, I can find some horny fat-assed broad with three chins who just likes to ball, but vast majority, blah-blah-blah, you're cute, but I'm married, you're adorable, but I'm in a relationship. But you guys have ordained promiscuity. Why would you want to curtail the feature that makes you so totally freaking cool? Monogamy is overrated, the bane of the modern society. Marriage is just legalized monogamy. You'll regret it as soon as you get your first wandering eye suck-off by some hot redhead, and your wife finds out and calls a fucking lawyer and takes half your flannels because you two were committed. Before the nuptials, she would have joined in, you know it, and all three of you heaving and moaning drunk on Chardonnay without the guilt, the regret, and the revenge. You think you want the right to marriage? Wait till you have it, you'll be miserable like all us straights. In ten years, when this all blows over and there's no more traction other than from the trial lawyers association, you'll bloody well thank me. Melvin "the Troll" Horgan will go down in history as a hero in the LBZU community as the Savior of Perpetual Strange."

"And we're out."

The nostalgia of annoyance. A couple years back, BGG had played the university arena, and the hours before the show had been spent pretending to work out in the gym and inviting cute coeds to a non-existent afterparty. Peery's Egyptian Theater had an unfinished basement with an AM-only radio and a version of Monopoly based around National Parks, except that someone (probably those fucking Harris brothers—Casey likely was wasted and Sam convinced the greedy moron the shit was real) had taken all but a couple of the bills, and the Community Chest cards all had pictures of boobs on them obscuring the instructions.

So, it was back to another solo pursuit with the Game Boy, and unfortunately, *Resident Evil* wasn't loading for some reason, but there were a couple of other games, including a go-cart game that allowed you to spill bananas on the road, which was modestly entertaining for an hour or two while Tiny and Billy worked on cues.

About four thirty, Marc Bauer walked through on his way to an apparent rehearsal. "You in a better mood today, Melvin?" he queried from safe distance.

"I'm in a great mood now, Giggler. You do XRK or BER?"

"Um, both. XRK at one, and BER at three."

"We won't get shit from BER, fucking Maroon 5 crowd. Maybe you charmed them. You do any harmonies, Giggler? Any 'Wake Me Up Before

You Go-Go'? But that's a station for thirteen-year-olds and their moms. XRK is legit. Still have that dyke, goth promotions girl."

"Monica, yes. Not a fan of yours, I don't think."

"Probably not. Her girlfriend blew Connor Oberst while I fingered her two years ago. Good times. On-air talent ask about us?"

"Bozeman Bob? He did. Asked how you were doing."

"Did he tell you 'bout the time I hurled in studio on the mike?"

"He may have mentioned something."

"Did you rep the after-concert party like a good boy?"

"After-concert party?"

"Yes, dingus. The event where as many of us get sucked off by as many sluts as we can fit in the bus. Holy fuck, you're dense. Only consolation is maybe we'll kill some fuck again and will be a moot point like last night. You didn't say shit about that."

"Hell, no. Tour manager was very clear. Are we up for rehearsal? You already finished?"

"Don't know. Goat's around here somewhere."

"Don't you have to rehearse with them? Don't you have to play?"

Melvin looked up with crazy eyes, and Marc Bauer stepped back. "You tambourine-shaming me, kid? Yeah, I didn't have parents who got me piano lessons, violin lessons when I was seven. Fucking nerve. I'm gonna assume you're as green as you are annoying. You ever heard of Mick Jagger, you fucking moron? Young Tom Petty asked Mick once the same fucking dumbass question you just did, and they had to make up a motorcycle accident to cover up the fucking beating little albino took. You fucking never. Unwritten law. Never again or I will beat your ass, so help me God. And remember next time, a radio show should be good for two to three sluts. Work on that." And with that, Melvin went back to Cheep-Cheep Island for show prep.

"Melvin, do you think you might tone down—"

"Giggler," Melvin offered with authority.

"Yes?"

"Giggler, you ever play any of these fucking games?"

"Of course. *Halo, Call of Duty*, TF4, GTA . . ."

"Then you know how hard it is to win, not to be killed, to be successful—when some idiot is talking to you? You know that?"

"Sorry, Melvin."

And with that, once more, Melvin had another prep room to himself.

***

Peery's Egyptian Theater was a garish relic of an age when people met. For every Peery's that had stumbled into middle age only to be reimagined and emboldened in the symmetrical patterns of urban renewal, there were six or seven others with overreaching blight now condominiums or chain stores. Whereas dance halls were tailor made for mosh pits, movie houses required more architectural maneuverability. For a more subdued event, the seats would trickle to the stage as originally constructed. For a more rambunctious crowd, the first ten rows of seats could be removed to foster a mini-mosh. Around the balcony were elaborate sconces intercalated with murals depicting a roaring '20s reimagining of Egyptian historical and religious events. If anyone in Ogden was prone to righteous indignation, or if any of the visiting acts ever cared to look, there might have been repugnance for these somewhat offensive portrayals that were retouched rather than replaced in the '90s for financial as opposed to artistic concerns. The considerable sums matched by a local private development team and the city withered as it became apparent that the B-list target comedians, musicians, and shows would still bypass Ogden for Salt Lake.

The theater also contained a pub and grub with no supervision and rudimentary security, allowing the lead singer from the warm-up act to swipe a couple of IPAs, the makings of a Seagram-heavy screwdriver, a package of red ropes, and a who-knows-how-many-days-old Danish or two while the conscientious performers practiced. When Billy noticed, about an hour before the show, the telltale signs of Melvin Horgan's inebriation—no change in shirt from the night before, unzipped fly, failure to shave—the response he got from his partner was "No point. Giggler can't summon a party, so I had to make one myself."

"Jesus Christ, Melvin."

"Jesus Christ yourself. We have a ten-song set to do for a hundred and fifty people. So, we suck and lose one download per person. By the time we pay the manager and the label and the fucking government, that's fifteen bucks. Well, I made up my fifteen bucks in Danish and red ropes, so I'm good for today."

By the time Billy Goat's Gruff hit the stage at eight, Melvin had to happily admit a miscalculation. It was a surprisingly robust crowd, consisting of college students who came either out of nostalgia from past shows at the university or curiosity about He Got the Giggler, and townies representing what appeared to be a North Utah hippie convention. There were seas of tie-dye nestled in a three-quarters-full auditorium, and an energy far beyond what they had encountered the night before in Boise. Whether the enthusiasm represented local pride for acts coming to Ogden rather than expecting the natives to trek to Salt Lake or some sort of carry-over effect from the positive vibes of the Boise show before Man Bun had collapsed was speculative.

Being short is, for the most part, detrimental. Sure, there's the requisite advantages of legroom on a plane or bus, and better slumber in a cheap Japanese hotel—although now we're getting esoteric, like fewer concussions living in a warehouse loft with low, overhanging vents—but the benefits don't remotely counterbalance the detriments. For Melvin Horgan, the one time he appreciated his paltry size was onstage. The lighting crew didn't exactly know how to handle his being a full head shorter than Billy and Bebe. It was frequently the case that anything but the overhead beams passed over him. As a consequence, he retained the ability at times to scan the crowd when the other bandmates, and in fact almost any other performer, would be blinded. It allowed him an opportunity to gauge reaction and pinpoint individuals, specifically women with whom he could potentially connect. Trench rock and roll. The gatekeeper peering out from under the bridge.

While the wandering eye lusted where wandering eyes lust, it was impossible not to notice the outliers. There were the unenthusiastic texters and surfers whose devices during the forced, non-hit, unknown songs lit up the audience in constellation patterns. There was always some overweight, middle-aged mom who used to be a "rocker" jiggling at terminal velocity with alternating intervals of rest and overaction, hoping to compensate in one show for years of missed spin classes. And inevitably there were a few hippies, relics of a blind era with abnegation of taste and self-awareness. Peering under the lights, one would find a gray-haired contortionist, fabricating rhythms to match some long-forgotten fertility totem etched indelibly into a deep-fried cerebrum. Gyrations of the hands in irregular patterns originally offered by some itinerant shyster who peddled beatnik incantations in exchange for drugs and free love overcame incipient rheumatism.

There was just such a specimen front and center at Peery's, contorting his kyphotic torso to grunge beats of a different cadence. *You jump up and around, you dumbass. You slam, you surf, you head bang. You do not gyrate or wave or, lord forbid, twist and shout!* All through the set, during tambourine interludes, when Melvin should have been concentrating on identifying groupies, he found himself transfixed on this old guy with Coke-bottle glasses and a morsel of hair halfway between a ponytail and a rat tail, gyrating behind a balding white tuft of residual hair. The man wore a blue-and-purple-dominated tie-dye. Who knows how Coke Bottle interpreted the "WTF" looks that Billy Goat's Gruff attracted this demographic. Probably too wasted to even notice.

It was a positive crowd, even stayed engaged through the raggedy new stuff and maintained momentum into "Froggy." Oh, "Froggy"—the anthem that bought their five minutes. And when the denouement came and easily half the audience, now nearing eight hundred minimum, shouted with Melvin, "*Pig detective sniffed his key*," Coke Bottle was just about the only independent voice Melvin could hear, and as he looked out, he had escaped the contortions long enough to yell out that terminal phrase with a vigor and passion that could only mean the old bastard was an actual fan. *If Coke Bottle comes to the merch booth,* Melvin thought, *swear to God, he's getting a free poster. If the geezer comes during Giggler, T-shirt. A free motherfucking T-shirt.*

And then, energized after hearing Coke Bottle the hippie sing "Froggy," Melvin did the unthinkable, with Billy now delivering the WTF sneers. "Thank you," he said into the mike. "Thank you. Nice. Fucking nice, Ogden. Can you believe we did that shit on *Letterman*? Almost three years ago, and I don't fucking believe it." Huge applause. "Now, I know that last thing you motherfuckers want to hear is"—this he said in a fake huckster voice—"'This is some shit from our new CD, so go buy this shit on the Infinity label,' but give it a chance. This one killed in Boise, and we all know you Ogden people are far more discriminating that those douchebags. This one is called 'Millicent DeGroenfeld Rice.' One, two, three, four . . ." And with that, the amazing, almost hypnotic appeal of the afterthought from a hangover inspiration was confirmed. Close to a thousand souls were entranced and in

Millicent DeGroenfeld Rice

unison, and this time, sensing the control, Melvin took care to enunciate the refrain more and more clearly each time: *"Millicent DeGroenfeld Rice, come on and make another slice / Friday night pole dance, Saturday found with your blood coagulating / by a Girl Scout in an outhouse at the zoo."*

By the time, the last refrain was shouted, and the throbbing mass turned over to the band for Billy's solo and Tiny's accompaniment, the tragedy of the prior night now distant. Even an existentialist, a nihilist, an abject pessimist, could see that this song, albeit perhaps a solitary anomaly amongst a CD full of unoriginal excrement, could lengthen the deal and make the tour. And maybe someone in this writhing throng of molten energy would see fit to tend to the loneliest member of Billy Goat's Gruff.

Coke Bottle. As Melvin surveyed the mob, he kept coming back to Coke Bottle. Here was this sixty-something-year-old guy with emaciated looks, like he hadn't had a proper meal in weeks, still bobbing and weaving to a personal beat while Billy cooked through his borrowed riff and Tiny escalated the pace. While the lights partially bleached the colors, they also faded him into a kaleidoscope whirl pointed towards an eleven o'clock sun. Melvin whacked on his tambourine in an approximation of time, his eyes moving from Coke Bottle to the jiggler at one p.m., and then to a young one lusciously doing the run in place while a presumed boyfriend grinded from behind. Back to Coke Bottle, who was still digging, and then a heavyset blond with an excess of makeup at high noon mini-moshing with a mousy Asian girl in a schoolgirl dress with knee-high black stockings. Back at ten o'clock was a frat-boy type, maybe a Giggler fan, bouncing his head in rhythm, maybe a convert, and Bobbie Sue or Mary Jane beside him, pigtails stretching up over and under her brow as she shook, coopting and deflecting the light in sunspot patterns.

One more refrain coming up to bring this bad boy home in fifteen, fourteen . . . and one more prowl around to Coke Bottle, but now Coke Bottle had turned down the frequency—he was still moving for sure, but like an airplane losing speed and, consequently, altitude. Coke Bottle looked up onstage and stared right into the craggy mutt of Melvin Horgan, as if he'd known his magnetism all along—as if every two-bit rocker in Ogden in the last ten years, from the Greg Kihns of the world to the Courtney Barnetts, came to Peery's and all inevitably fixated on Coke Bottle and knew the spot-on-the-rail Ogden hippie.

But the look was fading as Coke Bottle lurched backward, eyes closing and hand clutching his heart as he careened into an owl-eyed man with a beer, which soaked Coke Bottle's face and glasses as he spun onto the floor.

"Somebody get a fucking doctor!" palisaded through the PA as Melvin instructed his band members to quit with a slash.

Chapter 7:
Hipster Santa

Vic Sessions née Alphonse Crestwood was just arriving in his cubicle when he was summoned into the bureau chief's office. Vic was a Philly native who'd studied at the Curtis School and was making a half-successful career as a jazz pianist, even subbed for Paul Shaffer in the SNL band once or twice, before his career was derailed by psoriatic arthritis. It didn't take much, a demi-note in a minute riff was enough to lose gigs. A flake or two on a keyboard. This had been before AZT, and even the Cats were still paranoid about HIV.

Sessions became a DJ on JJZ in Philly and then on BEN until he turned state's evidence in the Michael Bolton Payola scandals of the early '90s and found himself ostracized in the industry. His FBI handlers took him in, and he'd been on the fraud/racketeering desk specializing in the entertainment and more specifically the music industry since then. It was hardly glamourous work, and when he chatted up a visiting businesswoman in the hotel bars downtown after work, it was the SNL exposure that was his closer. He could still play a little, but the years of prednisone, methotrexate, and Enbrel had stolen much of the vitality of his fingers and his face, and the sallow withering remnants of both could no longer be counted on. Vic spent most days in his office looking at Atlantic City and Vegas contracts, trying to sniff out influence deals the bosses could use as leverage. The performers always squealed. They were the weak links. An early morning summons from the bureau chief generally meant a new profile and demo to review to see if anything was fishy at Harrah's.

"Sessions, got one up your alley. You're the industry guy. Know anything about a band called Billy Goat's Gruff?"

"No, sir. Never heard of them."

"No matter. Curious thing. Audience members died the last two nights during concerts. May be coincidence, but neither stiff had much medical history. Negative tox screens. No clear evidence of foul play, but band's kind of sketchy. You know Whatley?"

"From Quantico, Whatley. The—"

"Yes, don't fucking say it, Whatley. She's in command. She'll be here in an hour, and you two are heading off to Colorado Springs for the next tour stop."

"Boss, you know I don't travel."

"No, I know you don't like to travel. Consider it a perk, Sessions. Hotel room, whole new town of stewardesses to annoy, and there's always Whatley. Overnight trip, Sessions. Go pack and Amtrak down South to Reagan. She'll meet you there. Brief is on your desk. Best have read it before Whatley meets you at the airport."

Vic Sessions didn't like to travel. Between having to get one of the shut-ins at the functional senior complex in Elkins Park—where he lived on the cheap—to care for the least likely miniature poodle an FBI agent ever owned, and knowing the acclimatization would exacerbate his psoriasis, and simply the loss of routine of a Wawa's pretzel and coffee breakfast, a Stouffer's mac and beef lunch, and a Bookbinders dinner that comprised the ritual of existence, the thought of even a day away from Philadelphia was disheartening. He hated travel so much, there was a bag already packed for one-day, weekend, and weeklong trips so as to evade the angst of preparation.

Nora Whatley was already his failure. Five years ago, when the bald spot was easily combed over and his complexion hadn't faded, she was a young investigator straight out of the academy assigned to an international drug smuggling ring that took down a putative Christian metal band from Canada named Winnepegged. He had tried to lure her to his room under false pretenses of reviewing surveillance tapes, but she had brashly remarked that she had been reviewing surveillance tapes with her dad since she was twelve and could muster the energy independently. It was an obvious play, and her rejection was both polite and flippant.

Nora was the daughter of the lily-white son of a Dixie agent from the Richmond bureau who had married one of MLK's cousins as a byproduct of a prolonged, unsuccessful surveillance looking for Communist influences in the movement in '69, shocking the Whatley family, which traced its heritage back to a cousin of the general himself. Whatley found himself excommunicated and resurfaced in the D.C. bureau, working directly in LBJ's justice department. His daughter was part of the third female class at Annapolis and joined the bureau at discharge and had been consistently promoted, even with her dad safely in retirement back in somewhat penitent Richmond.

Blue eyes in a multiracial woman were irresistible, entirely irresistible to Vic. Curly black hair scrunched into an efficient ponytail behind the efficient, company-issued black pantsuit, which mirrored his own. But sadly and inevitably, all business. If it was all business five years ago when booze and methotrexate were his only corporal poisons, it was hopeless under the duress of chronic steroids, with his face bloated like Humpty Dumpty.

They met five hours later in the bureau's Reagan gate. Commercial through Chicago and coach, for Christ sakes.

"Agent Sessions. Pleasure to see you again. Strange case, isn't it? Summary, please." All business, undermining the pleasantries.

"Yes, ma'am. Pleasure's mine. Tour of two Infinity artists—Billy Goat's Gruff and He Got the Giggler. Medium venues. Audience just under six hundred in Boise, nine-fifty in Ogden. Each show during the opening act, Billy Goat's Gruff, victim expired of apparent cardiac arrest about thirty-five minutes into a forty-five-minute set. Waylon Holstein, twenty-two-year-old barista in Boise. No medical history. Tox screen positive for pot but nothing else. Lester Mangrove in Ogden, sixty-two-year-old on disability for fibromyalgia. Traces of acid and pot. Hypertension but no other cardiac history. Autopsies pending. Holstein was towards the back of the room; Mangrove on the rail. He Got the Giggler is a new signee fresh out of college. Five guys, all college friends, manager a sixth. A couple of pot possession misdemeanors but nothing substantial. Entertainment families, no red flags. Billy Goat's Gruff is a quartet. Session bassist with no priors. A drummer, Tiny Atlas, with a remote history of GTA but mostly juvie stuff, nothing recent. Billy Markwell, guitarist. A few drunk and disorderlies and possession. Spokesman. Lead singer, Troll Horgan. Piece of work. Possession with some harder stuff, drunk and disorderly, indecent exposure, vagrancy, petty larceny. Nothing violent. Grunge is their thing, I think. Jumping and yelling. Angry but angst angry, not metal angry. Giggler is more mainstream rock and roll. Billy Goat's third tour—first one an opening act, second one a headliner, this one back to an opener. One national TV appearance, and one of their songs was featured in an episode of *Sons of Anarchy*."

"Good. Gut feeling."

"Coincidence. Waste of time. Natural causes in the old guy, and some medical zebra in the kid. Home by tomorrow."

"Honest assessment. CSI is already in place both venues. When we get to Colorado Springs, I'm taking care of analysis of vics one and two. You have recon and interviewing the bands. Giggler never played?"

"They didn't play Boise. Cleared the hall. After vic two in Ogden, Billy Goat didn't finish their set. Giggler came out, but apparently vast majority hit the exits while paramedics worked on Lester. They did about thirty minutes for a hardcore group of a hundred or so and quit by mutual agreement."

"Talk to both bands. Any crew present for both shows?"

"At the venue or in the PD?"

"Crew, roadies. Guys like that. Keep it informal, Sessions. That's why I asked for you. You're the least likely agent on the force. The closest thing we have to one of them."

"Ma'am, I'm a forty-seven-year-old former jazz pianist and DJ. Not sure I have much in common with a grunge singer named 'Troll.'"

"Make it work, Vic. As you say, probably a fool's errand."

* * *

The Black Sheep was a sleeper. An unimpressive dump from the outside that had a dynamic interior with a reputation for selling out even no-name, no-talent acts booked on reportedly national tours. There was an internal security system easily commandeered to agency requirements and monitored by local officials. Part one was easy.

Vic Sessions had little patience or enthusiasm for his mission, with its primary goal of providing a report explaining how the unlikely random phenomenon of two sequential deaths was coincidence as opposed to malfeasance. The process of interviewing the bands and the traveling crew was an onerous chore made only slightly less unpleasant by the fact He Got the Giggler hadn't yet become arrogant assholes. On the other hand, their stories were all uninteresting and consistent. The band was backstage in the prep room together with manager and crew, except for Marc Bauer, who was puking his guts out at the time of both emergencies. No one had seen anything unusual about Billy Goat's Gruff with regard to instruments or preparation, and none of them had mingled through the crowd. They all had pleasant banalities concerning the Billy Goat's Gruff members, except the Troll, about whom no one seemed to comment.

Vic started interviewing BGG with Bebe Mustang, whose answer to every question was "Bud, I'm just the damn bass player."

Next was Tiny, who barely seemed to comprehend that anything unusual had resulted from the shows other than "We didn't play songs nine and ten, for some reason."

From Billy Markwell came semi-appropriate remorse. "Fucking shame, really is a fucking shame, I guess," and the first revelation that both deaths occurred during the song "Millicent DeGroenfeld Rice," which was written by Melvin and placed on the set list by Melvin.

He saved the Troll for last, if for no other reason than that Melvin, knowing that interviews were forthcoming, was nursing his per diem at Fabulous TNTs, a nearby strip club with three stages active early afternoon with no admission charge before seven p.m.

Melvin "the Troll" Horgan appeared in the prep room about forty-five minutes before doors. Vic Sessions was prepared for the end of this wild goose chase, ready to take in an uneventful show and head back home to his own bars and strip clubs by the morning. Vic wasn't much of a detective, in the classic Sherlock tradition. He couldn't decipher soot on a footprint and just plain ignored tattoos and other potential criminal totems. He couldn't pinpoint an accent, analyze fluid splatter, or discern even the most fundamental of the subliminal indicators of duplicity. However, the fact that Melvin had, within three hours, consumed two beers and a vodka-based fruit drink was patently obvious. Melvin had about a six-day haggard beard and a T-shirt with the faded words "booger treats" under a faded picture of the Smails's grandson from Caddyshack.

"Mr. Horgan. Nice to meet you. I believe you were informed I would need about five minutes of your time before the show. My name is Vic Sessions,

Mr. Horgan. I represent the FBI, and we were called to just do some routine investigations of the events the last couple of nights."

"Events? The stiffs. Those events. What you think I can tell you, Dick?"

"Well. Maybe nothing, Mr. Horgan. Just before we start, I can tell you've put back a few. Just have to make sure you know you're not under investigation, and I'm just gathering information. But I can put this off."

"Dick, how much they give you per diem?"

"Per diem? Not sure."

"You sure as hell do fuckin' know your per diem. Mine's chickenshit. Twenty-five bucks, for the whole fucking day. Damn Infinity cheap bastards. C'mon. I'll answer your questions, Dick, but what's yours?"

"Fifty-one. Fifty-one dollars for food, eighty-nine for lodging."

"Now that's first rate, Dick. More than twice these cheap bastards. Of course, if you're the headliner, you get thirty-five. Fucking Giggler. That's two more beers. Twenty-five dollars and only twenty-two left after breakfast. Two beers, Coors, and one screwdriver at happy hour, and all twenty-two flew away—well, three of it in the G-string of this little Filipina. If you have some of your fifty-one left, not a bad way after the show."

"Melvin, about the guys in Boise and Ogden."

"Yeah, kid OD'd in Boise, must be. Old dude in Ogden. Had moves. Connection. Of course connection, I keep a fucking dart in my tambourine. A little ricin, a little curare. A little concoction I call midnight. The douche in Boise was wearing a fucking T-shirt of the cover of the fucking Little Prince. I needed that T-shirt. The hippy I thought looked to be ninety-seven. Gave me a cross look. Figured I could get away easy, disguise it as a heart attack. Is that your fucking theory? We attacked him from the stage. Hit two random bastards with a dart in the middle of a fucking song. Man, I knew you Dicks weren't the brightest lights. Go back and cuff up Giggler. That bastard would've done anything to avoid having to go onstage, pansy ass."

"Melvin, I'm not accusing you of anything. I'm gathering information."

"Gathering fucking information. I don't talk to Dicks. If Billy Goat Markwell got cut by the Giggler, wouldn't talk to Dicks. I'd get Tiny and bash that fucker's brains in until jelly paste was left. Then I'd make every fucking ingot of that bastard disappear, and Dicks wouldn't know shit. Now if I wouldn't tell a Dick my only fucking real friend's killer, because Tiny's more of a pet than a boon companion, why would I tell a Dick shit about some random shit that could not involve me unless I was Harry fucking Houdini reborn as the Joker?"

"I got it, I got it. Melvin, got to be honest. I don't fucking want to be here either, truth. Truth is that I think this is a bullshit case with no credible reason to think it's anything but random, and I resent the fact that I am here. I don't want to be in Colorado Springs any more than you want to be opening for Milli Vanilli there. So, answer me one question, and I will happily watch your lovely show tonight, and get my ass home where I belong. Who the fuck is Millicent DeGroenfeld Rice?"

"Millicent DeGroenfeld Rice is a dead stripper. Google it, Dick. Dead stripper. Yeah that was what was playing when both dudes croaked. Maybe dead strippers are exacting revenge. That's another brilliant theory, Dick."

"If it's a theory, Melvin, it's not mine. This ain't the fucking *X-files*."

***

Melvin sauntered off backstage with about thirty minutes until doors. Cameras had been set for hours, and a couple of local resident agency men had been given the day off from chasing meth runners and secessionist tax-evading ranchers to mingle into the crowd. If that meant showing up right at seven in freshly printed *Nevermind* and *Spoonman* T-shirts so as to appear less conspicuous, hallelujah. There were about three hundred actual patrons in the audience, maybe a third congregating towards the front, and the rest milling around the two bars or finishing up conversations away from the stage.

Beholden to an Eastern time zone circadian, Vic was already a little spent. Coach from D.C. to Chicago and the puddle jumper had annoyed his chronic lumbago, and as he tried to set up his proposed vantage point in the rear, his back started to rebel. If he was out at this hour (now his nine twenty), there was a stool and a sedative/hypnotic involved. There were no seats in the back of the hall, but there was a strange configuration exactly center stage of a small square table, low to the ground, suggesting it came from a Sunday School or grammar school (they'd make a detective of him yet). In the center of the table was a chair, not just any chair but a plastic, flat red chair, with its seat no more than eighteen inches above the level of the table. Another "clue." On top of the chair sat a projector, not a modern LSD projector coupled to a laptop, not even an antiquated Kodak slide projector, but a really old-fashioned, grade-school gray overhead projector, the kind teachers once used to display lessons etched on clear plastic sheets handed down over the years to be prism projected onto blackboards with equations such as $4 \times (3+7) = ?$.

Vic leaned astride the table with his right hand buttressed on the edge of the projector, which was at his waist level, and his body lurching to the right garnering minimal support in the knee from the edge of the table. From this position of relative stability, he surveyed the room and made notes of the agents and cameras, just in case, like Linus waiting for the Great Pumpkin.

At 7:25, five minutes until the appearance of a local second warm-up act, Vic was tapped on the shoulder by a man in red, all red. "Could you take your hand off the projector, please," the newcomer whined impertinently. He was wearing red jeans matching a red Old Navy tee and red sneakers. His tortoiseshells procured from the '80s stared widely into Vic's weary browns. The man was manscaped in a small, pencil-thin 'stache and a beard somewhere between a soul patch and a goatee.

"Why should I take my hand off the chair?" Vic replied, annoyed.

"Because it's mine" came the reply.

Vic Sessions thought momentarily about disclosing rank before reassessing the absurdity of the potential confrontation. "No problem. I am happy to stop leaning on your projector." Vic leaned down and, with a little forward torso flexion, allowed his hand to rest on the edge of the table, well away from the projector.

The man in red walked away, apparently content that his property was being respected, then returned no more than two minutes later and glared at Vic and said, "Could you stand somewhere else? I need this space."

"Correct me if I'm wrong, but you asked me not to lean on the projector, and I'm no longer leaning on your fucking projector."

"Well, now I need the entire space, and I have to ask you to leave."

"Then why didn't you ask me to leave the first time? I'm tired as shit. I've been up since six a.m. East Coast, and I just need something to lean on. Leave me the hell alone!"

The man in red walked away but soon brought back a man in green—head-to-toe green. This man was not the effeminate dandy of his compatriot.

His nose ring and copious facial hair around a pug nose had a wart hog effect. He was a head shorter than Vic and the man in red but had the immediate feel of a welterweight Greco-Roman wrestler. Vic knew he had backup, but as the man in green approached, he readied for confrontation.

Instead, belying his appearance, the man in green looked up to Vic. "My friend tried to ask you nicely to move, and you were insulting. I'm not sure why you're being so negative."

"I'm being negative. I'm being negative? Hipster Santa asks me not to lean on the projector, I stop leaning on the projector. Hipster Santa then asks me not to lean on the table, and I explain that I'm exhausted. Hipster Santa gets his Hipster Elf, and I'm being negative. I guess no fucking Omaha Steaks for me this year. But no worries. I'll take my aching back over to the pinball table." Vic had spied a *Buffy the Vampire Slayer* Bally machine strangely placed beside an ATM in the back of the arena. "And you can use this table and chair and projector for the naughty and nice list or whatever the hell you're going to do." And with that, Vic stormed away, hoping pinball was not hipster in Colorado Springs.

Vic Sessions still had a panoramic view from his abandoned pinball table, which as it turned out was unplugged for the show anyway. Until the lights went out, he avoided looking back at the man in red going through whatever preparations he might require.

A few minutes later, the lights dimmed, and out on the stage came a man and woman in matching silver unitards, with the man also donning a silver cape. He carried a flute in his right hand, and she had a guitar. "Good evening, everyone. Before you guys get to hear our feature acts tonight—Billy Goat's Gruff and He Got the Giggler—we are going to warm up the room a little bit. I am Hector Moncado, and this is my wife, Claudia. We are Aztechno."

An accompanying boom box provided an electric piano beat as Claudia played guitar and Hector meandered between passable artistry on the flute and techno be-bop in flat Spanish, which dragged down his wife's accompaniment. As Hector did his best to approximate Jethro Tull playing Vangelis, Vic noticed a projector screen behind the band, and on the screen danced visual effects of colors—red and blue and yellow in droplets sometimes separate and sometimes flowing together in second-grade science experiments of melding. Looking carefully, Vic could see the word "Pyrex" clumsily projected like an inadvertent microphone boom, and even the numbers and letter raised into the clear glass: 12, then PX79423. It wasn't much of a stretch to extrapolate why the man in red was so protective of his table and his chair, and his projector.

They provided low-tech special effects obviously for their friends' EDM gig, with the man in red in creative control, and the man in green orchestrating crowd control. How touching and special. Why the fuck didn't they just say they were the Gruccis of food-coloring-based performance art? Could have avoided all the negative energy.

"Thank you, thank you." Hector twirled his cape and waved to the crowd. "That was an Aztechno original, which we call 'La Iguana.' You may not believe it, but this is only our second live performance, polished as we are. You know why I wear this cape? My wife is beautiful, and I am what my wife calls 'gargorgeous.' What I lack in pure physical features, I make up for in machismo and animal allure, so now I will seduce you all—men, women, all of you—with a composition we call 'Capitán de la Noche,' 'Captain of the Night!'" Hector immediately launched into a flute solo and then turned on the backup synthesizers, and his wife joined in. In the six-minute offering, there was fortunately only about a sixty-second vocal section consisting mostly of Hector yelling out "Capitán, Capitán, Capitán de la Noche" repetitively while the little droplets melded and swirled behind in beat to the synthesizer more than flute or guitar.

Four songs and twenty-four minutes of play passed, and Aztechno reached the end of abbreviated set. "Thank you, everybody. You are in for a real treat today. Billy Goat's Gruff will be on stage in about twenty minutes, and then a really fantastic band from LA, He Got the Giggler, will take you home. Thanks for listening. We are Aztechno."

Hoping to re-establish a better reconnaissance position, Vic looked back, yearning for his projector or chair as an alternative to the pinball table, especially as the auditorium was filling, and someone would surely want to drop a couple of quarters.

But it was strange that Hector never thanked his buddy in red for coming out to provide visual effects. A quick shoutout would seem inevitable given his obvious self-promoting boisterous nature. And furthermore, while the man in red was not in position, the man in green hovered around the table, shooing away the crowds who entered the hall in greater frequencies looking for space in a parabolic curve centered on the middle of the stage.

Twenty minutes later, all was clear around the arena when the lights went down and Billy Goat's Gruff took the stage. The guitarist, Markwell, addressed the auditorium: "Hello, Colorado Springs. We're Billy Goat's Gruff from Portland, Oregon. Thank you for joining us tonight." And the band proceeded into a song that appeared to be about vomitus, whatever lyrics could be discerned over the clumsy uneven drumbeat and the grating inharmonious vocals.

Vic carried the predictable jazzman's arrogance concerning grunge. Like the essayist towards the romance novelist or an artist towards a carnival caricaturist, there was an essential bias that the worst of me surpasses the best of thee. Still, he knew Nirvana and knew Pearl Jam and fathomed the draw of the raw Cobain lyrics with a raw, stripped-down musical form. It might even be art, "Heart Shaped Box," "Lithium," "On a Plain." This was anything but. A bass player going through the motions with an unnecessary backbeat, the guitarist who hadn't evolved past quarter notes and simple chords and played even those with middling precision, the drummer's banging akin to a child weighing volume over complexity or subtlety, and finally the vocals screeched with an intensity to drive dogs from a steakhouse, to dissuade sailors on leave from a bordello. *Two dudes dropped dead?* he questioned himself with a grin. *They're the lucky bastards got off easy. Pass out the fucking Kool-Aid, Jonesy, my boy. Put me out of my goddamned misery. Mystery solved. Suicides.*

About a minute into the first song, identified per the setlist as "Dusty Heaves," Vic noticed that the Pyrex projector theater had sprung back to life. Only this time, the man in red was providing more superlative effects, combining not only the colored droplets but creating waves of motion using one of those cheap Disney World adjustable fans. With it, the droplets merged and collided in ebbs and flows in the Pyrex universe. What was his ultimate goal? The moons of Jupiter, the painted desert? But obviously the man in red belonged to the venue, not the talent. The assumption that low-level talents were co-dependent seemed unlikely now. But while the effects were rendered with greater complexity, the size of the band, and specifically the drummer, served to mute the effect, as Tiny's huge head ate into the bottom of the Pyrex projection, forcing Hipster Santa to move the glassware to a more remote location, stretching its image into a less true representation.

And so it went through the initial six setlist songs. There was a flurry of hardcore fans at the front engaging in some moshing during some of the quicker-tempo numbers. There was one crowd surfer who fortunately was initially dropped over the retaining wall separating band from crowd and seemed to get a hand down before security whisked her away and back into the crowd, where she resumed being queen of the hill and, this time, was likely escorted out, as she did not return. *May have just saved her life from the murder song.* Vic Sessions laughed before taking a look around the room at his team firmly in position and ready for anything from a subtle projectile attack to a full-blown domestic terrorism exercise.

All through the progression of vile composition, the bubbles swirled and twisted and combined and formed new colors and then disengaged into new rainbow patterns, and Vic had to admit that there was a value. If only the value was contained in an ability to defocus, there was a value.

Song number seven shifted back into music. Perhaps it was just the comfort of a familiar tune or the focus of the crowd, which proclaimed importance, but the reworking of a children's folk song into a modern urban parable seemed both artistic and relevant, even if Melvin's mutilated voice was at best a prop. For three minutes and twenty-two seconds, the man in red was forgotten, maybe even the mission forgotten, and as the song reached its conclusion and several hundred spectators rose, voices in unison, to disparage and mock police culture, Vic Sessions chuckled and hoped for a repeat stanza so that he had a second chance to participate.

But the nursery rhyme ended, and Billy Markwell thanked the audience and announced something new.

But before they started, Melvin Horgan took the mike. "Hello, Colorado fucking Springs. Not sure if you've noticed, but we've got some special guests today. Look around and you'll see a couple of guys dressed like they're at an Alice in Chains show from 1996. They're FBI. You'll see a couple of others look like they're the fucking Brady brothers. They're FBI. And you'll see one motherfucker looks like balding William H. Macy on meth—he's FBI. Now I'm not sure exactly why these fellas are here. May be friends of the Giggler, ladies and gentlemen. Might be fans of ours. In fact, they told me they were here to listen to this one particular obscure song. But do your best to welcome them tonight. Let them know how much you appreciate them keeping you bastards safe. This is for J. Edgar fucking Hoover in the back. It's called 'Millicent DeGroenfeld Rice.'"

And with that, Melvin "the Troll" Horgan lit into a tune that started out with unintelligible words and a catchy yet familiar backbeat and melody but was surprisingly peppy and alluring. The refrain cut like a knife, repeating the Millicent name and continuing through one rhyming sequence and ending hard on the word "zoo." This was better, more original than the folk song re-rendering and an order of magnitude better than the other tripe. Another stanza followed and the hall was buzzing. Down front, revelers moshed in random collision patterns like colored balls in a toddler's vacuum. The refrain came again, and there was mad jumping in some degree of crowd collusion. The man in red upped the ante, and the colored oil balls danced in circles as he applied gentle electric fan breezes from competing angles while the man in green introduced some darker brown and black pellets for a full third-grade psychedelic experience.

By the third stanza, the pace and fury of the still unintelligible lyrics had reached a critical flow. Parallel crowd surfers appeared in competition for attention with the slamming. The third refrain saw jumping with hand signals of slashing throughout the crowd, and even Vic felt some separation between floor and Rockport as the droplets in Pyrex appeared to expand and contract in three dimensions, as if that was within the capacity of the art form.

After the third refrain, Vic watched Melvin carefully. He noticed the singer peering low, under the lights, into the crowd as he kept rhythm on the tambourine. The bass player had receded into the background with a very simple back beat, but Billy Markwell was doing his best actual rock guitar impression and leading a Van Halen-style solo with an ever-quickening drum accompaniment. The crowd was, without hyperbole, going haywire, and Melvin, through it all, was scanning, ducking, and darting his head side to side across the audience.

First it was a cool effect of the oil droplets careening into the prism and tethering themselves to the glass, producing a psychedelic ripple on the swirling patterns remaining in the Pyrex. Next it was a few knuckles for the first time ruining the illusion of an omnipotent artist-God manipulating the stream like the parting of the Red Sea. Finally, it was the replacement of the Pyrex palate with a red arm that clutched across the screen, dimpled by the droplets adhering to the projector, then slowly giving way and disappearing down the side, leaving only the droplets shimmering in a cockeyed pattern of white light. Vic ran back to the projection table, but the man in red was by now prostate astride his beloved table and chair, with the man in green shaking him futilely. "Cut the music, cut the music," he screamed, barely registering five feet away, over the music, so he ran to the control booth, showed his badge, drew a finger across his neck in a slashing motion, and the microphones stopped in a cacophony of jeers.

Bystander CPR was initiated without effect, and the man in red was carted out pulseless and apneic a scant five minutes later. On Vic Session's order, the concert halted, the doors sealed, and a fruitless investigation ensued.

The man in red had showed up one day during a local show about nine months before, the manager said, and had this accompaniment, which he did with a modicum of enthusiasm. Thereafter, he would come in with a day's notice and provide backdrop effects for any band without their own AV team. The performer was always in red, his interference always in green. If a band objected, the manager would tell them to vacate, but most of them didn't seem to care. The manager thought the guy worked in a paint store. The promotions director swore he ran a little studio downtown. The man in green set them right through his sobbing. The guy was an elementary school science teacher who just loved rock and roll.

"'Millicent DeGroenfeld Rice,' Horgan. What were you doing up there, during that song?"

"Preparing my invisible curare gun, of course, Dick. What do you think I was doing? There were one hundred people between us, so I had to shoot off the ceiling, then ricochet off the side wall, a stairwell, and the bar, but I nailed him good, that fucking bastard I didn't know. Jesus Christ."

Vic Sessions stared at Melvin Horgan and thought hard about an aggressive reply, a sarcastic retort to punish the arrogant bastard and show him that whatever scheme was killing random concertgoers would be uncovered and curtailed with swift and appropriate punishment. But as this death made no more logical sense than the last two, he shrugged his shoulders and headed back to his $85.99 government rate room at the Hampton Inn—after briefly considering the potential alternative of the Filipino stripper—to review the surveillance footage and, with any luck, conclude that the deaths were unexplainable so he could get himself back home, looking into play frequency radio lists and suggest which private planes required search and seizure upon return the US.

Chapter 8:
Lenny Bruce of Grunge

Roger Smith was tan, but not as tan as he'd intended. Roger and his wife, Muffin, and son Chas and daughter Susu were in the Barbados when he got the call. Or maybe it wasn't Muffin at all. Maybe it was his secretary, Peggy, whose tits he'd embezzled (under the former administration) at a private island in the Turks and Caicos. Or maybe all of the above were left behind and he was in Phuket with his squash partner on a week-long bender of debauchery masquerading as a conference on international copyright law. The only truth was that Roger Smith kept his private life well beyond the gaze of Tee Nash or anyone else at Infinity but knew when it was time to scurry back to Manhattan.

It wasn't the FBI, it was the goddamned *Colorado Springs Gazette*. Day after the concert. Page six in what used to be the Metro page before small municipality newspapers all morphed into one large amalgam to hide the soaring ad to copy ratio. Headline: "Local man Dies at Rock Show."

> *Last night, local elementary school teacher Lonnie Rohrbach collapsed and died of cardiac arrest at local nightclub the Black Sheep during a concert performance by alternative rock band Billy Goat's Gruff. Rohrbach, twenty-eight, was providing special visual effects for the show at the time of his passing. He had no significant medical issues. According to his best friend, Mule Grimstead, also a teacher at Soaring Eagles Elementary School, Mr. Rohrbach was neither drinking nor using illicit substances on the evening of his death.*

> *Sources at the Black Sheep tell the Gazette that the FBI was in the facility investigating several other suspicious deaths at previous shows on the tour featuring Portland grunge band Billy Goat's Gruff and LA rockers He Got the Giggler. Again, sources say that all of the deaths occurred during the playing of one song by the Portland band. The significance of the song, called "Millicent DeGroenfeld Rice" remains unknown, but neither the FBI nor the managers for either band had any comment. An autopsy is pending. Mr. Rohrbach is survived by his father, Joel, and mother, Emma, in Estes Park.*

Somehow this piddling article made it up the food chain to the *USA Today*, and now Roger Smith had been summoned back to New York for damage control. Three concert dates had already been scrapped, and both bands recalled with the entire tour entourage to headquarters. A CYA statement had already been produced (on the airplane, while watching some Judd Apatow film), which stated, "Infinity Records is aware of three tragic deaths that occurred during recent concerts. While there is no obvious or plausible link between these unfortunate incidents, the bands and the label are cooperating thoroughly with the authorities. We all send our deepest sympathies to the families of these poor souls."

To Roger Smith, this was a cookbook play. Three deaths during the same song were no coincidence. It was something the dirtballs in the Billy Goat band were doing, or someone in their entourage, as a sick publicity ploy or, more likely, as revenge against the label for relegating them. If the Feds were to find anything, we'd know nothing; the band would be on their own, contract null and void for violating ethics standards. If the Feds didn't, they'd be pulled from tour and quietly release with a small severance to keep their fucking mouths shut, except for the bass player, who was a company man. Simple.

It wasn't your typical Infinity work morning. Roger was in the office at eight putting his releases on letterhead and then in his customary spot in the boss's office at ten to none, admiring the new Sam Gilliam mural adorning a part of the wall where two nobodies previously resided. Tee Nash was early. His entourage exploded into the office at nine thirty, well ahead of his customary entrance. After Tee and his backup harem, his eighteen-year-old cousin completed the posse. He had his phone playing, of all things, "Millicent DeGroenfeld Rice" by Billy Goat's Gruff—the refrain was clearly audible through the phone speaker.

Roger looked past Tee and the women towards the cousin, who appeared infrequently in the office and generally stood in a corner fixated to his phone. But today, the young man was engaged in the music and was standing right next to his uncle.

"Excuse me, excuse me, son," Roger offered in tones loud enough to be heard through the earbuds but not so loud to be construed as confrontational. "I'm not sure it's a good idea."

"Very astute, counselor, very astute. Dashawn, that shit might kill you, or me, or the counselor there. That's the murder song, cold-blooded murder song. You're in a damn office, boy. Show some respect."

"Sorry, Uncle Tee."

"You like that murder song?"

"Yeah."

"Why you like that murder song?"

"Dunno."

"Good a reason as any. So, Brother Horgan's song kills folks, or so they say. Three so far. Have you really contemplated, Brother Smith? Tried to make sense of this shit? I mean, I took this Troll for a lowlife. I mean, wouldn't leave my wallet out round the fellow, but something like this? Have to look the man in the eyes and formulate, Brother Smith, formulate."

"I've taken the liberty, sir, of writing a press release."

"A press release? Like a deeply regret bullshit press release. That's good, that's good and necessary. But what response do we have. When I go on *TMZ*, or *E* as they've been asking me to do non-stop, how have we handled this—what do we intend to do, Roger Smith?"

"Well, sir. The talent is expendable. Horgan's group was a mistake in overexuberance. Your predecessor was enamored of the grunge craze and lowered contractual standards. They have never made us a penny, and perhaps the positive publicity for the label in taking a hard line would provide some capital to compensate for any financial deficits. Giggler was always about the look. There will be three more like them we can find tomorrow. Battle of the Bands in any college town, you'll find a Giggler. And of course, if the Feds do find something, all the easier. Focus turns entirely to them, no umbrella, no public sympathy or potential exposure."

"Makes sense, it really does. Good corporate sense."

"Yes, sir. Not sure there's any alternative."

"I do want to talk to Brother Horgan. Not sure what that cat will have to say, but figure it will be entertaining, don't y'all think? None of this makes sense. Before we do this, Dashawn, you ever heard about Billy Goat's Gruff before? 'Dusty Heaves'? 'Froggy Went a Snortin"? Shit you listen to?"

"Naw. Never heard o' them until Lem told me. The murder song is dope."

"Your friends know the murder song?"

"Shit, everyone knows the murder song."

"Della, baby," Tee Nash called on the intercom to his "concierge." "Della, baby, get me the download data on 'Millicent DeGroenfeld Rice,' last seven days, please."

"Yes, sir, right away."

"You see, Brother Smith. One thing I've learned, people have fickle tastes. They're sheep. What you say—caution. Nothing wrong with caution. But in a way, this is caution, too. Don't wanna be premature, you know, slick?"

"Yes, sir." Della the stripper-turned-barista-turned-receptionist-turned executive assistant came in with a printout and handed it to Tee, who digested it, then looked up straight at Roger Smith.

"Seven days ago, two downloads of Millicent, six days ago one, five days ago—that's after Boise—a hundred and seventeen. Not bad, fifth of the audience maybe. Four days ago, two hundred and ninety-eight. Two concerts, two venues. Three days ago, four eighty-nine. Then the story breaks, seventeen eighty-nine. Highest download rate of any Infinity song that day. Yesterday, *USA Today* report out, *E News*, *ET*, eleven thousand five hundred downloads. Number one downloaded song in America. Number one in Infinity history. I have to talk to Brother Horgan. Other things to consider, Mr. Smith. Best course is probably, let 'em go, settlement. But let me talk to Brother Horgan."

* * *

Melvin was seven days into an eight-day suitcase and clearly down to the dregs of the Horgan boudoir. The jeans were the jeans, designed to ride out a prolonged engagement with only a ragged pair of sweats to provide a washing interlude or sleeping alternative in cold temperatures. The day-seven shirt was a freebee they'd put on everyone's seat before a Portland Trailblazers game at least five years earlier and had a slight rip at the shoulder and a greater rip in the back, which separated the halves of a Toyota logo. He was one day shy of socks and was therefore repeating a big-toe-worn pair of Haines bought in one of those ten for ten cents bags, and the underwear was still technically clean, although there was ample evidence of prior misuse.

He was led into the office but chose to walk ahead of his escort, knowing his place in the low-armed empty chair astride the suit and across from Tee Nash.

"Brother Horgan we meet again. At PS 208, I can remember this kid who kept getting called into the principal's office, habitually and repeatedly."

Melvin looked around the room. Unlike his last visit, he sat up straight and surveyed the room. He focused for a second on Roger Smith with a malevolent scowl and then focused back with eye to Tee Nash.

"You don't say."

"And turns out I am referring to the brother you see here today."

"You mean you. What you get in trouble for?"

"Oh, the usual, Brother Horgan. Stealing lunches, pulling hair, skipping class. Whatever, whenever." Tee remained focused on Melvin as if they were the only two people in the room who mattered—the only two to which this conversation pertained.

"Okay. But here's the thing. With all due respect, I ain't done anything wrong. I wrote a song. Suit"—and he glanced at Roger—"didn't like the lyrics and it needed approval, but you let it go. And you didn't bring me here because the song was inherently repugnant. You brought me here because you thought it would get you sued, and when you realized it wouldn't, your concerns evaporated. It was a you problem. Now we have some bad press because two junkies and an old hippie have died at our shows. Don't see how that's a me problem either. I didn't kill anyone. I was on stage performing, trying to make us both some money."

Tee Nash paused and stroked his chin before replying, "It doesn't seem strange to you?"

"Sure the fuck seems strange to me. I have no clue why three twats chose to die during our shows, much less during one fucking song. But does that mean I care? Not really."

"It's not of interest to you? It doesn't intrigue you why people seem to leave your concerts in body bags?"

"Well, to be honest, I think only one left in a body bag. I think the others were having some uniform blow into their mouths and another dude beating on their chest when they departed, but no. It's not something I think about."

Tee Nash again paused. Melvin thought to himself, *That ought to shut him up. I need to get the fuck out of here.*

"What do you, think about, Brother Horgan?"

Disappointed that the conversation wasn't over, Melvin decided on a strategy of uncomfortable, brutal honesty. "Normal shit. Getting laid."

"Brother Horgan, you ever been arrested?"

"You know I have."

"Ever assault anyone?"

"Rolled a drunk or two in my day. Been rolled, too—'bout even, take and been taken. I don't get this. Look, you want to fire us, fucking fire us. You put on tour with a bunch of no-talent pricks."

"Brother Horgan, hate to say it, but you boys are a bunch of no-talent pricks."

"Of course, we are, but we know it and don't give a shit. But you put us on tour supporting these assholes, and we blow up, we have a song that's fucking smoking, and you focus on some random dead fucks we couldn't possibly have killed unless one of us is Satan himself. So, go ahead and fire us. But just maybe you'll use your fucking brain and see we have a hit, and you'll have college ring here produce some asinine corporate spin, but let me be unconventional. Let me spin this my way, and we all go laughing to the bank."

Melvin looked over at Roger Smith, who by this time was staring out the window. Tee Nash stole a glance at his nephew and the lawyer, as if one of them might provide some insight or advice, but getting none turned back to Melvin.

"Spin. What's the spin?"

"Well, you corporate types specialize in apologizing without accepting or taking responsibility. Well, in this case, that's perfectly reasonable. You haven't done shit, so anything you say will be truthful other than regrets because most likely you don't give a shit about a couple of stiffs, and I know Joseph A. Bank here couldn't care less. And me and Billy, we'll give 'em just what they want. They don't want us to be white hats. They want us to be edgy at best, evil incarnate at worst. I can do that. Let's face it, I am that. Honesty buys publicity. Trust me. Or just fire us with a parting gift. Something tells me after this two to three thousand downloads, someone else will sign us."

And with that, Melvin turned and took his disheveled figure back to the company suites to play a *Call of Duty* game he'd bought used for five dollars from the GameStop in Times Square.

* * *

Roger Smith turned to Tee Nash and wearily muttered, "Interesting human being, there. Keen interpretative grasp of corporate culture and modern mores. Sir, I think fifty is more than fair. More than they'll ever see again. They can have say half of their standard royalties above the parachute. Both sides hold harmless. Something indemnifying us in case there is an investigation finding and vice versa, however absurd that would be. Sound reasonable?"

Tee Nash just sat without a sound, staring at a caricature of Count Basie on his side wall, absorbed in thought. "Sir, we could go a bit higher if you think it would mitigate the problem." But Tee Nash was silent, staring either at the Count or just randomly at some speck of a mite or gnat crawling up Basie's arm as he pounded out "Pennies from Heaven."

"Sir, have you made a decision, sir?"

Tee Nash turned around deliberately and paused a second to linger over his answer. "Flip the bill."

"I don't understand, sir. Make them pay us, it seems unlikely their agent would allow."

"No, dufus. Flip the bill. Giggler opens up for Billy Goat. Press conference, full-ass release form, and hope to hell these boys ain't responsible. Flip the motherfucking bill."

* * *

Four days was the timeframe to organize the next show. Tour stops had already been canceled in Reno, Yuma, and Santa Fe. The next obvious show was in Tulsa, Oklahoma. Cain's Ballroom—a big enough venue for a decent crowd but small enough to ensure a frenzy of demand over supply. Tee Nash made the talking heads rounds, pledging unwavering support while expressing regret for the three victims. CNN and Fox had panel segments with the strange bell curve of American politics. The Libertarians cried free speech and freedom from government interference and supported the show. The Tea Party blasted the immoral false sanctity of the artists and the influence of degenerates on pop culture. The far left sought to censure the song itself for its stereotypic portrayal of women as helpless objects and urged boycotts and protests. The vast middle simply downloaded and downloaded in numbers that logarithmically expanded daily, passing twenty-five thousand, eclipsing JT numbers.

* * *

The next concert was scheduled for a Friday night, and Thursday, a gaggle of reporters gathered in the Tulsa convention center for a press conference arranged by Roger Smith and attended by Tee Nash, Melvin, and Billy. Melvin and Billy had been shorn of their traditional road garb for a modest, business-casual attire, which fit Billy well but overcame Melvin's neck and ankles like a premature hand-me-down.

The opening statement, prepared by Mr. Smith, was read by Tee Nash: "Infinity Records is proud to bring the hottest band in America, Billy Goat's Gruff, to Cain's Ballroom for a show tomorrow evening. Dynamic new LA band He Got the Giggler will be opening. As many of you are aware, there have been some unfortunate events at recent shows, and Infinity Records is committed to the health and wellbeing of our concert patrons and will continue to work with the authorities to determine if there is a link between these tragic deaths. To date, we are assured that they are not connected and were in no way preventable. Our entire family is greatly saddened and wish to express our deepest condolences to each and every family member and friend as well as the communities affected. We have assurances that there will be exceptional medical teams and security at the venue here in Tulsa for any unforeseen events. Strictly as a precaution, there will be security entering

Millicent DeGroenfeld Rice

the Cain Ballroom both for staff and performers, and our concertgoers will be required to sign a release form before entering the venue. The rationale for these deaths remains obscure, but our commitment to the safety of our cherished fans is clear cut and sincere.

"For those of you who don't know, Billy Goat's Gruff is comprised of founding members Melvin Horgan and Billy Markwell, who are up here with me, as well as bassist, Bebe Mustang, and drummer, Tiny Atlas. Their third CD, *Space Needle Pricks* is available on the Infinity label, and the first single on that album, 'Millicent DeGroenfeld Rice,' is currently number one on the college charts, the modern alternative, and pop charts. Infinity is proud to make Tulsa the alternative music capital of the world tomorrow night. We will take any questions." He pointed to a tall bald man in a hoodie, who had elbowed out a mop-headed dandy for the first assault.

"Joe Mullaney, *USA Today*. Billy and Melvin, the record label has issued this statement and done a bunch of interviews, but we've heard nothing from the band. No publicists or lawyers. What would you like to say to the families?"

Melvin looked at Tee Nash and then in the wings where Roger Smith looked on nervously, and let Billy begin.

"Well," he said. "We're sorry to the families. Not sure what else to say. Very sad, what happened, real sad."

Melvin sat stone quiet.

"And Melvin?"

"I've got nothing to say. Or, to answer the question, I guess, I would say nothing."

"Nothing? Three people died?"

"Yes, and three people died of cancer and heart attacks, and murder and shit in Tulsa since this press conference began. You want me to 'express regret' for all of them, too? I didn't know those people. I certainly didn't have shit to do with them. Had I died on stage, it's not like they would give a rat's ass. Probably take a photo and post it somewhere. I wouldn't say shit. Because if I did, it wouldn't be sincere, and this world is already chock full of bullshit."

"But they were your fans?"

"Maybe, maybe not. Maybe they were our fans, and then maybe I'd regret if they didn't by a T-shirt or a copy of our CD. But maybe they were fans of the Giggler, which is the shit band we were opening for and now has to open for us, in which case they just happened to arrive early enough to see the warm-up, or to get a drink, but didn't know or care who the fuck we were. But look at it this way, if they hadn't have died, don't think we'd be getting tens of thousands of downloads and press conferences. Come to think of it, I'll take back what I said before about being sorry; they didn't buy shit before they croaked, but other people more than made up for it already."

"No remorse?"

"No remorse."

The blond in the mop top then came to the microphone. "Biff Malibu, *TMZ*. Tee, Billy, Melvin. So, we have three individuals, all dead during the same song. What's up with that? Theories? Speculation?"

Tee Nash put his hand on the table, a preplanned signal to let him go first. "Biff, we have thoroughly cooperated with law enforcement. I would have to defer to their offices, local and the FBI. It would be inappropriate to speculate further. Once again, regardless of Mr. Horgan's opinion, Infinity Records does send out our deepest condolences."

Billy then followed with "I never saw the first guy or the last guy. The old man in the Ogden show's heart must've given out, man. Melvin, you said you noticed him dancing the whole show, and he was ancient, man. Other two dudes, random. OD's, I guess."

Melvin gave a twisted smile for an answer he had rehearsed. "FBI don't know shit. I told him the Giggler had stage fright and did it to avoid having to play, and that agent believed me, too. Cavity searched the Giggler, but that was bullshit. You know, I've been thinking about this, intellectually, and looking at the evidence, and I think I know the killer. Who else is jealous as fuck at the success we're having and the fact we are the greatest motherfucking grunge band of all time? Kurt Cobain. Motherfucking ghost of Kurt Cobain, that goddamned schmecker, envious as fuck of all the attention, the love, the money. His wraith must follow us around getting more and more pissed as our crowd are rolling. Just like the cotton shooter he was, desperate we don't surpass what the fuck was the name of his band. He's drawn to our shows and gets so angry, he chokes the life out of some poor bastard, thinks it'll stop us."

A voice shot out of the reporter pool. "You're serious? The ghost of Kurt Cobain? Why not Eddie Vetter, at least he's alive."

"That cake-eating motherfucker. He's too deep up Steve Albini's rectum. Risk his XM channel or singing 'Take Me Out to the Ball Game' at the Cubs game, yeah right. You think the pantheon—me and Kurt—would sing at some fucking ball game? That pussy wouldn't be caught dead at one of our shows, and he was always scared shitless of Cobain anyway."

Biff Malibu, sensing a lead *TMZ* feature, followed up. "So, Troll, how are you gonna prove Kurt Cobain's ghost is killing your fans?"

"I'm a fucking musician, not a paranormal scientist. You're a reporter, even if you do work for *TMZ*. Get some paranormal fucker on the case, measuring ectoplasm or slime. Here's a hundred bucks towards hiring some ghost hunters. Even better, take two hundred bucks and go hire Peter goddamned Venkman. But as I sit here, I do think it's Cobain, bored shit down in hell because he can't fire the ack-ack gun without veins, but if it's not, it's that conniving whore of his. Only way that channel-swimming, no-talent bitch can afford her China White is his residuals, 'cause lord knows ain't no one downloading anything by Hole anymore except maybe 'Celebrity Skin.' I love that song. So, anyone here in Tulsa see Courtney Love sneaking around this Cain place tomorrow night, you bring her to me, not the cops, and whoever delivers her can have her after me but before Tiny."

By this time, there was controlled laughter from the crowd, and Biff Malibu could hardly get out his follow-up. "Have Courtney Love? Why between you and Tiny?"

"Look, we're not one for the authorities. If Courtney's following us around and disrupting our shows, we will show her our own brand of justice. We'd get her backstage. But you can't have some random fan go after Tiny, because once he does her, she ain't feeling nothing or no one else. Fucking mule that one. Unless whoever likes sampling her cold. But hell, it's not like a gang rape, that would be awful. More like a gang bang and everyone can appreciate that. We don't do Bill Cosby pass-the-roofie, groupie-friend-around-the-hotel-room kind of gang rape. More the old porn-star-on-a-crack-high-doing-bachelor-parties kind of half-consensual gang bang, so it's not so bad."

"Folks, he's only kidding. We don't condone—I mean, our band would never—"

"Fuck we'd never, Goat. It was your damn idea in oh-nine in Yuma. That drunk skank roadie would have run the gauntlet twice, wasn't for Bebe.

You're just mad I'd put the civilian in your slot. But enough of me doing you fuckers' investigative work. Next question."

Biff Malibu had a huge "I'm the lead story tonight," shit-eating grin at this point. "I'm sorry, Troll. Just one follow-up. Why are you convinced this is Cobain? Why not Jim Morrison or John Lennon or Hendrix?"

This time Melvin ad-libbed. "Are you really that stupid? Don't you know anything about the paranormal? John Lennon, that's crazy talk. How the fuck would he know how to get to Ogden, Utah? He ain't never played there. Dumbass question. Have to move on. You." Melvin pointed to a curly-haired, tall man with a ski tan.

"Aspen Majestic, *Denver Post*. Melvin, you clearly have theories about these unfortunate deaths, but it appears the authorities have theories as well. They seem to be interested in you. Why might that be?"

Tee Nash fidgeted, then placed his hand across Melvin's mouth and initiated. "That is inaccurate. Melvin was interviewed, as was Billy and about a dozen crew members, the other band . . . They have interviewed anyone and everyone who form a common thread between these deaths, and as far as we know, they are seen as random occurrences, tragic but random."

At this point, Melvin's gaze turned serious. He looked straight at Aspen Majestic and stood up, abandoning the tongue-in-cheek nature of his last response. "Mr. Nash. I do want to address this. Our media are fueled by lies. Lies fit narratives, narratives make sense. Sense equals blame. Blame brings on righteous indignation, and righteous indignation is what sells papers or gets ratings. That bullshit narrative of America. I, on the other hand, am honest. I speak my mind. And I am, by nature, unashamedly hateful. I don't try to hide it, onstage or backstage. The halfwits may mistake that hatred for motive, but I have neither motive nor bravery to face, much less kill anyone. Do I want people dead? Hell yeah. I have so many fucking people I want dead, starting with you, Aspen Majestic. I would love to see your smarmy, blond head on a pike hanging over top of the entrance to some dive bar in Boulder. But will I kill you? Fuck no. Don't have the energy to make a plan, too lazy to devise a getaway, and too puny to survive a week in prison. I have sociopathic tendencies, but I'm not a sociopath. Sometimes I wish I didn't have a conscience or, more accurately, fear of repercussions. That's not really a real conscience, is it? It's a pseudo-conscience at best, but it's a functional replica."

"So you didn't kill anybody?"

"Isn't that what I just said, moron?"

Aspen Majestic fidgeted and clicked his pen. "But you wish people were dead?"

"Yes, of course. So do you, although it's not socially acceptable to admit it."

"Who do you want dead, Melvin? Just give us an example or two."

"Let's start with the Giggler. Easily the most annoying fuck I've ever toured with. No loss to the world with that one. And that clown-lipped cunt Flo from *Progressive*. Doubt she's really named Flo, but hologram-proof dead Flo? That would be sweet. I could watch TV again. Ryan Phillippe, Ryan Guzman, Ryan Gosling, Ryan Reynolds, Private Ryan, anyone playing Jack Ryan—any and all get-by-on-looks, no-talent, pretty-boy, Hollywood Ryans in one mass Ryan grave. That's a good start."

"Maybe I should be flattered you group me with all those Ryans. But you didn't want to kill any of these people at your shows?"

"Why would I just want some random guy boxed? Only one I even saw before it happened was the hippie, and I thought he was kind of cool for a geezer. Let's move on, right?"

"Melvin, Lloyd Bodine, *Rolling Stone*. What would you say to your fans about all this? I mean, there's got to be some message you want to convey regarding the music, some appreciation for sticking by you through all this."

"I'm going to start by telling you, and working for *Rolling Stone* you must know this, the three core fallacies of rock and roll. The three myths that have to be debunked. First, it's all about the fans. Second, what drives us is the music. Third, it's not about the money. You know what we love about the fans—their money and their cunts. We play for the fans, but we can't differentiate one stinking burg from the next. Has one performer ever stood here in Tulsa, Oklahoma, and pronounced 'We love you, Tulsa' and ever fucking meant it? Short answer, from Neil Diamond to Bono to Henry Rollins to Billy Goat's Gruff—none of us love Tulsa. We also don't hate Tulsa. We are trying to curry favor and get the fans to buy more shit. That's all. It's a fucking job, a job that's a whole lot more fun and a whole lot less work than hauling boxes in some factory, but it's a job designed to make us rich and famous, 'cause rich and famous can even get a craggy-ass bastard like me laid. So, yes, we all appreciate the popularity of our music right now, but it's ultimately disingenuous to thank the fans, who are no more than a means to an end. But before you crucify us, what's a fan to an athlete? A means to an end. What's a fan to a movie star? A means to an end. And for that matter, what's an investor to a hedge fund manager, and what's a patient to a surgeon? Means to an end. Sometimes in a more altruistic endeavor, but always the same essential motivation."

At this, a hand shot up, and the room parted to allow one voice. It was Garland McCovey from the *New York Times*—the dean of rock and roll writers with '60s roots and twenty-first century sensibilities. His tie-dye was evident in accompaniments—tie, socks, and handkerchief. Otherwise, he was proper and corporate in a pinstripe black suit, a far cry from the *TMZ/Enquirer* crowd. "Sir, with all due respect and with acknowledgment of your current popularity, which can, after all, be fleeting, I would submit to you that your bleak view of your colleagues is not universally accepted. Did you ever see the Grateful Dead, sir? Not the touring version of today but the original spectacle, which toured nonstop for years, playing epic concerts of monumental durations? I daresay, Mr. Garcia, were he alive today, would take umbrage with your remarks."

Melvin grinned ear to ear, a satisfied grim of a lazy student who had stolen the answers to a test and was about to ace it. "The Grateful Dead, oh yes, the Grateful Dead. I knew one of you old timers would dredge them up. Not for the money. You know that after every show, that fat fuck Jerry Garcia would eat his own weight in hash Bananas Foster and cackle at his fans. They were the embodiment of what I just told you. Fuck the fans, fuck the music, collect the green. The Grateful Dead were the ultimate musical Ponzi scheme. No-talent hacks who 'jam' because they're too fucked up to remember more than twelve songs, so they make each one last ten minutes or more to obfuscate the fact that they know neither the words nor the music. Two thirds of the crowd are tripping. They've already bought in and too fucked up to know how random and disjointed the songs are, but on acid, it's all magic. Then the sober ones wonder what the fuck the fuss is about. They've been drawn in to hear high school musicians with eighth-grade poetry class lyrics. But they have an escape. The acid heads seem happy, so they join in, and the pyramid adds another level. Next show, those miserable assholes will convince one or two friends apiece to join the crowd, and there you have it. I may be the Lenny Bruce of this world, but that dead and bloated Jaba was its Bernie Madoff. If he hadn't croaked, he'd be making his smack cash singing American standards at Indian casinos. If there's a hell, he's down there watching 'Touch of Gray' commercials on a continuous loop."

"You, sir, are a fiend."

"That's not a goddamned question, Tony Randall."

"Do you care so little for art, for beauty?"

"What does one have to do with the other? I want to make money, that's for sure. But that doesn't mean it's not art, and it doesn't negate the creative process."

"I'm not sure how the filthy lyrics associated with the Millicent song could ever translate into art."

"Is satire art, professor?"

"Generally speaking, it can be."

"When those bastards called me the Lenny Bruce of grunge, I'd like to say I was flattered, but I didn't know who the fuck Lenny Bruce was, God's honest truth. But I found out. They said that after 'Froggy,' and 'Froggy' was a satirical song. So is 'Millicent.' It's a satire of fake morals. So, I read shit that Lenny Bruce said. You wanna know what he said about satire? He defined satire as 'tragedy plus time.' He said that if you gave it enough time, the public and shitholes like you would allow you to satirize it, and he called that ridiculous. Well, the public accepts this song as satire now. What's your problem? When can you satirize a dead stripper? When what you're singing has jack shit to do with the stripper herself. Of course, I don't have any clue why the poor bitch slit her wrists. But fact of the matter is that a stripper slit her wrists rather than face another day having you fucks gawk at her on the pole. I wrote a song about the way society chews up and spits out, and you're so fucking stupid, you take it literally. Lenny Bruce also called himself a surgeon with a scalpel for false values. Come to think of it, all these years I thought the folks at *Rolling Stone* were pretentious bastards who compared me to Lenny Bruce flippantly, but just maybe they were right!"

Tee Nash and Billy Markwell looked down at their watches as Melvin surveyed hands in the audience.

Roger Smith, from the back, sent repeated throat-slash messages to Tee Nash, who didn't see them.

Melvin did, though, and amongst the cacophony of "Mr. Nash and Melvin" requests, he called for silence. "Ladies and gentlemen, our handler suit is telling me to shut the fuck up. Hope everyone comes to Cains tonight for a killer show. Suit wants to remind you to sign your release forms. Hope you've all learned something, and sorry to burst your bubble about Jerry Garcia, Grandpa."

* * *

Backstage, Roger Smith cornered a perplexed Tee Nash. "That got out of hand quick."

"There's still time for a settlement, a release, an apology."

Melvin saw the huddle and inserted himself between the bosses. "That'll buy some tickets and some fucking downloads. You like that, boss? Satire of modern mores. No, just fucked-up reasons a stripper would kill herself, but man was that entertaining. You know my history. I once told a radio station in Omaha that the dog in our Dusty song died when Tiny had him battle a rottweiler in a dog-fighting league. I told a paper in Madison that Dusty ventured into a Chinese place across the street and became Kung Pao. I told a TV interview in Rockford that 'Froggy' was based after my late mother, who was killed by the MS-13 in prison for stooling. If you can't get good pub, get the worst pub possible. It'll sell, believe me, it'll sell."

Chapter 9:
The Etiquette of the Mosh

Benjamin Richmond had quickly determined that Tulsa, Oklahoma, was not going to adjust to him, so he figured out how he was going to adjust to Tulsa, Oklahoma. For a secular Jew growing up north of Central City in Jenkintown, PA, he had followed a pristine course. Qualified for Central High, partial scholarship to Penn, Rush Chairman at AEPi, Jefferson Medical School and Emergency Medicine Residency, and finally a first job at the Albert Einstein campus in North Philadelphia, he viewed with wonder every time his accountant father would drive him downtown for Phillies games. While the other kids were dreaming of being the next Schmitty or Lefty, Ben Richmond wanted nothing more than to stamp out disease from the mysterious and forbidden North Philadelphia neighborhoods he was not allowed to open his window while driving through.

It was a good first job. Four twelve-hour shifts a week, two to two fifty, with gradual raises and increasing vacations over five years, and eventual partnership. Plenty of time to take in games or shows, or club around downtown and pick off a stray, drunk tourist girl. He had an apartment downtown off Rittenhouse Square, an ICU nurse at Jeff who provided friends with benefits, six months with his folks around for spiritual support, and six months when they were safely out of range in Bal Harbor for relief. He had idealism for the mission of the emergency room physician, which charged his soul most of those forty-eight hours a week. There was a Kabalistic resonance to his work-life balance.

But then there was the one patient and one phone call that became his poisoned apple. Eleven p.m. on an otherwise nondescript Monday, an old indigent guy, a gomer, chronic drunk, schizophrenic, was rousted up down by Joe Frazier's place and brought to Einstein because Temple was on divert. One look at him clutching his kidneys and screaming out in pain roused the Oslerian instinct—widened pulse pressure, bounding abdominal bruit. Rupturing abdominal aortic aneurysm, one of the true life-or-death emergencies an ER doc will encounter. The ultrasound suggested it, CT scan confirmed it, and as Gomer Pyle waded through tests, his blood pressure dropped and dropped and dropped and his hematocrit dropped with it in spite of fluid and FFP, and blood.

As an emergency room doc, you handled whatever you could yourself, but unlike the television show *ER*, you need help and there are dedicated doctors for every specialty on call 24/7/365. Most of the time when you reached someone at inopportune hours, they were cordial and helpful. Dealing with the minority who were lazy were obstructionists was the most frustrating part of the job. Frank McClough didn't take calls very often for the vascular surgeons. He was grandfathered out and spent half of his time as an administrator and half doing elective vein-stripping procedures for cash. But a couple of the junior partners were at a meeting and another on maternity leave, so McClough was pitching in. Nothing unusual about his approach.

"Dr. McClough, this is Ben Richmond in the ED. Sorry to bother you. I have a sixty-seven-year-old, chronically unwell homeless man who comes in in extremis with back and kidney pain—hypotension but with a severe arm-leg pressure differential and abdominal bruit. Ultrasound and CTA confirmed an acutely ruptured AAA, BP now eighty over forty on pressors. ICU already accepted him but wanted a surgical evaluation. Hoping I could get you to take a look."

"Pressure is what again?"

"Eighty over forty, sir. Was one-ten over sixty when he hit the door, and a hundred over fifty an hour later. Very poor distal pulses. Concerning, sir."

"Yes, indeed, Doctor. Tell the ICU I will be in first thing in the morning. He may need surgery or stenting. First thing in the a.m."

"Sir. Are you sure he can wait until morning? Really barely palpable popliteal pulses, and the pressure is dropping. Tachycardic at 125."

"Trust me, he will be stable for six hours. Keep him NPO, I'll get him on the schedule for the afternoon."

"Dr. McClough, I'm not sure he's gonna make it that long."

"Tell the ICU I'll be there first thing in the morning."

Here, it should have ended. Pass it on to the ICU team. They want to get hot and bothered because doc is a lazy bastard; let them convince him to drag his ass in. Ben was just a messenger, just a middleman.

He's a fucking gome. No one would weep for him. He dies, he dies. One less homeless wretch talking to himself and panhandling on the cross streets congested by four-way stops coming from the Roosevelt Expressway up onto Broad. It's not your responsibility, Ben. Pass the buck. Instead, he said, "Doctor, I'm not sure you're getting the full picture. This man is going into hypovolemic shock. Hypotension, tachycardia, and active rupture on both imaging studies. We can only do so much without your assistance. And I'm not sure we have until the morning."

"Now, you listen here. I've been taking care of AAA patients for twenty-five years. Countless surgeries and countless cases with medical care only. One of us is in the position to judge what is and what is not an emergency, and just a hint, it's not you."

"Sir, I'm just trying to do what's right here. If you don't feel you need to come in, I will talk to the ICU team and do what's appropriate. Please let me know or call me back if we can expect you within thirty minutes. Again, I'm Dr. Richmond." Ben hung up and called the ICU attending, another fresh fellowship graduate, and decided to transfer the patient to Jefferson downtown on an urgent basis.

The next morning, Dr. McClough came in to find out the patient had been transferred downtown and had some other administrative crony initiate an investigation and immediately place Ben on paid leave for inappropriate and belligerent behavior. After a short hearing, and in spite of the fact that two nurses spoke up on Dr. Richmond's behalf to state that he was calm and reasoned in the phone call, and in spite of the fact that the patient had been in the operating room by two a.m. at Jefferson (and died anyway of sepsis five days post-op), Ben was fired about a month later. Of two of his colleagues he felt could exonerate him, the ICU doc and one of his partners on call that night—who had laughed about what a jackass McClough was and had been there listening to the call, by Ben's side—both feigned ignorance of the tenor of the conversation and stated that the medical issues were not clear-cut.

Not only was Ben fired, but he had to deal with reports to the National Physicians' Data Bank because of an adverse action from the hospital and was labelled a disruptive doctor. His lawyer advised him to go to a $4100 anger management symposium run by some offshoot of the Kaiser Foundation, where their answer to all clinical disagreements were the 4C's, which were collegiality, clarity, commonality, and he could never remember the fourth one, which might as well have been cuntiness because Ben was fast asleep by that part of the lecture. They did role plays in which everyone felt fucking validated all the time.

In spite of a successful graduation from this twelve-step bullshit, Ben was blackballed from every hospital in town. He expanded his search into Bucks County, Wilmington, and Northern Delaware, Trenton, and central Jersey, and York with rejection after rejection. He even got rejected in Chester and Camden, places where savage neighborhoods and lack of insurance coverage made jobs both dangerous and low paying. After a couple of months, the downtown apartment became downstairs at his parents' house, and friends with benefits evaporated.

Problems like this aren't resolved with headhunters or cold calling. Hopes faded during five months of fruitless job seeking and surviving on eighty-dollar internet surveys regarding antibiotic and anticonvulsant choices, and an occasional off-the-books shift at a doc-in-a-box in King of Prussia, covering for a guy with a racing form habit (aka Wild Bill Hickock), an incompetent addict who somehow could get a fucking job while he was blackballed for fucking doing the right thing. Then one evening a call came in. Guy who was a senior when he was a junior resident heard about his predicament and was running an ED at a small hospital in Tulsa. Tulsa fucking Oklahoma. But his group had a friend on the Oklahoma Medical Board and getting a license, getting a contract, getting credentialed, was hassle free. It was supposed to be a three-year gig to re-establish a reputation and re-emerge triumphantly at Abington or Lankenau or even Northeastern.

But time passes and routines become established. Tulsa wasn't as bad as he'd imagined. It might be correctly defined by Dennis Miller as the place where people paid $1.75 to get sent typed transcripts of *The 700 Club*, but on the other hand, people were really too bloody nice to be racist. Who would have known there was sushi in Tulsa—Koreans, not Japanese, but it didn't make you sick. There were apartments designed to mimic New York lofts in old warehouses with exposed pipes and ducts only with twice the square footage and a third of the rent of their Soho equivalents. There were pretty girls, maybe not worldly, but a subset of them would suck a circumcised cock without complaint or question.

And there was a music scene, and not only rambler-gambler bands. Fifteen percent of the African American population of the town had formed the Gap Band. And even placing Hanson in some purgatorial category you'd neither neglect or boast of, you had a passable alt rock band called Safety Suit, and at least a state claim on the Flaming Lips, who were technically from OKC but seemed to visit the downtown clubs with reasonable frequency. Between Cain's, the Vanguard, the BOK, the Brady, and the Performing Arts Center, live music became a solid substitute for the missing elements of real city existence. In truth, the ease of travel without traffic and proximity to his downtown loft made Tulsa a far easier scene to navigate than Philly had ever been. So even if the AA Drillers were a snooze and the ECHL was even farther removed from the Flyers, the off-call nights were replete with acts like Interpol, AFI, Dinosaur Jr, the Shins, Modest Mouse, Maximo Park—who you would never have thought would touch base anywhere between Chicago and Denver.

There was an occasional girl, and he would occasionally optimistically buy a second ticket but inevitably ate the cost of the companion ticket.

As year begot year and the trips back home, at first monthly, to see friends and folks became bimonthly and now quarterly, the concerts became more regular. He recognized the scalpers, Native Americans named Boho and McCalister, who stalked the entrances buying unused passes at twenty-five cents on the dollar and hocked them at face value while deriding the occasional citizen looking to give 'em away for beer money. The bouncers circulated club to club like long relievers, high school linemen trading their one commodity in the human sphere before they gave up to be nightwatchmen. They called the Polynesian ones, Samoan cops. The ticket takers and sales staff were the ski-bums of the industry, willing to get minimum wage for menial work in order to get free entrance to shows of their choosing.

About three years into the Tulsa experience, Ben found a partner. Tusk Johnson was a displaced engineer marooned at a small plant in Tulsa from a lucrative job in Eastern Oregon because of a misunderstanding with one of the administrative assistants. Tusk lived in the building in a ground floor unit, and after seeing each other both in the mail room and then in succession one summer at the Yeah Yeah Yeahs, Jet, and Broncho, they struck up a friendship that revolved around alternating buying the seats.

Quite a duo they made, inching to the front of a mosh, then sauntering back to the periphery when the crowd surfing and slamming started. A couple of oddballs, Tusk wearing a blond mop-top wig over his balding, military-cut, blond crew in a mixture of two outdated references to Dobie Gillis and Kato Kaelin. Ben sporting an even more outdated Rick MacLeish #19 and the mixed metaphor of a Phillies cap because the kids these days were into the hockey, and the baseball cap signified an allegiance to gang culture, although the dad caps not really.

Since the goal was to entice conversation from twenty-something women, the reality was that both were so far askew from their intentions as if they portrayed a metaphor only they within a crowd of 2,500 at Cain's could understand. They wanted to be Anthony Michael Hall accepted into the jock clique in an '80s teen flick, only to double-cross the cool kids and show up at prom with the quarterback's girl in a plot shifting swerve. They forgot that even when the nerds were invited to the house party, they were covertly a focus of ridicule.

It was Tusk who generally pushed the envelope on more contemporary shows. He spent his days on the road listening to XMU and Alt Nation and coming up with an internet radio payola list of hot, new bands, which would undoubtedly recruit hot, young fans. Any act that formed in in the twentieth century was likely picked by Tusk. Ben favored the more classic alternative bands, choosing nostalgia for the days when he fought sleep during training to watch a half hour of Weezer or Third Eye Blind videos.

Ben had managed to get floor tickets for Beck a month before, and they had weaseled their way into the legions of the superfans in the first couple of rows, almost garnering a guitar pick and a drumstick. So, Billy Goat's Gruff and He Got the Giggler was a Tusk production. He got the tickets after XMU started playing "All that Glitters" in heavy rotation. The tickets were for a Thursday night show, on a day when Ben was pulling a seven-to-seven shift, the last on a trail of four days in a row before three days off for a long weekend.

Usually, Ben would research the bands before the show, try to understand the influences, and stream at least a song or two, but with a four-day straight sequence of duties, it never happened. It was just another concert, and the subject of the unusual circumstances didn't come up until dinner before the show. Ben got home by seven fifteen, after a relatively slow day of one dog bite, two febrile illnesses, one chest pain, a code neuro stroke workup, which was ultimately a panic attack in an overwrought queer, a dog bite from a poodle of all breeds, E. Coli from Chipotle, a hypoglycemic crisis, and finally, ethanol poisoning from one of the frequent flyers. He put on some jeans, Vans, and an Eagles Tommy McDonald #25 jersey, which he wore because McDonald, who was his father's sporting hero but way before his time, went to Oklahoma. Another reference languishing in obscurity in a pack of twentysomethings. He met Tusk at the apartment, and then they got a quick meal at Tucci's, an Italian place where Tusk once had picked up a girl on her way to a show and thereafter held some sort of ritual compulsion, in spite of lack of any tangible evidence that the phenomenon would ever be repeated.

Tusk was ostensibly in appearance, personality, mannerisms, and verbal idioms from Minnesota, although his paper chemist father had run him around various forest-heavy areas kind of like an army brat through early childhood. He had craggy blue eyes and balding blond hair without his Kato wig, and looked like he belonged in a lighthouse on a fjord. He didn't eat green or yellow or any healthy colors. This meant Ben got all but the croutons and cheese from a "shared" Caesar salad, and Tusk got five of eight pepperoni slices, only fair.

"Well, whaddaya know about these bands tonight?" Tusk asked Ben.

"Not much," Ben replied. "I've heard the Glitter song, can't say I'd download it, but it doesn't suck."

"Well, you know, the warm-up band's headlining now. Bill got reversed."

"Bill got reversed? Never heard of that."

"Bill got reversed. You know anything about Billy Goat's Gruff?"

"Nope."

"You haven't seen anything about the murder song?"

"Nope, what in the hell is that?"

"Well, apparently, Billy Goat's Gruff was the opening act, and first three concerts of the tour, someone dropped dead in the crowd every time they played one particular song. That's the murder song. They did that 'Froggy Went a Snortin'' song a couple years back."

"I remember that one. Clever the first time, tolerable the second, stale the third, turn the station thereafter."

"That's the one. Well, the murder song is apparently the story of a dead prostitute, and some feller dies first three shows they play it. One old guy, two young ones. Now this is the number one song in the country. They canceled a few tour dates, and this is the first one since. Apparently we have to sign a consent form for the show."

"A consent form, as if we are making the assumption that some song killed three individuals? Gotta tell you, Tusk, that is completely ridiculous. A song can't kill someone. Can't even come up with a theory. Brain wave suppression, heart block, embolism. It's insane really. Must be one in ten million but can't think of any plausible explanation other than bad luck linking a heart attack and a couple of OD's to a couple of deaths or foul play. I guess the most likely explanation is foul play, but why? Who benefits? The band, but they're the first ones who would be blamed. The record label, but they have countless other acts. Why these guys? No, just random."

* * *

The venue was walled off like an Israeli airport. There was a line two blocks long, and before admittance, there were three or four employees handing out forms to be signed and handed in at the ticket window, granting the venue and the record label indemnity from prosecution. Then, after entering, there were armed police and an airport-sized metal detector, run not by venue flunkies but by TSA agents. As usual, keys and iPhone 5, passed scrutiny, and they emerged into a large ballroom walking past a merchandise area hawking T-shirts and posters and CDs. The graphics, on one side of the display, were of what looked like a modern glam band. On the other side was a cartoony depiction of a goat playing guitar and two trolls—a large bald one on the drums, and an intense short guy, with green hair and red eyebrows and what looked to be unusually large feet for a troll, wailing into a microphone.

There was another T-shirt that was obviously taking advantage of the recent ridiculous speculation: The goats and the large troll were largely unaltered, while the short troll was cloaked in a Grim Reaper get-up. The tag line read, "I survived Billy Goat's Gruff." While the other shirts were twenty bucks, the grim reaper shirt was twenty-five.

Tusk pointed and laughed as he passed the kiosk. "I'll get one when I make it out."

"Don't let the fucking opportunists, swindle you, man," Ben said. "I'll get both of us a Giggler T-shirt. Maybe they're the new KISS we've all been waiting for."

If the itinerary printed on the door was accurate, they entered to a three-quarter-filled room about five minutes into the Giggler show. Bastards looked the part of a rock band. The drummer wore a black T-shirt over which his shoulder-length frosted-blond locks ebbed and flowed like lapping flames in a Wild Mick Brown imitation. The bassist never faced the audience and displayed a wisp of Allen Woody arrogant chill. The guitarist paraded around stage with an ice dancer's shit-eating grin eschewing intensity for enthusiasm. And finally, there was the lead singer, made up in a Johnny Bravo finery of leather below and sequins above, with a Buck Swope look of futility, having realized several months too late that his shtick was forced and lame. He reminded Ben of the ubiquitous baby picture of a two-year-old in a dress-up sailor suit, not wanting to start crying to disappoint doting parents but clearly wanting to tear the thing off and run around the yard in diapers.

They played an uncomfortable seven songs after Ben and Tusk arrived with nothing even remotely worth a ninety-nine-cent download. A couple of times, the lead singer seemed to prematurely enter back into instrumental portions of tracks, but this was speculative, as the only tune Ben had heard was "All that Glitters," and that was only a few bars before he would abandon his XMU back to classic alternative to hope for someone with talent. They were pop masquerading as alternative. The rhymes disqualified them. "All that Glitters" had a hook, but it was made up of "gold" and "old," "told" and "sold." This was glam pop and not even good glam pop. The interlude couldn't come quickly enough, but it did allow some migration into the mosh as presumably Giggler fans either abandoned their spots or optimistically relied on compatriots to hold them against the horde of headliner fans looking to get within ten paces.

There was an etiquette to the mosh, as Brownian as human flow, disruption, and collision seemed to appear. You could push to the front, but you couldn't displace or obstruct someone pre-existing without tacit nonverbal approval. If you were tall, it was a serious offense to park yourself in front of a shorter individual. However, if a taller individual was already positioned, a shorter one could not have the expectation of displacement but could courteously request it. A place could be saved for a beer or bathroom run during a warm-up act or intermission, but never during the headliner. Crowd surfers did so at their own risk with no expectation of preservation of horizontality except from their crew. Body slammers started slow to allow conscientious objectors to shrink away, and they initiated horizontally rather than vertically so as never to displace the rail. Personal space was limited to six inches to allow some clumsiness in bounce dancing, slightly more if there was a long-haired bouncer to minimize ponytail feather-dusting and slightly less with a large-bosomed woman, to permit extra ricochets. As Ben had once commented to a surly, vampire type who complained that Ben would not move to grant his girlfriend an extra twelve inches of space, "Agoraphobia is an absolute contraindication to the mosh."

Tusk had a move that brought them in conflict with the rules. In general, Tusk liked the front. Logically, the front was better for true believers, but to pick off stray drunks, the back was more likely to house heavier drinkers and therefore disinhibited patrons. But Tusk liked the front, and since work precluded them from standing in line to get early access to the rail, looking for someone up front to turn around and then waving at them and holding up your beer provided a fraudulent yet credible rationale for fighting up while pretending to follow the rules. What made it difficult was height. Tusk was five foot nine and could find a final resting place in front of a shorter cohort. However, Ben would trail behind at close to six three and inevitably find nowhere to stand without obstruction. To compensate, Ben would move laterally from Tusk and try to find a spot on the side rail to minimize fatigue and eliminate line of sight issues from the passed over.

Tusk didn't care. Taking advantage of the intermission wanderers and vacating Giggler fans, as well as one or two moves in which Tusk would force his way forward, then wave to Ben so that the intervening patrons thought his place was saved, the duo managed their way down within about six rows from the rail right-center. While they were able to find some folks older than them at least in "telomeres," up front, they were easily fifteen years older than any of their neighbors.

To their right were a couple of goths. It took a while to sink in that here in the Bible belt, there were equal proportions of Bible-thumping, evangelical ideologues and pentagram-etching devil-worshipers. The goths were seldom tremendously friendly and would never spontaneously start a conversation. If spoken to, about half the time, they responded monosyllabically and the other half resituated, which could be helpful if they had better position for a potential evacuation upgrade.

To the left were the telltale mark of the frat boy down from Stillwater or Norman. There was the classic Tommy Bahama cargo shorts and imitation Ralph Lauren-patterned shirts, the uniform of the rich college douchebag from Austin to Gainesville to Durham to Charlottesville to Happy Valley to Madison to Ann Arbor. There were four kids—only one thankfully with sunglasses, that fad was fading the further *Risky Business* waned from pop culture—and two thankfully with exquisite Barbie-doll girlfriends to potentially grind up against if the bastards didn't circle the wagons when the music started and the crowd condensed.

Thankfully, the front and back were size appropriate, with a couple of frumpy Rosie-the-Riveter types not presenting an obstruction in front, and a loudmouthed, tall biker guy behind, who complained through the intermission about the Smiths songs blared on overhead speakers through the venue as a palate clearing interlude. Right around nine fifteen, the lights went down and the four-member headliners reached the stage to enthusiastic applause. There was a quick "Hello, Tulsa" from the guitar player, and they launched into a reasonably catchy tune about a mutt named Dusty, which Ben felt he had heard on the radio.

For a Tusk band, a show Ben was attending more to accompany his comrade than out of genuine interest or appreciation, the band got a three-song tryout. The Dusty song was catchy and even a little clever with a hook and hummable melody. However, it wasn't clear whether the vocalist needed to be overproduced into a more melodic voice or underproduced in a Dylanesque method to highlight his starkness. Otherwise, the band was nothing special—no real energy or rapture. There was none of the typical flying and flaring hands lapping through notes at superhuman speeds on the guitar, bass, or drum, and nary a keyboard to be seen on the stage. The lead had a tambourine, which he shook during instrumental portions, but the songs lacked a more complex instrumental intensity, which seemed to leave the sound barren and lacking.

Nonetheless, the clamor accelerated song to song, and while the band had failed their three-song tryout to the extent that Ben's phone came out to gauge ESPN box scores and a Twitter contest for "Elderly Superheroes" (Plastic Furniture Seat Cover Man, Elongated Explanation Man, Mighty Morphine Drip Power Rangers), the crowd seemed to be appreciative. The goths might not be representative, but the bulk of the crowd seemed so, for lack of a better word, happy. The douchebag college kids, fat lesbians, pimply nerds up front, all looked so much happier than Ben could remember ever being.

And this undeniable but inexplicable joy that exuded from the crowd couldn't be transferred or imbibed, as much or as often as Ben tried. The foolish giddiness of normal youth, which had been sacrificed to precociousness and eluded him in goal attainment and downfall, remained unobtainable and barely comprehensible. He tucked his phone back into a pocket for a hot minute, tuned out from the music and self-queried how this mediocre swill could make this rabble so elated and, conversely, why nothing short of one or two choice songs in the occasional concert could produce this effect for him. How come Ben could feel this way if and only if this was Franz Ferdinand and if and only if Franz Ferdinand was playing "the Dark of the Matinee," or if this was Cold War Kids and only when they played "Hang Me out to Dry"? But he had no explanation for what setlist.com called "Lola's Room" and "Gut Shrieker" was doing to the crowd. And then there was the inevitable realization that the crowd was not the outlier, he was.

His sixth-grade teacher, Mr. Bernard—a refugee from the British public school system, exiled by political correctness for incorrigible corporal punishment to a Quaker school, which swept his eraser-and-chalk-chucking habit under the carpet in search of a continental gentility—had once described the bottom half of his class as surviving on the sponge score and the monkey score in formal testing. The sponge score was the score a barely animate being could garner simply by existing in consciousness. The monkey score involved dumb luck, as in multiple choice exams. Ben often thought he was striving for the sponge score at these shows and reliably coming away empty and would drift away into people watching.

Billy Goat's Gruff droned on for another forty-five minutes as Ben lost track of time and was unable to correlate any comprehensible lyrics to the setlist.com itinerary from the prior shows. By now, it was close to ten fifteen, and Ben had been up since six and was almost ready to tap Tusk and ask for an early exit when for the first time since "Good evening, Tulsa, who's ready to rock?" the band paused to engage the crowd.

"Thank you, Tulsa. We are so fucking happy to be here." The guitarist pumping up the crowd was wearing a goddamned Tulsa Shock jersey with Diggins on the back. *Did he know that was a WNBA team?* That was fucking hilarious. "Tulsa, give it up for He Got the Giggler," and the crowd produced a polite cheer a few ticks short of frenzy.

Now the lead singer joined in. "We don't have a lot of 'hits.' Somehow *Saturday Night Live* and *MTV* don't want my beautiful face on TV, but *Letterman* let us sing this next mother one night. Fuck knows why. We got to meet Jeff Bridges that night, backstage. The Dude. We met the motherfucking dude."

The crowd went crazy as "Froggy Went a Snortin'" began. This one was worth putting away the phone for. Thankfully, Ben thought the drummer took the song off, which was fortunate as all through the concert, the drumbeat had seemed to reverberate through his organs, catapulting heart into lungs, lungs into diaphragm, diaphragm into spleen, spleen into stomach, stomach into liver. He was relieved he had a respite. Whereas the rest of the show had been sung with disdain, even contempt for the words, whatever they were, this one was chanted. It wasn't really sung, as singing would involve harmony and melody, and this guy had neither. But he was chanting this fractured folk song like a bar mitzvah lad imitating some Ukrainian rabbi, with precision and care.

The crowd, for the first time since the Dusty song, were bouncing in unison and repeating song elements, "mhmms" and repeated phrases parroted by vast swaths in the crowd. The audience participation was not encouraged nor recognized by the singer who cradled his microphone and chanted solemnly into the gray and black, eyes peeled into its pores. By the time the denouement and final proclamation were realized, the crowd seemed to know the punchline and delivered it in unison, with the singer nonplussed on being drowned out. At the finish, he finally looked out into the crowd and raised his right fist over his head in triumph and did an imitation of a microphone glide as Cain's Ballroom erupted.

"Alright, alright. I have something very important for you doomed bastards. Some of you might have heard that we have this here song called 'Millicent DeGroenfeld Rice.'" Huge applause. "Yes, yes, 'Millicent DeGroenfeld Rice,' which is number one on the Alt 18 and download charts, and just happens to be hazardous to your health. This is the only song ever to make it on the fucking FBI's ten most wanted list. Probably some FBI cocksuckers in the audience, and I sincerely hope that if one of yous croaks tonight, it's one of those bastards." Huge applause. "But you had to sign a fucking consent form to come in here tonight, and for that, we thank you. But I want to make each and every one of you a promise. We have played this song, and when someone turns blue and goes ground, they turn the lights on, and we stop singing and pretend to be all concerned and stop the show and send everyone home, but that's not fucking fair, is it?" Huge applause. "Right, it's not fucking fair to the thousands of you who don't fucking die. Why should you be forced to retreat home without hearing other shit you might want to download or hate? I don't fucking know. But here's what I, Melvin Horgan, promise Tulsa, Oklahoma, today. If one of you crowd members croaks, we ain't gonna stop playing. Just drag the body and prop it up until the EMTs arrive, and we will just keep on playing, fair deal?" Huge applause. "And if we off someone with this here song, ten percent of our merchandise sales will go to whatever charity that motherfucker wants." Cries and shouts. "Well, of course, whatever the fuck his family wants, feral cats or genital mutilation, whatever. And if none of you fuckers die, we keep the whole goddamned pot, okay? Daddy needs his Mary Jane, if I can find some here in Tulsa. You bastards toke here?!" Huge applause.

And with that, Billy Goat's Gruff launched into the murder song. Crazy thing was with no expectations, Ben realized quickly that it was compelling. The Ramones, updated by the Meat Puppets, with this refrain, which hooked you, really hooked you. Didn't much matter that you couldn't understand word one of the verses. Who could discern a word of "Lido Shuffle," and that shit had been number one forever when he was a kid listening to Casey Kasem. This crowd was more than energized, it was motorized, it was supercharged, and up now six rows from the rail, there was Dr. Ben Richmond, who just three hours ago had been reducing fractures and diuresing congestive heart failure, jumping up with the rest of the "freaks and hairies, dykes and fairies" and slashing his wrists the second time the Troll got around to the refrain.

Even Tusk Johnson, who was a dedicated head bobber and toe tapper, never a jumper or thumper, was bouncing a little, not a full Tigger like Ben, but at least a little Roo. By the time the third refrain came around, Ben was putting the murder song on a plane with "Matinee" and "Hang," with potential elevation to a theoretical plane with "Clint Eastwood" by Gorillaz and "Life on Mars," which were the theoretical electroshock therapy of concert songs. All the others were Prozacs, but the ECT might just make the effect permanent.

The third refrain finished, and an instrumental portion commenced with a safe and simple base backbeat, a loud, constant drumbeat with foot and both arms of the gargantuan pouncing on the skins simultaneously, and a guitar part far more nuanced and complex than anything the lead had previously offered. The singer wavered to the side with his tambourine, scanning the audience like a cheetah a-prowl.

Towards the center of the mosh, some slamming gave way to a long-haired blond teen in jeans and a yellow wifebeater, crowd-surfing first away from and then towards the stage, until he was delivered into the photographer's pit and quickly pushed back by security into the crowd to start the process anew.

Another, fatter kid in dungaree overalls tried to persuade the crowd to lift him, but he tumbled feet over head towards the floor in a motion that made Ben cringe, with shallow-pool quadriplegia flashbacks. But the kid survived his tipping and attempted another ascendance only to be unceremoniously flipped as the crowd obviously preferred the cachectic blond, who cost about seventy-five pounds less and flew gloriously and effortlessly, like a concert superhero.

All through the instrumental portion, Ben noticed the drumbeat starting to overwhelm, which was the first imperfection of the beauty of the murder song. The guitarist's first foray into competence was being overshadowed by drumbeats, which rained down like thunderstrikes from Thor, delivered in a slow but regularly increasing cadence and intensity. With the escalation, the reverberations and ricochets rocketed around the thorax and abdomen in a pattern both intensely pleasurable and deeply disturbing—like that thrill ride where you rotated around in a circle until gravity pinned you to the wall, when the floor is retracted in the dark, bringing about in unison fear of tumbling into an abyss, nausea, and a simultaneous powerful and intoxicating feeling of mastery over gravity, which you knew would be fleeting.

It couldn't have been a minute into the jam when the initial palpitation struck. The first one was a fluke, a bizarre thump where none was expected. As the song played on and the drumbeat mutilated the guitar and bass, the ricochets from one beat collided with the next and the next, and those collisions provided the origin of the palpitations, which seemed to logarithmically accelerate.

Ben instinctively stopped jumping but continued looking around, but nothing else had changed. Everyone else was still jumping, nodding, surfing, or slamming. Even the goths were slamming up against each other while jumping like basketball introductions.

As the drumbeat careened farther on into Ben's chest, he stumbled to a knee, then quickly picked himself back up and instinctively first tried to reach Tusk, who had gently slid up in traffic, out of arms' length, and then tried to get to the rail, like a drowning swimmer. But the oblivious crowd hemmed him in, until, with the drumbeat caroms fully sapping any residual composure, he fell on all fours and tried to turn onto his back again in an instinctive motion by an ER doc to get in resuscitation position.

Now, at some point, the crowd noticed him, and while the initial revelation of his calamity stretched the seconds, almost instantaneously, there was a parting around him, as if the throng finally had what it wanted, a middle-aged man gasping and fulfilling the promise of the show.

With his head supported now by Tusk, who alone had come to his assistance—but who, without a medical background or CPR training, was useless—he could look up onto the stage and see that fucking troll glaring down at him, snickering. And as the drumbeats made their final push from the thorax now up along the carotids and firmly into the cranium, overcoming consciousness and fading, the last thing Ben Richmond experienced, after his eyes closed—with that reptilian mug mocking his demise—and before the other senses surrendered, was, as the bastard had promised, *"Millicent DeGroenfeld Rice, come on and take . . ."*

Chapter 10:
Get Back

The hospitality suite at the Tulsa Omni was a far cry from the back of the travel van or sharing a room with Tiny or Bebe at the Travelodge. (Bebe refused to sleep with Tiny, who was prone to restless leg.) It wasn't the Marriott Marquis, where they'd stayed in New York for the *Letterman* appearance, but there were airplane bottles of Smirnoff and Jim Beam and mixers with brand names rather than fake supermarket labels. Each of the guys had their own room, but with the groupies cleared out by the Tulsa cops and medical examiners, there was no shot at company. So, Melvin sat in the big recliner in the lounge on the hospitality floor and watched an episode of *The Office* in syndication, and drank vodka and sprite while munching on Chex Mix.

"We killed a doctor, Melvin. We killed a fucking doctor" came a voice entering the suite from one of the adjoining rooms. Billy Markwell had removed his Shock jersey and came in bare feet as he entered. "It's not right, man. Something's not right."

"Cool your shit, Goat. Have a drink. They have Baileys. Order up some ice cream. We can do shakes. A little Baileys, a little vanilla ice cream. Fuck, they might even have some chocolate sauce. Like those shakes we used to make in Old Town back in the day, except it was with Kirkland's Irish Cream and Lucerne and a Hershey bar run through the microwave. Damn, those were fantastic. I'm fucked up, Goat. I got the Baileys, but you get the ice cream and the chocolate."

"Melvin, I'm serious. I don't wanna drink. That guy was a doctor, forty-one, in perfect health. Not drinking, and he fucking dropped dead. Same song, same point. No old guy, no junkie. A fucking doctor."

"Doctors die, too."

"Doctors don't die at concerts."

"Doctors don't come to crap-ass concerts like this. Probably a Giggler fan. Bastard had it coming. Signed their fucking form. What's the big deal? Number one song in the goddamned world, Missy Rice. Dead stripper. Dead doctor. Don't know why, don't know how, just know when. Ride it out, Goat. We've been down so long, maybe the world just figured we deserved a little time up."

"You're not—I mean, you don't know anything?"

"You, too? Shit, we've known each other most of our lives. I never. Look, I don't give a shit about anybody 'cept you, and Tiny, a little. But you know I'd never. Wouldn't even fucking know how. It's fun to tease 'em, though. Good for publicity, too. You think Stevie Wonder shows up to any other white-trash concerts? Only brothers who like us are the bastards happy we're killing off their enemies, one cracker at a time."

"They're gonna blame us. We're gonna wind up in jail if we don't stop."

"No, you see you got it backwards. Think of it. If we stop, and no other fuckers died, we're admitting there was something up with these four, and we were compelled to stop by our conscience or the label, or the Feds, because someone fingered us. But if we keep playing, and the bastards keep dying, then they have to keep trying to prove cause. And unless you or I are doing something—and I know it's not me, and I can't imagine it's you, and let's face it, Tiny can't tie his own fucking shoes, so it ain't him—they'll either prove jack and we keep rakin' in the dough or it's Bebe or someone in the crew or from the label or some sicko fan—either way, the three of us are in the clear. Stopping is the worst thing to do. That's what gets us fingered."

Billy left, and Melvin staggered out of the recliner up to the bar and separated off four bottles of Baileys from the remaining supply. He took the remote control and shuffled through the options looking for skin, but remembered he was in the Bible belt soon enough, saving himself from tearing through the channels a second time. Landing on a Fox News anchorwoman was the closest thing to a Cinemax softcore. They droned on about Benghazi, and Melvin turned it off and kept sipping.

When two of the four bottles were drained, he drifted off, only to be awakened when Billy re-emerged with a pint of Ben and Jerry's and some

Hershey's chocolate sauce in a single serving container. Billy mixed up a concoction and handed Melvin a chocolate-cookie-dough-Baileys shake, which had enough sugar in it to counteract the sedative effects of more booze and keep him awake.

"Cheers to Billy Goat's Gruff, the most dangerous band alive," said Billy.

"Cheers to you, Goat. And don't worry; if anyone ever takes the fall for this, it'll be me. All that Kurt Cobain bullshit. The Grateful fucking Dead. Why shouldn't I make whatever the hell this is into a sick joke. Karma's made my life a sick joke for twenty-eight years. I've been a fucking punchline for twenty-eight years. Whether or not I give a rat's ass, it'll come back to bite me; either way, I'm fucked. So just start with the premise that I don't really care that any of these four people have died, because that's the closest thing to the truth I can muster. If I pretended to care, some microphone or camera will catch me in a sick off-handed joke, and I will be detested and vilified. It will happen—I can't keep my yap shut, you know that. If I'm a douchebag and denounce caring, yeah, everyone hates me, but at least they kind of respect my honesty, and frankly, it's kind of entertaining to be the heel. You show remorse for both of us. It'll balance out the group."

"Look, I get it you've never been warm or fuzzy, but how can you not give a shit if our fans are dying if we may even a little bit responsible?"

"People risk their lives every day. Driving their cars, flying, crossing the street—there's a risk they know is there but don't get worked up over. Other shit is obviously dangerous. You're running with the fucking bulls, climbing the Eiger, jumping off a cliff in a flying squirrel suit. There's a danger and a rush. You accept the risk. That's what our fans are doing. They never heard of us before a week ago, but it's a rush with a one-in-thousand risk of dying, at least that's what they think. So nine hundred and ninety-nine live and they buy a fucking crap-ass T-shirt. We win coming and going. So, relax and enjoy yourself, Goat. Who knows how long this is gonna last? Whether its coincidence or some psycho, or Tee Nash's way to promote a band he knows sucks, let it ride."

Billy made another shake, and Melvin gulped it down and motioned for another.

Just then, Tee Nash entered the suite with a bottle of Moet in one hand and a tall, tattooed blond on the other. Behind him trailed Roger Smith and three other girls. Tee Nash was in a gray suit with the tie off and fly undone. "Brother Horgan! You know who I've just been talking to?"

"Cops, Feds. Fuck do I care."

"No, I believe that was Mr. Smith. No, Brother Horgan, I have been on CNN, *E*, *TMZ*, and NBC within the last hour, and the focus of their interest is, of course, you. 'Millicent DeGroenfeld Rice' is obliterating download records and *Space Needle Pricks* is the number-one-selling album in America."

"Who still buys albums?"

"Well, actually nobody, but they are downloading more than just 'Millicent.' And, Mr. Smith, tell Brother Horgan how booking is proceeding."

"Well, rather surprisingly, with our consent/release of indemnity protocol, we are sold out for three months. Every night to every other night. Starting to get some stadiums, arenas . . . Waiting on the big ones. Trying to find a mutual date for Madison Square Garden, but the United Center, Fleet Center, Quicken Loans, US Airways Center, and Staples Center are all in. And I think you will be pleased that Mr. Nash himself closed a deal to headline Friday night at Sasquatch."

"I got you your festival, Brother Horgan. They bumped Weezer down to second to last. Rivers Cuomo called you a flash-in-the-pan douchebag."

"Hip, hip, hip, hip. Give us some of that hooch to celebrate. Good work, boss. Billy, we get us a festival. Never played late before."

"Thanks, Mr. Nash. Melvin and I appreciate it."

"No, thank *you*, and to show our appreciation for a job well done, we brought some friends along for you." Tee Nash took out a vial of white powder and placed it with a Franklin on the table. "And some fine ladies as well."

Melvin took a swig of champagne and then clumsily rolled up the bill and snorted a line and sat back down into the recliner, distantly studying the freckled bosom of a strawberry-blond woman with pale, blue-green eyes, translucent and piercing, and a wide, pouty smile. Small hooped earrings sparkled, although her bangs hid about half of them. Melvin motioned her over, and she obliged. He slurred out, "Have a drink," and she chugged from the bottle of Moet. He pointed to another line, which had appeared, and she demurely accepted and then sat on his lap on the lounge chair and sank into him as he contemplated drink or drug.

The champagne and coke hit him hard, and any vestige of composure faded, along with linguistic aptitude. Melvin looked around trying to find Goat, who was walking back towards the rooms with a tramp-stamped Latina in spiked heels and a Flashdance blouse. He reached over to the table, nearly toppling the girl, and grabbed the champagne for another chug. "Whatser name, babydoll?"

"Lenore, baby. I'm Lenore. You tell me what you want, baby."

Melvin felt Lenore run her hand up his inner thigh, and then her fragrance and a faint smell of lemons encircled his champagne breath. "Tee Nash, movverfuckers. Man o'da peeps. I canna keep a'killin' 'em, you wantcha."

"Brother Horgan. Kill 'em. Don't kill 'em. Keep selling CDs and bringing in crowds, and Infinity Records will treat you right. Now, why don't you take thing of beauty for a spin. We have a travel day tomorrow and some press appearances in St. Louis. Show in two days. Have yourself some fun, then get some rest. Jet takes off at noon. Plenty of playtime and plenty of recovery. Ain't that right, Smith?" Tee Nash looked around, but Roger Smith was AWOL. "Smith! Ah shit. Brother Horgan. Just you and me and these fine ladies."

"Frine badies. Where da blow, Joe? Where da blow jus' go? Blow, baby, blow."

"I think between the ladies and Mr. Smith, it's been appropriated. But I do think it's time for you and Ms. Lenore to retire for the night. Baby, you know what I told you. This here's a star. Lead singer, number-one band in the USA, and"—in a whisper—"he kills folk. Treat'm well, baby."

"C'mon with Lenore, baby. I'll treat you right, like a superstar, baby. I will treat you like a superstar." But Melvin's inertia trumped his residual libido, and he remained adherent to the chair, peering off into Lenore, who motioned to get him up. "Up and at 'em, baby. Come on now with me, darling. Room's right over there. Oh, you and I are going to have some fun tonight, sugar. Leave it to me."

"Go on, Brother Horgan. It's your turn to shine, baby. Go give this fine thing a poke or two. This is where you start taking advantage of your celebrity, Brother Horgan."

Whether it was the impregnable reasoning of Tee Nash or a dusting of cocaine, which had lingered on some nose hairs and drifted into the mucosal membranes like a time-released cold tablet, Melvin propped himself up and shook his head with a Beetlejuice twist, grabbed onto Lenore, and pulled her to his room, bellowing, "I got this, boss. Yeah, I'm gonna get my rocks on, rocks on. Roxanne, you don't have to do-do-do-do-do da-da-da is all I wanna say to you. Uh-huh. Fuck the Police, ha-ha."

Tee Nash turned to the lady next to him and whispered, "That bitch know she gotta stay the night, now," and getting an affirmative nod and finding himself alone with the choicest morsel, he didn't bother retreating to a room.

* * *

Back in his junior suite, the cocaine glow was again waning, and Melvin contemplated whether prophylactic vomiting was indicated. If he excused himself to the bathroom, the mood might be spoiled, as even a pro like this lovely strawberry blond would be reluctant to be anywhere near his mouth, no matter how many tiny bottles of hotel Listermint he consumed. On the other hand, vomiting during a fuck might well be grounds for contractual nullification, leaving Melvin once more alone and extending a celibacy streak, which by now had extended way too fucking long.

In the end, he decided to risk the Roman shower scenario, and Melvin found himself emerging from a decision-making fog with the girl on top of him as he sat on the sofa in the foyer, grinding away with her dress off but bra and panties intact. His shoes were off, but maybe he had removed them hours ago, and one sock was still on, but the other was over the television, blocking part of the view of a welcome message. He couldn't remember the girl's name, but she was encouraging him to engorge or something. He poked around at her bra, looking for a clasp or a Velcro band, but his fumbling caught her attention, and she discarded the bra with a flick and a snap. Red-freckled breasts danced in his sockets, and little blue venous imperfections seemed to create spirograph trails imprinted on his retina as they danced over him in a futile attempt at stimulation.

Noting her failure, the girl traveled south and removed his jeans and started stroking his flaccid form to engender a response. Still nothing emerged as he pushed her off and headed towards the bedroom with his briefs half down. This sabotaged his ambulation, ataxic as it was from the booze and coke, and he stumbled down after a couple of steps, not even to the doorway. "Fuck that hurts," he muttered as his skinned knee landed on the leg of a poorly placed chair.

"You okay, baby?" Lenore asked as she came and supported his weight, and, after a halting limp or two, deposited him on the near side of a hotel king-size bed with all-white sheets and comforters now marred by subtle red oozing from the open, raw skin.

"I'm alright, alright. Okay. Alright." Melvin rolled around on the bed a few turns, like he was trying to douse a fire, then landed in a ball on his left side, turned away from the girl and the door. She came over and spooned him, having disrobed completely. She grabbed his cock and tried to get him back over into a position she could work with, but he remained oppositional and incapable.

Before he trailed off, he brushed her hand away from his penis and looked back into her glowing, ethereal, aquamarine eyes and whispered, "I'm so sorry, I'm too fucking drunk. Don't take it personal. Never could have believed I'd have a chance with anyone so beautiful. And then I fuck it up. Don't deserve it, dead doctor. Makes no sense, dead doctor, dead cock. You're plenty hot. I'm just drunker."

"Baby, it's okay. I can try again. If you get going, don't worry. I can catch up, and we can come together." She sang the last two words with a British twang in what must have been a John line.

But it was to no avail, and the prostate figure of Troll Horgan—naked excepting for one white, mid-length tube sock with a red stripe at the top and a blue stripe just below with a fading yellow tip tinged from the inside with the splotched residuals of at least a dozen loads of self-stimulated jizz on the right foot—cowered away from Lenore, who by now reasoned that her effort had been sufficient, and the client was unlikely to awaken before she was off the clock at eight a.m. So, accustomed only to short spurts in fine silk sheets, she took advantage of the opportunity and set the alarm on her Motorola to seven forty-five and trailed off on the far opposite side of the bed. It was two fifteen a.m.

At 5:27, according to the hotel clock radio, Melvin Horgan sat straight up in bed. He was at that seminal moment where sleep is instantaneously arrested by the Bernoullian arrival of a swiftly rising column of whateverthefuck was left undigested in the gastric antrum. Rising up in bed like a sleeping antelope hearing rustling in the grass, he sprang up and sprinted to the toilet, depositing white-brown vomitus tinged with morsels of the hospitality suite's complimentary signature Rice Krispies Treats mostly into the target with only small misplaced streams heading down the side of the porcelain and onto his right cheek and eventually, with gravity, onto the neck before he could make out a washcloth in the darkness.

Cursing relative sobriety, he leapt back into bed only to land on Lenore, who was sleeping soundly. She was startled and shot up, temporarily disoriented in the darkness. She reached out for her phone and its light reveled an ashen Melvin settling into the other side of the bed. She turned on the bedside lamp and looked down at the phone. "Not that I'm encouraging you, love, 'cause I'm tired as hell, but you do have time left on the clock."

Melvin rolled over and looked at his bedmate, a look of terror creeping over his eyes, and he recoiled from her, landing in the far corner of the bed. "Who the hell are you? What are you doing in my room, and where the fuck did the other girl go?"

"Other girl? Shit, baby. Just you and me. Simple and free." Again, she lyricized the last line.

"Fucking Chicago? That other bitch disappears, and all you can give me is sappy crap from Chicago? Don't think of you people as trumpet rock and roll fans."

"Listen, honey, just because I'm a chocolate goddess don't mean I can't appreciate the sweet crooning of Peter Cetera."

"Yeah, you Black, which is fine. But the girl sucking my cock last night was strawberry blond, pale-blue eyes, big freckled titties. She was a fucking white girl, and where the fuck is she?"

"Honey, your boss paid our fraternization fees last night, and he done took the only white girl. You were given Lenore, you were happy and left the party with Lenore, you tried your best with Lenore, and then woke up next to Lenore, and you got another hour or so with Lenore. And, sweetheart, I'm damn certain I'm Lenore."

"She was a motherfucking white girl! I don't fuck Black whores. She was a fucking Caucasian."

"You don't what, what?"

"Oh, I ain't no racist. I fuck Black girls, but I don't fuck Black whores."

Melvin was wide awake now with a pounding headache. He scanned the room, looking for his companion from the night before. He sat up on the bed onto his knees, and Lenore shot out of bed, the sheets folding back on themselves and drooping towards the floor. She covered her bare breasts and collected her knockoff VS bra and panties, collected her knockoff DK suede skirt and her knockoff GV red blouse, and he watched her dress quickly and quietly in the bathroom. She found and picked up her knockoff JF black stilettos and carried them towards the door.

Melvin's mostly naked body didn't budge from the bed as he continued to scan the room. He then ignored Lenore as he crept into the bathroom half expecting to find a dead girl in the bathtub or the closet. He wore a look of terror each time he opened a door or looked behind a curtain still essentially naked, his hair parted haphazardly, which maximized his bald spot. Spittle coalesced around his right lip and cheek, ribs provided the only differentiation from flab, and the proportionally miniscule flaccid penis drifted harmlessly to the left, away from the door and away from her. He pretended not to look at her and returned to the bed, pretended to use the television remote control, but she had—as was her habit in upscale accommodations—pilfered the AA batteries some time earlier. "Well, let me tell you, you may not fuck Black whores, but based on your performance last night, you don't fuck white girls either. You was so fucked up, I could have been a goddamned mermaid and you'd have no clue. It was me. I sucked your cock, and it tasted like four-day-old figs marinated in vinegar. And I licked your balls, and they tasted like cat litter mixed with baby vomit. And thank God you didn't come 'cause something tells me your cum would make spoilt milk taste like a vanilla milkshake."

"Out," said Melvin. "Get the fuck out, you goddamned bitch. Get the fuck back to your dime-bag crack house, sucking your Bible thumpers and cookers for Jacksons. You like to sing, cunt? Your mama's waiting for you, drinking her Mad Dog booze, and wearing her Goodwill sweater. Get the fuck back home, Loretta," and he gave her the middle finger and stood up, naked except for the one sock still hanging on, waiting on her to gather up her remaining possessions and leave while some kid in a red jacket walked by dropping copies of the *USA Today*.

Chapter 11:
You May Be Right, I May Be Crazy

Nora Whatley was briefing the team. The Whatley/Sessions partnership had expanded over the month to include Muto, the dedicated CSI pathologist, Thompson, who was a poison expert, and Barnathan, who was, for lack of a better term, a spiritualist. There was an inside man on the road crew as well. Since the Tulsa show, a thirty-three-year-old barista had died in St. Louis as the first female victim, a twenty-six-year old security guard had collapsed during a Peoria concert, and a thirty-seven-year old female cop, present as part of a city detail, had passed during the Lincoln performance.

Agent Whatley went around the room for status reports. Dr. Muto had six victims all dying of sudden cardiac arrest with no prior cardiac history in five, and only some mild hypertension and mild coronary artery disease in the Ogden hippie. No common hormonal dysfunction. The barista and the teacher had some depression history. The doctor had some anger management complaints but no active treatment. The security guard had asthma and migraines and took inhalers. The cop took Synthroid. All but the hippie had all vaccinations. None had any significant childhood injuries and no infections. Essentially, no patterns.

"Horgan's not a sociopath, if that's what any of you are thinking," Muto announced, stroking a small mustache. "He knows right from wrong. He's schizotypal with a sprinkling of paranoia. Unusual behaviors, odd speech, eccentric thinking, few close friends. He may go off the deep end—many of them do—but he's not a serial killer. Doesn't fit the profile."

Next was Thompson. The Boise and St. Louis victims had moderate and small amounts of THC in their system. The hippie had past but not current LSD use. No cocaine or meth in any of them and therefore no pharmacological rationale for heart disease. No occult poisons either. No ricin, radioactives, curare, strychnine, or any other obvious external toxins, infectious agents such as anthrax, or pathogens.

Vic Sessions was next. All six victims had deteriorated and died during the instrumental portion, more specifically, near the end of an approximately eighty-five-second guitar solo after the third refrain of the song "Millicent DeGroenfeld Rice." No deaths occurred during other songs. There was no witnessed strange behavior by the band. Only the lead singer, Horgan, was even a potential suspect since all the others were occupied with instruments, but several of the victims were well out of visual range of Melvin Horgan. Through the inside man, none of the road crew had a violent criminal past. In short, no clues, no suspects.

When Vic had finished, Barnathan, a slight East Indian man with a wispy moustache, dressed in a snappy tan Burberry suit, arose from his chair and asked, "Sessions, you're the music expert here. What do you know about songs associated with death?"

"'Gloomy Sunday.' A Hungarian song from the thirties about a man who wants to kill himself after his lover dies. Paul Robeson did an English version, but Billie Holliday's was sublime. *'Sunday is gloomy / My hours are slumberless.'* In Hungary, after the original recording, there were dozens of reports of suicide associated with that song, and the Hungarian who composed it went crazy and killed himself as well, years later. There were unsubstantiated reports over here related to the Holliday version, but nothing was ever proven."

"Sessions, 'Gloomy Sunday' is a suicide song. A song imbibed with such sorrow that a certain percentage of those who heard it were driven mad with sadness and ended their own lives. Science scoffed at the thought and considered it impossible. Always a plausible explanation trumps an inexplicable one. But sometimes, the debunking loses sight of the realities of history and legend. Anyone know the song 'Barbara Allen'?"

"Sure, Scottish folk song, many renditions."

"Most widely collected song native to the English language. First referred to in the seventeenth century but refers to a real phenomenon in the Scottish Highlands in the fifteenth century in which mass suicides followed a particular tune played to eulogize the lost love of a nobleman who was poisoned by a rival. A true suicide song which morphed into a modern form. Study 'Gloomy Sunday' and some of the original versions of 'Barbara Allen.' They share line structure and syllabic cadence. May be a coincidence. But what if there is something inherent in the structure of the songs that drives brain chemistry, and the flux of dopamine depletion makes people suicidal. What if?"

"So, what in the hell does 'Barbara Allen' have to do with 'Millicent DeGroenfeld Rice'?"

"Good question, Sessions. Absolutely nothing. It's the correlation, the lineage over time, from a historical event to a legend to a song to an evolution into a modern form. Those who do not know their history are doomed to repeat it, but ancient history may be hidden or lost in folktales or legends. Now, what is a banshee?"

"A fucking Scooby Doo villain. Old Man Greeley, the nightwatchman who wanted the rubies for himself."

"No, Sessions, try again."

"A wailing Irish woman who portended death. That good enough?"

"Okay, as legend has it, a banshee literally means, in Gaelic, 'woman of the fairy mounds,' but as we know it, a banshee connotes a myth of a fairy hag whose scream would predict death. Just a legend passed down in Celtic culture. There are versions in Ireland, of course, but also the bean nighe in Scotland and the Hag of the Mist—I can't pronounce the native term—in Wales. But what if the banshee's scream wasn't a scream? What if it was a song? You see, the banshee is also referred to in pre-modern times as the 'keening woman,' or lamenting woman. And, all of a sudden, the scream isn't a scream at all, it's a song. And then the hag isn't a hag, she's a beautiful woman with a song that portends death. Now we're starting to sound more familiar, the story of the so-called 'bean chaointe' or keening woman known in Irish and Scotch lore, who would sing a lament for one about to die either in proximity or as a warning of someone in danger far away."

"Again, I fail to see the relevance."

"Prudence Corliss, born Desirae Turley in what is now Northern Italy, was born into a troupe of what was a precursor of operatic singers. She and her kin traversed Western Europe in the lands of the Franks and the Gauls in the early thirteenth century, performing stories in verse and song. Desirae was by all accounts a beautiful Alpine blond with a lovely soprano voice and second only to her aunt as highlight of the show.

"When the troupe made it to Wismar in the northern part of Saxony, Desirae caught the eye of the second son of the Duke of Mecklenburg, who sought to take her for his wife. Unfortunately, the duke was enraged that his son would consort with a common performer and forbid the match. However, by that time, Desirae was pregnant and her troupe ostracized her. Her lover concealed her, but they were betrayed, and as the baby was delivered, her daughter was taken from her and brought to the castle to be raised, and Desirae was cast out alone and told both she and her daughter would be executed if she ever returned."

Vic fidgeted and pretended not to listen as Barnathan droned on, somehow purporting to track the itinerary of a troubadour dead seven hundred years through Europe in the Middle Ages, eventually placing her in Tudor England.

"Now, this is where things get interesting. These were low-level entertainers putting on bawdy plays at fairs and festivals, lowest common denominator entertainment of which Desirae, out of necessity, participated, but she had a beautiful operatic voice, and she was allowed to great acclaim to sing 'Lammas Ladymass,' 'Sanctus,' and other religious-themed songs of the day. But eventually, she was allowed to write her own song, in Italian, called 'Mia Figlia,' as an ode to the daughter she had lost."

Vic kept his mouth shut so as not to prompt his boss's ire as Barnathan essentially provided a setlist for this imagined heroine whose relationship to a dead stripper remained obscure.

"At Dartmouth, she performed the song at the Duke of Devon's summer festival, and one of the duke's cousins took a fit and died. The next week in Bath, a daughter of the earl also had a seizure and died, prompting Desirae to leave the troupe and head north on her own. Emboldened by the power of her song and rageful at nobility, she reappeared with different names, most often Prudence Corliss, and snuck into fairs and festivals, performing, watching at least one noble-born die of something described by a barber surgeon of the time as an 'unmitigated fit,' and disappeared into the night. No one knows exactly how many succumbed to 'Mia Figlia,' but eventually, all records of deaths, Prudence Corliss, and Desirae Turley cease. Whether she was eaten by a pack of dogs, developed a conscience and went home, or moved her act to parts of Europe without a historical record is unknown, but the legend spread and was twisted until the Irish developed the term banshee as the woman whose wail didn't cause but, to their reckoning, portended death. As history became corrupted, the lovely Desirae became a hag, a demon, or a goblin to potentiate the effect of the legend."

Sessions had spent years with self-important "artistes" and no tolerance for the pretentious, fabricated meandering of his colleague with no plausible relevance to the situation at hand. One of the pleasures of his current position was the subjugation of speculation to fact.

"Now, perhaps it's no coincidence that Desirae's daughter grew up in Mecklenburg, which is the ancestral home of the DeGroenfeld. In fact, the DeGroenfelds were nobility in Mecklenburg, and although this is speculation, I do believe that, somehow, whatever spirit allowed the song about that little girl to kill in the thirteenth century imbues this rock-and-roll song about her ancestor with the same dark power."

"Are you fucking done, Barnathan?" Vic finally had had enough.

"Sessions!" Nora Whatley interrupted, attempting to regain decorum.

"Prove me wrong, Sessions. Not like you have any better theories after how many deaths? Ban the song. It's cursed by some ancient evil. Ban the song, stop the deaths. Simple."

"Simple, just fuck the First Amendment because of some made-up shit. Screw you and your bullshit story. The fucking banshee was puppets and projections designed to scare tourists away from the grave of an old Irish guy by a greedy magician named Marlin Merlin. Our agent Shaggy figured it out and alerted inspectors Velma and Daphne. Come on."

"Sessions!"

"Come on, boss. You guys are criminal scientists, and I'm a pianist with a fucking autoimmune rash. I know painfully little about medical forensics or toxicology, but I sure as hell can smell out a load of crap. Can we go back to science? Bring these guys into a venue. Put a volunteer up and strap them into monitors. Do bloodwork, heart monitors, EKG, EMG, EEG, whatever these guys want, and see if anything happens. Sure makes a whole lot more sense than a modern banshee."

"Inspector Whatley, I understand that not everyone appreciates the parallels between these events and can incorporate the inexplicable into their analysis. I'm not saying that forensic science is obsolete. In fact, I believe quite the opposite. But science alone is incomplete without an understanding that we can't always explain every forensic mystery without admitting there is an unknown."

"I volunteer. I fucking volunteer. And if I have to listen to any more theories about the Creeper or Mr. Hyde from this charlatan, I hope I'm the latest in the line of Scottish nobility to fall to the curse of the banshee."

* * *

The next Billy Goat's Gruff concert was in Detroit at the massive Masonic Temple, a palace of the Gothic Revival, born out of a transient fascination with the mystical and spiritual in the '20s and as good a place as any for a song about a suicidal stripper to kill a pre-suicidal agent.

The auditorium had been prepared for the show later in the evening, with a scattering of seats removed for a rudimentary mosh, and the majority of the 4,400 others cleared of trash and debris, at least temporarily.

Inside the massive structure, Vic Sessions was being prepared by Muto for his private concert. A full forensic analysis was planned, at least as complete a forensic analysis as could be performed on the living. All over his torso were affixed EKG leads to measure heart rhythm. A blood pressure cuff adorned his left arm, and an IV decorated the right. Tangled mats of hair gave way for EEG electrodes in a connect-the-dots pattern approximating a crown on his head. In his cock, a catheter collected all urine flow. An oxygen sensor covered a finger and tiny needle electrodes measured nerve conduction as well as tissue pressure in the thighs. "I can't carry my side piece because I have a fucking bag of urine strapped to my leg, Muto. Not that I ever carry my gun, but what if I need my proton pack. Goddamn it, Muto, what if I catch Slimer coming to do me in and instead of my industrial-strength, Barnathan-approved, phantasm-collecting gizmo at my side, all I can do is hope if I spray piss water on the angel of death, I'll be passed over. Passover, I like the sound of that, Muto."

"Sessions, shut the fuck up. The Foley and blood collection devices will work automatically every five minutes or at my command. If you feel at all in danger, you have a kill switch. Try not to die."

"But if I do die, do I get the Bronze Star, or the Purple Heart, or whatever the fuck we have in the bureau? I guess I should know this, was probably on the entrance exam."

"The exam is why Whatley's an inspector and you're ten years her senior and a field agent. Yeah, maybe. The Memorial Star, if you die. Shield of Bravery if you live and someone accuses you of heroism."

"Accuses me?"

"Accuses you. Anyone who knows you, ya damned prick, would say you're doing this just to stick it to Barnathan if you live, and put yourself out of your misery if you don't."

"Words of encouragement, Doc. Nice pep talk. Find another orifice. Stick another tube. You know you wanna."

"Sessions. Hit the kill switch if you have to. Where would we find another music industry insider to completely sell out."

"Any damn street corner, Doc. Any fucking subway platform. Any radio station outside of drive time. I'm a dime a dozen."

The band showed up for their private show about ten minutes late. Sessions was napping in his designated mid-mosh hospital bed, body occupied from head to toe with monitors, electrodes, catheters, and dressings.

"Hey, boys, look!" said Melvin. "We're the fucking USO, giving a private concert for the fucking English patient."

"*The English Patient*, Troll? You're gonna admit you saw *The English Patient*?"

"Fuck, Sessions. You and I have both been in our fair share of Red Roof Inns. What the fuck I'm supposed to watch on a Wednesday afternoon? Soaps, *Sesame Street*, sports? I watch whatever movie is on whatever fucking channel ain't that shit."

"You mean, you're not writing and rehearsing? What a shock, considering what a tight sound you boys have. Melvin, that tambourine of yours must make your Juilliard professors so proud. The Jimi Hendrix of boink, boink, boink, boink, boink. What a talent. Tiny, how 'bout a little Whiplash for me? Can you do that for me, big guy? Billy Goat's Gruff, featuring Fleabag on the guitar. Play me that chord. You know, your one chord. The one chord you ever play. The Pete Townsend of grunge—that's what they're calling you, if by 'they' you mean not a single fucking person. Rock on."

"What's your problem, Dick?"

"No problem, Melvin. Excited to hear some of that number-one magic."

"Good, because I was worried you were disparaging our musical talent, which would be ironic 'cause way I hear it, you was no Thelonious Monk before you got grayscale. So, instead of throwing Buddy Guy in the face of Tiny, who you know can't fucking defend himself, you got something to say, I'll hop down offstage and we can parlay."

"Oh, Melvin, such an angry young man. You got a golden ticket. You can't take me having a little fun with you. Lighten up. Kill an FBI agent, then maybe find an eight who doesn't mind fucking a celebrity two. Perfect day for a troll."

"Yeah, I'm a troll, and I'm a two, but people been making fun of me my whole life. I got experience. And I know when it's good-natured, but believe me I'm an expert in self-loathing assholes, so welcome to the fucking club. Might be a short membership."

This was not a band that ever practiced much together. Billy and Tiny were used to training, but Melvin and Bebe were seldom involved. The usual convention of the drummer setting the beat was laughable. Tiny was a rush end, not a signal calling Mike linebacker. So, Billy gave the one, two, three, four, but the first time Bebe came in on cue, Tiny was a little late, and they started over. The second time all was well, and the murder song commenced. Melvin Horgan embraced his vocals like a crooner, except instead of a velvet fog embracing the mike, his was a stucco gale. He gave Vic Sessions an upwards stare as he sang in his reptilian impression of the Chairman of the Board making eyes at Natalie Wood.

Back in the control room, the monitors hummed. Sessions was a little hypertensive ("Go see your doctor," Muto had told him. "You're my only fucking doctor" had been the reply). But a resting heartbeat of eighty-five, belying a little bit of nerves, and a pressure of 145/90 held steady. EEG and EKG were normal, and all the bodily fluids squeezed out appropriately. But these were the verses, and none of the deaths occurred during the verses.

Better off without you," and then the final refrain, as toe-tapping as cacophonous drivel could get, and then the guitar. During the guitar solo, Melvin was just lurking onstage, feigning rhythm and interest on that meandering distraction of an instrument commissioned to Tracy, the forgettable Partridge, or Val, the unappreciated Pussycat. Muto was a doctor and not a music man. He would have figured it out eventually, but Sessions knew right away. The instrumental portion began, and the slow constant beat of the drum was at first just out of step with the heartbeat, one seventy-two and the other eighty-five, but the intensity of the *thwack* shocked the aging torso of the agent, and while the beats, a half or even quarter second away, were dissonant, even thoracic ticklish when they beat close together, there was a capture, and although the heart tried to escape, tried to sabotage its parasite, it was unable, as in a tractor beam, and eighty-five became seventy-two—and Vic Sessions knew it. He'd counted time by heartbeat and knew his chest thumped when Tiny Atlas thumped. He wasn't alarmed. It was an easy feeling, as if he had just been able to let go and let something else carry the load of lifting for a while. A rickshaw for a pilgrim supposedly on a sacred and personal mission. Cheating, but not really.

Tiny's drumbeat functioned as a defibrillator, triggering firing of his ventricle so every *thwack* was immediately followed by a *thwump*. *Thwack-thwump, thwack-thwump*, ramping up unevenly but inexorably as the pace of Billy's solo and Tiny's accompaniment quickened. Now about thirty seconds in, the pace heightened by about a third note and faster *thwack-thwump, thwack-thwump*, up to a feeling of soaring. If your heart is doing only two-thirds of its work, perhaps the brain and the lungs and the kidneys and the penis reclaim their lost circulation, and you think more clearly, and breathe more deeply, and pee more forcefully, and engorge and maintain more robustly. Vic liked the feeling.

Around 120 drumbeats per minute, there was a confluence, where the *thwack* and the *thwump*, the catalyst and the reaction, came instantaneously, and now the coupling was complete. Muto saw it as a change in rhythm. He thought it was a high-rate atrial fibrillation, but he didn't realize that what he saw as atrial waves were quarter notes from Tiny and noted the rhythm change about thirty-seven seconds in but held off the kill switch. For Vic, there reached a point where the euphoria of his heart taking a thirty-second nap from performing its own work was overcome by the loss of coordination between the atrium and ventricle, resulting in diminishing efficiency and consequent blood flow to the other organs.

In 1940, the Tacoma Narrows Bridge, otherwise known as Galloping Gertie, responded to a windstorm by matching resonance oscillation patterns with the gale and started convulsing before ultimately collapsing. Everyone watched the footage in seventh- or eighth-grade science class. Vic remembered the footage from eighth-grade physics with that old fruit Hossler at the Friends school, showing it to the class while he sat in the back sticking out his tongue like an iguana while plotting how to cop a feel of his next thirteen-year-old willy. That old queer showed up bruised and beaten one day and then just disappeared, most likely without repercussion, to peddle his sickness in some other exclusive school in some other exclusive suburb. This memory exploded into his consciousness as his heart bounced with acceleration. Aeroelastic flutter had brought down bridges, planes, rockets, but in this context, it was the drumbeat taking over and contorting the heart as the muscles of the right and left ventricle went into a contradictory spasm, a death spiral, so to speak, just like Galloping Gertie plunging into Puget Sound.

To Vic, it was palpitation and lightheadedness. To Dr. Muto interpreting the various rhythms and leads, it was slowing of brain waves, lowering of blood pressure, and raising the heart rate and appearance of ventricular tachycardia, a rhythm to be followed inexorably by ventricular fibrillation and death. He hadn't figured out the drum thing, but he had figured out as the alpha waves receded and the blood pressure dipped, and the ventricular rate continued to rise, that the end was near. He could also tell that Sessions was not hitting the kill switch. After ten seconds of V tach with the pressure down to 80/40 and his friend smiling defiantly up at the singer while he struggled to maintain his wits, Dr. Muto hit his kill switch, and the electric guitar and the bass halted, but the drum kept beating faster and faster, just with less reverb, as the microphones were off.

Vic Sessions wasn't suicidal. He had no more desire to die than he had to live. In fact, the whole experience had him flustered. On the one hand, he was unmistakably dying. He had no concept of the science, only knew it had something to do with the drumbeat. Muto, on the other hand, who he could see running—hands over ears, the fool—headlong towards him, or maybe not towards him, in slow motion, knew it was a death rhythm, knew the rate was climbing, and the blood pressure was dropping. He knew V tach was soon to become V fib, and that was the end of the story. But he didn't know about the drums. Muto knew the science; Vic supplied the art.

Enjoyable was not the word; it was uplifting, your brain floating uncoupled from your heart because some behemoth with two drumsticks and no discernable talent was able to assume the burden of your autonomic nervous system, become your atrium. *Maybe if I survive this, I should get a fucking pacemaker,* Sessions thought. Set it to 120, retire, and sit outside in all four seasons drinking and chasing this feeling. But then Tiny was much higher than 120 beats per minute, and the feeling of soaring was starting to give in to a crash. He tried to look for Muto, but he remained transfixed on Melvin Horgan. *God that would be a ghastly last image, and worse yet, Barnathan might actually have been right.*

Chapter 12: Sasquatch

"You may not know this, Giggler, but I didn't really care for you much when I met you."

"You don't say."

This was as close as Melvin Horgan had ever come to holding court. Even if it was just him and Marc Bauer, with Tiny Atlas asleep in the back of a luxury Dreamliner, which had brought Billy Goat's Gruff to headline the Sasquatch festival in the Green River Gorge. To be fair, Melvin had sent some flunky down to gather the lead singer of He Got the Giggler, and it was only the two of them.

"Yeah, I may have said certain things which may have been interpreted as offensive."

"Like when you said, 'I want to kill the Giggler'?"

"Yes, but realize, some of that was hype. You know hype?"

"Hype? Hype is Oasis and Blur. Backstreet Boys and New Kids. We were two struggling bands. Aren't we supposed to support each other?"

Melvin had to admit, Marc Bauer had balls. He would have never questioned the headliner when BGG was a three p.m. band.

"In theory, yes, I suppose, but, Giggler, truth is, that ain't me, supportive. You got looks, I don't. You got height, I don't. You got some musical talent, I don't. You even have a fallback, and I fucking don't. It's not jealousy or envy, or pure malice, someplace in between. It's like I'm the fucking evil stepmother, and you're not exactly Snow White—not Snow White, maybe Jack White, a solid six but no better. I still want you out of the fucking way. That's just me. Not sorry, just that's me. But here we are. I want you to know I was the one who brought you here. Your first festival, Giggler. Not main stage. Five p.m. between some local flute band and Ween, but your first festival. My way of saying, I don't dislike you anymore. After a few plays, 'All that Glitters,' I can say ain't half bad, Giggler."

"I don't quite understand, but okay, thanks."

"Alright, now get the fuck back to your bus."

It was Thursday, the day before Sasquatch opened at a large amphitheater on the Columbia River, closest to Seattle and Spokane but accessible from Portland as well. Infinity Records had an aircraft carrier of a bus for the band. The only downside of the Gorge Amphitheatre was the lack of availability of a hotel fancier than a Comfort Inn in the vicinity. When Billy Goat's Gruff had played a seventy-minute set on the third stage three years earlier, they'd slept in their van—well, at least Tiny and Billy had slept in the van. Lord knows where Bebe would disappear to, and Melvin spent his nights passed out in the fields covered in heterogeneous excrement and vomitus. For this show, they had the run of a mini mansion in town, the summer home of something called an otolaryngologist from Walla Walla.

With newfound prosperity, Melvin had abandoned his Game Boy, which, it turned out, was outdated technology, and he now had a PlayStation portable he'd bought secondhand in a GameStop outside St. Louis, along with a *Call of Duty* game and a *Grand Theft Auto* selection.

When Marc Bauer left, he put on some headphones to drown out Tiny's snoring and went on a mission to clear out a cadre of Hispanic gangsters and pilfer their pot while puffing on his own. This was a flagship van, fitting for the hottest band in the Infinity stable. There was a full bar that had been restocked as soon as they reached the Gorge. There was satellite TV and reclining chairs that swiveled.

Melvin completed the mission by blowing the head off the lead biker and mowing down his lieutenants in a muscle car replica and was told he had made five grand, which made him chuckle, because the pot alone was worth ten times more than five grand. He put the game in his pocket and opened the door and crept outside to finish his joint.

Billy was walking up to the bus incognito in sunglasses and a Knicks hat he'd bought at a game during the last summons to Infinity headquarters.

Melvin whispered at him as he entered the bus, trying to let Tiny rest, "Goat, how's the scene? Traded in any passes?"

"Nope. No one's here yet but the cops. They're fucking swarming. Suits, too. They gave me a new script to read before the song."

"New script. Let me see that." Melvin grabbed a single piece of paper with text in a twenty-point font, as if someone assumed dumbasses like them could only read big refrigerator magnet letters. "You ever talk like this in your life? 'The members of Billy Goat's Gruff want to ensure the safety of our friends and fans. To that end, the paramedics are here and ready to provide assistance.' Oh, Jesus Christ, I'm not gonna let you get laughed off stage. I'll take this, man."

"Suit made me promise."

Melvin put the piece of paper down under a half-empty PBR bottle, then took a miniature sausage and goat cheese flat bread off of a large tray, took one bite, and put it next to the beer, toppings leaking onto the now oil-spotted paper.

"Suit works for us now. Was Inspector Brown Pants down there, or did they retire him to stud after we killed him? Can still see his body flailing each time that quack gave him the juice."

"He was there. Said he wanted to see you tomorrow before the show."

He wants to see me. That could be entertaining. Melvin took another swig and then went to grab two more, handing one to Goat.

"Probably wants to thank me. Must have got a medal or something. Purple Heart—no, that's a war thing. Whatever the fuck Feds give for a Purple Heart, although I don't think GIs get a Purple Heart for shitting themselves. Maybe a promotion for bravery in the line of fire."

"Can't believe the bastard made it; shocked him so many times. Didn't think we'd ever see him again. But he can wait until tomorrow. Tonight, got a couple of Bacardi girls in early; wanna party. Invited them to the house."

Bacardi girls. Why didn't that sound appealing? Admittedly it should have been appealing, but for some reason, Bacardi girls were not on Melvin's agenda for his first night headlining a festival. "Thanks, Goat. I got plans, but get Tiny some pussy."

"What you got, brother?"

"Oh, some Canadian model came here with Tegan and Sara but decided she needs to mix in some cock." It was a good if not a plausible lie.

"Well, if you change your mind, I'm meeting them at their kiosk at eight and heading to the house. Gonna grab a quick nap."

"Whacking off in your shag green sock, you sick mofo. I know your nap routine. You can't compete with Tiny. His come and ours don't. We're losers, Goat. Temporarily successful losers, but nose-picking, flatulent, prematurely ejaculating losers." Melvin took a drag and looked out over the Gorge, threw the butt towards the river and watched it fly and fall, then kicked it out with his boot. "But go take your nap, get primed. I wish you well, my brother."

"What the fuck's wrong with you, Melvin? All you whined about for months was how we were gonna lose our contract and be nobodies again, and here God knows why we're successful, and you're whining more than ever. Can't you just accept success and be chill? We're successful. You're not supposed to be bitter and jealous anymore."

"Don't know any other way. I'm fine, hungover's all. Life's grand." Melvin grabbed his fresh tallboy PBR and squeezed past Billy before heading back outside to a deckchair someone had placed between their bus and Giggler's large van.

Maybe Melvin would have been able to relax if there wasn't one fucking conversation that didn't underscore the fundamental incompatibility. Take the PBR. Why in bloody hell did Verne at the catering outfit hassle him about the damn PBR? With that shit-eating grin and feigned, obsequious, puppy-dog servitude: "You know, Mr. Horgan, we can get you any beer option you can think of. How about something more befitting of your success? We have a lovely Terminal Velocity Porter." *What the fuck is wrong with PBR?* he thought. *If I want PBR, if PBR reflects the full range of the sophistication of my taste buds, who gives a shit, Verne?* But instead, Verne had to propose a theory, a formulation to explain why a rockstar given an unlimited budget would elect to settle on a brew appropriate for indigent hipsters or lower middle-class fraternities at directional state colleges. The last thing the world needs is a passive-aggressive sycophant.

So, in an attempt to restore balance to the relationship, Verne gave a casual chuckle and provided his theory of demeaning pandering, of hectoring adulation. "No problem, Mr. Horgan. I'll bet PBR's sponsoring your tour, aren't they?"

"Now, Verne, I may be mistaken because I didn't go to business school or marketing school, or university, or frankly any school after my mom just stopped caring when I was fourteen, but I just have a theory that corporate America, with few exceptions, won't hitch their fortunes to a bunch of no-talent lowlifes whose five minutes come from remorseless concert murders. Not exactly a Coke and a smile, Verne. I don't think we get sponsorships, except maybe from some self-important haunted corn maze. No, can you get it through your thick head, I just fucking like PBR?"

Autograph seekers were an unheard-of diversion in other times. Now when their bright, expectant faces greeted him in the park on a weed run or at a minimart, the quotations reflected a vitriol previously reserved for more talented colleagues. "To Mickey from Troll, hope you are the next to asphyxiate." "To Gertrude from Troll, only with two bags and dead drunk."

The only escape was in the game. Only in the game was chaos congruent and animosity inconsequential. This time, a Haitian gang leader had a package of munitions riding from a safe house to a buy with another rival gang of rednecks. Taking his motorcycle, Troll sped down the causeway, catching up to the Haitian leader and shooting out his tires. When the gang leader and his henchman exited the car, Troll blew them away with his machine gun and went for the stash when the fucking low-power indicator started to flicker menacingly. He turned the game off and started back towards the bus, where he had the charger, but stopped suddenly, placed it in his pocket, and meandered down the path to the venue past the various checkpoints.

At each of several stages, roadies and janitorial crew were preparing for the festival. The amphitheater housed multiple events each summer but nothing as grandiose as the festival and the normal cadre of creature comforts—Honey Bucket portable restrooms, ATM stands, booze and food merchants, and chair and tent rental places were being augmented, upgraded, and cleaned. Around the stages, speakers and lighting displays were rearranged with tweaking on the bigger stage and creation of the smaller ones, which were added to allow lesser bands like Giggler to experience the festival atmosphere. The main stage, where they were scheduled the next night from nine thirty until eleven, was the focus of several lighting men and an audiovisual team obviously preparing a video screen for some other band who had prepared better images than colored dyes in Pyrex.

Someone had asked Troll if he wanted Infinity to conjure some video images to play during their songs. They suggested a kaleidoscope haze with recurring pictures of a troll and a couple of comical goats or a rollercoaster, with a couple of trolls in the front of the car and goats in the back. Melvin countered by offering that a montage of snippets from the movie *Elephant* should play in the background during "Millicent," which the lawyer quickly nixed, and that ended any thought of video accompaniment.

All around the festival grounds, First Aid stations dotted the venue in Chinese Checkers patterns. Apparently, the imminent threat of what the press was calling percussion roulette, due to some apparent FBI leaks, was not the only festival-related morbidity and decidedly rarer than dehydration, overdose, and scrapes and bruises from fighting over prime real estate on coke or meth.

In the main infirmary, which was hidden in a grove remote from the main stage, Melvin found Vic Sessions sipping on an Arnold Palmer, sitting atop a makeshift stretcher, oxygen tubing in his nose with a portable green tank at his side. Christ, the guy had aged ten years in the month or so since the mock concert. The thinning hair had surrendered nearly completely, with only irregular tendrils from sideburns to bangs to protomullet. His face and eye sockets had shrunk in, as if some internal termite was eating away at his countenance. Flab drooped from his tissues as if he's been kidnapped and starved. On the other hand, perhaps the benefit of nearly dying in the line of service, if he was still indeed in the line of service, was a dress code exception. While the other agents sweated the venue in suit and tie, Vic was dressed for a Tiki bar in khaki cargo shorts and a bright-colored plaid shirt, which focused on green with a smattering of yellow, red, and blue.

Melvin watched him from behind a large elm, then paused in disbelief at the breadth of the deterioration and was wavering on whether to approach when Sessions looked his way and spoke. "Horgan. What the hell you doing down here, superstar? No one down here but roadies and us company men."

"Dick, didn't see you. Yeah, I was doing some walk-throughs. Main stage walk-throughs."

"Walk-throughs? Walk-throughs, that's what you're going with? We've been following you for months now, Horgan, and closest thing you get to a walk-through is that fucking Loser medley. Love that. If you sang that instead of the crap you call songs, I think I'd actually buy a ticket. Walk-through? Which part you gonna walk through, the screeching or the offbeat tambourine? Bloody hell, Goat and Tiny rehearse their little hearts out, not that it would help either of them, but you, Melvin, what you really doing down here?"

"Okay, whatever. I'm not working. I'm just taking a fucking walk. I was bored up at the bus, and I wanted to get out a little, pass time."

"Melvin, why you feeding me this bullshit? Maybe we don't know each other well, but there's a certain connection, you know, when you've all but sent me to the other side. I don't think you've ever taken a walk just to 'get a bit of fresh air' or 'experience nature' in your whole miserable life. It's okay. I'm not a 'take-a-walk' guy either. You take a walk, you are going somewhere, getting something, looking for something. Me, too. I'm not a take-a-walk guy. That fucker owns sandals. I don't own sandals. I took a walk in Philly, I was checking out the bars, getting a bottle, turning up somewhere I figured some piece of ass would be. So, Melvin, don't disillusion me, because I appreciate you for your honesty. What exactly are you doing passing by the infirmary the day before your big show?"

Melvin looked at the sallow eyes of Vic Sessions, took in the oxygen tubing bathing his nostrils and the strands of tissue gathering around what used to be biceps and triceps and quadriceps and many other ceps ravaged away by whatever happened in Detroit. "What the fuck happened to you?"

"It's an improvement. Ought to thank you."

"What were you thinking?"

"I was thinking some moron thought you were killing people as the personification of the Banshee myth, and I was going to show that idiot what's what. Still can't shut him up."

Melvin looked at Vic and felt the dissonance of remorse or even pity. Having been the source of pity for as long as he could remember, this felt bizarre. Pity for his looks. Pity for his lack of brains. Pity for his inability to engage in the simplest of social connections. Pity for being an utter failure.

Pity had been a tough way to grow up, but it was better than the contempt, which was its less empathetic cousin.

"You're telling me the government—*my* government now that for the first time in my life I am likely a tax-paying citizen—is paying one of you fuckers for banshee theories? Strap that bastard in the fucking chair."

"He didn't volunteer."

You had to give the guy credit. He wasn't cowering. He was taking his comeuppance like a man.

"When you was losing your shit, did anything happen? Give me something, and I'll give you a hundred bucks towards Rogaine, no, two hundred bucks towards those weavy extension things. See anything? Hear anything?"

"I can't take your money. But truth be told, I just heard your godawful voice and then you stopped, and it was just guitar and bass and drum, and then I started to fade, and next thing I knew, Doc was standing over me. You wanna confess to something, Melvin? I can't comment on any active investigations, but you're welcome to confess."

Is this why this bastard's afoot. I can't believe after what happened that he would still think I had anything to do with whatever was happening during Millicent. "I haven't done nothing."

"Well, I guess that's consistent with the fact that we haven't locked you up . . . yet. Melvin, what the fuck are you doing down here? And don't tell me the taking-a-walk bullshit again."

"Nothing. Stupid idea. Go back to sleep. I'm gonna go find me this Bacardi girl Goat got for me back at the house."

"And do what?"

"Dick, gonna show her dick, Dick. And if your biceps and triceps are any indication, not something you are capable of showing any longer. Times like these, good to be alone, alleviates the inevitable disappointment of abandonment."

And with that, Vic Sessions started to laugh. Not a giggle but a full-throated laugh, and Melvin was pissed. He turned and started to walk back to the bus, not wanting the conversation to proceed.

"Hey, wait a second. Don't leave all angry. Yeah, I'm not in use right now. Ha-ha. I'm Viagra-proof limp. But, remember, I know everything. Black girl in Tulsa. She was a hooker, sure enough, but mouth on her. Barista in

St. Louis, few bucks got her to talk, and then remember Zoe in Lincoln? Redhead. Big, heaving titties. Said she was an elementary school teacher; was going to scold you for being a bad boy. Ha-ha. That was Muto's idea. Agent Sheehey, fucking gorgeous. I had to convince her there was no way you could actually close. You wanna see the video? You'll never guess where the camera was hidden. 'Fuck, get out of here, you fat bitch. Can't fuck every fugly groupie bitch.' Girl's five-foot-eight, one hundred ten pounds dripping wet, former Miss Utah, and that's the best you can come up with, 'fat fugly bitch'? And you hadn't even drank that much with her, at least until after your disappointment."

Melvin turned back around and got in Vic Session's face. The stench of cheap beer with the flatbread sausage and cheese made the FBI man recoil.

"Fuck you. Come find me when you see pussy you don't pay for. Love to see some snaggletooth blowjob whore not touch you without rubber gloves and double condoms. Standards for the standardless."

"You know, Troll, I was at the end of my arc. This just shortened my downslope. But you, my friend, are at your absolute zenith and still an abject joke, even to yourself. I'd ask you if this is guilt, but number one, I don't think you're capable, and number two, I'm not sure what personal experience or exposure you have. And I'm quite sure if you had anything concrete to do with this mess, we'd have you locked up in a cell with some jailhouse Romeo, but then you'd probably start to work again."

"I do feel guilty I didn't tackle that fucking sawbones before he shocked you awake. Stay up late every night fretting why the fuck I didn't let you end your miserable life the way you wanted, some sort of agency martyr. Maybe you thought if you died in service, they'd have a ceremony and then some plaque somewhere, and five years from now, someone would actually remember that you fucking existed on this planet and prevent you from fading into total obscurity."

If Melvin thought this would enrage Sessions, he was dead wrong. The agent's eyes suddenly were aglow with a light that had been lost since his near death. Sessions laughed again and went as if to give Melvin a bear hug from which he balked.

"Oh, that's the Melvin I know and love. Emboldened. Top of the world. Yeah, I'm a forgettable nobody. Got it. Let me ask you, 'Come On Eileen.'

Great song right? Great song. Dexys Midnight Runners. 'Poor old Johnnie Ray.' What was the name of the lead singer, that guy with the overalls? Probably fucked everything that moved for two months. One year later, you think anyone could have picked him out of a lineup? Think that guy will rate a mention on the evening news when he OD's, if he hasn't already. You're a one-hit wonder, Melvin, one hell of a hit but a one-hit wonder. Either you fade into obscurity, or perhaps you might have an ignominious public embarrassing fall, if you're lucky, that is. If you're less fortunate, OD like the rest.

"You think I expect this to last? I stay above ground, and two years from now, introducing season sixteen of *Dancing with the Stars*. He's some washed-up football player from some shithole state in the south; she's the cunt who was America's sweetheart twelve years and three rehabs ago in some inane sitcom and a couple of formula movies. He is the way-too-good-lookin' aide to President Clinton who was mayor of Cleveland or Akron or some shithole in the Midwest until he fucked his campaign manager while his wife had snatch cancer, and he is a no-talent prick from Sac Town who wrote a number-one hit that killed a sawbones and a hippie and came a sliver short of taking out a Federal man but now needs to lift up some whore by the crotch to get proximal to pussy. Ha-ha. Sounds nice. Sign me up. You'll be watching every fucking minute and telling some widow drenched in Charlie, you once knew that guy." And at this, Vic Sessions started to laugh, and then the laughing turned to coughing until laughing took back over and could be corralled. "Oh, Melvin. Don't ever change. You go find your Bacardi girl. I may not be out stalking much these days, but chances are, wherever you take her, I'll be watching. Do me a favor, let her sit on your face—it improves the view considerably. I have to live vicariously through you lot these days. Goldilocks and the Three Bears, we call you guys. Tiny is the papa bear—too hard. Melvin, you're the mama—too soft, ha-ha. Billy is baby bear. Just right!"

"You fuckin' perv."

"Perk of the job, Melvin."

Melvin Horgan thought briefly about giving Sessions the finger, but perhaps that was too much considering the recent near-death experience, and he abandoned the infirmary nook and wound his way back to the trailers and busses.

* * *

At two a.m., when Melvin returned, barely coherent, to the house, high on coke and booze from the bus on a shared bender with a former NWA hype-man traveling with a South African brother-and-sister rap act, he found three girls in various degrees of nudity sprawled with his bandmates on the floor. Tiny still had socks on, and his massive cock spread over the unconscious face of a petite blond with asymmetric implants. A Black girl with '80s hair was in his right arm, squeezed up to his mighty body. Billy and a brunette had a throw rug over their midsection, with dry-cleaning requirements, if the security deposit was a concern. One freckled breast, with a tooth mark or two, peeked out from under the wool.

Melvin stumbled into one of the bedrooms and pulled off his clothes and tried to self-stimulate but gave up when lefty fatigued. He threw the lotion on the floor and went into the bathroom and drank some water to see if it would stay down.

He came back to bed, stepped backward with a muddied stare, and audibly accosted the shadows. "There you are. Where the fuck did you go? Stop fucking laughing. You can be part of the solution, fucking cunt. No, don't go away. We can talk in the morning. Where the hell did you go?" He searched the corners of the room and the closed door to the hallway. The bathroom door was open, and he checked inside. But then the spins took hold, and he had to lie down.

With that, Melvin Horgan trailed off to sleep and stayed comatose through an early morning Tiny foursome.

* * *

It was past one when Melvin woke up, and the carnage from the night before had been sanitized. The no-name local bands would already be on stage, warming up the early arrivals, the hardcore who required a full three days of performances. Melvin poured himself a screwdriver to accompany some catered arrangement of pastries, fruits, and breakfast meats. Tiny and the girls had devoured most of the good stuff, leaving a few trampled croissants and a lot of blueberries with a few random pineapple pieces and an orange slice or two. The burning in Melvin's esophagus ached for a Zantac, but they were back in the bus, so he coughed up a little blood and took a few more bites of croissant to calm the acid whirlpool streaming across his antrum and cresting about a third of the way up the esophagus.

"Troll. Hey, I had an idea. Let's do a cover tonight. Give 'em something they'll never forget."

"You don't think they won't remember when some fucker starts convulsing, then keels during 'Millicent'? I think that's pretty fucking memorable. Don't you think that's enough, as well as the magic that is Billy Goat's Gruff?"

Melvin was barely awake, but Billy shone in the light of fresh fornication amplified by the understandable but increasingly annoying optimism. "C'mon. Let's try something new."

"I've got something new—almost ready. Tee told me we needed a new single. Almost done. He also told me we needed to add in some fucking audience participation, but fuck if we're gonna do that."

"Just something simple. Something punk. 'I Wanna Be Sedated.'"

How do you tell your best friend to fuck off without telling him to fuck off? "How we gonna teach Tiny that? And I don't wanna rehearse. I wanna go listen to the bands. Have 'em kiss my balls. All the shit we had to do when we were the two o'clock band, hoping to have Third Eye or the Presidents just fucking mention our existence. 'Weren't those Billy Goat's Gruff fantastic? Give 'em a hand.' Pick someone and pretend to like their shit. That's what I wanna do—figure out who we wanna pimp, and see what we can get for it."

"Well, Bebe can play just about anything, and Marky Ramone's just a jackoff like Tiny. Just have him bang in time, he'll be fine. And I know the chords. You just have to know the lyrics."

Melvin smirked. *If Goat meant this as reverse psychology, he was good.* "Damn it, Goat. I've known the goddamned lyrics since I was ten, but we ain't the Ramones, and we play our own shit. We'll play our shit, let 'Millicent' play out. By that time, these bastards will be so fucking high and drunk that after the blood lust, they'd love us for Rocky Mountain High, much less if we save 'Dusty Heaves' for the encore like we planned."

"But if we add it as second encore—when we come back on before 'Dusty.'"

Second encore. What are we, the fucking Stones? We have three albums and most of it sucks. We're lucky to be able to string out what we have without embarrassing ourselves. "They paying us more for a second encore? They're paying us for a ninety-five and we're giving them ninety and five. 'Millicent' ends the set, then 'Dusty,' then off. Maybe if you've got those Bacardi girls again."

"Nah, JT's here for Saturday. When Timberlake's here, the rest of us get scraps."

"Fuck."

Chapter 13:
I Wanna Be Sedated

During the day, the main stage of the Gorge Amphitheatre provides panoramic views of the White River, which rolls behind it with cliffs beckoning from the opposite shore. The mounds of grass cascade up the hills and the cliffs provide some natural resonance to the music coming from down in the valley.

The sun shone bright on act after act, stage after stage, until the late setting sun of the northwest finally started to announce the arrival of commercially recognizable acts. That was the strategy of the festival, build to a crescendo day after day. Let your crowd gorge on overpriced beer and institutional-quality, fatty meals while unfamiliar, less-popular acts play, and then congregate after short beer breaks for the main acts, the draws, the headliners.

If you headline a festival, you're the headliner of the headliners. Sasquatch featured, on average, twelve acts a day, and if you followed their tour schedules, about half were substantial enough to headline their own tours, while the others were satellites in the orbits of more successful entities. To headline a festival was validation, and with it came more of the trappings such as passes and freebees, and a prime place backstage from which to hold court and receive tribute from the less successful. It was like the diamond medallion status of artists. First class, no baggage fees, triple miles, free entrance to the lounge where you could get complimentary blow and blowjobs.

You could debate whether Friday or Saturday night went to the biggest act. It wasn't Sunday, half the crowd, the half that worked had already left. Saturday there was a bigger crowd but a less coherent one. All day drinking and drugs and, by the end, tattered attention and overload. A fair percentage had checked out pharmaceutically or spiritually. Friday, the crowd wasn't as large, but the enthusiasm was maximal, and since only a few had been present since opening, and most had come from the likely sobriety of employment, engagement was nearly universal.

There was still a modicum of sunlight when attention shifted to the main stage for the closing act. About half the crowd had skipped the final act on the second stage to squat in front of the main amphitheater for Billy Goat's Gruff, and the other half meandered over after some South African Rap consortium. "Claudette Wants Flowers" opened and got the response you'd expect from a billboard college tune that climbed as high as number fifty-six on the "I Don't Give a Fuck" charts. Polite but not overly enthusiastic.

After the finish, with the audience still meandering down from the other stage with overlapping conversational noises temporarily trumping musical voices, Troll came to the microphone. "Oh, holy crap, Sasquatch, we are headlining. Any of you remember we were here in 2009, playing—what was it, Goat?—a two-fifteen to two-forty-five slot on Saturday on a backstage between some garage band where some sponsor's kid was on drums and a no-talent white rapper from Missoula? And here we are fucking headlining." Eighty-decibel applause. "We just might have been to a few more of these things. That guy from Walla Walla still selling wacky weed brownies in that old Mystery Machine van out in the B lot?" Seventy-five-decibel agreement. "Shit, I lived off those things in oh-eight. Brownies and Beasts. Anyone know what that's like?" Ninety-decibel agreement. "You guys enjoying the show?" Seventy-seven-decibel agreement. "Any of you guys see He Got the Giggler?" Forty-decibel scattered applause. "That's cold, people. I know they suck. In fact, I know they all suck but us, but that's fucking cold." Seventy-five-decibel applause. "Now the record company suits and the pricks who run this place and their shysters want me, well actually, they wanted Goat to read some statement they prepared about the song we're playing later. We ain't playing it now because half of you that don't go ground and shit yourselves will leave, and we want to play the whole set before the ambulances give us pause. But I took the liberty of a little re-write." Seventy-decibel applause. "After all, I'm the fucking songwriter. I should be able to write a warning letter for my fucking song better than some suit, right?" Eighty-decibel applause and three or four shouts of "I love you, Troll."

"So, my little trolls and trollettes, this is my warning to you. All our other shows, you would have all signed some fucking indemnity form. Well, they damn well know that not every one of you came in through the front entrance. Shit, 2007, I pretended to be an Aramark chef and came in the employee entrance. In 2008, Goat and I dug our way under a fence. Impractical to have forms when maybe half of you wouldn't get one. So, here's the deal. Every time we play this one fucking song, one of you croaks. Here's the good news: So far, it's been just one per concert. So one of about five hundred diehards in Boise, one of maybe fifteen hundred in Tulsa, two thousand in Detroit, and so forth. But here at Sasquatch, there's maybe fifteen thousand of you, which means chances are more of you will die driving home blitzed or high to Gig Island or Beaverton or wherever the fuck you're from than will die here at the Gorge today." One-hundred-decibel applause. "Okay, okay. So, relax and enjoy the most dangerous band in America. This one's called 'Tiger Drag.'"

The infrastructure of the Gorge was a modern marvel. Speakers lined up three stories on both sides of the stage, four abreast, and then, extending across a boom suspended over the stage, exploded sound a quarter mile up the amphitheater. Like a cook handling metal pans without a potholder, like a boxer without a helmet, like a surgeon who refuses double gloving on an AIDS patient, Melvin Horgan was perhaps the only performer who regularly refused ear protection.

Deafness just wasn't enough of a threat to justify the burden, minimal as it was. Maybe the volume was a stimulant. Maybe he just assumed the chance he would live long enough for deafness to ensue was minimal, but either way, he endured toxic sound levels night after night. But no other night was near as intense as at the Gorge. There were no neighbors to complain, and the amplification needed to blow away the crowd in back required ototoxic decibel levels on the stage and in the mosh.

"Tiger Drag" cascaded in kaleidoscope waves through the ripples in the Gorge, ransacking otoliths like vandal marauders. But it was worth it to see this derivative tripe adored, really adored. The ovation upon completion was beyond anything at any of the prior tour concerts, and it was only the second song. But the adulation was not lost on Melvin, who went off script. "Goddamn. Thank you very much, everyone. I'd tell you I love you all, but you'd know that would make me a fucking liar." Eighty-five-decibel applause. "We love festivals. We would play every fucking festival in the country if we could. Back a few years ago, we got in here, but we tried almost every fucking festival in the country, and they turned us down. We even asked to do Lilith Fair, but I guess they didn't believe that the photo of the cartoon Josie and the Pussycats we sent in was actually Billy Goat's Gruff. But one festival we did play other than here was Bumbershoot." Sixty-decibel applause. "That's in Seattle, and for you Portland people, your fucking festival turned us down three years in a row. When we played Bumbershoot, we were so fucking poor, we still had day jobs, if you could call rolling drunks and rummaging trash for recycling a day job. Well, they gave us each six backstage passes for friends and family, and we don't have any friends and, you know, fuck our families." Eighty-decibel applause. "We were determined to use those passes to our advantage. So, I wrote this song about our backstage eBay experience there, and I apologize if you were the Wiccan who blew me—at least I didn't know your name and include it, and since we're still within the statute of limitations, bitch swore to me she was nineteen." Ninety-decibel applause. "This is 'Bumbershoot.'"

And, for the first time, spontaneously, the crowd joined in once the simple, repetitive pattern became obvious. *"Who'll give me a blow job for a three-day pass,"* with an eruption of twenty thousand voices together on "three-day pass." *"Who has an ounce of chronic for a three-day pass,"* with another explosion of voices echoing through the Gorge. *"Who will trade an eightball for—"* and this time, Melvin felt confident enough to point the mike towards the crowd and let the audience drive the volume. And so, it continued through the twelve barter opportunities cited in the lyrics and then repeated for each of the twelve through even a screechier second stage at an elevated but equally unharmonious octave. This was another level of adulation, the ability to drive a full song of audience participation, and not even with a hit that more than the diehards knew. It was audience-participation driven by personality, a story, and innate enthusiasm, all concepts which would have been utterly unfathomable prior to "Millicent."

After "Bumbershoot," it was smooth sailing through the set. Fifteen songs and a one-song encore. Fifteen originals and "Angry Chair," which they had been covering since the ramen/baked bean years. Little stories for each of them. So, they didn't really get scolded by Lena Durham in the green room at *Letterman* not to drink all the fucking Diet Cokes (as mixers), but it was a great lead in for "Froggy." "Money Grab" wasn't written about Pearl Jam, just that cake-eating prick Vetter (that one drew mixed cheers and boos probably along the Seattle/Portland schism). And it was a dream come true, an envisagement only imagined all those years in the trenches. Fourteen up, fourteen down, and rapturous applause echoing through the Gorge, from Ellensburg to the Wenatchee. From Moses Lake to Royal City. Hell, maybe down in Yakima the old timers were wondering what that rumbling was, whether St. Helens was once more stirring or whether the Fold Belt was shifting in its vast northwest expanse across the state.

After the applause settled from the synchronous *"Pig detective sniffed the key,"* Melvin once again hit the microphone. "Okay, okay. I don't want to be here forever, one of you needs to be on my cock by eleven. Look, I could tell you we've got one more for you, and you would all pretend to be disappointed, but we all know that's the premeditated hoax of the headliner. It's not our last song, but it is one for which you'd better have your fucking affairs in order." Decibel-level-eighty applause. "Who's gonna get your bong, or your record collection. Who can fuck your old lady, other than Troll, of course. Now, I'm not a doctor, but I've heard the rumors, the theories, and the quack cures and all of this bullshit. Let me just say I can neither confirm nor deny that the FBI forensic docs think weed can prevent Millicent DeGroenfeld Rice Syndrome, but it's sure worth a fucking try." Decibel level 105.

And with that, Billy Goat's Gruff launched into "Millicent DeGroenfeld Rice" with a passion beyond their normal capabilities. Like a pitcher whose fastball elevates a tick or two in the playoffs, or a sprinter inevitably breaking records at the Olympics, the volume, intensity, and precision of guitar, drums, bass, and vocals exceeded the mediocre capabilities of the individuals. Even Tiny stayed on beat with Whiplash precision.

Of course, the crowd responded in trancelike resonance, hitting their cues for aping Melvin's hand gestures, Cobainian pogo sticking, "ice" rhyming augmentation of the refrain, and in more juvenile pockets, moshing in perfect Brownian approximation of the rush of guitar notes, many of which were not in the official sheet music, but all of which augmented the overall presentation.

The instrumental portion of the song lasted a little over a minute, and during that interval with the tambourine serving as a prop, Melvin would scan the crowd for the doomed, and if the doomed weren't readily evident, for a pretty but entranced face. But the sheer magnitude of the numbers and the distance from stage to mosh along with the intensity of the lighting precluded this, and Melvin found himself pulled over to the side while Billy took center stage for his solo.

With no enticements in the audience, no grim-reaping parlor game, Melvin drifted as far as the need to maintain beat would allow. "You glorious bitch," he muttered, well away from the microphone, glaring into the lights just barely outlining twenty thousand acolytes. "You inspirational cunt. Look at what you've done. Holy fuck. Bottom feeders. We were bottom feeders. Bottom feeders headlining Sasquatch. When you fucking offed yourself, how could you have fucking imagined, imagined this?" And the guitar and drum instrumental flowed through the crowd and into the ridges between the mountains and shook the tents of the few who had retreated for the night or never emerged from their smoky cocoons.

The band was tight, Tiny hitting his cues and escalating his drumbeats as maliciously as Troll had ever heard him. And as they reached the conclusion, where Tiny brought it back down, and Troll gave the refrain one more go, there was no way from the stage to visualize the inevitable commotion, so after the refrain and the incipient flourish, all four members posed on the stage as the lights faded, and they waited for the roar.

But the roar was more of a rumble as the crowd craned their collective necks, looking for CPR anywhere in the rabble. But there was none. And with the realization that the promise was unfulfilled, any putative cheering turned haughty. Billy Goat's Gruff was being booed off the stage. Billy and Melvin came together. Bebe was already backstage in encore position, ready to re-emerge, and Tiny sat transfixed at the drums, waiting for his mates to react.

"What the fuck, Goat. No one dies, and these assholes are giving us the bum's rush. Fuck them."

"Let's just get out of here," said Billy. "Wait a few, come out, and give 'em 'Dusty' and get out of here."

"I'm not leaving this motherfucking stage. Goddamn these people."

"Say something, Troll."

Melvin crept to the microphone, and the hissing intensified. "Hey, hey. I know you were all hoping for your girlfriend's creepy best friend to—" but the sound drowned out the microphone, and when Melvin tried to approach the mike again, the noise again drowned him out.

Melvin walked back up to Billy and whispered in his ear, then went back to Tiny as well. While the crowd was temporarily lulled into a dull chorus of displeasure, the notes sounded and Melvin belted out, *"Twenty, twenty, twenty-four hours to go / I wanna be sedated."*

Chapter 14:
The Addictive Lure of Infinitesimal Danger

"What do you mean, a class action lawsuit? For what?"

"Breach of contract seems to be the gist of it. False advertising claims, Mr. Nash. I wouldn't be too worried about it. There's no implicit or implied contract. They really can't win in court, probably just looking for some go away nuisance money."

To Roger Smith, a fortunate side effect of the national sensation of Billy Goat's Gruff was the engagement of his boss. No more entourage. No more showing up late and leaving early. Anytime the press called, Tee Nash was present and corporate.

"Who the fuck would sue us for not dying, counselor? I keep waiting for one of these dead bastard's families to come after us, and now we're dealing with people who wanted to die?"

"Well, technically, the complaint is because they claimed that a death had been promised, just some random death in the crowd, and in the absence of a death, the contractual terms were violated. But again, sir, it's a ludicrous claim, almost completely frivolous."

Roger just wanted to blurt out laughing at the farcical nature of this claim, but relied on his day as a collegiate actor, channeling his inner Robert Wagner, ever the straight man.

"Almost completely?"

"Well, sir. They will likely quote Horgan's boasts that the death would happen as a contractual promise. But I think we can refute that as unenforceable. And I can't imagine any reasonable jury in eastern Washington would accept that argument. I don't think it's a major concern, at least not at this time."

Roger Smith glanced past the Afro Sheen bookends of the EcoArt custom black-ebony and platinum desk, and past the Warhol, and out into the New York sunshine, and thought back on his time as an intern at CAA: a twenty-three-year-old Ivy League debutante imbibed with the promise of the control and manipulation of beauty. While mastery of money or monopolization of righteousness drove his classmates at Columbia Law, he was solely obsessed with beauty—artistic beauty and physical beauty, not limited to one race, one sex, one genre. Of course, he tried LA first, but it was a nepotistic morass, and Greenwich was home. The New York houses welcomed his pedigree, but it was Infinity that made him second-in-command so many directors ago, when so many luscious boys and girls hitched the northern highways and the southern byways to follow Dylan or Baez. But now, he was a babysitter. The talent, the bosses, the press were all an exercise in creative babysitting.

"Sir, this is not a heavyweight, making the threats. It's a firm out of Denver. This is no Angelos, no Michael Lewis, just a guy. Sir, what is pressing is the sales bleed since the event. Downloads down nearly fifty percent. We got their Ramones cover out quickly, and that's seen some action, but overall, this thing may be running its course."

"Fifty percent? Significant, I see, Brother Smith. No shows since? It's been—what?—a week since the fail? Maybe we need shows. A comeback killing. Something to re-inspire confidence. What's the schedule?"

"East Coast leg of the tour. We tried to get them a foreign tour. Anywhere with a strong download rate—Japan, UK, Germany, Australia, but so far, no one will admit them. So, just the East Coast. The plan was Atlanta, Charlotte, Richmond, Washington, Baltimore, Philadelphia, Pittsburgh, then Hartford, Boston, and finally, we have the Garden Halloween Night, and that's the finale."

"Advance sales?"

"Strong. A couple of sellouts on the pre-sales, but ever since last week, we're seeing a stream hitting the secondary markets, not a good sign."

Roger wondered when this thing faded, which was inevitable, would the boss lament more the loss of exposure or income.

"This has got to get back on track by the time they reach the Garden. I'm not putting on a half-empty show in my own fucking hometown. So, any theories?"

"Well, sir, since we don't have any concrete ideas what causes the deaths, there are only hypotheses about what didn't happen in the Gorge. Our FBI sources indicate that Tiny's drumming during the guitar solo is somehow connected. Something about the cadence and intensity of the drum solo is felt to be responsible for capturing and corrupting the heartbeat. The speculation is that this capturing requires an inside space with a certain degree of reverberation of sound to potentiate the event. An outside concert wouldn't create the same resonance with the heartbeat, therefore no capture, and no arrhythmia."

"Then why don't we have scores of dead assholes playing that shit loud at home, in clubs?"

"Sir, Tiny Atlas is generally replaced on studio tracks by more accomplished drummers. He really only plays live shows."

"Session players, makes sense."

The phone rang, and Tee Nash was talking to someone at marketing about an album cover for a hip hop band, and Roger Smith shifted slightly in his chair, and something in the summer air whispered damp, foretelling a squall, bringing him back to *Cat on a Hot Tin Roof*, his one turn in the spotlight, albeit in a minor role of Doc Baugh, freezing on stage, not because of stage fright or forgetting his lines but just marveling at the beauty around him and getting lost in the moment. There was that one solitary instant in which he'd thought he might be talent, but then there was the embarrassment when he realized he couldn't, and he'd relegated himself to the family trade.

"No, motherfucker, I didn't say show a titty, I said *expose*. It's fucking artistic for showing a titty. It's classy, not dirty. One more session, my dear God, one more only, and get it the fuck right."

More and more, Roger's mind wandered. Just another three hours and he'd be on the D train, heading to the stadium. *CC and Josh Beckett. A cool night in the early summer, lineups . . . What'll be the lineups? McCann, Texiera, Jeter, Arod, Gardner, and who's that new right fielder? Think Roger, think.*

"Brother Smith."

And then louder. "Brother Smith!"

"Yes, sir."

"Focus, Brother Smith."

"Mr. Nash, I'm not sure this is my particular strength. I'm not sure legal counsel is the key to restoring download volumes."

"Outside the box, Brother Smith. Do you really think musical talent made Troll Horgan the biggest star in our stable?"

"That's not for me to say."

"I'm asking you for an opinion, consiglieri. I expect counsel."

"No, musical talent is not the basis of the success of Billy Goat's Gruff." Roger glanced back from the window at his boss who had the angry eyes of a man possessed. The role reversal was stunning. For years, he was aching for his boss to be more engaged. Now, he felt himself increasingly checked out.

"Okay, of course not. Dumb fucks obsessed with danger, but not too much danger. A little danger is a narcotic to these morons. We rely on the addictive lure of infinitesimal danger. Half of the crowd at a Billy Goat show has seen more than one concert. We have half-wits following these idiots around the country, dosing on the thrill of a one in two thousand or whatever chance of becoming famous. I doubt either of us, Brother Smith, can understand the thinking of the rounded portion of the bell curve, but apparently that's the thought process that compels a twenty-three-year-old auto parts salesman from Santa Fe to take a week off for three shows in the Midwest."

"Still, Mr. Nash. While what you say is probably true—"

"It's certainly true."

"Okay, certainly true, but how is that something we can harness?"

"I don't want to harness, Brother Smith. I want to ensure."

"Ensure?"

"Yes, are you deaf? *Ensure*. Now have we got any reports of deaths in the community from the downloads."

Roger now was burning internally, on the verge of quitting, trying to recall how much pension he would sacrifice by resigning rather than retiring or being fired. "No, sir."

"Of course, 'no, sir,' because what is different about the studio recording?"

"I'm not sure. Maybe the conditions, the volume, the room configuration?"

"No, the drummer. You just told me. Concentrate, damn it. On the studio recordings, studio drummers are used because Tiny Atlas can't actually play the drums. Studio drummers can't kill anyone. So, what is required is an acoustically pristine small venue and Tiny Atlas banging the hell out of those skins. So, no more outside shows, no more large indoor venues for now. Back to the clubs. Back to tipping supply and demand and making these shows an event, a tough ticket. Raise the fucking prices. Make these shows like hang gliding: privileged danger. And, Smith, next show should be somewhere remote, someplace far away from hospitals, paramedics, fire stations. Build it if you need to. I don't want anyone saved. We need a body."

"Mr. Nash. You know Infinity was doing just fine before these boys. No Sony or Columbia, but for a smaller label, it's not like we were losing money. Might I suggest we may be better served just letting this play out, minimize risk, and get back to the business of promoting music and not dodging lawsuits and allegations."

"Smith, I mean no offense. I know it's in your nature to be cautious, and if I utter the word 'pussy,' I don't intend it in the playground fashion, inferring femininity. If I say you're being a pussy in business terms, it's because maybe I'm too green in the corporate world to remember whether it's the bulls or the bears that are the pussies. Really doesn't matter, some white cat a hundred years ago, maybe two hundred, came up with the nomenclature. Irrelevant to me. Pit bulls and pussies—that's what I'd call it. And, Smith, I'm a motherfucking eighty-pound pit bull, and I'm gonna run this motherfucker like a pit bull. Now I probably do need a pussy or two by my side, tempering the enthusiasm. But, Smith, since these boys started their run, we turned three major hip hop acts and signed a fourth. We got the *American Idol* runner-up and American rights for the *Australian Idol* winner. Overall sales are up twenty percent, independent of Billy Goat. That's what face time does for you. We're beating Tommy Mottola at Sony and David Geffen to sign new talent. No one in the industry can compete when I'm on *TMZ* tonight, *GMA* tomorrow, *ET* next day. Who says we can't get a JT or Wahle? But it ain't happening without getting back our mojo, and right now, we need another death or two to maintain momentum."

Roger Smith stared off outside where a kit of pigeons waved to and fro, occasionally alighting on the residential roof across the street with wash laid out and hopscotch patterns drawn in pink and orange astride the rows of lines and linen. The world was such an amazing place. Perhaps it was an illusion, a figment, but the pigeon-shit white blotches on the asphalt of the hopscotch chalk boxes made dice. A two dot on the second one-foot square, and a diagonal three on the right, most of the first two-foot stomp, and then two onesies later, a big, wet, fresh-looking one just in the center of the square. Roger stared at the patterns and wondered a second whether some cheeky kid had steered his etchings to enclose the pigeon droppings in symmetrical patterns, but the lanes weren't haphazard; they paralleled the lines. But this was no kid creating pop art. Nature did that. Even pigeon shit could be utterly beautiful.

"Smith? Where you at today, Smith? You need to let me know if the Feds back off so I can arrange our contingency plan."

"Contingency plan, sir." Roger reluctantly refocused away from the window. "I'm not sure I follow."

"And you're not gonna follow. That's another department, not Legal. Ha-ha, not Legal. I just need intel, that's your contribution here."

"As far as I know, the concerts are still surveilled, but after the Detroit incident, the task force disbanded, and it's just a couple of agents, with Sessions in the lead."

"Sessions, he's faded. That's a window, Smith. Maybe I ought to talk to Sessions."

"Mr. Nash, that's not a good idea. Sessions may have some physical impairments, but there's nothing to suggest he's compromised cognitively, and he's no friend of Horgan after what happened."

"No friend of Horgan might be a friend of mine, though with appropriate enticements."

Roger Smith paused before responding. There was a reflection in the window that seemed to accentuate every struggling line of his face, adding ten years to his already-degrading profile. He glanced around the room at the Warhol and Gilliam and the surrounding works attending the masterpiece like maids-in-waiting, with the newly purchased African chieftain woodcarving balanced like a pendulum on a concave wooden base, swaying slightly, the Carrier window unit acting as chaperone. "Sir, there are some lines, I have to advise you not to cross. There's no coming back for yourself and for the company. I'd hate to see—"

"Smith, that's enough!"

Roger Smith now stared back at Tee Nash defiantly. The habitually insouciant Mr. Nash's voice elevated to a level he generally reserved for the blue conclusions of stories told jokingly about fucking country singers' wives or retired quarterbacks' daughters. Elevated beyond the bravado claims comparing his member to that of Bam Bam Bowser, elevated beyond the hyperbole of purported playground rivalry pickup games with borderline NBA stars.

Nash remained silent, and Smith looked down at his hands, twirling his Princeton ring and waiting patiently for the inevitable hardscrabble lecture, the uptown ingenuity. There was an arrogance in power without erudition. Surely there was arrogance in power with education, but the arrogance of the former was more pervasive, as it came with a foolhardy self-confidence that the educated had learned to marginalize. Maybe it was just the antipathetic anticipation of getting reamed out by someone whose rise to power was entirely dependent on monosyllabic rhymes with weapon synonyms.

"Pussy'll be pussy. Smith, you have given me your input, and I have noted that we are at odds, so to speak. When I took over this calamity, I cleaned house. But I kept you, Smith. Why? Because people said, 'Smith is smart. Smith is loyal. Smith knows this business and can solve a goddamned problem.' Now I've had no reason to complain, until now. But what I'm sensing now is Smith ain't smart, Smith ain't loyal, and Smith is creating problems. That creates a basic incompatibility."

Roger Smith didn't squirm. He glanced back out on the rooftops to make sure that his discovery hadn't self-immolated, then sat up straight and, with square-jawed, prep-school certainty, responded, "Mr. Nash. I have been loyal to Infinity Records for twenty-five years and have always given counsel in the best interest of Infinity. And while I work at the behest of the Board of Directors, I am acutely aware of my responsibilities to you and your office. I believe I am giving you and the company wise counsel. I believe I am loyal fundamentally to the firm, but to you as well, and I am trying hard to solve a profound and unusual dilemma. I appreciate the fact that you are shrouding your intentions. That's smart on your part. But I am also concerned that there are contingencies in place that could cause harm to Infinity Records and its chairman, and it's my job to mitigate that harm. And while clearly you have not indicated to me any discreet plans intending any malfeasance, understand that if I become aware of any such transgression, I would be both ethically and professionally compelled to reveal my suspicions."

Tee Nash pulled up his sleeves with the obsidian cufflinks and furrowed his brow. He started into a sentence, in fact what would likely have been a measured and unemotional one, checked his thoughts like a baseball swing, and in a staccato, escalating tone, replied, "Attorney-client privilege, bitch."

Roger Smith worked hard not to pivot or squirm. He had lost all trepidation, all fear of being fired. He was reverting to the factory setting as if he had been playing a soap opera role for twenty-five years and was just now learning of its cancelation. It didn't take twenty-five years to typecast a C-list actor or a B-list attorney. And after twenty-five years of acting, the last several had become more and more of a caricature of the babysitter fixer yes-man, no more intellectually challenging than the aging actor, once the Strasberg pupil playing old lecherous Dr. Denton making feeble double entendres during the unrealistic mishmash the soap opera writer construes as rounds. So, when the actor who had done nothing but Dr. Denton for twenty-five years finally gets killed off and tries to read for a part in some Art House movie or AMC series, he errors to the technical acting class techniques overly stilted or flamboyant, or avant-garde. And similarly, when the attorney decides he ought to once again be an attorney, there is a recession back into intellect over instinct. Back to those second-year axioms: a valid legal argument was better than a bruhaha. When you know you're right, pound the law; when you're not really sure, pound the table.

"Ah, Mr. Nash. Another civilian whose legal expertise comes from Dick Wolf. Sure makes it sound easy what we do, what we learn, how we apply the statutes to what you would call real-life situations. And you bring up 'attorney-client privilege.' Well, let me tell you about attorney-client privilege, because it's not what you think it is, sir. You see there are elements here. Am I your attorney, or am I a business agent? I mean, I negotiate contracts, provide advice. In some ways, I've been more business advisor than attorney. That would negate privilege. But, more important, if you have committed a crime and I am your attorney, I take any communication from you as privileged to enable your best defense. On the other hand, if information is given either asking me to participate in or be party to a crime, not only is that not privileged but also I am compelled to report any such imminent threats to the court. Compelled. And let's say I can aver I heard a threat but no statement of certainty and yet later that threat is carried through, I am still compelled to come forward. So, you see, attorney-client privilege is not what you should be counting on, Mr. Nash."

Tee Nash was momentarily speechless. He fidgeted with the carved African tribal pendulum and checked his phone, then sent off an email. About thirty seconds passed, and he looked up after sending the message. "Smith, Brother Smith. Why so serious? Did I get your goat there? That's all just bullshit, man. Just bullshit I say sometimes. What did'ja think I was going to do? No, wait, don't answer. I ain't doing shit. We cool. Status quo is okay, but not going to do any crazy bullshit. We cool?"

Roger Smith leaned back as far as his flatback red English leather chair would allow. He slapped his left thigh with his left hand and then put his hands behind his head and leaned forward. He squinted through his eternal twenty-twenty vision, made it twenty-fifteen, maybe twenty-twelve by focusing on Tee Nash. "Mr. Nash. It has been a pleasure to serve this company and to advise you and your predecessors. I have always done my best in that regard, even as my duties have strayed from my training and supposed expertise. Contracts, mergers and acquisitions, corporate law . . . I married that with my desire to promote things of elegance and beauty to the masses. But as time passed, I've been less of a lawyer and more of a corporate conscience. Frankly, it's neither rewarding nor fun. And now this.

"Sure, we're cool. I don't think you're going to send an assassin into the crowd in Richmond to ensure your continued presence in the news cycle. That would be insane, and you're not insane, right? Especially now that you know that I'd be compelled to report my suspicions to the authorities at the highest levels. The untouchable ones. And you're not crazy. You're smart enough to realize how foolish that would be. No, I don't worry about you. And since you're smart, and you know now that I'm not really positioned to perform my job with enthusiasm, with the verve you deserve, you're gonna put me on paid leave. That's the smart thing to do. Six months—no, eight months. That's the Einstein play. Let me go on special assignment. Board will okay it; they think you walk on water. And my special assignment will be to forget what I know. I think I can do that in eight months. Forget about what I know is never going to happen because you're so damn smart. And at the end of that eight, make it nine months, you'll have someone on payroll much cheaper than me to do contracts, and a counselor a little more to your choosing for the day-to-day, and I'll be in the wind. By that point, I'm going to assume this is all moot; those morons still can't be America's sweethearts. Either the bodies stop dropping and they climb back down whatever hole they crawled out of, or the Feds find something, however they do it, or some street painter's compendium compels people to rape their mother—that would be even more shocking and less tasteful. Our crowds and downloads would wither, and Infinity Records can meander back to the music business."

Tee Nash didn't say anything. He let out a laugh or two; put his shoes up on the table. He muttered something that sounded like "crazy mofo" and seemed to be formulating, composing. He was glaring at the ceiling, then suddenly smacked his fist on the table and returned his feet to the floor with a large smile on his face. Roger crossed his legs and ran his hand through his Rogaine-curtailed thinning hair. He wasn't sure whether he had won or lost this very sudden power play. Finally, Tee Nash stood up and came over and offered his hand to Roger Smith, who shook it warily.

"You gangsta, Smith! Mayflower Gangsta. Maybe that's my comeback song. 'Mayflower Gangsta, the Fresh Princeton.'

"He's a Mayflower Gangsta
Slays a nigga with a writ and not a trigga
He's the Fresh Princeton
Motions on retainer no smack and no gun
In Greenwich Connecticut, born and raised
In the country club is where he spent most of his days
Chillin' in the hot tub, Lime Rickeys at the pool,
getting in nine holes in the evening after school
When a couple politicians who were up to no good
Started integration in the neighborhood
He had one little negro call him a dork
And his daddy said, 'Your law school is in Harlem, New York'

"Mayflower Gangsta
Keyser Söze, no indecision, avoid this nigga's jurisdiction

Fresh Princeton
Burns a motherfucking cross on yo lawn and it's all constitutional,
Revolutionary, this bitch is institutional."

Tee Nash came out of song, out of character. "You like that, Brother Smith? You get me license to sample that beat-up Will Smith shit, and we are good. You are free. Just do me that, Brother Smith. You get everything you want, just get me permission. Gonna make you famous, Roger Smith, the Mayflower Gangsta."

Roger Smith knocked his Princeton ring on the table. Proximal emancipation was actually more wrenching than continuing to play act. But this was a fair trial. One last manifestation of his accrued talents. And in the spirit of some old game show he'd watched in East Egg with Smith senior, he said to himself, *I can get that song in three calls,* and he scurried back to his office to phone Burton Jones, his counterpart at Columbia Records.

Chapter 15:
The Dutch Golden Age of Hallucinogenesis

Melvin Horgan was in the midst of a really vivid dream, the kind of dream that might amaze a normal human being and prove that the axiom that you only use 15 percent of your brain is accurate. Had he been paying attention, in the dream, he was writing a masterpiece, the "Suite: Judy Blue Eyes" of grunge. His dream song, had he been paying attention, might have saved the genre against the onslaught of pop divas and neo-crooners who were dominating the airwaves against all non-homicidal bands. In the dream, he had finished the composition and was laying down an anthemic tune not borrowed, not sampled, but entirely original. But as he worked in a dingy hotel room strangely similar to the Ellington in D.C., a knock came on the door, half in the dream, half in reality, and before the opus was memorized, or perhaps because of the narcotic cocktail that had ended the conscious phase of the previous evening, the inspiration faded forever.

Melvin waddled to the door, favoring the leg without a recent bruise he didn't remember receiving. He looked for a light switch, flailing along the wall, and found one, but the left switch was a false alarm, a bridge to nowhere, and the right resulted in the illumination of a ten-watt bulb over the portico, revealing the likely source of the knock and little more. Once more came the *thump, thump, thump,* and now with validation, Melvin inched towards the door.

He remembered there had been a concert the night before. Somewhere unfamiliar, a town they hadn't played before, in the south, Richmond, maybe Norfolk. Somewhere before the D.C. show. But that was hours ago, before the lingering effects of whatever concoction lubricated the performance and its aftermath, and he clearly remembered that there was an aftermath, deposited him wherever here was. A dingy bulb wasn't particularly revealing, but the few clues suggested an unfinished basement. There was a concrete floor punctuated by a small rug in the middle, like an oasis. In fact, he had woken up on the rug, which was green and white and brown. Had the light been better, he may have recognized a rug depicting a golf hole with white sand and blue water hazard at the margins of a green turnpike fairway. There was Troll drool intercalated in the fibers of a grove of trees about halfway down the left-side of the fairway.

Melvin had not made much progress from the light switch to the door before the leg with a freshly clotted gash gave way, and he lacked motivation to continue, but the subsequent knock was piercing and insistent.

"Is there a Melvin in there?" A female voice, brassy but muffled, evolved from the conclusion of the knock, and then led into another rapping.

"Enough, I'm coming." Melvin hesitated at the door and, before opening, queried, "What do you want from Melvin? I mean, it's the middle of the motherfucking night."

"Melvin placed an order."

"What kind of order?"

"Listen, bud. Are you Melvin? Melvin asked for someone to come, and here I am. One hour and twenty minutes, two-hour guarantee. Not like I was awake at one a.m. But here the fuck I am, and Melvin's credit card is already out five hundred. So, Melvin evidently felt a five-Franklin minimum was justified. But I can't earn the other five hundred if I don't find Melvin, so let me in please."

Melvin sat ashen, his back against the door as if feigning protection, an additional line of defense that would miraculously withstand a battering ram, or Jack Torrance with an axe, or whatever was going to inevitably break down the door and rain down terror. He thought, shouldn't he be hiding? But there was no obvious secret door, no false floor, no rope to connect to a swinging anvil. At least nothing he could identify through the meager light. But just as Melvin was prepared to pick a hide-and-seek spot in a corner behind a bookcase unlikely to confuse a toddler, he made an assumption. *Fuck! I sent for a whore. And I already paid her, or maybe Tee did because we're now three for three since Sasquatch, and some fucker bought it tonight. And if the whore is already paid for, I'm sober enough to come. Who am I to look a gift horse, or if not I'd be wasting five hundred of my own funds if I was the one who placed the order. And maybe it's what I need to reconnect my brain and my cock because I sure as hell need to reconnect my brain with my cock.* And with that, he yelled out, "I'm Melvin, I'm Melvin. Hold on, I'm gonna let you in," and swept back over to the door and fumbled to open the lock and chain.

The door opened inward, and in the brighter light of a hallway—a hallway decorated with pink and light-green flower prints on a white wall and dark-green carpeting adorned with horns of plenty and gourds—superimposed on the remnants of this Margaret Mitchell memorial, stood the least likely woman to represent the plantation. This was a modern Amazon, a hulk of a woman, thirty-five, forty, maybe with a close cropping of graying hair in a mohawk with some scattered, almost abandoned purple-and-orange highlights. Nose ring, six or seven right and three or four left ear piercings with a feather on the left, cross on the right, and a studded tongue. Who knew what else was pierced or inked up and down whatever was not exposed. On the neck, just a hint poked through of a cacophony of colors, with one scene blending into another and only fragments independently recognizable, one dragon hidden within a carnival ride was on the left arm, and a baby eagle or falcon emerging from a gigantic egg on the left clavicle, rising up the neck.

"Okay, Melvin. I'm Hals. You got me here. What is it you want?"

"Hals, want? What the . . .?" came stammering out as Melvin backed away from the door, spying to see if his putative hiding spot could be reached in cover.

Hals drew out a trunk-like suitcase on wheels. "Look, buster. I don't get many two a.m. requests, but it's common courtesy not to flake when I've ventured out. This isn't the best neighborhood in town, but I'm fucking here. So, if you know what you want, let me know. You've already paid. But if you don't, make up your mind or at least let me go home. I can leave you a card, and call me in the morning."

Melvin's initial terror had turned to wonder as he looked up at this woman, a head taller than him, standing majestically in the doorway like some Norse Goddess.

"We're leaving in the morning, I think. Not really sure when, but I think we leave in the morning."

"Then I would encourage you to make up your mind. Or don't. I do good work, but at this point, I'm gonna get paid either way. But just between the two of us, looking at you, I'm itching to get to work. Looks like you need me."

At this, the spell was at least transiently broken, and Melvin bristled, "Need me. How the fuck would you know? Need me? Need you for what? I'm fucking perfect. I was fucking perfect before whoever called you, and I'll be fucking perfect when you're gone."

"Perfection? Yes, of course. How was I so blind to have missed that? You won't be needing my services, then. I can scram. Still a little time for a good night's sleep."

"Now, wait. I didn't say that. I'm not sending you away. I just am not really sure . . ." Melvin thought hard and focused on the large woman in front of him. ". . . what exactly it is I want."

"Generally speaking, you don't call me without a rudimentary understanding of what it is you want."

"Sure enough, I understand that, Hals—what kind of fucking name is Hals?—but maybe when I called I had more certainty, and now I maybe need more guidance."

"Guidance? I don't provide guidance. You know what you want, and I stay and do it, or you don't know what you want, and I melt back into the night. Either way, Melvin."

Melvin hesitated in thought. He felt down below where his dick was getting erect, and wondered if this carny first oarswoman could accomplish what a cacophony of corporate pros and groupies could not. He still had no recollection of his phone call; how he would have contact info in a city they had never played, and how could he have directed them to wherevertheﬁuck he had landed? Simplicity overwhelmed him, even if the thought of overpaying did materialize. After all, it might be Tee's money anyway. "Just suck it. B. J. and the Bear."

"What the fuck, Melvin? Wrong idea, mate. Wrong idea. This ain't a massage, and there ain't no happy endings. Unless what you're looking for is Greg Evigan getting off by a fucking chimp, I think we're gonna have to call it a night. Next time you call one-eight-hundred-tattnow, know what you're after, and don't fry your fucking brain."

Now confusion reigned. After a millisecond of hope that being dominated might elicit a response where submissive beauty had failed, Melvin looked up at the woman and tried to regain composure.

"Oh shit, wait, wait. Yeah, I'm starting to remember now. Yeah, I was just shitting you, Hals. Hals? Isn't that a fucking cough drop? Why the hell are you named for a goddamned cough drop?"

"Goodbye, Melvin. In about four hours, you can find an open shop down on Shockoe Slip. And the other, just ask the goddamned concierge. I'm sure they can get you twenty-four-hour service for 'B. J. and the Bear,' or whatever floats your boat."

"Hold on, hold on. I'm an asshole, yeah, I know, but concierge? Still in a hotel? I suppose I'm still in a hotel. Which fucking hotel? This doesn't look like a hotel room. Fuck, tattoo. Yeah, I remember that now, five hundred now, five hundred on arrival. On eight-hundred something or other."

"Yes. And this is the goddamned storage area of the Jefferson Hotel. Hell of a time convincing the front desk I was directed here."

The Jefferson Hotel. Some of this was coming back. At the show, a beautiful sorority-type dropped dead in the front row. As they tore off her clothing trying to revive her, she had a beautiful piece of ink on her abdomen, a large heavily rooted tree, and as they pounded on her chest, he kept staring at that thing—a flowering dogwood, he'd heard a paramedic say. He came back to the hotel and smoked some weed and popped a shroom, and must have had a fit of inspiration. He refused to consider it contrition. Needed to get away.

"Yeah. Storage area. That's right. Hair dryer burned out and didn't want anyone to know I was using it to try to start a chemical reaction, yeah, yeah. Told Goat I was heading downstairs, and what the hell was I thinking? But I wanted a tattoo. I'm not generally a tattoo guy, no offense. Not a personal appearance thing. Not a needle thing either."

"Then why did you call? Why did you lay out a grand for an emergency, late-night tattoo? What did you want?"

He thought back on the young woman having her chest pounded on, black and blue marks appearing under her ribs, and imagined the bruising melding into the dogwood tattoo and the flowering leaves withering and dying.

"I have no idea. But let's do it. You're here, with your big box of pigments. Crayola for Juggalos. I'm ready. Defile me, Hals, you wicked woman. Endow me with something cool, hipster male for a boob job. Give it to me good. If one thousand isn't enough for a chest manifesto, I'll pay more. Do me, Hals, do me good."

"And what exactly were you thinking of, Melvin?"

"Dealer's choice, Miley Aguilera. Whatever you think suits a national phenomenon. Give me a backstory. I will tell the world about Hals next time I'm on the *Today Show*. Free publicity, Hals. Can't beat that. Make me beautiful."

Is this some sort of penance I subconsciously concocted, he thought. *Because I don't do penance. I'm Melvin Horgan. And I fundamentally don't give a shit.*

"Sugar, that's not really the way it works. I don't choose for you. Customers either come in with exactly what they want, with a sketch or picture, or a concept I help them flesh out. But it's not like getting the chef's menu at a restaurant. We're à la carte, baby."

"Okay, I get you. How about one of those tribal things? I think Billie Joe Armstrong has one of those, or maybe it's Adam Levine, or could just be the Rock."

Hals went over and inspected Melvin, who at first instinctively flinched away before allowing her to palpate and probe both upper arms, pinching his muscle mass between her slim fingers, which were etched with fine inkbrush figures. "You ever seen an old man, ex-Navy, seventy-five or eighty?" Hals said. "Used to be a big, strapping buck with Popeye arms from rowing, or hauling, or whatever those swabbies did all day who went out in '72 in Saigon, or '45 in Okinawa, or '52 in Pusan, and got themselves a lovely, vibrant anchor right on that ever-loving right bicep, commemorating their love of the ocean, love of the Navy, or maybe of some beautiful native woman to remember, some girl they'd spent their leave with. But then they come home and stop lifting anchors, or whatever gave them those biceps, and become an insurance man or a security guard and grow fat and flabby on Ho Hos and Pepsi until the biceps that once belonged on a Roman vase shrivel and shrink and the skin folds and tucks under itself until that anchor is a puckered-up mess that resembles a Calder mobile—wait, you wouldn't get that one—a bunch of crushed wire hangers on his arm, much more than it could be taken for a proud symbol of the sea. And the problem here, superstar, is that you already have that geezer bicep. You've already got the folds of skin wrinkling and crinkling in such that I would have to pull your skin taut for ink, but upon release, it would immediately revert to a jumble of blacks and whites in no discernable pattern unless you were to roll out your flabs with push pins like a treasure map. But if that's what you want, the motherfucking customer is always right."

"So, I guess you're not planning to set out a tip jar. Not really pressing for return business, are we, Rosanne? My fucking luck, I make a drunken plea for a suck and fuck, get my mother lecturing to me—that is, if my mother was going through a Billie Jean King meets Axel Rose phase. Look, bitch, if I want to hear about my motherfucking inadequacies, all I need is a plane ticket to Sacramento and someone to hide the Quaaludes. Don't expect the truth from the motherfucking service industry. And just because I'm the Troll don't mean I'm ignorant of who Alexander Calder is, arrogant cunt."

And now, as if the insults, weed, and shroom simmered together with his bringing up the unmentionable, he saw his mother laughing at him at middle school graduation, telling him that was all the schooling he needed to pump gas. Then she was screaming at him when post-marriage boyfriend three took off for good after he vomited on the asshole's pants after getting drunk for the first time, at twelve, on the Jack and cokes they gave him. The displaced anger welled up, and Hals was no longer the Amazonian savior; she was a bigger, badder version of dearest mom, deposited into a world where Melvin had some ability to defend himself.

"Return business? Ha! Chances your average rockstar cruises back into Richmond, Virginia, for ink? I think I'm safe in assuming if I forged the motherfucking *Mona Lisa* of tattoos on your torso, or Escher's *Relativity* crammed on your back, it's not like we'd ever cross paths. Pre-paid business is the benefit of this here on-call position."

"Just forget it then. Go run back to Large Marge and strap it on, baby. You give, don't you, Hals? You're a giver. I can see that in you. A spiritual cunt who does tattoos. A cuntattoo, Hals. Go, get the fuck out of here." Melvin reached into his wallet and, unable to recognize the contents even when squinting, had to scramble over to the glow of the dingy bulb. Once the contents were illuminated, he reached in and threw a bill on the floor. "A tip.

Bet you didn't think you'd be getting a tip tonight, Hals, baby. A Franklin. One hundred dollars, Hals, for you, as a thanks for this re-awakening to the intrinsic cuntiness of all women. And if I could request a small favor for my generous tip, considering no service was performed, I want you to set up a profile on some dating site with a picture of some little Veronica Ratchet and agree to a date with the most pitiful bastard you can find. Bastard who cares for his mama and volunteers at some mission, and stand his motherfucking ass up. Wait, here's two hundred." He threw another bill with a wrist flick, and it circled and landed on the green of the putting rug. "Before you do that, take the extra bill and get yourself made up to look, like, straight. Makeup and sundress and wig or shit, and actually go out with the guy and lead him on real good, and just when he thinks he's gonna score him some, Hals, get your lady friend to come by and, after casual conversation, start making out and thank the fucker and tell him he finally turned you. Ruin him, Hals. That would be the cuntiest thing ever."

Hals glanced down at the two bills strewn at Melvin's feet and momentarily paused, as if calculating whether nearing proximity to him was worth the profit. But then, silently, she turned her back and headed back towards the door.

"Take it, bitch. You know you want it. Take the fucking money." Melvin gave a malevolent laugh. "You don't have to do shit. I was just joking. Take the money. Tip for reminding me. Remedial education in human nature. Take it."

By this time, Hals was at the door, reaching out and preparing to exit. At the last moment, she turned around. "Maybe I'm a fucking idiot, but I'm gonna give you one more chance, Melvin. Man, it would be much easier to go home and tell the girls I had this confrontation with irascible nogoodnik Melvin Horgan, wasted and locked in the storage room of his hotel, and got into a beef in which the only retorts of this alleged 'Lenny Bruce of grunge' amounted to sixth-grade, rug-munch jokes fresh as 'that's what she said.' But, Melvin, something compelled you to call me at two a.m., not a whore, not a dealer, not your apparent bitch of a mom. You called for me, and call me a moron, but I want to figure out why."

Melvin propped himself up with his bad leg sprawled out straight behind his body, which clung to the top of a dinner chair draped in plastic, indicating ongoing repair. Wanting to curse but temporarily unable to, he belched an opening into a cough or two and finally into a hack, as seamlessly as a gymnastics combination. He wouldn't look at Hals, who hadn't moved except to put down her case. Melvin looked off into a bookshelf that harbored prop titles no longer recognizable as purveyors of class, empty binders of bypassed classics, kept as if some manager reasoned Wharton and Henry James might come back into fashion. And really, Hals wasn't a factor, she wasn't his confessor—she wasn't there anymore, maybe had never been there. Maybe just a remnant of the smack, or a creation of that odd-colored shroom, and he was no longer able to talk.

I don't know. I've been kind of seeing someone or thinking I'm seeing someone. Maybe when I was wasted, I thought she could inspire me, but I was just drunk, and I don't want it. I'm certain I don't want it. There was a muttering that Melvin couldn't clearly discern coming from the door, some *Peanuts* adult-speak, which may have been a question and may have been his imagination. He went over to the books and knocked a couple on the floor. Thackery, Galsworthy, Stendahl, Cooper, all went tumbling onto the floor, which swallowed and processed them like carbonite. Forgotten, purged by Melvin's swing, doomed to oblivion save for the occasional eight-hundred-dollar *Jeopardy* answer or a Yorkshire nursing home's book club. "Just some bitch I fucked. Must've been a good one, but don't need her on my ass. No, fuck no. I don't need no fucking tattoo." And with that, he walked over the pile and past the golf rug and out the door, to ask the night clerk if he was even staying at the Jefferson Hotel.

Chapter 16:
Don't Look Back in Anger

Natalie Dormer's agent wouldn't allow her to sign on with such limited screen time. The montage mentioned previously wasn't sufficient. Ginnifer wouldn't disrobe and was therefore eliminated from contention for the part. Natalie would, but after *The Hunger Games* and *Game of Thrones*, there had to be ample screen time for Best Supporting Actress consideration. Without it, she wasn't interested, and the casting directors were pessimistic of finding anyone comparable. Ms. Dormer would require additional screen time. Tell Dalton Trumbo to write her another motherfucking scene.

"Hey, Vassar!" Vince the Wop had finally settled on a "V" name for Millicent DeGroenfeld Rice based on her obvious peccadillos, which differentiated her from the Victorias, Veronicas, Violets, and Vixens. "Where's Vassar?"

"Out on the floor, Vince. Where do you think she'd be? She's just off station two and is roaming the floor. Girl hasn't taken her breaks for three years" came the voice of the cashier, never looking up from a frayed copy of the July 6th, 2009, *People Magazine*.

"Somebody go and fetch me Vassar." Vince stuck his neckless head out of his broom closet of an office—the manager didn't rate a tryout couch—and looked around to see if anyone was stirring to follow his order. No one budged. "Someone go find me Vassar," he proclaimed emphatically, "or there'll be consequences, see," he continued in his mob voice, equal parts tyranny and parody.

"Were there consequences when I blew your ma?" came the voice of Sheila, the head bartender. "Go find her yourself. Burn a calorie or two,

Vince. You can neutralize that one-calorie Fresca you had with your meatball sub breakfast. Dietary equilibrium for a fat ass."

Vince looked over at Sheila and imagined tugging down her goth-dark ponytails and shoving himself down her throat, past her studded tongue, as he did each and every time he looked at her, then shrugged and walked the other way.

Out in the lounge, he crept stage to stage, but no hint of Vassar. Vixen was doing her no-talent babydoll boop-boop on the main, and Victoria was eating bills out of the cleavage of a kept Eastern European thing on number two. A couple of girls roamed the hall, looking for privates, but no Vassar anywhere in the lounge.

Millicent didn't smoke. You wouldn't find her in the alley puffing away on a "vagina slime" or a J and certainly nothing injectable. She didn't binge/purge, so her bathroom trips weren't protracted, and her meal breaks were generally grab and go's. She wasn't one to break policy to pocket under the table, turning tricks in one of the surrounding flop houses. There was only one other locale—the Champagne Room.

The VIP lounge at the Good Guys Club was obviously named to connote sophistication and élan. Every club had some private area conjuring special girls and special treatment, but in reality, it was just a conduit for Jacksons to flow like Washingtons did on the floor. The Champagne Room was a dismal, old office that had been outfitted with a leather chair in the center and some glow hearts and stars on the walls and ceiling. The only champagne influence on the space was the stains spilled from flutes of Asti poured out of Dom bottles in just a little white lie. The customers were generally drunk enough that they'd never notice or care, especially when half the volume went splattering on the seldom-cleaned shag during the five-minute sessions of detached grinding. There was a gaudy sign on the door in intricate script, indicating the room, with a notice below—Vince's touch—which said "VIP's only" with a red/white cardboard adjustable indicator to notify whether any VIP experiences were ongoing.

Vince walked up and noticed the red. Only Vince and the bouncer, theoretically tethered to a theoretical panic button, were authorized to enter on red. Vince did so quietly, just opening a slit, and glanced in to see the back of the head of a short dark-haired man in a suit, ridden by a strawberry blond, grinding and waving her hair in his face to "Wild Wild Life" by the Talking Heads. Fucking Vassar off-script again. But Vince wasn't particularly feline, and Millicent spied him and started shaking her head and prodding him to leave as best as she could while maintaining adequate focus on her mark. Vince gestured towards his mouth and pointed at Millicent, who had re-established focus, but when she looked up, she nodded and sat up on the man in the chair, thrusting her chest into his nose as she tried to wave Vince out of the room while assuring him she would come find him.

Vince was satisfied that his message had been received and was about to leave when he saw the man raise his hands, transfixed by bilateral, lateral occipital cleavage stimulation, and place his hands on the outside of Millicent's breasts and push them together while she continued on his lap. Immediately, Vince turned the light on and rushed to her side. "Sir, club policy. No touching allowed. No touching, strict policy. You're gonna have to—"

"Vince, dear. We're okay. Get out of here. I will come talk to you. Taunggpaan partai, Lwin. I'm sorry. He's a crazy man who comes here and pretends he's a bouncer. A crazy man, but he's leaving. Next one's on me, 'Once in a Lifetime,' okay?"

"Okay" came the reply, and the light went off as the last refrain medley of "Wild Wild Life" took over and brought the purchased lap to a close. Millicent wearily climbed off her customer and pressed a button and resumed the position as "You may find yourself" was spoken simultaneously by David Byrne and Millicent DeGroenfeld Rice.

***

Millicent entered the office six minutes later, Good Guys T-shirt over a red bikini top, and filled in paperwork. "Vince, what the hell. Policy? What policy?"

"What policy, Vassar? You're not a rookie. No kissing, no hands on breasts, butt—"

"I know the damn policy," Millicent interrupted, "but I also know that there's no bouncer except at the door, no camera in the VIP, and no one to watch it if there was. So we make our rules. That guy's a regular. He's harmless. Pays well, tips well. My regular, and I had to give him a free ride, which I really don't appreciate."

"Sorry. Just trying to protect you—could have been a crazy Chinaman."

"Jesus Christ, Vince. Chinaman? Inappropriate. Chinese diplomats don't come here. They have money. They go to Dupont."

"Japanese, then."

"The Japanese embassy and consulate staff have class. I've never seen anyone here. Lwin is from Myanmar."

Vince looked perplexed. "I thought your mother died. How's she sending you gook pervs."

Millicent was used to ignorance and stupidity from Vince, who was not really a boss, as the girls were independent contractors than employees. But this was outrageous, and it was worth a somewhat hollow threat and the risk of being jettisoned or shifted to Tuesday and Wednesday afternoons during the slowest of off-peak hours to confront abject bigotry.

"My God. One more racist word from you and I'm gone. Myanmar. It's a country in Southeast Asia. Used to be Burma. The embassy is on S Street down the road. We do get a fair amount of traffic from the embassy. It's a poor country. And I don't mind him touching me once or twice. It's easier than having him try to kiss me. He goes for the chest, I arch back out of range. And if you cared so much, hire more security. Just don't go around like a goddamned mall cop, hall monitor, security guard motherfucker harassing my regs. I like the guy, even learned a little Burmese."

"I had no idea. Damn 'Myomurmese,' how the fuck could I? Well, screw. Sorry. But I'm gonna make it up to you, sweetheart. I got you an easy score. Saturday at the Mayflower, got you for a private. Big spenders. Make up for the freebee twenty times over."

Millicent shook her head in frustration. *Does he remember the last seven times he tried to get me to go off-site?*

"I don't do privates. You know that. You have any number of girls who will. I did a couple of privates when I came on and swore I'd never do it again. I know about the money, I know about the tips, I know you'll send security, and I'm not going." Millicent stared into Vince's eyes, neither in anger nor defiance, but more to reinforce her determination to never even be asked again.

"I know you're a conscientious objector," Vince said, "but please. Just listen to me. I really need you, kid. I took the job for six, but Virginia's dad is having surgery Friday, and go figure, Veronica's boyfriend is graduating law school in Baltimore. I'm down, and it's a big contract. What can I do? I don't have the numbers unless I siphon from here, and I've already cut to bare bones. You're my last hope. Asked you last—swear to God."

"Jesus Christ." Millicent got a pained look on her face, one familiar in all people of principle who assume their integrity doesn't have a price when they realize that abandoning their core principles may have a price. "You know why I don't mind what I do here? Why I can take my clothes off and grind and pretend to care, pretend to be engaged when the basic principle of taking my clothes off for strangers disgusts me? It's because I can trade the disgust for control. I never had control, Vince, until I came here. It's the ultimate control, in which these poor schmucks have the illusion of control, but we actually have a monopoly of it. It's the control that gets me through. The control trumps the horror of the meaningless objectified nature of the life. But at the Mayflower Hotel, you know how much control I have? I've got none. I have the illusion of control, and they monopolize it in reality. And that's why I don't go off-site, and I don't do privates."

"You think too much. It's bad for you. Gives you worry lines. Every woman has her price, V. What's your price? You're getting a grand for the appearance; tips are all yours. Do as much or as little as you like. Security guaranteed. I'll guarantee you an extra five, baby. Fifteen hundred for one night, plus tips. Can't beat that, it's one night."

Fifteen hundred dollars for a night was a lot of money. Millicent was hardly a big spender. But that was vacation money or concert money or annual subscription to the ballet money. There hadn't been a real vacation in years. *Germany*, she thought. *What if I went to Germany, where my grandmother came from—Schwerin and Rostock, the magical places of her childhood—and then maybe ferry up to Denmark and see Copenhagen. And what else can I get the jerk to give me, especially if he doesn't think I care about the cash?* She paused and started to shake her head and walk away, then turned back.

"I don't really care about the money. But here's what I want. I want to pick my own music. 'Pour Some Sugar on Me'—I get it, it's sex. It's a double entendre for morons. But not everyone's a moron, and some of our customers would actually like to hear some decent music, would rather hear a decent song, even if it doesn't overtly flaunt fornication. I want to make my own playlists when I'm onstage. You let me do that, and I'll do your fucking party. 'Don't Look Back in Anger,' Vince. Yeah, it's not a stripper song, but I'll blow wads on 'My Soul Slides Away.' Best word in rock and roll, 'slides,' sexy, too. But I can make it mine, Vince. 'Pour Some Sugar on Me' will never be mine. 'Girls, Girls, Girls' will never be mine. 'Gravity Rides Everything' is mine. That's something I slither across the stage to and fucking mean it. That's my price, Vince. I go to this Mayflower shit, and I get my own music choices—not once a week but all the time"—and here she hesitated—"and the extra five hundred dollars."

Vince the Wop's expression became thoughtful, the kind of feigned reaction people of average intellect acquire when they realize that a conversation is about twenty IQ points above their paygrade and have no way to respond, positively or negatively, without sounding like an utter moron. Vince the Wop generally would have responded and allowed himself to be the unknowing moron, but he remained tongue-tied with an appearance mimicking *The Thinker* if Rodin had used Vinnie Barbarino as a model.

Millicent waited a few seconds and a coy smile emerged. "I'll send you a playlist," she offered, and then walked back into the main area. "Cherry Pie" was going to start in three, two, one . . .

* * *

A staple sexy scene of every adult-themed drama is the preparation montage of the female protagonist preparing for a night on the town by putting on her alluring dress and preparing hair, lashes, and lipstick—makeup application would ruin some illusion and is omitted. These scenes are sensual because the audience knows they imply an impending seduction. It doesn't really matter whether that seduction is in pursuit of love/lust or some more nefarious purpose, it is seduction nonetheless, and since the protagonist is in charge of the dramatic process, the audience views the preparation as alluring.

Now, let's consider our montage in the cramped, three-room apartment of Millicent DeGroenfeld Rice. There's nothing sexy about a six-hundred-square foot, one-bedroom, one-bath space in an eighty-year-old D.C. apartment with low ceilings, awkward angled partitions, and grainy original hardwood floorings, originally designed for low-level bureaucrats. There's nothing sexy about a closet of gaudy knockoffs in bright pastels rather than white and black and red, which encompass about 90 percent of regular movie dresses. There's nothing sexy about preparation for a workmanlike performance of a disaffected refugee. Maybe it's paced and shot more like a collection of troops putting on their military gear en route to a suicide mission. But it's not sexy.

But a montage is called for, and when it's said and done, there's Natalie/Millicent in a yellow, low-cut thing with a bikini underneath and red, calf-high boots from the DSW, and the requisite stripper accoutrements—fake classy bag, garish nails and lips and eyebrows, and well-designed but ultimately tacky costume jewelry.

The six women meet at the Daily Grill for a drink and appetizers before the concert. Vassar, Venus, Vamp, Vixen, Valkyrie, and Valerie. Hard to know what the citizen customers thought of the gaggle of beautiful young women at the table by the door. They were a pornographic fellowship of the ring. *Reservoir Dogs* meets the Bangles. One was clearly a decade older than the others but more elegant and worldly (Vassar/Millicent). Another (Vamp) was the sassy Black girl from PG County with ample street smarts and a well-disguised heart of gold. One (Venus) is the lovely blond from Culpeper, naïve and desperate not to have to return to Mom and stepdad. Number four (Vixen) is a failed New York model, too short for the runway but imagining this gig as thrilling as her last. Next, we have a Rosario Dawson-type (Valkyrie), who, as a proud Latina, won't take crap or suffer fools. Finally, there's Valerie, truly a wonderful soul, stripping for extra dollars to put her through a master's in social work, a do-gooder. Six of them convene for a drink and a meal and a plan to get them through the night.

Millicent is the last to arrive, and Vamp is holding court with Valkyrie at her side, mentoring the three inexperienced girls. "Here's the most important thing to remember. It's just like work, except all lap dances, and there's no cut. The club already took theirs, so any tips are yours and yours alone. Any extras yours and yours alone. You can make a week's salary in one night. Some girls survive solely on weekend bachelor parties and privates. Well, look, welcome to the party, Princess. Now, Princess can give you the dissenting view because she doesn't do privates, except when she extorts an extra five large from Vince."

The six of them were sitting in a circular table with Vamp and Valkyrie both in their late twenties and veterans of the game in the middle with the younger, less-experienced girls huddled around them. Millicent, derisively called Princess for being aloof. Normally, Millicent had little to say to either of them, but she was fond of the younger girls and didn't want to be entirely adrift in the tutorial.

"Capitalism, Vamp," said Millicent. "You got a problem with capitalism? I didn't think so. You'll make it up, extras as you put it. Nothing wrong with privates. Just not my taste. It's like when you're twenty, dropping E and clubbing is a kick, but ten years later, it's kind of sad."

"I can't imagine what it must be like after twenty years," deadpanned Valkyrie with a malevolent purr.

"I don't know. Let's ask your mama," retorted Millicent. She stared at Valkyrie for ten seconds and, seeing no response, started to laugh.

This seemed to soften the mood, and the rest of the party giggled, even Valkyrie, putting up a hand and toasting with her Moscow mule.

Millicent called over the waitress and ordered a Tom Collins and duck confit. "It's not a matter of liking or disliking these shit shows. I'm just over it. The celebrity parties, you're just an ornament, and the bachelor and corporate events are just a bunch of drunk morons trying to use their 'charm' to get their extras for free. I just got tired of both, and I'd rather be home with a DVR and a bottle of wine."

"I didn't think you drank, Millicent," said Valerie, whose red satin dress looked more appropriate for a charity event than a job.

"I don't drink at work. At the club, booze would be giving up. I refuse to do that. You drink to mask the elements you detest. I want to feel them. It's strange, but I feel better about what I do if I fully experience the parts that are revolting. But I know I hate the entirety of this scene, so showing up two sheets to the wind might make the night a little more palatable."

Vixen was the loveliest of them. A green-eyed twenty-two-year-old blond with high Bulgarian cheekbones, a way product of a Swedish lush and an Eastern European, low-level goon with a wandering, indiscriminate dick. She was dressed all in white like an angel. "But, Millicent. That's so cynical. Don't you ever think about someone kind who might take an actual interest?"

"Oh, sweet child. The *Pretty Woman* myth. You know who wrote *Pretty Woman*? J. F. Lawton. J. F. doesn't stand for Jane Fonda. It was written by a man. You know who was the director? Garry Marshall. Amazing. Not a chick. It's propaganda. Karl Marx called religion the opiate of the masses, baby girl. *Pretty Woman* is the opiate of the strippers and the whores. Keeps you toiling away because you never know when the baseball star or the movie star or the rock star or the CEO is going to fall madly in love and whisk you away from all this. If they could, they would show you that drivel once a week. Teach it to you like the plantation owners taught their slaves 'bout Jesus and the rewards of the next world. Don't succumb! Ha-ha. Vamp. I know you're not a *Pretty Woman* fan. You don't think one of the Wizards are coming to rescue you."

"Oh, Princess. Give these kids a break. You're telling our kids Santa ain't real. Don't listen to her. She's Laura San Giacamo, this one. The ugly, jealous roommate. You keep dreaming, bitches. You never know."

"You never know. That's what Vince said," offered Venus in her elegant Virginia drawl. Her long blond hair pulled backwards instead of flopping forward as it often did to hide her buck teeth and crooked orthodontist-neglected overbite. "Wasn't there a girl at the Good Guys who married some football player?"

Millicent laughed and replied as someone between savior and matron. "I can't tell you it's never happened, and that some slumming deb revealed herself to her advantage to someone with a savior complex. But, for one of us, might as well try to land the cover of *Vogue*, sorry, Vixen. Might as well become the next Bond girl, first lady of Argentina, channel-four weathergirl. Sorry, sweetheart."

"Well, I don't care what Millicent says, this is going to be fun, more fun than the regular slobs in the club." Valerie giggled, a natural dirty blond who had transformed into a Snow White ingenue to inspire club profits. "I know this is some rock-band party, and the Mayflower is one of the oldest and nicest hotels in D.C. Does anyone know who we're there for? I checked, and there's Death Cab for Cutie at the Verizon, and Cage the Elephant at the 930."

"Billy Goat's Gruff."

"Who?"

"Billy Goat's Gruff," repeated Millicent. "C-list, four-member grunge band touring with something called Bear Hands. That's what we got."

"Billy Goat's Gruff? Anyone ever hear of them?"

At this point, Valkyrie looked perturbed as if the conversation was going off the rails and announced slowly and boisterously, "They're clients. That's all. Other than that, they're nothing. They are a pile of twenty-dollar bills ready to transfer themselves from their wallet to your G-string. If you want them to pay one hundred at a time, a thousand at a time, they can be that as well. That's your call, all of you."

The waitress came by with the confit, which was an outlier amongst two beet salads, one kale salad, two Caesars—one with salmon—and a pear-walnut-goat-cheese vinaigrette. The preparation was on baby greens with pommes de terre à la sarladaise. Millicent cut into the crispy red skin, and there was an expulsion of fat.

"What is that?" asked Valerie. "It looks decadent."

"Duck confit? This is the regional dish of Gascony. It's duck marinated in salt and garlic and then poached in its own fat to make it extra tender. Try it. There's plenty."

"Cooked in its fat, yuck."

"Oh, just try it." Millicent carved off a bit of the breast meat and put her fork into Valerie's mouth, barely avoiding a choo-choo train tunnel enticement as the girl moved her mouth from the fork. "Not bad, huh?"

Valerie licked her lips, and a wry smile emerged. "It's delicious, Millie. Can Vixen try?"

"Sure, of course." Small morsels were favorably received by all except Victoria, who was a vegan.

"How do you know about this stuff?" Valerie asked Millicent. "I've never even heard of duck confit."

"Bitch was inspiration for *Pretty Woman*, right, Vassar?" Vamp laughed. "She got plucked from the streets by her own Dick Gere, got a taste for duck confit and Tom Collins before he done lost his taste for street meat and found himself a new girl, and Vassar goes back to what she knows, right, V?"

Millicent ducked back into her chair and chuckled. For just a second, she revisited nights with Sly Dobbins in New Orleans, exploring French and Creole gastronomy as a positive byproduct of languishing. Not everything about those days was worth repressing. "I lived a spell in New Orleans. Duck confit in the Easy is like chicken Caesar salad here. Everyone serves it, albeit a little differently. This here is more French. I like it Cajun—a little spicier, but either way, it sure as hell beats kale salad. Don't you think, kid? Oh yeah, and a Tom Collins is just sugar, lemon, gin, and soda water, not exactly a champagne cocktail."

"Millicent, why do you do this?" The unspeakable question. It was Valerie. Sweet Valerie. Baby face, straight, brown hair, long and flowing, with probing blue eyes. She would make a great social worker someday, when the ones and twenties added up to pay tuition a semester at a time rather than sporadic night courses. And, in time, she would learn to offer solutions, not probe problems. The one question you can't ask a girl in the business. You're either going to get a lie or a truth so painful, it should only be slowly and gradually extracted from a psychiatrist's couch or a police interrogation.

Vamp and Valkyrie immediately intervened, dispelling the requirement that Millicent respond. "None of your business, bitch," Vamp interceded with a protective scowl. Enforcing an unwritten rule.

"I'm—I'm sorry. I didn't mean to. I mean, I didn't know."

"It's okay, Valerie. I don't mind. But it's a question you can't ask. You want to be a social worker, but I'm guessing the first thing they teach you is how not to appear judgmental. No drug addict lets in a damn judgmental do-gooder. It's the same way with us. Most people are immediately judgmental, and frankly its fucking exasperating. And they make up assumptions that either criminalize or victimize us, depending on their bias. We do this because we're on drugs, or because we're trying to stay off drugs. We do this because our stepdad fucked us, or because our stepdad wouldn't fuck us. We do this as conditioning therapy for our poor body image, or we do this because we adore our bodies and want to share. Either way, it's judgmental, and so we lie either to validate their assumptions and garner sympathy or deliberately try to shatter them. Either way, it's a wearisome game you'll quickly tire of. You'll understand when you realize it's been five years, and you don't need it for the tuition, but you're still active, and no one understands why, and you keep getting peppered and peppered until you're done answering forever. And that's why you don't ever ask."

There was an awkward, long silence in which the younger girls were transfixed, and the veterans just drank. Millicent finished her Tom Collins and motioned for another.

The women finished their food and drink in relative silence, punctuated by meaningless, culinary small talk, the kind of vapid, time-sapping filler that typically populates desperation dinners with flailing couples or uncomfortable reunions of incompatible, semi-estranged relations—"You have to" exclamations, with the emphasis squarely on "have," which is generally not the word spotlighted in any normal phrase, as in, "You *HAVE to* try this chocolate flan." All animus, all gravitas, and all veritas tumbled away, cleared with the empty glass of Tom Collins number one.

They were expected in Room 1003 at ten. Their contract held them until one. A grand each for three hours of partying with some band and their entourage, with the potential for more in tips and individually negotiated optional arrangements, for which Vamp spelled out usual and customary. Valkyrie gave the warning talk: don't undercut the other girls or there will be repercussions. Millicent talked about security or the lack thereof. A primer to the world of private parties, or the *Dummies Guide to Limited-Term Prostitution.*

As they drove away in two cabs, Valerie leaned up against Millicent in the back seat of the cab and squeezed her hand like a fourteen-year-old headed to her first middle school dance.

Chapter 17:
Take the D Train

"Our numbers, okay, boss? Back to the status quo?" Melvin Horgan had earned a better seat in Tee Nash's office. He now had a leather swivel chair with a head rest and armrests that irritated his muscle-poor cubital tunnels. Other than the chair, his appearance looked reminiscent of his first summons. Same flip-flops. Same T-shirt. Probably the same socks and underwear as well. The only other meeting participant was a new corporate lawyer, a light-skinned Black woman who looked like an actress playing a young Black lawyer—overly prim and proper and professional, too perfect for a third-rate shop in the real world. Too much color in the dress and jewelry, as if trying to overplay for the camera rather than downplay to connote substance over style. *What happened to college ring? Wasn't this his chair?* he thought. But there was no reason to ask. He may not have earned this status at Infinity, but it was his new reality.

"Our numbers are fine, Brother Horgan. Exemplary, and back on top, in modern alternative and college charts. We've fallen behind in the pop charts, but that's only to be expected. After all, this really isn't 'pop' in any sense of the word, is it?"

"No, I don't suppose we play 'pop.'"

"But here's the salient issue. You have three weeks, and then Madison Square Garden, New York City. Before then, a light schedule. Hartford, Boston, Buffalo, Philadelphia, and then the Garden. *Today Show* morning of and then the Garden."

"Five more shows, and then we're off tour. Free agents, really." And with that, Melvin faced Tee Nash with a knowing grin.

"Brother Horgan, I don't want you to worry about that. Infinity has you covered. Your initial deal is completed. Tour commitments completed. We will have that addressed; I assure you. But what we need is something new, something for them to remember you by. Something to keep Billy Goat's Gruff front and center so that in a year or so, when you get back on the road, you are still relevant. The news cycle hasn't forgotten you."

Melvin looked up at Tee Nash and smiled. Melvin didn't own a normal-person smile, but it wasn't an evil smile either. It was a mustered, twisted smile, as if he was trying to remember a funny joke but was tortured because he couldn't quite remember the punchline. "Yeah, I got something new I think you're gonna love. But I'm off contract for anything beyond this deal. There's even a part for you, Mr. Nash."

"Something for me? I love it. Melvin, you are our first priority. Isn't that right, Ms. Pinckney?"

The lawyer in the corner nodded affirmatively.

"But we need to get you properly prepared for the Garden. It's not like Boise or Tulsa, Melvin. It's the motherfucking Garden."

The motherfucking Garden. Melvin's eyes rolled. The New Yorker's view of the world was kind of like his view of a woman, with Manhattan as the pussy, the Garden as the clit. It came back to scale. Melvin had never expected to play a paying gig, much less the Doug Fir, much less the Crystal Ballroom. Anything beyond the Crystal Ballroom was icing, extraneous to self-image. Gotham-centric ideation repulsed him, the same way everyday guys trying to eclipse their station by micro-critiquing red wine and cigars made him want to vomit. The Garden represented culmination, not validation. Melvin's career was made the first time a reasonably hot chick blew him after a show. The Garden wasn't going to supplant that seminal highlight. It was just going to be one more show, and one more corpse. Melvin tried to think of some benefit of being in New York; they'd played some shithole in the Bronx on the first tour but stayed in some highway motel in Yonkers with a TGI Fridays as its hotel restaurant.

He looked up at Tee Nash and solemnly asked, "Can you get me on *Stern*?"

* * *

The balance had shifted since that first summons to New York on a red-eye coach ticket, staying in the spartan corporate apartments, with a twin bed cot in the corner of a ten-by-ten room with a poster of some long-since deceased Infinity jazzman as the only adornment and a white towel commandeered from a middle-school gym. There had been a shared bathroom with a leaky no-pressure shower valve and brown-tinged water. But now, there was a superior room at the Four Seasons, with mints and nuts and a concierge just for the floor. There was a giant tub with those tiny little shampoos with French names and feminine scents. Prints of New York scenes covered the walls with arrogance, letting the guests know that there were seven famous landmarks superior to anything that Des Moines or Birmingham, or whereverthehell had to recommend itself.

Melvin drifted back to the apartment to write. There was something he was working on, but he didn't want to spring it on corporate yet. He wanted to capitalize, get a new contract, an extension of the original three-disc deal to five or six, with a greater take of the concert gate, a greater download share, and then Tee Nash would see his follow-up to the masterpiece. But instead, Melvin boarded the D train and headed south towards Washington Square Park. The concierge directed him with a knowing smirk. There's no off-Broadway down there, no Tavern on the Green in that park. He scurried into the car with a Dylan fragment about the all-night girls circulating through his limbic system. And, for the first time, he saw the promotional materials on the Subway rail next to the impotent urgings for English lessons in every language from Arabic to Urdu, next to the street shysters promising visa assistance, or "I only get paid if you get paid" rejoinders, and bilingual ads for McDonald's breakfast. And here's an ad for Billy Goat's Gruff and their "Pay Your Premiums" tour coming to the Garden. Get your motherfucking tickets now.

Melvin couldn't stand it—there was one in every car, and he exited prematurely and walked the rest of the way down Fifth Avenue, past a total of eight street musicians, including the ones in the subway, seven of whom were obviously more talented than he was. There was a Chuck Mangione type in the subway hall—hell, it could have been Chuck Mangione, trumpeting a jazz tune with an audience and a healthy coffer. Just outside, a lone skinny white guy with a ponytail and a wifebeater banged African tribal sounds on the bongos with a ferocity and rhythm that put Tiny to shame. A little further down the block, an immense Black man, maybe kin to Clarence Cleamons, was making "New York State of Mind" palatable on his sax. All three were fantastic, but Melvin's hands never left his pockets, where they clutched his wallet and cell phone as if to shield them from marauders.

Further down the line reigned an obese, dark-skinned soprano belting out "Last Dance" with a boom-box karaoke accompaniment, letting the world know that were she thin and beautiful, she damn well would have been famous.

Number five was the failure—the one buffoon of a performer that even Melvin, bottomed out, could assuredly discount as a rival. He was a gaunt old fogie in a shaggy coat too valuable for a street person to take off or put down with a years-long accumulation of facial hair alternating between blowing a harmonica—as if it were a kazoo—and singing "Take Me Out to the Ball Game" in a flat warble, substituting the line "buy me some peanuts and cracker jack" for "leave me a dollar for coke and Jack," while he waved around an old copper flask.

Melvin laughed as he heard the song through a second time and tossed the guy two dollars before heading back downtown towards his destination.

Moving down closer to the park, there was a trumpeter in fatigues blaring out military marches with a small surrounding crowd. Coming closer, the man looked to be in his early sixties with a bald man's ponytail and a stump below the left knee. One of the crowd saluted, and Melvin obliquely shifted to the other side of the street to sidestep the collection box and didn't return to the park wall until he was well past the performer.

Finally, at the far entrance of the park, there was a Boy George type in goth makeup and a gray Salvation Army, dollar-store dress, playing, of all things, Springsteen songs, only at half tempo, and singing them in an a Capello crooner arrangement. That tickled Melvin, who wondered if somewhere some fruit was crooning "Millicent" or "Froggy" on a street to get loaded. It didn't mean Melvin left a cent in the collection box, but he did linger until the lack of remuneration would have been awkward and then retreated into the heart of the park.

Melvin had visited the park before, destitute and cunning. He'd peered around the grounds for paraphernalia clumsily tossed away after a shake-relieving score. Like a homeless man hooked on nicotine searching for a prematurely discarded fag to sample until his fingers or lips charred. You could purchase anything here, from the cheap smack cut many times over with the purity of a Dutch prostitute to an exotic Fijian mushroom rumored to have orgasmic paroxysms between hallucinatory triple features.

Melvin meandered like a citizen literally just taking a walk. For many minutes, he dared not approach any of the evenly spaced merchants, scattered along trails as if serving as mile markers. And Melvin found himself finally outside the park, in Greenwich Village, and realized he hadn't eaten all day. He found a quaint café, the kind of place that served croissants and marmalade to accountants and lawyers. This fucking place even served ramen noodles. Twelve-dollar ramen noodles, the staple of the years of degradation and poverty. The shit you could get twelve of for a dollar and just need a burner. Cheaper than Campbell's, cheaper than bologna, and cheaper even than entrails and snouts and whateverthefuck else comprised an Oscar Mayer hot dog. He'd told Tiny one time he could get high off the flavor packet of the spicy chicken Top Ramen, and watched while Tiny snorted it, then chased him around Old Town, Melvin laughing all the time until Tiny caught up to him and made him eat the rest of the package after a love tap in the stomach. That was back in the days when they played for drinks and tips.

So, Melvin ordered a twelve-dollar ramen and sat there with a Rolling Rock Tall Boy contemplating whether an egg, some spinach, and a few pieces of pork belly (he could swear the motherfucking noodles were the same) and a broth augmented by a little miso and fresh chicken stock was worth the extra $11.92. A couple of sips later, after trying to cut the pork belly with the sumo spoon they provided and instead, in the absence of other utensils, massacring it with his hands and teeth and depositing smaller fragments back into the soup, he determined he was no longer hungry and went back for the beer, finished it, and ordered a second, dripping the last vestiges of the first into the broth and occasionally returning to see if in time, and as a ramen microbrew, it might separate itself off further from its more economical cousin.

Melvin lingered for a good half an hour, an extraordinary time for him to sit marginally sober, tethered to a table, without a TV or a game or some individual to amuse or disgust him. People-watching is a pastime of either the idle rich or the working criminal. Normal people didn't have time or enthusiasm for watching a crowd and "playing games with the faces." It was a job for those hellbent on a mission with ill intent or those stoking their egos by imagining the inherent inferiority of those around, inventing stories placing dullards beneath themselves in intelligence and social significance. Melvin didn't watch people, and he didn't take another Rolling Rock after number two was devoured. He remained outside at this little fusion café in the Village, trying to replicate a thirty-minute blackout without drinking.

Towards the end of this vigil, a stranger, presumably a passerby, stalked the table, eventually presenting himself. The stranger was a middle-aged, handsome man with Germanic features and wavy light-brown hair—each follicle was headed in its correct swirl. He wore a three-piece tan suit with fancy brown leather shoes and a red-and-yellow tie. "Melvin Horgan, are you Melvin Horgan?" the man asked with a Cary Grant affectation. "But of course, you are. I've seen your picture every day on the train. Melvin Horgan. What are you doing here, man? You don't play the Garden for another couple of weeks."

"I'm really not. Look, man, I'm just getting lunch, okay? You want an, uh, autograph or something? I ain't got any free tickets."

"No, man. Already have my tickets. Pre-sale. Floor seats."

"Floor seats. Nice. You're not scared?"

"Scared? No, I'm not scared. But during 'Millicent,' I think my bladder might be full, or I might need a beer. So, I'm not scared. I'm a coward, but I'm not scared."

"Well, nice meeting you. You know, I'm new at not being anonymous. I'm not really sure how to react, how to behave."

"You should probably get used to it. People just did a piece, rag, as it is, calling you the O. J. Simpson of grunge. You know the whole testimonial thing. Second-grade teacher of the dead girl from Richmond. Doc from Tulsa's ma. You're notorious."

"Notorious, eh. I guess not too notorious. What's your name by the way?"

"Jason."

"Okay, Jason. If instead of my ugly mug sitting here, it was O. J. Simpson, would you have come over to meet the celebrity?"

"Hell, no."

"Right. Me neither. Well, mister. I'm not really the conversational sort. You want my autograph or something?"

"Uh, how about a selfie."

"Sure, what the fuck."

The stranger in the suit smiled, and Melvin scowled, and within ten seconds, Facebook and Twitter were ablaze with a Melvin Horgan sighting in Greenwich Village. Meanwhile, Melvin thought through the revelation that he was irrevocably linked to perhaps the only man in America felt to be more complicit in mass murder without direct repercussions.

* * *

That evening, Melvin sat contemplating scribbles of lyrics he had been test-driving for a song he planned to call "Random Slayer," an unapologetic anthem glorifying and taking credit for the deaths and omitting any remorse. But the refrain was hookless, and the whole piece never challenged. It was what a lazy music critic would have assumed his next effort to be. But now he had something fresh, an idea that might never be haute art, but would be anything but predictable.

The last time Melvin Horgan had sat down to write had been in a glorified cell in a flop house in southeast D.C. The neighborhood was so brutal, even the roaches were scared to come out at night. There was no creative process, just blind stabs, most of which found dead ends like an elaborate Ice Maze with Melvin destined to be Jack Torrance floundering until freezing to death . . . until "Millicent DeGroenfeld Rice" gave him a map—better than a map, a cheat code. He hadn't had to navigate his way through that damned maze. It was like he'd learned to walk through walls.

Here in New York, both aesthetically and creatively he could not have been more comfortable. He wrote with his head lightly supported on one end of a white leather chaise lounge with his stubby legs unencumbered by what could more appropriately be termed a short man's sofa. A bottle of Evan Williams was counterbalanced by a mere medicinal dose of cocaine, obtained not illicitly in the park but civilly through the concierge, the way athletes and movie stars do, with a hotel charge for sundries and a generous tip for discretion. Minibar staples, the drained Smirnoff's and Gordon's and Cuervo 1.7-ounce bottles were arranged to spell out "OJ" in big letters on the bed. Washcloths with cocaine-induced ejaculation fluid were left out for the service staff. To Melvin, a luxury hotel meant that they would clean up however many jizz stains you could muster without complaint.

For four days and four nights, Melvin worked on his opus, his bridge from Dexys Midnight Runners to the Spin Doctors. One-hit wonders faded away, beset by the inherent pressure of the fact that no one wanted to hear anything but that one fucking "Come On Eileen" or "Spirit in the Sky." But hit a second time, and you're guaranteed a gambling casino in Missouri when you're fifty. "Jimmy Olsen's Blues" makes you a novelty band. "Two Princes," and you're gonna drink for the rest of your life. *Space Needle Pricks* had been written nearly in its entirety on defense. Now he was on the offense. Other than "Millicent," the hits—"Dusty Heaves" and "Froggy"—had been written on the offense. Everything else was a combination of sampling and resignation.

But this song had chops. Lyrics he wasn't ashamed to sing out loud, a hook refrain, and a quasi-rap tune he could almost entirely envision in spite of his rudimentary musical knowledge. Every word diabolical and contributory to the end of formulating a song the hipster morons would listen to out of spite but also enjoy from the aesthetic sense.

On the fourth day, with the refrain completed and only fine touches on the first and third stanzas pending, Goat showed up unannounced. Unannounced was less a social faux pas but a necessity, since Melvin's iPhone lay uncharged on the bathroom floor and the hotel phone had been disconnected.

Billy Markwell had morphed. It was not like the money and fame had made him Bono. He wasn't jetting around the world in Gucci sandals, giving photo-ops in Somali orphanages, or prefacing every show by imploring the audience to visit some Save the Dolphins website. He hadn't bought a Ferrari or hired a life coach, but he had bought a pair of Rag and Bone jeans, a Michael Kors shirt in black and gray, and some checkboard Vans to replace the Big Lots and Overstock.com wardrobe carted around in duffel bags on chess-team-school-bus van cruisers.

"Goat! Wasn't expecting you, man. Kind of busy."

"Melvin, man. We need to talk. No, that sounds bad. We need to make some decisions. Contract offers. We, um . . . We made it, man. You can't believe the numbers. Insane numbers."

Melvin looked at his oldest friend, who had shared grade-school alienation and high school angst and post-graduation wanderlust. Countless hours spent in a shared dual envy and hatred of pleasant society, of workaday complacency, of ordinary citizens, of the meaningless merger of doctors and lawyers and engineers, and salesmen into an amalgam of normalcy—all of this was trumped by one goddamned smile of complacency, and for a fleeting instant, Melvin wanted to bash his friend's brain into pulp. But his only available weapon was a flimsy hotel pen, the kind that writes for about four hours, then explodes in your pocket, eventually splotching your hand and anything you touch. Melvin hurled it towards Billy Markwell's midsection, which barely registered a thump. Melvin muttered, "Goddamn it, Goat. I'm writing. I'll call you later."

"Melvin, look. Sony, Columbia, RCA, and Infinity all want us. We need to make a decision."

"Infinity."

"You haven't even heard the terms."

"Infinity. They signed us. Just Infinity. Now, you're bothering me while I'm working. Go the fuck back home."

"I don't think this is how you negotiate."

"Fuck negotiate. Green Skittles. I want a bowl of those lime-green Skittles. The kind they used to have because they replaced them with the godawful apple ones. I want a bowl of lime Skittles before every show, before every interview. The rest of it—who the hell cares?"

Melvin went back to reading and re-reading the third stanza, trying to displace one word for another, while Billy Markwell looked through some papers strewn towards the bathroom door, not exactly crumpled but not exactly preserved either. "Haunt me with a smile? Isn't that a Pumpkins' song?"

"What the fuck, Goat? Keep out of my shit. Yes, it's a fucking Pumpkins' song. 'Disarm,' same fucking thing. That's why it's trash, and it's fucking impolite to go through other people's trash."

"Sorry, Troll. It's not . . ."

"Not what? Burned to a crisp? You're not as dumb as Tiny. It's got wrinkles and ridges in it. It's fucking trash. Get out of here. Go back to Portland and your Jew lawyer bitch. I know about it, Goat. I'm happy for you. I'm sure she's a nice girl. Let me work and go home. Take her for a walk in Forest

Park and go buy some of those fucking three-dollar doughnuts and take her out to the organic, vegan, gluten-free steakhouse." Melvin looked up at Billy, who looked stunned, blindsided. He sat down on a white velvet-upholstered ottoman.

"Melvin, it's not like that. She's cool. She's a photographer for the *Willamette Week*. You love the *Willamette Week*. Remember when we had our names in the free paper the first time, ad for our third show at Biddy's. You picked up thirty of 'em, papered the wall."

"Go back to the cunt. I'm writing. I don't bother you when you're rehearsing. Here's five hundred dollars. Go buy Jolene a golden retriever puppy. No, here's a grand. Go buy her a labradoodle. Name it Millicent for all I fucking care."

"Her name's not Jolene."

"Of course, her name isn't fucking Jolene. No one's ever been named Jolene. More songs written about Jolenes than there's ever been Jolenes. Now go home and fuck Jolene, or I'm going back to Portland, and I will ram it up her ass for you, got it?"

Melvin went back to working at his desk and deliberately turned his back on Billy, who stayed fixated in the foyer. After a couple of minutes, Billy got up the nerve to blurt out, "Why do you have to be such a fucking ass."

"Because I am a fucking ass. I would have thought you of all people would know that," Melvin said softly, his eyes never turning from his work.

Billy had tears in his eyes. "Just because my dad and your mom told us time and time again we were losers, assholes, doesn't mean we are. Just because they were incapable of love, doesn't mean we have to be."

"Love," Melvin cried. "You think this girl loves you. She loves your money and your fame. No one will ever love either of us just because. We're mutts. Yeah, we're getting our fifteen minutes, maybe twenty if what I'm writing is as good as I think it is, but no way we're not eventually alone."

"I don't know if this is love. I've only known this girl a few months. But we've had nothing, been nothing for so long, and this is something. And even if it's not Jim and Pam love; it's enough to prove to my pops he was the asshole. And if I can feel that way, so can you. Your mom was wrong. No one should reject their kids the way they did to us. Find someone and prove her the fuck wrong."

Five minutes passed without comment until Melvin finally spoke. "Tell Tee Nash I've got a new song, and he's gonna do it with us at the Garden. Tell him to send over the contracts."

When Billy left, Melvin did a last survey of his new masterpiece. Every bar in its place, every cadence in order and measure, except where he didn't intend regularity. Musical and production notes were neatly indicated in the margins. Tee Nash here at the refrain. Melvin here with the stanzas, with where Bebe would harmonize, and Tee and Melvin would share leads. Reminders to Tee that the emphatic syllable was "shit," suddenly prompted worry that "shit" couldn't go over the radio. "Wipe the shit from your shoes." First track of *Morning Glory?* Probably okay, then. Shit. He put down his sheets.

Underneath a three-day-old *New York Post*, he pulled out another set of sheets with the title "Hooker Song." The lyric Goat had uncovered was written, crossed out, and written again. "Haunt me with a smile." Derivative tripe. *How the fuck to explain a recurring fleeting vision of some unknown bitch, not really a haunting? Seems more real. Maybe an apparition. A haunting has to be menacing or melancholy. An apparition can be neutral. This chick is neutral. She just fades in, maybe inhabits some whore, appears to me, then, having fulfilled some spectral sorority hazing task, fades into nothingness. Maybe I'm a fucking panty raid. Not sure how to turn that into a coherent love ballad. So, it's not really haunting, and not really a smile. Damn, how did Journey ever do this? She is beautiful, though. Maybe I'm going nuts. I freak out when I see her, but I don't run. I want her here. Goat gets something real. Maybe this is the closest I ever get, probably more than I deserve.*

Melvin pulled a bottle of Gordon's out from under the bed and gathered some tonic water from the minibar fridge. The ice bucket had whittled down to a few stragglers, and he shifted them into a sanitized water glass, mixing in enough gin superimposed on his pre-Goat consumption to hope to be visited once again, if only to better define the central figure of the composition, to try to ascertain whether he could differentiate between haunting and apparition. But the manic energy of the composition had faded, and Melvin sank down into a fourteen-hour compensatory nap.

Chapter 18:
Ruh Roh

It was six p.m. on a Tuesday, and Vic Sessions, now formerly an FBI agent, was engrossed in the Seinfeld episode where Mr. Bookman, the library cop, presses Jerry for an unreturned Henry Miller novel. At some point, he would make dinner, but he had never seen this one, which had recorded the night before, so dinner could wait a bit. Three *Seinfeld* episodes a night fulfilled a quota and got him through boring solitary evenings. The dinner hour was one thing, pausing when the water boiled and then fast forwarding through the commercials while barilla cooked and ragu simmered. There was a discovery factor since Thursday nights in the '90s weren't spent at home watching television and the agency was a life calling. So many of the episodes were new to him, no more than three a night, though. Four a night would just be sad. When more than 80 percent were reruns to him, he would refrain, switch to something else he'd neglected. Fragments of conversations amongst the civilians rendered clues towards future binging. Sometimes he would spend hours at Best Buy, trolling the television aisle, looking for shows popular enough to reach DVD status but available on basic cable. Or maybe one day, he'd purchase a DVD player or spring for pay channels, but the pension was smaller than he'd anticipated, at least until the disability claim was adjudicated.

The cardiologist who had retired him quoted with irony that something called an EF, which explained how efficiently his ticker pumped, was low enough to preclude him from fucking but not low enough to get him on the transplant list. The sallow complexion and clear prongs in his nose delivering colorless, odorless life were clearly a contraindication to a choice consultancy on CNN or Fox. Barnathan had recovered from an indignant termination and hooked on with the SyFy network as a creative consultant on their current attempt to model Scooby Doo for middle-aged dullards willing to sublimate reality to join one failed soap actor and a shampoo commercial extra in a scripted attempt to legitimize the Creeper in a junkyard in rural Washington State.

Chester Pavilion was an independent senior care facility on the main line just short of the Villanova campus. Oxygen delivery, emergency response assistance, and on-site physical and occupational therapy facilities were provided, but there was no meal service or non-urgent nursing assistance. The rooms were former dormitories, parceled off and refurbished with wide walkways and bars adjacent to the toilet and bath. There was a mini kitchen and room for a sleeping nook, a desk, and a small alcove for a television. In the corner sat a suitcase, which opened into a battery-powered mini organ, a retirement present from his friends in the agency.

Vic Sessions had tried to play when he moved in, but the older residents complained about the noise, and Vic took his suitcase on wheels into remote parts of the city to play to the squirrels and chipmunks a simple semblance of the music he had once intended to draw a living from. The budget was tight. If he ever got a full disability retirement, there would be a tax-free sixty-five—easy to live on. But, for now, the cardiac deterioration had been judged to be unrelated to the incident with the band and secondary to congenital heart disease. He'd been sent to an independent medical exam in Jenkintown, where he underwent a battery of tests leading to that conclusion by a jaundiced octogenarian who hacked and stuttered his way through the examination. Unfuckingrelated. Accelerated cardiovascular and pulmonary disease caused by pre-diabetes, borderline obesity, and nicotine use disorder (from a weekly Cohiba in the cigar room of the Four Seasons), with no material contribution from the well-regulated and rapidly reversed service-related cardiopulmonary event. He hired a back-of-the-phone-book lawyer, who was fighting with the agency over the discrepancy, which amounted to a thirty-five-thousand-dollar difference. For the present, he had needed to abandon his apartment, sell off most of what he'd apportioned over the years as trophies of his bigger cases, and retreat into a spartan retirement with occasional attempts freelancing for spending cash.

Vic Session's once thick and flowing black mane, which cascaded as he played with a Tatumesque frenzy, now was beyond the Rogaine pale, leaving him with only a few follicles on his forehead reaching haphazardly in disparate pick-up-sticks patterns into barren areas. In the Indian summer heat, cargo shorts and a wifebeater substituted for a Saks-store-brand suit; slippers for Edwin Wright wingtips.

Straying from TBS into the news-ish bundle of stations, he found Melvin Horgan, who'd created a stir on Opie and Anthony by claiming that his song played backwards could raise the dead, and if he knew where Millicent was buried, he would serenade her, give her a piece of his massive troll dick to thank her for the karma of the hit song, and then play the song again to put her down, to make sure the deaths continued.

Venturing with his remote into increasingly lower channel numbers, he entered into the reality quadrant of the cable box. Here, he found the true-science explanations of the multiple Billy Goat's Gruff deaths, with theories ranging from communicable prion disease to dart-propelled nanotechnology administered as pre-meditated murder to a mass hysteria akin to the Salem witch trials to the Barnathan banshee hypothesis. Everything but the truth, or at least the best approximation of the truth from Vic's final report, until the FBI closed their investigation permanently.

Ever since the resuscitation, congestive heart failure required hydrochlorothiazide, bronchiectasis necessitated albuterol, and Symbicort, and for chronic pain, gabapentin and oxycodone. All of this poison combined with Enbrel and prednisone for psoriasis kept Vic in a zombie daze much of the day, generally in relation to the gabapentin. When sleep came, it often merged consciousness with REM in paroxysms of reality, in which the senses incorporated real time into virtual-reality dream, as the descending channels meandered past, remote buttons possibly being depressed as the control became trapped under his slumbering body, or possibly dormant on his chest lying on the sofa with oxygen tubing wrapped around it compressing the up or the down. That night it was into children's programming, some kind of award show with Melvin Horgan and Anna Kendrick handing out the award for best performance as a vampire, witch, zombie, or werewolf in a movie. Did Troll really say, "I hate that bastard," when Zac Efron was nominated for *Vampire Taxi*?

And the channel changed, and there was a cartoon of the Scooby Doo crew, although it was young Vic Sessions as Fred with his ascot and a large brown Great Dane curled at his feet, lifeless, with just a drop of blood oozing from his floppy right ear onto the cement floor, a morsel half-eaten astride him on the concrete, a fritter of some kind with little bits of peanut butter and coconut giving it uneven texture. A sinister figure, looking like the subject of the Scream except with yellow hair in a brown leotard and cape, sat tied up on the floor, his feet surrounded by marbles and glue. The police sergeant took the mask off the banshee, revealing Melvin Horgan, who yelled out, "You would never have caught me if it wasn't for those meddling kids," as a tall, goateed teenager wept in the background.

And then the dial automatically continued downward into the sports stations, and Vic saw himself standing in a mist on a golf course, the tightly mown greens of the fairway segueing into brown wherever the sun materialized. Vic was wearing trousers, and over his shirt was a bib which read "Horgan." He was carrying a golf bag, and out of the gloaming, a voice pierced through. It was the voice of Ben Wright, commentating, "Second shot coming up for the wee American, Melvin Horgan here at the twelfth. Lovely drive past the burn and avoided the thick stuff, taking the ball down the right side of the fairway for a good look at the back left pin placement. He has 195 yards to the pin, 185 to the front to clear the spectacle bunkers. Horgan coming off a birdie on eleven, trying to chase down Justin Rose at six under par and Matt Kucher at five; Horgan now at four under. Caddie Vic Sessions hands him a seven iron. He's aiming his natural draw, trying to aim right and let the wind bring it back to the left. Horgan takes a mighty lash, and he's snap-hooked it up into gallery to the left of the twelfth green."

The camera panned up to the gallery behind a greenside bunker where a man in a red T-shirt and red pants was slumped forward, his head overlapping into the bunker with bright-red blood splotching the sand, trundling down into the middle of the sand trap, forming patterns like beads of rain on a windshield. "Oh my Lord, not again. First at the Colonial, then poor Mrs. Nicholas at the Memorial, and now again here at Carnoustie. We can only hope and pray that it's not serious. But look, the ball caromed off the gallery, and that is Horgan's ball twelve feet below the hole, just a touch of red on the dimples. And now Horgan is at the green; he's at the bunker with his glove, but he sees a man slumped over in the trap, with emergency personal scurrying up, and keeps hold of his glove. And now as he sees where his ball has ricocheted and realizes he will have a good look for birdie, a wry grin appears."

And again the channel changed, and the scene was an army camp, in the low-def world of nostalgia land—not the black-and-white nostalgia network whose only commercials hawked insurance bilking and elevator stand-ins for the lower middle class, but the shows that might pull a 1.5, enticing neo-cons in their '50s and '60s into remembering back to when they were "rebels." Flowing now more towards inhabiting rather than watching the scene, Vic stood at the bedside, getting screamed at by no other than Alan Alda. "What's your excuse this time, Frank? That's two dead kids. Real kids, Frank."

"What are you talking about? You think I'm fucking Frank Burns? Let me clue you in, pal. Larry Linville's been dead for years. I'm Vic Sessions. I'm a musician. I'm not a surgeon, and I didn't kill any soldiers. Where is he? Where's the Troll? Where's the motherfucking Troll?"

And Vic went hurtling through the ward, looking from patient to patient, under covers and through blankets. He pulled off the masks of nurses in the operating room. He pulled the bandages off dying boys looking through the scars and eschars for that reptilian countenance. He rummaged through the mess, into the men and women's showers and finally into Colonel Blake's office.

"You've gotta help me!" he screamed. "There's a killer in the camp. Little guy, gargoyle of a face. He's the Troll. He's the Troll." But by that point, Wayne Rogers had caught up to him and injected something in his buttocks, which, like television injections do, made him succumb instantly to a slapstick *kaboom*, as Sidney Freedman wrapped him in canvas straps for the long ride to Seoul. And later, when Vic was awake in the back of the truck—Dr. Freedman waiting for his driver, the canvas straps plastering his arms against his body, and his legs banded together like in a potato sac, a gag tempering any further non-scripted blasphemy—he saw Alda again in front of the truck in one of those holier-than-thou preening poses. "Goddamn it. Radar, call the colonel. Another kid, and this time, it wasn't one of Burns. And as a corporal came from the colonel's office and in front of the truck, Sessions started gesticulating through the gag, wildly shaking and yelling as best he could, his tied-up legs and elbows bouncing off the inner crated metal: "That's not Gary Burghoff. That's not Gary Burghoff."

And the channel changed once again, and Vic saw himself standing behind a podium in a television studio in front of a large audience. He looked down at his monitor and saw the figure "$1200" displayed below. There was no oxygen, and his stomach was chiseled and trim, his fingers pink and plump. He was himself again. He looked to his right and thought he recognized the man next to him in a red T-shirt, who met his eyes, bristled, and looked away. He turned to the left, and there was Melvin Horgan, who gazed malevolently, then pointed down at his display, which read "$2300," and showed Vic his middle finger.

A young woman with cards turned to the three of them and provided a cue that they were coming back on air, and a man who might credibly be Alex Trebek started reading into the camera: "And we're back and ready for Double Jeopardy! In first place is challenger Melvin Horgan, a rock-and-roll singer from Portland, Oregon, with twenty-three hundred dollars. In second place, our returning champion, schoolteacher Lonnie Rohrbach, from Colorado Springs, with eighteen hundred dollars, and trailing, a retired FBI agent from Philadelphia, Alphonse Crestwood, with twelve hundred dollars.

"And here's our categories for Double Jeopardy!: Potable Poisons, Jazz Pianists, She Blinded Me with Science, Fairy Tales, Serial Killed, and Quarterbacked Where. Alphonse, you're in third place, but a lot can change in Double Jeopardy! Your selection."

Vic hesitated. He looked around, not sure how or when to speak, and not particularly interested in the competition or outcome. He scoured the audience for clues on how to get back, to escape. But, with nothing forthcoming, after an uncomfortable pause, he offered, "Jazz Pianists for two hundred."

"He implored you, 'Don't worry, be happy.'"

Vic instinctively went to push a buzzer in front of him, but he hadn't positioned his trigger finger properly and lunged for it as the buzzer rang.

"Melvin Horgan."

"Who is Bobbie McFerrin?"

"Correct. Your selection."

"Serial Killed for two hundred."

"Abigail Folger, Voytek Frykowski, Sharon Tate."

Vic pushed his buzzer, trying to regain control.

"Alphonse."

"Who was Charles Manson?"

"Correct."

"Jazz Pianists for four hundred."

"Better known as a bandleader with classics like 'Take the A Train' and 'It Don't Mean a Thing if You Ain't Got That Swing.'"

Vic again clicked confidently, assuming he would be able to continue.

"Melvin."

"Who is Duke Ellington?"

"Correct. Melvin Horgan in the lead. Select again."

"Potable Poisons for two hundred."

"This poison made from a plant extract was used to kill Socrates in Ancient Greece."

Again, the reaction times, deadened by the damned oxygen and heart troubles. A fraction late. A fraction slow.

"Lonnie?"

"What is hemlock?"

"Correct. Lonnie, you're back in control."

"She Blinded Me with Science for two hundred, Alex."

"With her husband, a pioneer in the science of radiation. She won Nobel prizes in both physics and chemistry. Lonnie?"

"Who is Marie Curie?"

"Correct."

"She Blinded Me with Science for four hundred."

"She spent the better part of five decades studying and reporting on the chimpanzees of Tanzania."

The damned reflexes. *Click, click.*

"Alphonse?"

"Who is Jane Goodall? Jazz Pianists for six hundred."

"That is an audio Daily Double. Alphonse, you are in third place with eighteen hundred dollars. What would you like to wager?"

"I'll wager all eighteen hundred, Alex."

The audience gasps at the confidence displayed.

"Alright. An aggressive wager. Listen to this recording. Who was the composer and pianist for this jazz staple?"

As a kid, Vic had been a summer latchkey kid, as both parents worked, and he raided the record collection, played over and over the standards, none so frequently as "Time Out." "Take 5" wasn't a six-hundred-dollar tune. This was a fucking insult. His own dream a fucking insult.

"Who is Dave Brubeck?"

"Correct, and with that, you vault into the lead."

"Quarterbacked for two hundred."

"This category, we will give you a quarterback and you tell us where he went to school. Peyton Manning, 1994 to 1997. Melvin?"

"Where is University of Tennessee."

"Correct."

"Fairy Tales for two hundred."

"When three billy goats attempted to cross the river, they were threatened by this hungry creature. Melvin?"

"What is a troll?"

"Correct. Melvin, you have the board again."

"Fairy Tales for four hundred."

"Most of our modern fairy tales were popularized by the Brothers Grimm and this Danish writer famous for *The Little Mermaid*. Lonnie?"

"Who is Hans Christian Anderson? She Blinded Me with Science for six hundred."

"With her husband, she formed the world's most famous team of paleoanthropologists looking for links between apes and humans. Lonnie?"

"Who is Mary Leakey?"

Vic despaired with every success by his opponents. He had a vague feeling that this was an escape hatch, that a win would bring him back to the real world and maybe even an awakening from this month-long nightmare of disintegration.

"She Blinded Me with Science for eight hundred, Alex."

"Marine biologist who is considered a transformational figure in global conservation and alerted the world to the danger of DDT in the oceans."

There was a pause. No one else was answering. Vic bristled. He had to know the answer or else his subconscious wouldn't be asking the damned question.

"Alphonse?"

"Who is . . . Rachel Carson?"

"Correct."

"Serial Killed for four hundred."

"Elizabeth Stride, Annie Chapman, Catherine Eddowes. Alphonse?"

"Who was Jack the Ripper? Serial Killed for six hundred."

Son of Sam or Ted Bundy, it has to be.

"Hugh Scrutton, Thomas Mosser, Gilbert Murray."

Again silence. Not Bundy or Sam.

"Alphonse?"

"Who is Ted Kaczynski or the Unabomber?"

"Correct. You're in the lead. Select again."

"Potable Poisons for four hundred."

"Although the name means 'beautiful lady,' and in small doses, it dilates the pupil, it is a notorious poison felt to be responsible for the death of Roman emperor Augustus. Melvin?"

"What is belladonna? Quarterbacked for four hundred."

"Johnny Manziel, Class of 2013. Melvin."

"Where is Texas A&M? Quarterbacked for six hundred."

"Pictured, class of 1999."

A glorious shot of Tom Brady taken during some NFL production, some rare helmetless photoshoot. *Plays in New England, from California . . . Think, motherfucker.*

"Melvin."

"Where is University of Michigan? Quarterbacked for eight hundred."

"Now a broadcaster, but Todd Blackledge won a National Championship in 1982."

Local guy, local guy.

"Alphonse?"

"Where is Penn State?"

"Correct. Alphonse in the lead now with sixty-two hundred, followed by Melvin Horgan at forty-seven hundred, and our defending champion, Lonnie Rohrbach, with thirty-two hundred Alphonse, the board is yours."

Alphonse stared out into the audience and saw rows of indistinguishable moptops clapping and nodding. This wasn't just a dream. He was convinced it was a conduit, a wormhole back to before this case, maybe even before he was Vic Sessions, before the ravages of psoriatic arthritis making it all a cruel joke with a do-over. All he had to do is win. "Jazz Pianists for eight hundred, please."

"This legally blind stride empresario from Toledo, Ohio, was renowned for the blinding speed required on compositions like 'Tiger Rag.' Alphonse?"

"Who was Art Tatum? Jazz Pianists for 1000, please."

"Finishing off that category. This composer of 'Round Midnight' and 'Straight, No Chaser" was supposed to appear on the cover of *Time Magazine* in November 1963, only to be bumped by President Kennedy's assassination."

Vic hesitated just a split second. He knew the answer, but there was no way any of the others would—

"Melvin?"

"Who is Thelonious Monk? Game on, motherfucker."

"Um, correct, Melvin, but I need to remind you—"

"Remind me what? You'll fucking edit this right on out. Quarterbacked Where for one thousand."

"Jared Zabransky of Statue of Liberty fame, 2007. Melvin?"

"Where is Boise State? Goat, you life-saving cocksucker."

"Correct, two minutes left in Double Jeopardy! Alphonse leads over Melvin by three hundred, with Lonnie trailing. Melvin, please select."

"Fairy Tales for six hundred."

"This imp can spin straw into gold, but his downfall is overconfidence that his name won't be discovered. Lonnie?"

"Who is Rumpelstiltskin?"

"Correct. Time running out. Lonnie, your selection."

"Potable Poisons for six hundred."

"And that would be our second Daily Double. Lonnie, you have thirty-eight hundred and trail Alphonse by thirty-two hundred."

"Two thousand."

"Although it is found in octopi, newts, and snails, the most frequent human victims are iatrogenic from improper pufferfish sushi preparation."

Lonnie leaned over at Vic and Melvin, brandished a middle finger, and yelled with gusto, "What is tetrodotoxin? Don't fuck with a middle-school science teacher."

"That is correct, Lonnie. Time running out, your selection?"

"Serial Killed for eight hundred."

"Waylon Holstein, Benjamin Richmond, and Lonnie Rohrbach."

We've all had that test-taking dilemma—the obvious answer or the gimmick. Only this time, it wasn't for the difference between a 94 and a 96, a 740 or a 760, a B+ or an A-. To Vic, this was the difference between escape from an eight-month penance back to his underappreciated status quo. He prophesied an antidote to Melvin's poison, which had infiltrated his lungs, heart, skin, hair, and even his teeth. He saw a return back to R. Kelly trafficking seventeen-year-olds across state lines and narcotics deals funneled by promoters through roadies inside the ropes at essentially every festival. Horgan or Atlas. Horgan was the obvious one, but it was Tiny's drumming. But Atlas was just a patsy. Horgan was the one who kept putting it on the setlist, knowing the eventuality. Tiny might be the trigger, but Melvin cocked it and pulled.

"Lonnie."

"Who is Melvin Horgan?"

"I'm sorry, that's incorrect. Anyone else?"

Well, when you've got a fifty-fifty shot and one answer is eliminated . . . Vic clicked.

"Alphonse, for a commanding lead."

"Who is Tiny Atlas?"

"I'm sorry that's also incorrect."

"That can't be, both incorrect. It's not the fucking banshee."

"Melvin? Want to take a shot?"

"Yeah, I'll bite," and he clicked in. "Who is Vic Sessions?"

"That is correct. Eight hundred dollars, and we've reached the end of Double Jeopardy! with Melvin Horgan in the lead, with seventy-five hundred dollars, Alphonse Crestwood in second, with sixty-two hundred, and defending champion, Lonnie Crestwood, trailing but still alive with five thousand dollars for our Final Jeopardy! category, Nineties Grunge."

"Alex, Alex. There's no way that last answer is correct. Vic Sessions didn't kill anyone. Fact checker, I think you need a fact checker. I know for a fact Vic Sessions did not kill these people."

"Alphonse, all of our questions are triple-checked. Vic Sessions is correct. When we return, on to Final Jeopardy!"

When they cut taping, Vic exited his answer space and approached Alex Trebek, gesturing by pointing at himself. He looked down and he was being trailed by an oxygen tank, with those infernal prongs back up his nose. His paunch kept hitting the dolly pulling the oxygen tank, his wasted, sallow fingers clutching the dolly. "I'm Vic Sessions. You hear me. The answer is wrong. I didn't kill anyone. I'm a goddamned FBI agent." Security interrupted him before he made it all the way to the podium. "Get your fucking hands off of me. This is a joke. Vic Sessions. I'm fucking Vic Sessions," and he coughed once, and then it kindled a second and a third.

"Alphonse. Calm down and get back to your stall. You're not out of it. But if you don't calm down, you're going to get disqualified."

"Disqualified, you glorified pitchman. Without a lucky break, you'd be hawking Riverside Toyota's end of the year clearance sale. I've seen Quiz Show. This is bullshit. I'm calling the cops, the papers. I'm calling Alan fucking Dershowitz. You're not going to get away."

And with that, the security detail had Vic fireman-carried, with two people and another for the oxygen, into the pitch black of an open room at the end of the hall behind the studio. He heard a crash and a tug as the oxygen was tossed in, followed seconds later by the bum's rush into the darkness.

And in the darkness, the nasal prongs were no longer positioned to maintain life's balance between carbon dioxide and oxygen. Slipping into glycolysis with hot liquid dripping on his chest, Vic started breathlessly screaming for help, appealing to Alex Trebek, appealing to Muto, and finally appealing to Melvin Horgan for help before waking up gasping for air in a pool of bile-tinged mucus, having fallen from the dinner chair, propped in front of the television with a TV tray, onto the olive shag. Vic cleaned up and started his evening nine-thirty routine of brushing teeth, getting into plaid wool pajamas, attempting unsuccessfully to masturbate to visual images of the Olsen twins, and finally to slumber a good three hours earlier than what he was accustomed to.

And as he lay in his motel-liquidation-sale mattress contemplating his inability to self-pleasure, thoughts drifted to anger. How dare his fucking self-conscious. Who gave a fuck what anyone in the public, anyone in the agency thought of him? "Disgraced FBI agent" was assuredly his most common introduction and almost in the context of "eluded the grasp of." No one understood, he was no detective—just a failed pianist and whistle-blowing DJ who got in over his head to gain a job that occasionally got him laid.

But for his own self-conscious to betray him was unforgivable. There was no reason to invent new failures; there were enough real ones to occupy his waking hours until the corrupted heart allowed him to pass. Sleep should afford rest at worst and a fleeting glimpse of what once was and what should have been, not a Burtonesque re-telling and exaggeration of failures. Furious but without a safe outlet, he took a safety valve, two Ambien washed down with a ninety-proof swig in a Preservation Hall shot glass, and postponed further self-reflection.

* * *

When Vic woke up the next morning, air-hungry from a unilateral nares' dislodgement, he had indeed sublimated the futility and resumed the waking routine. The job required flamboyance with an air of desperation. The oxygen intake contrasted the black-feathered hat and the bell bottoms and zoot suit lapels and purple jacket, picked up cheap at the Goodwill because the pants weren't provided to complete the ensemble.

Most days, he would take the mini organ onto the bus downtown accompanied by an eight-hour tank and a Halloween candy dispensary bowl he'd snatched from a stoop in Germantown where it had lingered unappreciated into the third week of November, rationalizing its confiscation on the basis of benign neglect and a just-in-case replacement stash of Kirkland AAs and 9-volts required in sequence to power the organ and speakers. He would pull out his "honored citizen" Septa pass and sit in the handicapped section with the second seat housing his paraphernalia. The ultimate destination would depend upon the day of the week and time of the year. The Riverfront was busy year-round but with competition from other performers, and the annoyance factor of trinket peddlers and bums. Independence Mall had the best traffic but was patrolled by cops ordered to keep pristine pathways to maintain the myth of continuity with our forefathers' time when God forbid a fifer (or whatever you would call him) might play for copper coins where the richest colonials were congregating. Fairmont Park was less for tourists and more popular with locals during April, May, September, and August, between the frost and the humidity.

But, most weekdays, Vic would come downtown early to get a spot in Kennedy Plaza near the Love statue, perhaps trying to draw karma. Not only did the bus drop him off less than one hundred yards away on JFK, but the thousands of businesspeople flittering about were perfect fodder for the five-minute interlude amongst the food stands. In the off-hours—nine to noon and one to four—hotel and tourist traffic provided a steady stream of flow. The cops here were more willing to ignore a performer with an expired bureau ID as an alternative to official licensure.

There was an ambiguity about making a supplementary living on the street. There was a moral hierarchy that you had to either accept or formally reject. The untouchables were the panhandlers offering no more than a temporary assuaging of upper-middle-class guilt. The other end of the spectrum, the brahmen, were the pretzel and hotdog salesmen who were unobtrusive and operated on a true supply and demand imperative. The only complaint one could offer is that at times, the sheer volume meant that the consumer had to choose, and picking one pretzel peddler when traffic was low registered as a rejection to the others likely prompted more than one neurotic, over-sensitive tourist simply to stay hungry or search for a nearby bodega.

The remainder of the street economy were the peddlers and performers whose presence and services might be either welcome or annoying, depending on taste.

When starting to supplement his pension in this manner, Vic had stretched his imagination to rationalize why this was any more useful to society or deserving of payment, either charity or volitional, than the ever-present kids who wiped your windshield as you waited to turn left onto the Schuylkill Expressway after the refineries on your way into town. In utilitarian terms, was an unnecessary glass cleaning any more or less valuable than a song that couldn't be avoided without altering one's trajectory?

Vic played mostly jazz standards, venturing into pop selectively when the crowds were decidedly younger and unlikely to appreciate. Occasionally, he would slip in some vocals, realizing that his metallic alto was somewhat muffled by the oxygen flow, but that the guilt factor might outweigh any diminution in quality. At times, he was correct, as small crowds congregated around the tank-toting pianist, who had to take longer air toke breaks between songs and would pair up the snappy with the sedate to dial down the respiratory rate from "Take the A Train" to "What a Wonderful World." Indeed, the guilt factor was often independently sustaining, and there was even one homeless crooner who mimicked Vic, using fake tubing and an empty tank marked "helium" that he had never returned after a failed stint as a balloon salesman.

On this morning, he assumed a spot in the park near the statue but on the way to JFK, so as to capture both the local business traffic as well as a share of the tourist volume. He carefully laid out his Halloween collection plate, maneuvering the creepy hand at the back left corner to be inconspicuous, and unfolded the organ and played a few warm-up chords, before starting into a simplified version of "Straight, No Chaser."

The most exasperating part of the audience was the loitering freeloaders. If someone wants to walk on by intent on scurrying down the boulevard to pilgrimage up the Rocky stairs, God bless 'em. You thank anyone who antes, no matter how meagerly. But the loiterers who hang around the music, never quite looking you in the eye and never contributing a cent, they suck the life out of you. It was a bystander day as his opener blended into "Don't Worry, Be Happy." The pop crossovers with raspy lyrics would normally mobilize the outliers from toe-tapping bystanders into contributors. But, on this day, a half dozen meandered within listening range with the telltale lack of eye contact. There were a couple of likely homeless, but three retirees and a tourist with a Liberty Bell hoodie and a green White Sox cap holding a pretzel, who had stopped his progression towards the art museum. Maybe $1.30 from Theo Monk and $2.00 from Herbie, less than minimum wage. The standards were failing that day. "A Train" was a shutout. "Wonderful World" played as slow as possible garnered a buck fifty, from one of the other performance beggars no less—the old Black guy who played Marvin Gaye and Barry White—took money out of his own plate, but zilch from passersby. "The Thrill is Gone" was too obscure to get more than a cumulative two bits. "I Got Rhythm" was too old for the crowd—nothing doing. "Baker Street" was a slump buster; made ten bucks on it the weekend before. But only a single from a fat, gyrating, braless brunette who meandered over from the statue when she heard the piano version of the classic sax riff.

The hour was shifting as the locals scurried away to jobs, and only the tourists remained in the open. Etta James was a shutout. Cab Calloway barely registered. By this time, Vic was winded and took an hour break, waiting ten minutes behind a throng of school kids on a field trip from Frederick, Maryland, to get a pretzel from the nearest vendor and watching crowds gather around the Asian break dancers and the comic juggler. He started back up at eleven when the lunch crowd meandered into the square and joined the straggling tourists with the "I did the art museum" crew already having forced their way back up JFK for the walk to Independence Square.

When he came back on, he did so with ammunition. This was going to be the Philadelphia hour featuring the greatest jazz and soul icons Philadelphia had to offer. He announced this and waited for the appreciative throng, but the pretzel line only grew while the hotdog peddlers new to the square for lunch carved out their slice of the prosperity.

But this was an act, and the words were no less essential than Miranda rights, even if they were the sidewalk Sinatra equivalent to "if a tree fell in a forest."

"Philadelphia Soul is not just a football team, ladies and gentlemen. It is the embodiment of the spirit of this city, the legacy of the founding fathers and the spirit of independence. Join me, Vic Sessions, on this journey through the legacy of the Philadelphia sound. In the fifties, Harold Melvin and a group of friends started their career as the Charlemagnes but later changed their name to the Blue Notes and were a staple of the local scene for many years. In the early seventies, they hired a backup drummer who soon became lead singer for Harold Melvin and the Blue Notes. That gentleman's name was Mr. Teddy Pendergrass, and although Teddy is gone, his legacy lives on. From Harold Melvin and the Blue Notes and the great Teddy Pendergrass, here is 'If You Don't Know Me by Now.'"

It was a simple tune, and the piano notes while simplified from an ideal composition blended well with the raspy alto, if you could imagine Rod McKuen doing R&B. On a normal day, the history lecture and familiar hook was effective promotion, but today it fell flat. "Thank you, thank you," he coughed at the end of the song directed into the breeze. "Chubby Checker wasn't born here, but he moved to Philadelphia as a teenager and was discovered by Dick Clark. You might think Chubby was a one hit wonder, but he had a long successful post-'Twist' career, married Miss World, fathered a WNBA player, and became an entrepreneur and social activist, but we do know him best for that infective 'Twist.'" And with that, a largely instrumental and not particularly twisty version of "The Twist" rang out into the park without substantial notice or interest. As a consequence, Vic hurried through, not fully elucidating the pregnant pauses, which punctuated changes of cadence and note in the original. At its conclusion, the only nearby souls seemed driven by Brownian motion through the square as opposed to bonds of attraction.

"Only in Philadelphia can the top pop duo since Simon and Garfunkel meet like this. During a battle of the bands, Philadelphia hail rang through the hall and performers scattered. These two dudes ran to the same elevator and figured out that they both were at Temple and both were disciples of soul, students of the blues. Daryl Hall and John Oates went on to become one of the best-selling duos of all time and members of the Rock and Roll Hall of Fame. This one was originally recorded by Lou Rawls but later went to number one with Hall and Oates, although I do it the Lou Rawls way."

Vic had in his repertoire "Maneater," "Rich Girl," "Adult Education," and "She's Gone," depending on the audience. This was a "She's Gone" crowd, or lack thereof. "What went wrong" seemed an appropriate query. "Thank you. John Coltrane is to jazz what James Joyce is to novelists or Steven Hawking to scientists. His genius dwarfed his compatriots, who struggled to grasp what he could see plain as day. Coltrane was primarily a saxophonist, but his compositions for quartet were sheer genius. I can't do 'Giant Steps' as he intended, but I'll do my best."

Coltrane was a pheromone for hipsters. When all else failed, they would come marauding, their hard-earned barista or NPR, or nonprofit thinktank dollars flowing into the collections as if compelled. Bowler donned flannel-wearing, goateed dandies with saffron- and latte-scented Susan B. Anthony dollars regurgitating from their mutilated faux-Masai gullets. But today, the hipsters spent their lunch breaks buying vinyl or comic books or eating pork belly crumpets. Another bust but undaunted, and as the lunch crew continued to wander into the park, Vic changed directions again.

"Born in South Philadelphia, Jim Croce—taken too young in a plane crash—was a storyteller in the best sense of the tradition. Croce went to

Villanova and had real jobs like the car wash before his career took off. You might expect 'Bad, Bad Leroy Brown,' but that was set in Chicago, or 'You Don't Mess Around with Jim,' but that one's in New York. 'I've Got a Name' is my favorite, but Croce didn't write it. I wanted the quintessential Philadelphia Croce song, and frankly, I can't be sure about this, but I grew up here watching the roller derby on WPHL, channel seventeen, I think, in the sixties as a kid, and something tells me Jim Croce did, too. Maybe he even had a crush on one of the blockers and came up with this classic." And out poured "Roller Derby Queen." Part novelty song, great story, awesome hook, no cash except a buck from an overweight woman in sweats with shortly cropped blue hair, who may well have been called "Spike" in her day.

The lunch hour persisted as swarms now entered the sunny refuge of the park, escaping institutionalizing break rooms and commissaries. The Philadelphia icons tumbled by. Boyz II Men, Stan Getz, even the great Patti Labelle came and went without remuneration. The carefully constructed ladder of the Philadelphia sound led nowhere. The people crowded around, needing benches more than raspy vocals and mediocre keyboard stylings. Several hours down and essentially out of voice, he had barely enough for a touristy plate of bucatini amatriciana, much less the good stuff he used to get as a routine in South Philly.

The lunch hour was ending, and the three-piece suits were starting to gather up scraps and trash and head back towards their Broad Street offices, with the pantsuit crowd following behind. The tourists continued to wander through the park in diagonals, heading down to the art museum or heading South towards the Franklin Institute, or back across Broad towards the water to Independence Mall and the Liberty Bell. Vic was packing up, having already stuffed his $13.75 into his pocket and was preparing to break down the organ and head to the bus when he had a thought for an encore, not like anyone was gesturing or waiting. But, regardless of the take, Vic felt his performance merited an encore, and he looked at his phone on a lyrics site. He knew the music; the damn rhythm was chopsticks simplistic.

Vic couldn't yell. His vocal cords were half frozen from his arrest. But he simulated the cacophonic frenzy of the stanzas, while he lingered and enunciated on the refrain. He started with a challenge: "Any brave motherfuckers out there?" And then he transitioned into the bizarre first stanza of the murder song. *"Millicent DeGroenfeld Rice, come on and take another slice / Friday night pole dance, Saturday night lying with your blood coagulating / in the outhouse at the zoo."*

At first, a couple of the tourists meandered over, as if it was perfectly natural that the most notorious piece of music in modern history was intended to be played in proximity of the Love statue, but soon, they were joined by a group of suits who turned around from returning to the office.

By the end of the second stanza, there was quite a crowd. A chubby Hispanic woman in green dress and flats, her hair let down from a Babushka and her purse swaying at her side, danced with a young Black man with a Brian Dawkins replica jersey. A cute red-headed mother pranced with two ginger kids, holding hands to form a circle while they jumped in unison.

As Vic entered the third refrain, there were easily one hundred people, virtually the entire park in his vicinity clapping and singing along. He simulated the guitar/drum work and then repeated the refrain a few more times before an improvised scat finish to broad applause, with the crowd lingering around the collection vesicle after completion, until Vic was able to get at his coffers and counted $220.50 and one card propositioning him. He gathered up the money and chuckled this time as he added the meager prior bills to these and put them in the wallet. He counted out the coins and put them in his pocket, save one quarter, which he held onto as he headed back to the bus stop, this time headed into South Philly to L'Angolo. Even if it was a last hurrah, he couldn't even think of taking his last bath until he'd washed down a caprese and a paccheri with a fine demi carafe of a good Amarone.

Chapter 19:
Backlash

"Hey, Goat. Remember that first interview we did on 94.7 after 'Dusty' popped? Eight a.m. on a Sunday with that nose-pierced motherfucker doing some sort of internship from the retard high?"

Billy Markwell didn't respond. He was in the corner of the Great Hall, calming down Tiny. Bebe was outside smoking, and Melvin sat in a brown leather swivel recliner next to Tee Nash, stopping his spinning only long enough to take a sip of a mango mojito sorely miscast in a tall, thin orange-juice glass. "This asshole couldn't have been more than sixteen," he offered while twisting and at least momentarily facing a group of grannies from Nebraska who'd won the Powerball, "and he kept asking us about those damn hash brownies. You got any more hash brownies? You got a recipe for kick ass—asswipe really said kickass on the goddammed radio—hash brownies? You bring any of those hash brownies to the studio today? It's eight a.m. on a Sunday, motherfucker. Played Dante's night before, finished up at one. Hung, sure, but hash brownies? Kept waiting for all the bullshit questions we get now. Nothing about the songs or the contract or the tour. Just the fucking hash brownies—oh yeah, and what happened to the dog. Chow mein, motherfucker. Wonder what the fuck that yahoo up to now? Bet he's pumping gas back in RIP city, telling everyone how he knew us back then."

It was a tree-falling-in-the-woods scenario. Their boss was occupied on the phone, engaged in energetic discourse with Roger Smith's replacement, who was urging discretion with regards to their upcoming performance. Tiny was folded in a ball on the floor in a corner, vomiting into a bag of cinnamon apple chips. Billy kneeled over him, repeating comforting platitudes and reassuring him that he did not have to be present for the interview as long as he could venture on stage for their performance. Getting no response, Melvin reached over for a remote to change the channel, but it was just a closed-circuit feed, and every channel showed a fat, smiling Black man bantering with a smiling Ms. Minnesota type and a plastic he knew to be Matt Lauer. The volume was down, but their expressions didn't change as the subtitles expressed topics as diverse and dysthymic as the ill-fated consortium of lottery millionaires who had already been trimmed by two through heart attack and cancer (an amazing story of friendship), the aftermath of devastating hurricanes in Florida, and the promised Times Square debut of a new hit song by the murder band, Billy Goat's Gruff (but don't worry—they've promised not to sing "Millicent DeGroenfeld Rice").

The lottery winners were going on first, earlier, as the band was being saved for the later spot in the eight o'clock hour. Maximum viewership. NBC was promoting the hell out of this. The old ladies exited the green room into makeup. A five-a.m. pepperoni slice grumbled as it churned and passed through the pylorus, broken down into sub-particles. Liquid magma laced with sturdy acid-friendly bacteria whirled through his stomach like waves of lava in some ancient volcano being shifted and rolled like waves in a massive planetary prehistoric storm. But his esophagus held firm, and although the liquid rose up, trundling up the antrum and threatened to re-emerge, a decade of conditioning gastrointestinal exercise kept the fluid subjugated. After years of ramen, burritos, Old No. 8, and the Beast—a slice and two-thirds of a bottle of Evan Williams shared with a Seventh Avenue whore were like milk and cookies.

Melvin tensed himself to try to tighten the untightenable involuntary sphincter muscles of his esophagus, but unlike most normals, who would prefer to avoid the discomfort of retching and the malodor of vomitus, the Troll simply wanted to avoid the inevitable well-meaning and folksy question one of the green-room handlers would inevitably ask, "Oh, are you having nerves?" Nerves—when he was doing shows back at East Bern and Bunk back before "Dusty," when they were more or less a Nirvana cover band with sprinkles of Alice and Sonic Youth and some truly awful original compositions, some asshole had asked him about nerves after he yakked during a sound check. "No, it's four-day-old Kung Pao" was the reply. "Guess it turned."

Melvin briefly drifted off and awoke as the lottery winners were on set laughing, placed in between Matt Lauer and the beauty with the chubby Black man chortling next to her. There are difficult interviews a morning TV host has to perform: a philandering preacher, an actor promoting a film off a string of critical and financial bombs, a politician defending scandal, or a performance-enhancing athlete denying circumstantial evidence. Lottery-winning grannies were less of a challenge. Origin of the partnership, how you picked the numbers, how you'll spend the money—there has never been another question asked to a lottery winner unless the ticket was misplaced, traded, or incinerated, or only recently discovered buried in a two-month-old *Home and Garden*. "I picked number nine because that's the number of young men who had me in my very first gang bang, sonny," whispered the stooped dowager with the rolling walker and a Quasimodo hump. "Twenty-two is the number of times I cheated on my sweet, departed Edgar, dear," whined the perky blue hair in the blue pantsuit, who stood up straight but had a ptotic right lazy eye. "I contributed forty-seven, which was the last year my snatch got wet," offered the prim Mrs. Drysdale type in the librarian glasses. How could anyone remotely interested in these old biddies be a grunge fan? I guess this is what is meant by crossover. Billy Goat's Gruff performing in the Neal Diamond timeslot. Sweet Millicent Rice—exsanguination never seemed so good, so good, so good.

Rockefeller Square accepted Christmas carols, barbershop quartets, doo wop and ebony hip hop. It swung to swing, crowned crooners, and saluted Americana. Rock bands were welcome if they described teen love, everlasting love, lost love, unrequited love, forbidden love, ancient love, even "Muskrat Love," but songs about dead strippers were destined for dingy caverns with sticky floors and no seating. Stripper songs belonged in rooms with black backdrops, which camouflaged headbangers in black bandanas and black T-shirts and black jeans with black fingernails, save the one red representing something they killed or wanted to kill slamming in the mosh and sometimes floating onstage only to be forcibly evicted back out into the black. Stripper songs sung by no-talent hacks belonged in places where expulsion was nigh impossible short of arson. Masturbation, fornication, inebriation, mutilation, self-immolation, if tasteful and relatively discreet—all is permissible, every show a teleported fragment of Christiania. You may find yourself with a beautiful song, performing on a beautiful stage, and you may ask yourself, "Well, how did I get here?"

"Ten minutes, Mr. Nash. You and your crew, ready for final sound check."

And with that, Melvin looked up and a commercial for Poligrip had replaced the grannies and headed outside well in advance of Billy, who was still trying to motivate and calm Tiny. Arenas and clubs, stadiums and bars were all essentially similar except in expanse. There was a back room and a stage set apart from the crowd in a raised area and lighting that gave the audience the illusion of a greater degree of interaction than what the performer experiences. It takes effort for the artist to filter out the lights and identify audience members, while the audience achieves the illusion that the artist is performing just for them.

But outside, with the sun rising over the park, and thousands of fanatics (not of the band but fanatics in search of a half second of fame on the broadcast) jostling for positions at the rails, the interaction could not be avoided, such that in the minutes waiting for Billy and Tiny, and then on hold awaiting the promised light, which would lead to an introduction and a world premiere, he could scan the crowd, read signs, and truly interact.

The signs told the story. Front and center was a destination wedding party from Carbondale, Illinois, with the primary sign holders blond, rat-faced, and cheese-fed chubby. Then to their right, the Gilliland family from Murfreesboro, Tennessee, imploring to meet the overweight weatherman with three generations only one of whom had not yet discovered barley and malt calories. Off to the left with the ubiquitous and likely fictitious "first trip to NYC" sign, a collection of necks from Jonesboro, Arkansas, all clad in red, white, and blue overalls, whooping and hollering up a storm whenever the hosts came in view. Signs were everywhere. Sioux Falls wanted to marry Ms. Nebraska. Kokomo wanted Matt Lauer's autograph. Lo and behold, Allentown, PA, had a BGG fan or two, at least that was what they wanted the world to think.

And then Melvin saw her. Between a bespectacled Asian apparently in meteorology school in Delaware and a sexual proposal for the grannies, the missing strawberry blond stood stone-faced, glaring in the general direction of the band.

Alternating bursts of sun and shadow gave only transient recognition, but when the long shadows of morning cloud cover receded, it was unmistakably her, although why the hell she would have shown up in Rockefeller Plaza was unfathomable. The others waved and fought for camera time, wailed and pleaded to be recognized and interviewed, but the woman stood stationary and transfigured by the morning rays into a radiant glow of sunlight personified.

While the road crew finalized the instruments and microphones, lighting, amplifiers, speakers hiding cables and micromanaging the sound board, and the performers did instrument and sound checks and checked their cue spots and visualized their notes and lyrics, Melvin stared off into the distance in the direction of the woman, buttressed only by the lack of tuning required for the tambourine and total commitment to his lyrics.

The sun passed by, and the flourish of light and shadow temporarily obstructed his view, and when visibility returned, she was gone. Melvin scanned the crowd without success and thought about getting a closer look but instead replaced a pensive quizzical look with his pre-performance vocal ritual. But when he finished and looked to opposite side of the crowd, he spotted her again, with that same dispassionate stare she'd worn before; this time, she was sandwiched between a barbershop quartet from Troy pleading for an audience in four-part harmony and a rotund Asian woman from Ypsilanti carrying an asthmatic Lhasa Apso like a parrot on her gigantic shoulder. He started after her, only to be admonished to maintain his position, as they were coming back from commercial imminently. As he prepared to argue and glanced back, she was once more gone.

Melvin was still scanning the audience when the cameras went red. "And now, what all of you have been waiting for," offered Matt Lauer. "The number-one band in the country, Billy Goat's Gruff, with Tee Nash, and the world debut of their new song, 'Getting My—um, a word I can't say—Back."

Melvin hesitated a second before looking at Tiny and hitting his tambourine in conjunction with Tiny's drum to introduce the beat. Bebe added a rather conventional Mitch Ryder-sampled riff, and with Tee Nash beside him, and channeling his inner Eminem, Melvin rode the wave of a Markwell chord into:

Richard Sanders Polin

> *"Evicted from Riviera*
> *Hertz money gone to appease the bereaved*
> *Innocent or guilty, it really didn't matter*
> *Any way you look at it, juice got squeezed."*

And now there was reversion to the tambourine and backup vocals, adding emphasis to the end of each line Tee Nash enunciated with precision and furor.

> *"Going to get my shit back*
> *Load the Remingtons on the Bronco gun rack*
> *Round up the boys to get my shit back*
> *No hesitation, Palace Station, midnight sneak attack."*

And now Melvin, again with Tee backing him, both strutting on stage like Beastie Boys. Hell, Melvin never felt more like Kid Rock than he did up on the stage white-boy faux-rapping with Tee Nash.

> *"Pension ain't sufficient to sniff out the killer*
> *So I sign photos, sign jerseys, sign my Topps seventy-one*
> *I'd sign your grandma's motherfucking titty*
> *If it's under the table money and the Goldmans get none.*

> *"Boys let's get my shit back*
> *Rifles getting loaded on the Bronco gun rack*
> *We're gonna get my shit back*
> *Palace Station, no hesitation for our midnight sneak attack."*

While Tee Nash bombarded the crowd with the lyrics, Melvin soft-pedaled his backup, all the time scanning and scanning and scanning to no avail.

> *"Beardsley motherfucker, not sure how he got it*
> *Jerseys, private photos, wedding videos with Nicole*
> *But now we're off to the Palace Station, the bastards framed my reputation*
> *But they'll never sell my soul.*

Millicent DeGroenfeld Rice

"Gonna take my shit back
AR-15 in the Bronco gun rack
I'm getting my shit back
Palace Station, no hesitation for a midnight sneak attack."

As this chorus repeated and repeated with rehearsed "ad-libbed" versions from Tee Nash, Melvin continued his search for his itinerant hooker in the crowd, without success. But what he did see was connection with the crowd. Whether instant popularity was related to commiseration with the song's protagonist, a lack of understanding of the point of the connotation through inability to appreciate the lyrics, or a simple appreciation of the marriage of grunge and rap was immaterial. Whatever the reason, Melvin was reasonably certain he had a follow-up hit, and that was almost as reassuring as the existence and safe reappearance of his spectral seductress.

Some songs flourish at the end, others crash, and still others taper. Melvin liked the faux ending in which the audience sensed a denouement and gave a measured applause only to be bamboozled as the trailing end picked up and persisted in a brief jam before finally reaching a terminus. You could get two ovations if you played your cards right, which was especially satisfying on live national television in front of an audience of yokels. But having pulled it off, Tee Nash and Billy Markwell brought it home while Melvin stroked his tambourine and scanned the audience fruitlessly through the ovation and acknowledgment thereof.

"Billy Goat's Gruff with Mr. Tee Nash," Matt Lauer proclaimed with enthusiasm as the Rockefeller Plaza crowd exaggerated whoops and hollers, hoping for camera pans. "We will be back with an exclusive interview with the band after this break."

There was an outside set made up with chairs for Matt Lauer, Tee Nash, Billy Markwell, and Melvin Horgan. They were short-backed chairs with red leather cushions so pristine, they may have been hand-delivered from some Amish seamstress in Lancaster by horse and carriage for a one-time appearance under a celebrity's ass in New York. Softball questions had been promised. No accusations or queries about remorse or regret. Just a couple of comments about the rise to fame and excitement about the upcoming show. In response, Melvin had agreed to dial down the Sam Kinison. But while the nation was hearing about Velveeta and Swiffer and Red Lobster, and some new Matthew Perry vehicle, Tee Nash was trying to understand why his star was stretching and straining his head behind the chairs towards the audience instead of focusing on the pre-approved and pre-arranged questions, which were soon to be confiscated from the host but made readily available on the teleprompter in advance of the return of the red light. "One minute, Troll. Hang with me, Brother Horgan." But Melvin was elsewhere, oblivious to the grips and gaffers readying the set for the end of the Perry promo and return the morning to Lauer.

When the red light reappeared and a wide-angle shot captured the four men gathered around in a semicircle with the poster-bearing throng behind them, three were focused, eyes-forward, and the fourth focused back into the crowd, twitchy and furtive.

"It's eight fifteen now on the East Coast, and we're back visiting with hip-hop star and record mogul Tee Nash as well as the founding members of one of the hottest bands in the world, Billy Goat's Gruff, Melvin Horgan and Billy Markwell. Their latest song just world premiered a few minutes ago. Melvin and Billy, a few months ago, you were relative unknowns, and here you are with a number-one hit. What does that mean to you?"

Billy looked to Melvin, who hadn't returned from playing "Where's Jane Doe" and panicked, having forgotten Melvin's rehearsed response. Tee might have remembered, but before he could provide a third-person platitude, Melvin turned around and blurted. "Where is she? Where's the whore?"

"Melvin—I'm not sure, that's not appropriate. Savannah's not—I mean that's not something we can—"

"No, not Hillary Duff. Never mind. Just thought I saw someone I knew. New York, I mean unknowns. We were never playing for recognition. We always had a loyal fan base, and whether it's some tiny club in Portland or Madison Square Garden, it doesn't really impress or change. Hey, if there's someone out there who disappeared on me in Tulsa, or maybe St. Louis, and Richmond—I think Richmond—stick around, meet me later. What was the question again? Sorry, boss."

Billy looked distraught, understanding that his memorized piggyback lines made no sense, but that he had to say something, preferably something either connected or clever, or both. "It has been a surreal last three to four months, but I guess Troll must have gotten laid at least once. That's the impact of being famous."

Perhaps, Billy thought this was funny, but Melvin flipped him the bird, narrowly escaping the censor.

"Tee Nash." Matt Lauer hesitated, looking back and forth at the teleprompter, then right at Nash and finally into the camera. "Billy Goat's Gruff is undoubtedly Infinity's number-one band, but they reached that status through controversy, and now on their follow-up, perhaps just as controversial, you are a contributor. Any concerns about backlash?"

Tee Nash stared back at the interviewer and did a meme-worthy double-take. "No, Brother Lauer. I don't worry about backlash, because like this genius sitting beside me, I consider art a challenge to the status quo, not a confirmation of it. I will admit, the first time I met Brother Horgan, I didn't know what to make of him. But I came to understand he is gangsta. Maybe not in the way I was gangsta back in the day, Tupac was gangsta, Snoop was gangsta, and even Bam Bam was a little gangsta. Just like our music was a challenge, so is this. Doesn't mean he wanted Millicent to have this unintended consequence. He wanted to rattle us all, and he did. This tune is just a natural progression, maybe a spiritual sequel, and I'm damned glad he granted me the ability to participate."

Melvin then seemed to flip a switch back to engagement. He hesitated for a second and then, before anyone could speak, pointed a finger at the host and started, "Elite society is so hypocritical. The mafia are heroes. Revisionist tales substituting codes and honor for callous killing win Oscars and Emmys. Write a screenplay about some scoundrel but portray him as sympathetic or vulnerable, and praise and awards flow like shit down the subway. But I write a song—and you have no idea, would never bother to ask if its serious or satire, and you ask us about backlash. Mister, you sit there with your Burlington Coat Factory catalogue looks and your FM DJ voice, and your Brooks Brothers wardrobe and think you know anything about backlash. Backlash is when you try to talk to some random four at a show, and they pour a beer on your head—that's backlash. Backlash is when you haven't eaten in a day and think you're gonna flip a drunk for a fiver, but he's just resting and fractures your nose. Backlash is when you tell your pops you're gonna be a rock-and-roll guitarist, and he smashes the one you worked all summer washing dishes to afford against the floor and makes you sweep up the pieces. Right, Billy?"

"My mom's worse. She bought me a broom for my twelfth birthday and told me I better start practicing, and that's pretty much the most thoughtful gift I ever received."

"And that was backlash for?"

"Failing sixth-grade English."

"No summer school, no tutor, no help with homework, just backlash. You see white Bryant Gumbel, you ask us if we expect backlash. We are backlash."

"I didn't mean—"

"Oh, don't backtrack, Brother Lauer, ha-ha," said Tee Nash. "You woke the demon. Can't get him back in the cave, don't even try."

"No, Tee. I'm cool. Ask me anything, You couldn't get me on *Stern*. I'll do a *Stern* interview with this guy instead. Can the script, Seacrest. Ask me something someone wants to hear."

"Well, I think this is getting away from us just a bit. Billy Goat's Gruff."

But the light stayed on. Some producer, maybe someone slighted by Lauer with a dish towel Christmas present, maybe with hindsight subtly avenging a more personal affront, wasn't going to go to commercial three minutes early when she had a five-second delay to work with.

"We're still here, America," said Melvin. "I guess our host is finally learning about backlash. Congratulations, Matt. May I call you, Matt? Do you have another question?"

"Um." The teleprompter was blank, but it might as well have projected a huge middle finger at the host. No co-host or weatherman or serious newsman was coming for relief. Lauer stammered and coughed and stalled and finally just kept smiling and gave America a Philip Seymour Hoffman smirk and a finger towards the camera, repeating, "You, you, you, you," before Melvin started to ask and answer his own questions.

"You really should spend some more time listening to Stern. I know you can't ask all the same questions. You can't ask me my penis size or anything like that, but you can make your lines of questioning more interesting. Something more people would be interested in rather than how we felt when we was teenagers sixteen years, sixteen hundred joints, and sixteen thousand beers ago. Any answer we provide to that is fabricated crap. And I know your average promotional interview is fabricated crap. Naomi Watts ain't coming here to promote *21 Grams*. Awesome damned movie but small budget. She'll go on Bravo or IFC, where movie nerds go and talk about *21 Grams*. She comes here to chat about *King Kong*, which sucked balls but made her a fortune with a kicker for promotions, so you ask her the banal tripe that the studio suits ask for, and she laughs with you at some fabricated anecdote about Jack Black and Adrien Brody, and no one's the wiser that it's all greenscreen, CGI nonsense and the interview might as well be CGI. Really, you're laughing at the dumb saps in the audience who're gonna waste eight bucks on that crap and consider it delightful."

"Brother Horgan, I think it's time we bid adieu."

"Just a minute more, boss. I haven't answered all the nice man's questions yet. Inquiring minds. Why O. J.? It was inevitable. Eventually, someone romanticizes every villain. It was going to happen in twenty-five or fifty years. Jack the Ripper, Bonnie and Clyde, Billy the Kid, Bugsy Siegel. Bad people, evil murderers all softened and in a way worshiped. Why wait a generation for O. J. Simpson? Look. I've never met the guy. May be guilty, may be innocent. I don't really care. I wrote a song taking his perspective. But if you don't like it, America, then don't listen. If you do, come see us at the Garden or download the song."

"Hey, Troll." Billy must have decided either that this was enough or that he wanted to take over for the stunner host.

Melvin crossed his legs and adjusted his flip-flops and took a sip of water. He leaned back in anticipation.

"*Do* you ever feel guilty? I mean, about all the people. I mean, I know none of us understands this, wanted this, but do you ever feel guilty, because—" Troll knew Billy was conflicted about their success, although it was not something over the past months on the road they had ever directly discussed. Theirs was a brotherhood that hinged on shared alienation, not shared intimacy.

"Wait, Goat. Let me answer this. The deadliest extreme sport in the world is BASE jumping. James Bond shit, jumping in squirrel suits off of buildings and mountains. Death rates of one in sixty. But it becomes more and more popular every year. Now modern BASE jumping started in 1978, with a dude named Carl Boenish and a couple of buddies who started jumping off mountains and buildings and antennas and bridge spans. Do you think they should have felt guilty when people voluntarily started copying them, falling to their death? I doubt it. Free will. Maybe the first couple of guys were collateral, but the last fifteen knew and accepted the risks, and makes me proud, not guilty. We're giving these Gen X, Y, Z, millennial sheltered babies a chance to live without going to Afghanistan or jumping off the Eiger.

"I guarantee you Carl Boenish and his buds were never here with the real Bryant Gumbel being grilled about their feelings about some dumb schmuck in Idaho's suit not working and splattering his brains into the Snake River, because, frankly, Carl Boenish wouldn't have cared. And neither did the guy who invented hang gliding. And neither did the dude who invented cave diving. And neither do I. You come to our shows, you have a fart's chance of dying, God knows why. But you have a 19,999 out of 20,000 chance of surviving and feeling more alive than you ever have before, not to mention seeing the only grunge band since Nirvana to outsell the one-named divas and the crossover crooners, and the Saturday morning cartoon-ready boy bands, and the pasteurized suburb approved hippity-hoppity crews."

At this point, a red light appeared on the camera, which Tee Nash knew was a signal to wrap things up, so he interrupted, "And to think when I met this man, you couldn't get two words out of him. And now he's a master of the modern soliloquy. Bravo, Brother Horgan. I think he's handing it back to you, Brother Lauer. But before we go, announcement: New York. Second show. We're adding a second date. I mean, we've been sold out for weeks. We'll stay another night in the city. Billy Goat's Gruff featuring Tee Nash at the Garden. Tickets available now for our second big show."

And with that, the red light faded and presumably some announcer restored NBC control over its programming, and Melvin threw down his lapel mike and took off into Rockefeller Plaza, hurdling a short wall and absorbing gentle pats on the back before being absorbed into the crowd in some sort of peristaltic assimilation.

Chapter 20:
Subreddit/Horgan

Billy Goat's Gruff had over a million Facebook friends. That account had been set up by Infinity when they signed. They'd had just short of five thousand friends before the tour, with the site in a state of benign neglect—tour dates and pictures from the "Dusty" tour and the *Letterman* video, with a promise that a new CD was on its way. The Twitter account was non-existent until Millicent popped, and now the band's site had passed six hundred thousand, and Melvin's personal site had passed a million followers, with the millionth (a barista on the Ball State Campus) getting a signed copy of all three albums on vinyl). Someone in promotions managed the accounts, ignoring the Satanistic ritual invitations and born-again remonstrations and kindly retweeting an occasional fan claiming to have a birthday, a terminal kid or best friend, or an upcoming resection of some fungating brain mass. There were the requisite thanks to the good people of wherever-they-had-played-the-night-before, as well as promotional tweets. And finally, they hired an unemployed comedian—who had been canned from the bullpen at *Jimmy Kimmel* for wearing one of those Obama Joker T-shirts in his then-girlfriend's Instagram post—to write sarcastic "Melvin-like" 140-character comments on modern life.

> "Gino's is really the best slice in New York like Coors Light is really the world's most refreshing beer. #FalseAdvertising."

> "If they make a movie about my life like #8Mile, @RosanneBarr is either gonna be my wife or my mother."

> "If Philadelphia is the City of Brotherly Love and Boston is the Cradle of Liberty, then Baltimore is a fucking dump."

> "We were going to do a video of 'Millicent DeGroenfeld Rice.' I wanted Lindsay Lohan, but her agent said she wasn't available. Loved her in 'Just Married.' Trying for Ruth Bader Ginsburg instead."

> "Coming to Dallas and we want all Cowboy fans to come out for a series of 50,000 1 song free shows."

> "I'm a huge fan of Justin Timberlake. So talented. What a great job playing a pretty-boy, arrogant douche in 'The Social Network.' How the hell could he have done that so effortlessly?"

> "In 1967, Jimi Hendrix opened three shows for Herman's Hermits before they changed the order based upon greater talent and appeal. That'll never happen again, eh Giggler?"

There were pictures as well of Billy and Melvin in school, or at their first gigs, or washing dishes, or hauling their gear or the headliners' gear for small venues on obscure tours where roadies were an unaffordable luxury item. Right after they absorbed Tiny, they played a thirty-minute set at the Alibi Bar in Portland, and someone named "@JesusRemnant" had posted a picture of the three of them: Tiny in mid-stroke, Billy playing his beginners' chords with an advanced strut, and Melvin, leaning into the microphone like some bastardized Bizarro crooner.

It was the day before the first Garden concert, the last event in the American portion of the *Space Needle Pricks* (Subtitle "Pay Your Premiums") Tour. Not that there was going to be a European tour. They'd been rejected for Visas by England, France, Germany, the Netherlands, Spain, Italy, and a bunch of smaller countries with names that bled into long-forgotten *Jeopardy* answers. Only Japan, to date, had not provided an unconditional rejection, and the decision there remained pending.

Tee Nash had rented an East Egg mansion for the week leading up to the show, with ample room for his entourage as well as all the band members, including the Giggler crew and a few hand-picked visitors. But while the others mingled in the ballroom, spraying champagne like World Series champs, eating hamachi nigiri off the body of a nude model who eventually morphed into a snorting table, and sharing model-strippers and a giant orange bong with black crystalline flakes like family-style night at an Indian joint, Melvin was shut into the second-largest bedroom, peering at his phone.

The day before, a private detective hired by the firm had found him not far from the Plaza, sulking around outside an Argentinian Steakhouse, looking in a window at the happy hour martini crowd. He had been whisked onto the Island but refused to participate in the festivities, first binge-watching Season 1 of *The Sopranos* and then *Shameless*, and then *Game of Thrones*, as if in a reverie.

His room was, in fairness, larger than the entire apartment he and Billy had shared in Portland in the early days. He lay in a king-sized bed, which sat under a faux fresco of a religious baptism, painted with the priest gazing licentiously at the haloed infant. On the near wall was a gigantic mural of a '50s Bowery scene, with cartoonish hucksters and shysters chasing around Mort Walker and Chic Young beauties while more realistically depicted street people withered and despaired with empty tin pans and sleeping mutts. The mural's neighbor was a peaceful French provincial scene. The room was decorated as if Martha Stewart and Hef had both been given the charge to design their dream bedroom and decided to compromise by selecting accoutrements one by one, like a fantasy draft.

Melvin was naked under purple satin sheets, save for a pair of yellow-tipped, ankle-length white athletic socks with the rest of his clothes strewn on and around a Chippendale chair around a dark oak desk. A blue, gray, and white ski sweater and a never-washed pair of jeans made the chair while Fruit of the Looms, a Philadelphia Phillies promotional T-shirt, and a quite expensive Helly Hansen jacket, black with a yellow collar, didn't rate even a chair back hanging. One flip-flop straddled the underwear while the other propped up the collar of the T-shirt. His iPhone was perpetually connected to a power source in the headboard as he scrolled, oblivious to the goings-on downstairs, even when they bled into his chamber.

The room was phased to remind of the old days. The bathroom light was buffered by a three-quarter-shut door to reveal the perfect admixture with a twenty-watt nightlight close to the door on the opposite side of the room from the bathroom. The light matrices combined like gamma rays, creating a hot spot of luminescence and a trailing off into the corners of the room, cloaking the bed in case of interruption.

Melvin held his phone in his right hand while his left blanketed his crotch—not, as one might expect, for self-satisfaction but more for the relative spike in body heat that a physiologist would attribute to blood flow, a psychologist would blame on erotic narcissism, and a romantic would pin on deep loss and longing. And then the kneading, rolling, and squeezing of a free 100-percent-natural stress ball. With the other hand, Melvin slowly shuffled through his Twitter account. Someone had set it up on his phone, entering some unassailable password so obscure that hackers would have to be the proverbial million monkeys with a million typewriters.

So many names. A choreographer from Manchester, UK. A barista from Dubuque. A high school rebel from Hattiesburg. An IT geek from Lyon. A coffee shop owner from Ankara. An entertainer from Yuma, An amateur jeweler from Adelade. A comic with a podcast from Culver City.

The list was endless, and as soon as he scanned a few, more followers joined. He switched to mentions, retweets, messages.

"DoggyStyle89" wanted a retweet for his cousin with throat cancer, of course his biggest fan, but suffering from throat cancer on her twelfth birthday in Limerick, with a picture of a grotesque gargoyle of a human in a wheelchair with a breathing tube, hands sundered askew like a crazed conductor.

"ScreenLookerMcGruff" wanted to know if he wanted to come to a bachelor party in Kenosha—just for kicks, not to play or anything.

"ChillyWilli" wanted to know if he liked Indian girls or had ever been to India or would like to come visit Kashmir after she graduated in June.

"FifeandDrum51" asked how he felt he could save his soul from everlasting damnation, and whether he felt that he had a demon inside of him and how it ensnared him.

A fourteen-year-old girl from the St. Louis suburbs showing off her braces.

A straight male dancer from Spokane with a detached-looking Afghan.

A prankster offering imagined comic opinions from the perspective of Tiny Atlas's biceps and who wished his location remained obscure.

A hotel porter from Darbyshire who promised 100,000 followers.

From Twitter, there were links to message boards and sub-message boards on sites like Reddit and Quora, and Tumblr, linking together victims by blood type, histocompatibility antigens, dental history, caffeine utilization, leafy green vegetable consumption, childhood vaccine avoidance, and eczema. "Molly T.," from a server at Vassar, was convinced every victim of the murder song had eczema. There was a string of posts discussing the relationship of the song to a coming apocalypse, and another rearranging letters in Melvin's name (as Mel Horgan, a name he had never been called in his entire freaking life) via a cipher and deriving Beelzebub.

Billy Markwell's guitar was once owned by Charles Manson, claimed "Gobbledygook75." It emanated pheromonic signals, homing in on the weakest in the audience reeking vengeance on the never-believers. "Chromedome" was of the opinion that the band were Russian agents working with the KGB to obfuscate the real reason behind the killing of high-value targets with an undetectable Russian nerve gas agent.

Democrats called Melvin a fascist pig; Republicans, a Commie pinko. The wealthy considered him trailer-trash slime, and the poor thought him an arrogant oppressor. The feminists regarded him as a misogynistic pig, and the defenders of male privilege saw him as a sellout. The East Coast New York Scene scoffed at his credentials to approach Lenny Bruce, or even Lou Reed or Joey Ramone. On the West Coast, Seattle rejected him, Sacramento passed him off to Portland, and Portland called him a commercial sellout and refused to acknowledge him beside James Mercer and Isaac Brock. Really, other than the rare Pentagram-loving Troll disciple, there was agreement only in terms of the utter physical, emotional, and spiritual depravity of Melvin Horgan.

Then who the fuck is downloading songs, showing up at the concerts, buying hastily made T-shirts with the grim reaper, or the "Dusty" EP cover? The world hates Melvin Horgan, like it hates chemical warfare and kiddy porn, he reasoned, lying in bed, meandering through the net. And yet the anachronism persists, the paradoxical and inevitable progression of ten more and now seventeen more, climbing, climbing. No one would follow a convicted child rapist. "Ooh. What's he gonna say next? I'm gonna so dislike it. I'm gonna so block Gil the kiddie rapist, because he's such a kiddie rapist and I hate kiddie rapists. But, oh my God, he just retweeted me. That kiddie rapist just liked my tweet about the Monday blahs. And look now since Gil the kiddie rapist liked my tweet, twelve other people liked my tweet. Even a woman in Alberta, Canada, liked my tweet, all thanks to Gil. God bless you, Gil."

Richard Sanders Polin

A sixty-four-year-old publican from Darbyshire standing under a sign that said "The Horse and Hare." A comedian/soccer mom from Grand Rapids with two daughters who looked nothing like her and a Subaru Impreza. A street musician from Philadelphia whose profile picture was Daryl Hall and called himself "Payolaf." A college junior at SUNY Albany who must be the only male on the internet with a duck-lip selfie pose. A nursing fellow from Olympia with a profile picture taken overlooking a Ferris wheel on Pier 57 in Seattle, where Melvin had once slept off a drunk, who listed herself an expert on luxury watches and bubbles.

Melvin was down to 135 pounds, his eating now restricted to the unsalted peanuts he kept in jars in the bathroom, with shells strewn across the floor, and dried apple rings he had sent to himself in bulk to keep him regular. He was down twenty pounds from his normal touring weight but still drinking mightily, and his veins bulged out like the Alps on a topographical map of Europe. Blue fluctuations were evident in his neck, his arms, his feet, even onto his torso in places where normals hide veins deep beneath skin and adipose for just a faint blue marring an otherwise pristine trunk or torso. The last few days had been a perpetual feast downstairs, but for Melvin, other than the booze, there were only peanuts, apples, and a half-empty bag of peanut butter-filled pretzels, which he rationed four to a meal like a camp prisoner.

Sleep was confined to times the whiskey superimposed on protein malnutrition overcame the racing mind, which compelled him to stay on his phone, sifting through the followers. A couple of hours here and there was the best his beaten-down melatonin could muster. He was tethered to a power cable and his penis, delving follower by follower down the phone, looking for a clue as to the one.

A hematologist from Monroe, Louisiana, with a profile picture from Jamaica with beads in a mullet. A poet/philosopher from Aberdeen who called himself "RoberttheBruce1989" and had at least four corgis. A teenager from the United Arab Emirates, obviously from a rich family, seen beside a swimming pool with servants in abundance and wearing an Eton jacket and Polo swim trunks.

"Me1999" whose posts were chiefly retweeting Jacksonville Jaguars touchdowns or paradoxically University of Georgia goalpost stormings.

The ironic arc of the past six months had circled back to the vilest swill available on the Island. The dalliances with Newman's Own champagne, lavender craft cocaine, green-tea, caramel-peach IPAs, and Glenfucker 347-year-old whiskey blended in an albino goat's belly at two hundred dollars a thimble, artisanally prepared only by direct descendants of William Wallace, with only ten bottles a year allowed to leave Cuntalagan. When you're a troll, you understand that you're never more than visiting, on vacation in this blessed world, so don't develop a taste. So here, the reversion back to Stroh's, Bud, the Beast, the Rock, seemed less a demotion but a recalculation, punctuated by figures like $3.99 and three for fifteen. =

Rosemary's Babydoll, an Asian with a neck tattoo of a cigarette standing beside the Frances Scott Key Memorial. A male nurse from Prague with a huge tuft of hair mysteriously missing from his head amongst an otherwise plush forest crop. A Laotian seamstress apparently with seventeen siblings who seemingly preferred '70s disco. John fucking Daly. No, it said John fucking Daly, and he was verified.

Eventually, the searching would become more frantic, concentrating only on light-skinned female Caucasians between twenty-five and forty. This would allow hundreds of profiles scanned in minutes, finger manipulations performed with simultaneous, fevered, excited, and knowing fatalism. He would never find her. If she evaded him from his bed, and from his audience, how did he expect to track her down through millions of Facebook and Twitter followers, many of whom had nonsensical meme motifs in lieu of identifying pictures. But he persisted in a digital death march, oblivious to the rhythmic squeaking of bed frames all around, often producing complementary syncopation intermixed with the sounds of whatever the DJ or host was spinning, which went through phases of the Mysterious T anthology, Hall-and-Oates-style vanilla soul, early MTV video one-hit hair bands, and glorious jam session masters from Earth Wind and Fire and the Commodores from T's personal collection.

Two or three times over the course of days, Melvin peeked his head out of the room, even ventured through the crowd to the kitchen or pantry. One time, he got a cab and drove five minutes and back to a gas station mini market, where, for some reason, he had the compunction to take a dump in a blue-blocked urinal stall reeking of Cheetos-laced vomitus before buying two six packs of Busch and two giant Slim Jim sticks before retiring back to his room. Other than his bandmates and the executives, everyone was a stranger. Random groupies of varying ages and ethnicities, but no missing link, and back to bed he went.

The last ten—the followers who had been with him from the start, when the fake account for the fake rock star was initiated. Tee Nash, Billy Markwell, Tiny Atlas, Infinity Records, *Rolling Stone* magazine, Melvin Horgan News, Roger Smith Atty at Law, Billy Goat's Gruff fansite, and *E News*. That was it. No disappearing hooker. Nothing on Facebook, Instagram, nothing. Melvin placed the phone on the headboard and folded the covers over him, the way he'd used to when tripping Dusty used to wander through the house looking for seconds. He took a couple of tugs and quickly realized the futility of that project and re-emerged. The stereo downstairs was playing "Raspberry Beret," and from the cadence and vigor of the mattress squeals, it sounded like Tiny Atlas was in action a floor up and a couple of rooms to the left of Melvin's hideout. Nobody could thrust as slowly and deeply as Tiny, and he imagined the heaving giant brutalizing some rail-thin model into either rapture or desolation. Still no arousal.

Melvin cursed under his breath and returned to his task with visions of some groupie in Anchorage 2008, images of a punk girl in Dover in 2010, twins after Tucson in 2011, which generally didn't fail him. But it failed him today. Had been failing him a lot lately. Occasionally, he considered whether his obsession would allow progression, but her memory was off limits as an aphrodisiac, sacrosanct.

Who knows how the mind flows, channels, when the normal circadian predictable cycles are altered, and you enter the doldrums? You seem to reach REM quicker and without the protective barrier to shade illusion from reality. Sometimes you just drift back into memories, which you relive like they happened yesterday, and sometimes you're so slightly in REM that although you see and experience these images, the other aspects of physiology, generally shielded, remain tangible. It's an eerie amalgam of dream and reality with sleep terrors and somnambulism—the crested wave between reality and dream most of us have access to as children when we spend our last conscious hours feeling the excitement of flying or web-slinging across the stereotyped repetitive skyscrapers of REM New York.

So, here was Melvin, underneath the covers, astounded to have materialized back to a club he recognized as the Bunk Bar on the waterfront in Portland. And he watched silently as Billy thanked Roman whoever, who had booked them to lead off with a three-song set on a four-band bill highlighted by an all-girl punk band called Pussy and the Josiecats.

It was just the three of them on a makeshift stage in a sandwich house, a gig for which Melvin recalled getting paid an IPA and an order of the best fucking tots on the planet. There were maybe fifty people in the audience, and many of them were conversing or eating when Billy introduced the band. Tiny didn't give cues, so Billy counted them in, and the next thing he knew, Melvin was mouthing "Dusty Heaves" while meandering in the air, watching himself on stage singing "Dusty Heaves." He watched the crowd as at least ten, maybe more, of the don't-give-a-fuck majority turned towards the stage and put aside their munching or chatting. And suspended above the stage, he felt himself emerging. The half-asleep erection as it grew, however, shifted him from REM back to a wakened state, and the image of the Bunk Bar stage faded and was replaced by an imaging of Madison Square Garden and twenty thousand, filled to the rafters. Just as quickly as he had sprung to life in his dream state of the past, he wilted in anticipation of the future. Melvin opened his eyes, cursed, and went back to examine the new followers on his phone.

A humorist, poet, and philosopher from Sante Fe who nonetheless wore a Best Buy Geek Squad jacket. A hot mother of two from Göteborg, Sweden, who listed something called team handball as a hobby. A hippie radiologist from Ashtabula with a Bernie Sanders bumper sticker as his profile picture. A seventeen-year-old high school junior from North Platte with an angel tattoo on one arm and the devil on the other.

Chapter 21:
Our American Cousin

"I'm not fucking wearing this. Tell Tee Nash I am taking this piece of shit and lighting it on fire. I wear what I wear."

"Mr. Horgan, Mr. Horgan. Mr. Nash warned me you'd be upset, but he said for New York City."

"Fuck New York City. Fuck Grand Central Station. Fuck the Guggenheim. Fuck the Yankees and the Mets and the Giants and the Jets. Fuck the motherfucking Tavern on the Green. Fuck Greenwich Village and Central Park. Fuck Harlem and Spanish Harlem, too. Fuck the Garden, Fuck this show. And fuck Tee Nash if he thinks I'm going on stage dressed up like Toby the Faggot Lumberjack." Melvin Horgan sat in front of a triple-paned, body-length mirror and gazed down at slender-cut, fuck-me Rag and Bone button-fly jeans. Jeans that cost more money than the last ten pairs he'd owned, purchased from Goodwill or, when he was flush, from the Gap outlet store between Portland and Salem. His shirt was a designer taupe on red background, blue-and-black checkerboard flannel—kind of like when a fancy restaurant tries to perfect and augment the Twinkie or Ho Ho. How kitsch. His flip-flops were replaced by platform shit-stompers, which did give him two inches. "Fucking jeans belong on binocular guy in a playground. Shirt from a fag costume party. Isn't that clever. My Beau Morris is Toby the Erotic Jolly Woodsman, and I'm a weeping willow. I'm not fucking doing it. I didn't ask for Lenny Kravitz to do a dress up. Just give me my clothes back."

The wardrobe man didn't say a word. The jeans and Ghostbusters 2 T-shirt, the white tube socks with holes in the soles and the toes, and the green-soled flip-flops were gone, God knew where. He drifted out into the hallway and passed the word online that the Troll was indignant and insistent that his clothes be returned. A few minutes later, a small parade accompanied Tee Nash into the hallway to get it from the horse's mouth. Tee strode gracefully into the changing rooms and, with a big smile, let out a "Brother Horgan" like most men would express a sigh.

Melvin just glared down at the Brooks Brothers brown socks, exposed when the shoes were kicked up into the wall.

"Brother Horgan, has anyone told you where we stand with 'Getting My Shit Back?' You've surpassed 'Millicent.' We've crossed over, both of us, crossed over. Number one adult alternative, number one R&B, number one on the pop charts. Crossed over, just trying to maintain that crossover appeal."

"Fuck, Tee. I don't 'cross over.' I didn't get into this to be Timberlake. I don't want to cross over like that. I can barely accept that I crossed over from food stamp guy, and not just food stamp guy but guy who rolls drunks for smokes and trades 'em for food stamps. You and Goat can cross over. I wanna wear my own fucking jeans and my own fucking shoes and shirt and look in the mirror and see the same fucking douchebag I've seen for the last thirty years. Is that asking too much?"

Tee Nash looked up at Melvin, who had risen and started pacing during this last pronouncement. "See you backstage. Don't be late and don't forget your cues." With that, he vanished back into his entourage. The wardrobe man eventually knocked and placed a grocery bag at the dressing room door and scampered off. Melvin took the new clothes and folded the socks in the shoes and the shoes in the shirt, and the shirt in the jeans. He sat there for a second, images of himself attacking from the various angles of multiple surrounding mirrors, with nothing but survivor's underwear, holes in the elastic, stains around both sides showing how he had turned them inside out, forward, and reverse to prolong wear, like rotating tires. Ten minutes maybe more, he sat there, going over the setlist and his oratories. When it became evident no one was returning to dissuade him, to persist in the argument, he slid on his jeans and slithered into his T-shirt, looked around to see if anyone would bother him here, and got the first uninterrupted three hours of sleep he'd enjoyed in New York, in a plush chair, legs spread out on an ottoman.

The ready room at Madison Square Garden sparkled, as if, after every performance, the old room was purified by fire to emerge again like the phoenix. There was nary a spot, splotch, or imperfection on the sofa, chairs, rug, drapes. Neat rows of Fiji water lined up in a five-by-five array in a walk-in refrigerator next to five-by-five rows of Coke, Diet Coke, Sprite, Dr. Pepper, Dr. Brown's Cream Soda, and New York apple and mandarin seltzers. Heineken, Heineken Light, Amstel, and Amstel Light, even Grolsch in those replaceable top bottles, as if to remind of the Dutch origins of the city. The vast food spread included bagels from Absolute with lox and the lightest cream cheese whipped into a sublime mousse, Ray's Pizza—five varieties, including one with an Italian boar sausage, which had a James Beard award—and if one was inclined (though Melvin and the boys weren't), huge slabs of hamachi and maguro swimming on little puffs of sushi rice, as if to split the difference between sushi and sashimi.

Photographs on the wall showed the Boss deep in a swoon; Jersey crooning to an adoring crowd; the Piano Man swaying, leading an audience sing-a long; Paul McCartney in front of a wall of fire, hands in the air, screaming into his microphone and commanding the stage; Paul Simon and Art Garfunkel in a delicate truce during a reunion tour, sharing their harmonic synergy; Bono in sunglasses, regaling over a packed hall, pointing towards some lucky section in the distance; Lady Gaga in a Rosie the Riveter costume, delighting her home crowd; and many more legends. And now fucking Billy Goat's Gruff—a session bassist, a drummer who can't drum but can terminate existence, a guitarist who puts forth good effort but who's stymied with seventh-grade skills, and a lead singer with a muffled scowl of a voice and no musical aptitude beyond that of your basic groupie—was going to join them.

Melvin thought to do his vocal preparations, but each time he started, the sound arrested as he stared in disbelief at his predecessors formulating his unworthiness. There was a difference between being a fraud and a phony. Melvin had been a phony since the first time he belched into a microphone. But he had never perpetrated a fraud. The fractional differences between his sins occupied his ruminations, displacing his vocal snippets and eventually leading to another brief nap as He Got the Giggler took the stage for a five-song, fuck-you opener.

Melvin sat suspended on that borderline of sleep and wakefulness, opening his eyes long enough to see Marc Bauer on the closed circuit, preening like a prancing Westminster poodle, emoting his heart out for an eighth, maybe at most a seventh, of the paid audience. Even from backstage, the humming of the music meandered with the amalgam of voices, countering and ultimately negating it. Negative decibels. It was like they were bankrupt. A fucking Monopoly game that started in Boise, Giggler in the race car with double fours and then double fives. A light blue and an orange before Melvin'd even rolled, and he got a four, one, and three—not with doubles—and had to pay fucking income tax. That was where they started, and here they were done and Giggler was bankrupt, thanks to the comeback of the century. Negative decibels, and later tonight, there wouldn't be a stray peep in the house during "Dusty" or "Froggy" or "Bumbershoot," unless Melvin called for it. Reversal of fortune.

And this comforted him, their collapse comforted him, and he was back on the outskirts of REM, but now picturing himself walking around backstage at the Gorge in a fugue state, high, maybe on mushrooms, for some reason he assumed it was mushrooms, and he was asking directions to be trephined. Somewhere at the festival, intercalated amongst the venders of wooden mailboxes and shark-tooth jewelry, and found-art windchimes, was a Lakota shaman who'd trephine you for seventy-five bucks, and Melvin watched himself beg for a chance to be reunited with his memories. But the shaman would not trephine him until he drank a concoction of a cinnamon-spiced horchata spiked with human bone marrow and a sprinkling of absinthe. The shaman's shack smelled of lilac and tobacco and rum, and there was a rug pinned to the wall, of stick-figure natives, each balancing a spear on the shoulder of his brother ahead.

He drank the potion, and the memories flooded into his brain: an amazing amalgam of childhood, adolescent, and adult remembrances appearing in splotches back and forth in time, like an art house movie, but then twisting away in a funnel cloud to mix with other lost memories at the show, as if this tent was a drain for every neuronocidal activity of each and every of the thousands of concertgoers filling their bellies, noses, and veins with contraband. And his mind was overrun by images of the intercalating stick figures, spears now turned to point and marching in precision towards him. And it was like this was the only memory left in his brain, the memory of these rug warriors who had turned on him and were chasing him around the tent of the shaman, who was now unseen in a small enclosure in the corner of the room, chanting lines in his native tongue from a repetitive three-line prayer or poem (who could know) in some rhythmic anthemic cadence.

And as they pursued him, he ducked under tables, over chairs and, in his reverie, through concrete barriers and metal walls, and he was trying to remember something vital, something to allow him to escape. As he hurled his body down a cavernous corridor in what was once a tiny shack, windows and doors appeared, some ornate like gothic cathedral entrances and others cookie-cutter. There was a guy beside a door who beckoned to him and pressed him to go in, to escape. It was none other than Kurt Cobain, with the side of his temporal lobe, on the entry side, black and discolored, and on the exit side blown away with fungating brain oozing from the open scalp and skull. Cobain didn't say anything but motioned him towards a white concealed door, but Melvin didn't go in; he kept scurrying down the corridor, followed closely by his pursuers. He continued down the hall, and this time, there was a castle double-door with dual soldiers with spears guarding the entrance, but with John Lennon from the Yoko honeymoon, two-gurus-in-bed era, flowing beard and moustache and hair down to his shoulders, trying to get him to enter, but still Melvin ignored him and rushed down the ever-expanding hallway.

Doors propagated all around, and arrows whizzed by, one grazing the hairs on his neck beard, but he shrugged it off and zig-zagged down the corridor until he saw a door to a movie theater—one of those great, garrulous red-velvet monstrosities Regal or Cinemark uses to make you think you're in some old-time movie house when you're really entering screen thirteen of sixteen in an offshoot of a strip mall. But the usher stood by the door, and it was Lenny Bruce, and he said, "Get the fuck in here, Schmegegge."

Melvin entered this room, thinking he'd be safe. The door locked behind him, and Lenny Bruce was gone, but this was another green room, and there were posters of bands all around him. He saw Nirvana, and all of a sudden, in a wave, it came to him—the riff that opened "Come as You Are"—and with the riff, the words and music flowed back to him, and he knew them completely. And then there was Alice in Chains, and a spigot turned on "Black Hole Sun," and he started to hum it as the tune and lyrics trundled into his consciousness. But now the black-carpet men were bleeding through the walls, oozing into the room with their swords perched on the next one's shoulder, and marching inexorably towards him in a diagonal, rhythmic swale, and as they moved closer, they raised their swords in unison, ready to strike, as faceless and indistinguishable as *Fantasia* brooms.

And just then, in short bursts, Melvin remembered a note, then a chord, then a line, then a riff of "Millicent," and he hummed and then sang the chorus, "come on and make another slice," and one by one, the figures morphed into people, and those people started to choke and die, and they were suddenly recognizable as the dancing hippie and the ER doc and Hipster Santa and Petit Prince, and all the others, as if the song was some missing reagent. They stumbled and fell, clutching their chests or their throats, until only one remained.

The sole survivor was masked and continued to come at Melvin more slowly and deliberately, with feline patience. The sword was transformed into a clarinet, and the figure stalked Melvin, repeating the chord Billy played over the murder beat. Melvin got pressed into a corner with the figure ever nearer, playing the murder chord closer and closer to Melvin's face, and it seemed they were about to send it through his soul when suddenly the figure pulled off robes, and its shape was undeniably feminine. She lunged for him, and he was now terrified, on the ground, in an empty room of nothingness, everything having faded away. She reached for him on the ground and started to pummel but with sparring blows, toying with him, spanking.

He realized that she was not out to hurt him, and he attempted to wrest control, turning her over on her back and pinning her down. She squirmed from under him, but only to knee him gently in his privates, which excited him, and Melvin pushed back down harder, moving his right hand to her left breast, which firmed as her resistance diminished. Finally, he had her pinned down and submissive and rubbed his face against her mask and the visible remnants, and after a pregnant pause, she kissed him. She pulled him down to her, and now he had the right breast exposed from her robes and fondled it while they continued to kiss.

And then he moved down and kissed her breast, and as she moaned, "Yes, yes." His hand slid down into her labia, and he felt the warmth and wetness as he fondled and entered. And still, "Yes, yes." Finally, he left her breast and returned to kiss her, leaving his hand running loop-de-loops, searching for her spot, and when he came back up to find her lips once more, with his free hand he removed her mask and beanie and saw her beneath him, now whispering, "Yes, yes."

Melvin stopped caressing and kissing and paused, mouth agape, staring into the eyes of his lost prostitute, who stared back at him with elfin innocence and then gently pulled him back in with her right arm and reached for his penis with her left.

But almost instantaneously, as her lovely lips, red without cosmetic embellishment, encountered his, Melvin noticed a subtle tactile transformation: crackling of the lips, thenar muscular atrophy, wrinkling of the breast, parching of the sweet, vaginal flow. And as he looked down, she had aged twenty, maybe now thirty years, but still with such a beautiful smile of desire. And after an initial recoil too rapid to emotionally calculate concern versus revulsion, he screamed and woke up in a cold sweat just as Tee Nash entered the room and proclaimed, "Showtime!"

Chapter 22:
Joey Ramone's Shorter Brother

For the past seven shows, the setlist had been identical—fifteen, close with "Millicent," clear off the stiff and a two-song encore. "I Wanna Be Sedated" was permanently in the encore and "Rock and Roll High School" had slid in, replacing a cover of STP's "Vaseline" that Melvin lacked the range for and Billy had to cut half the chords to keep up with. For the Garden, "Sure Shot" was added as number sixteen, giving Tee Nash a second song onstage and another New York icon, the Beastie Boys, to use to suck up to the audience. It was the only song Melvin had rehearsed.

Everyone else was in place, grazing around backstage and waiting for the roadies to ready the pyrotechnics. Melvin snuck two lines and a vodka Red Bull and popped up from his makeshift bed and headed to join the others. Backstage there was pyrotechnics, a ten-member road crew, security, and three huge video screens. All manifestations of a status on par with the transcendent.

As he stepped out to a roar, it seemed more of a dream than the shaman's hut. Twenty thousand people stacked for admission to the Lottery, not just admission—souls who wanted to be granted permission to participate.

But the downside of the arena was the sacrifice of recognition. The people were separated not by a small camera well or roping but by a goddamned medieval moat. Individuals were not separable, signs were only legible if the font was massive, and sounds were muffled like a Peanuts teacher. Melvin missed the big-chested blond holding up a "Marry me, Troll" sign and screeching out "I love you" proclamations when the pre-and post-song roar faded. But he also missed the middle fingers and the "You suck" assholes, lately congregating towards the front, as well as the odd "Repent, sinner" signs from holy rollers willing to cheat death to curry favor to their Lord and Savior.

"Dusty Heaves." That was Melvin's Lord and Savior. Without "Dusty," there was no local fan base, no record contract, no "Froggy," no *Letterman*, no "Millicent," no Tee Nash, no Madison Square Garden. "Dusty" was as much of a friend and comfort as Billy, a confidant and companion for life. When was the last time they had played a show without "Dusty"? Best thing he'd ever written. Most original. "Dusty" was what differentiated them from dozens of garage bands playing the five-dollar cover bars in Old Town and on the Eastside. "This fucking mutt," best opening line of a rock and roll career, save maybe Radio Free Europe or Longview.

Strays. Strays aren't supposed to be here. Strays have fleas. Strays forage and struggle to survive. Strays sleep under benches, and strays drink sewer water, and strays get kicked and cursed and hunted down. It was a strange set of thoughts to register while on a stage in front of twenty thousand people, mimicking a strut he once saw Liam Gallagher do in a video, like Liam banging on a tambourine, demonstrating ineptitude.

But then he realized—the Gallaghers were strays, cut from the same cloth. And Cobain was a stray, the Kirkwoods were strays, REM were strays—more talented strays, surely, but all anomalies, cast-offs.

And then as the final refrain finished, and the effects faded into the dark of the auditorium, Melvin was alone in a garage with his best friend and a microphone, and he spoke to an imaginary throng. "Thank you. Thank you very much." He paused for effect. "New York fucking City. How the hell are you?" Appropriate applause. "It's good to be back. We have actually played here twice before." A few scattered claps. "Panderers. No one fucking saw us play. No one who can afford tickets to this shit." Big applause. "We're gonna be here for a while tonight. But first, here's a song from our new CD; it's called 'Tiger Drag.'" Moderate applause.

"Tiger Drag" was followed by "Bumbershoot," which had become something of a minor download hit and a concert favorite. And while Troll could never be an audience manipulator, cultivating attention amongst limited attention spans with interactive audience sing-alongs or audience "faa-la-las" or "whoo-hoos" like pop acts, "Bumbershoot" was an opportunity to play with the crowd and amend lyrics, really, as he saw fit for the venue. What he could do was amend lyrics as an insipid, repetitive ditty to the glee of the brainless throng. Given that the original version of the song was really just various methods of expressing a barter of cunnilingus for three-day access to a musical festival expressed with subtle difference in intonation, phrasing, and cadence, it was moronically simple in some alternatives, providing a local flavor. He could even create little stanzas: "*Who'll give me Yankee tickets for a three-day pass / Behind the fucking dugout for a three-day pass / Ain't taking Mets tickets for a three-day pass.*"

That got 'em going. Half the audience jubilant, and the other half riotous, with the whole damned throng engaged. Then the standard shit, blow job, blow, smack, everything but the damn handheld video game, which was his enduring legacy from festival barter.

Melvin stepped up to the front of the stage, under the lights, and, for the first time, recognized the full magnitude of the studio crowd, differentiated some faces in the front, and some signs moving back in the crowd, the faces muffled and subdued. Yellows, blues, and greens danced above him, focusing first on Billy, then Bebe, and finally someone tried to capture Melvin, who dodged and swerved away from the light so he could keep an eye on the crowd for any eye contact, for any potential late-night pussy. For her.

He had experienced it before as an audience member—a perfect harmony between performer and crowd. A synchrony of adulation. But when there were twenty-two thousand indoor fans, the sound waves resonated, not through the heart, like the coarse, euthanizing drumbeat of "Millicent," but into the brain, like a whole other soul inhabiting, swirling, intermingling through whatever debased morass remained of his conscience, and creating a turbulence, not to cleanse but merely to churn his essence. His tambourine beats slowed down like underwater breathing, but the instrumental hum stepped up, cocksure and prodigious, and Melvin pounded on, trance-like, transfigured in this cranial chaos of intersecting lento and strepitoso, until, instinctively, he caught a telltale phase shift Billy used to transition back to the last primal scream of desperation. "*Last chance, give me something for a three-day pass*" was uttered to mimic the unraveling conclusion of "Territorial Pissings."

Riotous applause. Riotous applause for "Bumbershoot." Whole damn place on its feet with primal screams of adoration in soprano and tenor for some shit he wrote in ten minutes, scribbling the last words so he could make it into the hallway bathroom to puke Kraft Dinner made with the Beast and a little smack instead of milk or water.

"Holy crap, New York. You knew that one, right? And that's not even on the radio. You can't say 'Give me a blow job' on the radio, right? I can ask for the Yankee tickets, cocaine, Game Boy, even." Someone out there yelled, "Weed!" "Yes, even weed. But you can't ask directly for a blow job and get airplay on WNBC, can you? And the fact that you know it means you actually know our catalogue, and I like that. You like that, Goat?"

"I dig it, Troll."

"Well, let's give 'em something they might know a little better. And Tiny, why don't you sit this one out. Let's welcome out on stage Brooklyn's own Marky Ramone."

You had to give it to the audience. You could fuck around with the order, but they kind of knew what was coming—setlist app, those motherfuckers. But the cool thing was the roars that came on opening riffs.

"Rock and Roll High School." It might have been the first video the Troll ever saw, or maybe just the first that set him on this path. Joey Ramone, caterpillar mop top hiding his repulsive ferret face, and a mealy off-key warble. A tall Marfanoid Hyde who collected blond babes using fourth-grade repeating lyrics and simple chords that must have been borrowed from the Sex Pistols or X or some greater talent. If it could work for Joey, it could work for a balding homunculus who sang like Petty into cellophane after inhaling low-dose helium. And now he was on stage with Marky fucking Ramone. Holy crap, Joey would probably be up here, too—paying homage to the next one if he hadn't croaked a decade before.

"Rock and Roll High School." Roars. "Froggy Went a Snortin.'" Roars. "Claudette Wants Flowers." Roars. Even "Fuck Charles Goren." Roars.

By the time Tee Nash was ready to join for the penultimate song of the set, there was not one ass on a seat or the floor in the whole motherfucking MSG. The mosh was pushed up so tight, there was room for another thousand in the back, if the fire marshal would acquiesce.

"Lola's Room" ended to roars, and there was no hesitation or reluctance to be the barker, the front man. "New York, New York. Thank you, New York. We've got a song or two left. Billy Markwell, what did you tell me when I informed you I had written this next song?"

"I think I told you we were going to hell."

"Yes, you did, Goat. Not the first time you've told me that, brother. Going to hell. But let me ask you, Goat, if we're going to hell, you enjoying the ride?"

Billy Markwell answered with a paint by numbers copy of a Charlie Daniels riff.

"I'm glad to hear that. Now, I asked someone else about this song, didn't I, Tee Nash."

The boss walked on stage, in three-inch brown platform loafers and a tan linen three-piece Armani suit, to a colossal roar.

"And what was that you told me, boss?"

"I told your ass to save me a part, Brother Horgan."

And with that, an extended version of "Shit Back" exploded in the Garden. Tee had Michael Hampton and Billy Bass Nelson from the Parliament lined up at the back of the stage in a concert-uncredited cameo, assuring that the twenty-two thousand would be blown away, and blown away they were.

Melvin's job was simple. He had the verses, sung to a sparse drum and bass accompaniment, but more of a rap than a song—Melvin Horgan impersonating Marshall Mathers impersonating Ice T. And then each time the refrain kicked in, there was such a cacophony of perfect synchronicity of instruments and voice that Melvin, who was supposed to harmonize, slunk back under the lights to listen and spectate. And he found a spot, under the floods but over the floor lights. This was the perfect cavern of colored lights—yellows below and reds above—from which to glimpse out, like from an arrow port in an ancient castle, into the crowd and get some definition of the faces and the signs and the unfettered adulation—for what, he couldn't figure. For some words and dots he'd written because he was angry or jealous or desperate or miserable. And one of them—strutting or dancing or simply swaying with one hand, maybe holding up a fathead or a "Marry me, Goat" sign—wouldn't make it past the next song, wouldn't be alive ten minutes hence, and as he peered out through that peephole into the slaughterhouse, he knew irrevocably that no matter how much they loved him and no matter how many times they performed to a similar end, he would never really care.

The song finished in a bold, improvised clash between the guest performers, leaving Billy and Bebe playing air instruments to look engaged, while the ringers interspaced notes that sonically coupled in the air of the Garden, literally guitar-thrusting itself into the private regions of the base and grinding, then engorged again and thrusting, thrusting, while the bass notes were rapturous, exploding in air in climactic exhilaration. It was really too much—spectacular, to be certain, but not at all what the author intended. It was a melodical usurping, and it pissed Melvin off. The whole band had been pinch-hit for, and he could hear Bob Sheppard, the Yankees PA guy: "Now guitaring (guitaring) for Markwell, from the Parliament Funkadelic (delic), Michael (Michael) Hampton (Hampton)." It was high time for someone to die.

When the roar receded, and the guest performers left the stage, Melvin again assumed the mike. "Tee Nash and some friends from the Parliament, fucking awesome. Fucking awesome. On bass, Bebe Mustang. Let's give him a hand. Not a lot of people know this, but Bebe's sister was my first lay, right Bebe? I was fifteen, and she was—what?—thirty-two, Bebe? Still in that special—what was it?—a halfway house. Sweet memories, Bebe. Coming in your thirty-two-year-old sister's mouth while she was coloring pictures of Frosty the Snowman. You never forget your first, even when she's Simple Simon, twice your age, eh, Bebe? No, nooo?"

Bebe just stood there like a loyal professional performer, shaking his head and silently refuting the Troll.

"Bebe Mustang. I just proved it—coolest-of-the-cool motherfucker. Someone said that shit to me, I'd rip their fucking tongue out, and I don't even have a sister.

"Tiny Atlas on the drums. Biggest cock in rock and roll, and that's the motherfucking truth, no matter what Melissa Ethridge says—she's close, but Tiny's bigger. Anyone interested, we have this deal: I stretch you out to get prepared for Tiny—believe me, it's better that way.

"And Billy Markwell, Billy Goat. My best friend since we was in middle school. He learned the guitar and I couldn't get past 'Chopsticks,' so I play the fucking tambourine."

Melvin paced back and forth before continuing, stopping and starting once or twice to encourage louder roars. He turned once more to the audience. "You know what's coming up next, New York? You know what to do, just go to the lobby if you want. Go the fuck home; we don't need you. Hell, Tee Nash asked me to stall with this microphone shit. Fuckers halfway to Long Island by now, damned craven motherfucker. We have had a lot of people commenting about this song, and the—what's the word?—consequences. Turns out, a lot of people care deeply about the cause and effect of 'Millicent DeGroenfeld Rice.' Truth is, I can't explain it. Before, we were nobodies. Now we're playing the fucking Madison Square Garden. Remorse. I'm always asked about remorse. Thirty thousand people croak in the Indian subcontinent a week from starvation; not once have I ever cared about that. Why would I lose a minute over one person every couple of days over here? So, here's a song you may have heard about. It's about some stripper who"—here he spoke in an awful British accent—"*did herself in.* And because I was hungover in a bathroom where someone left a paper, we're famous and about twenty people are dead. This fucking world."

There are bands, Melvin thought in advance of the cue, *that try to force last songs of the concert, fuck the encore. You could play anything in the encore, and the mindless fucks will wail with glee. They're getting extra songs. Oh boy. Boston got three, but we got four; they must like us more. No, we ran out of fucking ordinance time in Boston, you smarmy bastards. You can't force the last song. Cobain knew that. It's not "Teen Spirit." That can open, but to close, "Territorial Pissings." That's a closer. Scream yourself offstage. The audience is in a frenzy, and he gets some extra time for the vocal cords to recover. Something building to a conclusion. "Let There Be Rock!" Not a beginning or a middle. A definitive end. An exclamation point. A climax with the encore and a bit of cuddling and snuggling and maybe some fingering while the Viagra kicks in and you can do it again in the next town the next day. "Man in the Box." A sense of finality, the essence of this band, what they signify, what their underlying mission is. And now, as if amplifying, the new zenith of what can be accomplished at the end of a rock show in three verses, four refrains, and a goddamned derivative angel-of-death solo.*

We give these millennial twats an inkling of what it was like on D-Day or in the jungles of 'Nam without having to serve. We give them a thrill and bragging rights to their twat girlfriends and boyfriends, twat brothers and sisters, too. Bragging rights in the twat universe, as if they did risk something for the greater good as opposed to just playing a giant one-in-twenty-thousand game of Duck, Duck, Goose with the grim reaper. A chance for the slack-jawed tools who live life in the corners, perpetually looking at the ground, hiding on their devices, retreating from their Xbox existence to walk tall for a week or two until the sense of accomplishment fades into some more elusive goal of slaying a warlock or dragon or progressing to the final competitors of a virtual battle royale.

Melvin retreated to his corridor of visualization as his vocal part ended and the death solo began. Twenty thousand people on the ground and three decks was a *Where's Waldo?* challenge for sure, but he wanted to watch. Melvin started in the mosh and scanned the patrons. He found signs, fatheads, and more signs, fading in and out based upon the pattern of illumination. There were upwards of fifty of them at the event, scattered in the mosh and the stands. The official ones were licensed, but most were crude magnifications of his face hastily pasted on placards, circle awkwardly on square.

Somehow, he knew she would be there. The tunnel of illumination, like a worm hole, came in and out of view, but he was certain he saw her, near the front, but maybe ten or fifteen rows back. He craned his head and tried to stare at her as she faded in and out. Her head bobbed behind a green-haired punk, to the right of a hulking Black man in a dog collar, and to the left of, well, himself, as she—the light coming into a more discernable fractal array—revealed herself to be in the arms of a frumpy mouse in a pink party dress with black lipstick, jet-black hair in a pony. This girl stood ten, no twelve rows back, with a fathead Melvin Horgan in one hand, riding it high above her head into the air, and a fathead of his prostitute in the other.

His own fathead he got. But the rationale for a fathead of a disappearing migratory tart escaped him, escaped him, escaped him. Unless . . .

Chapter 23:
I Want It Now

They arrived at the Mayflower in formation, a V, more accurately an upside-down V, a flying wedge really. Vamp was the ball carrier with Valkyrie in the lead, Venus and Vixen in the second row, and Vassar and Valerie on the back line. They marched in choreographed hip-hop cadence into the lobby, brushing past a young Asian and an elderly Black doorman, who opened French doors in their over-ornamented Buckingham Palace replicas.

In the lobby itself meandered a business group with a sign indicating Georgetown University Faculty of Arts and Sciences, English Department. A bespeckled man in a corduroy jacket with tan leather elbow patches was divided from a frumpy blond in a suit and tie as they wedged through the gathering and across the lobby and up to the elevator.

Down the lobby hallway they strutted, and for reasons she could not explain, Millicent thought of the *Madeline* books her grandmother used to read to her as a child, the orderly processional of the orphan girls in Paris. They stayed in formation into the elevator, and the six of them rode alone and silently up to the luxury suite on the seventh floor of the grand old Mayflower. Down the yellow corridor, they marched deliberately, resisting the urge to touch the gold-patterned wallpaper adorned with frescos of crocuses and lilacs. The door was propped open, and Vamp whispered something to Valkyrie as she peeked in, and then when she was satisfied she swung open the door. They stopped just inside the doorway as Vamp held up her hand to wait and survey the scene. Millicent craned her head to assess what kind of mess she had reluctantly volunteered for.

What she spied was about fifteen men and a couple of women already in attendance. The unexpected aspect was that there was no loud, modern music playing, just a sixty-inch TV playing *Willy Wonka and the Chocolate Factory*. They were at the part of the move where Veruca Salt sings "I Want It Now." They were mid-scene when the women entered, but as soon as Mr. Salt plummeted down the rotten-egg chute, the scene started up again from the beginning, entering the laying room, and soon enough, "I want a goose that lays golden eggs for Christmas" led into the most remarkable acting performance during a song in movie history. When Veruca exited through the chute once more, with no one paying attention to the new arrivals, one of the guests, a sawed-off older man with proportions that looked like an achondroplastic dwarf, incompletely genetically penetrated, exclaimed to the crowd, "I would so do her. I am not a kiddy fiddler, but I would so do that kid. Look at those lips! I would gladly do fifteen to twenty for those fucking lips." Not getting a response he continued, "And if I don't get the things I am after, I'm going to scream."

"Please don't scream again, Troll."

"I just want you to acknowledge, Goat, that you would give let's say at least ten years of your life to have those little girl lips around your cock. I know you would, we all would." The man he was talking to, a short sallow blond with sideburns about a third of the way towards mutton chops, took out his phone and entered something and replied, "That's Julie Dawn Cole, Troll. Not bad looking for an old broad. Yeah, I'd hit that."

"Not now, moron. She's old, haggard. Fuck that—1971 Julie Whateverthefuck. Immortalized in time with that party dress and shoes, and those lips. 'I want the Troll's dick, and I want it now.' Tiny, you'd fuck that girl."

A massive light-skinned Black man, sitting facing the TV, with a tall dark girl on his knee, laughed and said, "The little girl, Melvin? That's silly. I might hurt her."

"But if she just sucked you off, Tiny. That would be okay. That wouldn't hurt her."

"She's a little girl, Troll. That's funny."

Millicent immediately regretted her decision to come. She tried unsuccessfully to tune out.

Millicent DeGroenfeld Rice

It's a couple of hours. You are trained to find the alpha in the group, then the beta. Who's the money man, the spigot. Work the spigot. He will keep feeding girls towards the followers. Push the secondaries towards them. Vamp and Valkyrie get the alphas and the betas. You sister, get the spigot, the sophisticate, the money. But it can't be this moron, preening on about molesting a twelve-year-old in a fifty-year-old film. Keep quiet—let Vamp work the room and the spigot will declare.

"Who could control himself—those cherry-red lips and Veruca, what a fucking actress, pivoting on a dime from psycho, angry bitch to calm sweetheart to homicidal maniac in thirty seconds while singing, 'And if I don't get the things I am after, I'm going to scream.'" The little man ran over to a paper towel rack in the kitchenette of the suite and pulled the towels with him across the room. The big man and the greasy blond laughed. Otherwise, across the room, there was some acknowledgment of the rumpus, but no choreographed accompaniments and barely a ripple in the conversations on the outskirts. Skinny-jeaned, big-hair leather guy kept talking to Daria Goth, one firetruck earring and pasty, chubby sound-or-light guy kept flirting with failed MMA roadie, obviously not gay, here by obligation. On the far side of the room, big-mustached dragon tattoo was showing something on guitar to goateed, hair-band neophyte, a confluent tattoo, leather-vest handlebar and somewhat chiseled friend of a friend, either a punter, kicker, or long snapper or a participant from one of the Caucasian-dominant competitive sports.

It was seeming more likely that the little guy was the alpha and also the spigot. He was Vamp's then. Cocaine residue apparent on a black table by a kitchenette. The drug of choice of hotel guests everywhere—immune to the smoke detector and devoid of paraphernalia and cleanup. Valkyrie, for one, would suck your cock or pussy dry for a couple of lines, tough, in-control bitch she pretended to be.

"Hey, everyone. Our girlfriends are here. It's about fucking time."

Only the blond and the big guy seemed to hear. One of the roadie-types craned his head, then returned to flipping coins off his elbow, catching them in his palm. Empty minibar bottles on the floor by the television spelled out "Blow Job." Underwear and socks were stuck in the chandelier. Bigger bottles on the kitchenette counter were arranged in descending order of height with mixers in a mirror image of shortest to tallest. Millicent turned to the bar, scanning to see if there were sufficient ingredients for a proper sidecar. Silence lingered as the gargoyle paused the video with an image of Veruca running away from a . . . flock? Murder? Parliament? Conspiracy? No, a symphony of Oompa Loompas seared on the screen. Deliberately, he approached the six women, flat-footed flip-flops scraping along the floor, almost tripping as the edge barely evaded a power cable connecting a not-yet-used blender to an outlet across the room.

"Girlfriends!" the little man exclaimed. "I'm a bit fucked up right now, so you may have to remind me which of you lovely bitches is with me."

The posing began: Wednesday six p.m., best you got pouts and purrs designed to entice the one Yugoslav attaché to bypass the other five girls on the floor. Only Millicent wasn't scrutinizing the alpha. She was craning her neck, thinking about which of the golden-ticket holders would be left once Veruca went down the bad egg chute. The alpha took a lap around the girls, still in formation. When he returned to face Valkyrie at the head of the pack, the six spread out, with Vamp flanking Valkyrie and Millicent the farthest to the right.

"Honey. Don't tease," pleaded Vamp. "You know there's nothing any of us wouldn't do for our men." She sauntered up to the alpha and put her arm over his balding head and around his back. "Now where do we start?"

The man pulled up to Vamp and smelled her '70s curl and took one more survey like a general assessing a platoon at attention. "What's your name, honey?" he asked Venus.

"I'm Venus." Her Culpeper drawl accentuated by nerves brought out an extra vowel or two in the pronunciation.

"Okay, who is it that just loves white Southern girls? Tiny, this is Miss Venus. Teach her a thing or two, fix that overbite while you're at it. Don't worry, sugar. Tiny's a good strong buck, just what you crackers go for."

Vamp looked curiously down at the little man assessing her squad and tried to remain in charge. "Be kind to Venus, boys. She's just a young'un, an innocent babe."

Venus glanced up at Tiny and looked down, hesitating before inching towards the behemoth by the television.

"Don't worry, babe. Let you in on a secret. Tiny's only half Black, so you're only half going to hell."

There was scattered laughter from leather coat and grubby blond. The big guy hardly seemed aware he was being discussed and wore that W. Bush stare of ambivalent ignorance.

"Now what do we have here?" Melvin ran his clubbed nails across Vixen's nape, front to back. "This one's my little baby bear. What's your name, doll?" Vixen looked up to him with doe eyes and a Betty Boop finger on mouth pout, which could bring the house down on a Friday night. But before she could speak, Vamp interceded, "That's our Vixen. She's new." More clearly, she hadn't earned the alpha or the spigot.

"New, maybe you need to be broken in, baby doll."

"Darling, I didn't catch your name. But I'm Vamp. Who do I have the pleasure of—"

"I'm no pleasure, Vamp. I like that, Vamp. You can call me Melvin."

Vamp leaned in and whispered just loud enough for the other girls to hear. "Melvin, we want all of you to have a good time. And we will put on a great show and show you a fabulous time. But we're strippers, darling. We're not pros. D.C. law, we're topless, not full, but fully ready for a little roleplay. It's a distraction, something fun to do. But we're dancers, hon. Not hoes. Now, someone's generous, wants to strike a deal for private, can't say I've never. But that's the lady's prerogative. Anything else, any pressure, anything out of bounds, and we will call it a night, and our manager, Vince, has a retrieval team you don't want to meet. We clear, Melvin, honey?"

"Clear? I think I'm in love. Vixen—welcome and feel free to mingle. Vamp, who's this lovely creature next to you?"

Valkyrie stood tall and proud. "I'm Valkyrie," she exulted like a marine.

"Valkyrie? Ain't the Valkyries supposed to be Nordic? You're fucking gorgeous. I'd let you carry me by the dick to Valhalla any day, but you're a Spic. Maybe you should call yourself Vatos or Valencia, or Violetta. But Valkyrie, that's weird. No offense. I'd let you sit on my face anytime, but just seems wrong."

"Valkyrie's not a race. It's a state of mind."

"Well, quite literally, it is a race—a race of Norse warriors. And Norse warriors don't generally look like they're one day of forgetting sunscreen out from shuffling tarot cards and wearing a Kaftan. I like you, though. I'll keep a song on my dance card for you. 'Living La Vida Loca' or 'Constant

Craving.' But what do we have here?" Melvin moved down the line to Valerie as Valkyrie stared through him in disgust. "What's your name, angel?"

"I'm Valerie!"

"Of course, you are, Valerie, you are absolutely adorable."

Valerie lit up with a smile indistinguishable from a smile she would have given in response to the same comment from a playboy billionaire Leo DiCaprio, the Bachelor. "Thank you for the complement, Mr. Man."

"You don't belong here, with these others. Goat, look at this girl. This is John Cusack's girlfriend from every teen movie. It's that girl from that toothpaste commercial you used to jizz to. Wholesome, that's the word. You're wholesome. What the fuck are you doing here with"—he pulled up close to her and whispered—"these tramps. You should leave—maybe take Goat with you, he's the best of us—and leave." With that, Melvin paused and stared directly into her chest.

"Mister, mister. These women are lovely. They're my friends, and I'm proud to work beside each of them."

"Valerie, that's enough. Let the man have his opinion," reasoned Vamp.

"Yes, let the nice man have his opinion. Darling, I've changed my mind. I need a redeemer, and it shall be thou. Maybe I need some wholesome, at least for a night. Let me put you down for 'Goody Two-shoes,' and can you strip to 'You Light Up My Life'? I want that one. I would like you, dear, misplaced Valerie, to grind your twat over my prick during 'You Light Up My Life.' Do that, and all of your sisters will get smiley faces or gold stars." Melvin gave Valerie a saccharine grin, to which she held back tears save for just a hint of lacrimal cloudiness.

Melvin continued to the last of the women, Millicent DeGroenfeld Rice, aka Vassar. Who knew if Vassar had a maternal instinct, or whether it had been systematically eradicated over the years, but for reasons beyond the obvious resentment for the treatment of her co-workers, she was seething by the time Melvin cozied up his snaggleteeth up to her one-eighth, maybe from the confit, one-seventh of a double chin.

Melvin, as he edged up to her, feigned a double take. He then backed up and chuckled, not saying a word, no "what's your name," no lurid glares. Millicent, as he backed away, shot at him, "You have a problem, Iggy?"

"No problem, no problem at all, Gypsy Rose. Only I guess one of us is confused. Maybe it's me. I was under the impression we were throwing an end-of-the-tour party with coke and smack and booze and titties, and it looks like you are here for a PTA meeting. And it concerns me that there's a fourteen-year-old at home begging for help with some calculus problem and his mommy is away because she got her dates wrong. What's your name, madam? Whom do I have the pleasure of addressing?"

"Her name is Vassar, and you're damned lucky she's here. She's not usually one for private parties. She's practically management," returned Vamp with something of a half-hearted scowl.

"You mean, she's got seniority?" Melvin doubled over tickled by his rather obvious retort. "And what the fuck, Vassar? Like the college in New York? I assume that's not your real name; you guys have the V thing going. Vassar, is that because you're established in 1861?" Again, Melvin peeled off, this time hiding behind a sofa to disguise Amstel bubbles oozing through his nostrils.

The dilemma of the service industry. Is the customer always right? It's either a declarative statement or a rhetorical question. In the theoretical, physical violence or credible threats of physical violence negate the assumption that the client is infallible, but how about emotional intimidation, bullying, or even unwanted ribbing? When does the employee rage? Where is that line crossed, and how does it happen that different individuals straddle disparate lines? Maybe Vamp would have ripped out his larynx—one well-aimed thumbnail designed to neuter his voice box eternally. Valkyrie may have aimed for his manhood with a sharpened stiletto. But Millicent felt she couldn't realistically retaliate. "Pretty funny," she said. "Look, this is supposed to be fun. Yeah, I'm a few years older than my friends here. But I've learned a thing or two you might appreciate, if you give it a try."

Melvin came back over to Millicent and sniffed her like a dog sniffs a hydrant. He brushed against her bosom and peered down below her leather skirt at her bare legs.

"Learned a thing or two, from who? Martha Stewart? I'm not here to learn how to make a casserole. And fun is the name of the game. Popping Valerie's cherry, that's fun. A threesome with young Tina Turner and Rosalita here, that's fun. Watching Tiny widen the sweet neck's twat two sizes, that's fun.

But trying to concentrate on tits and not being able to take my eyes off of your varicose veins, just not that fun. Not fun at all, in fact."

Millicent tried to stare ahead, pick a pithy remark, and not for God's sake look down, but she couldn't help a glance down, and she recognized a couple of blue discolorations in her calf. Zits for the middle-aged, heralding an incipient transition from youth into middle age. With this harkening mingled an understanding that this hovering through life was unacceptable. The room had gone silent. The television muted and conversations paused, anticipating Melvin's next move. Like a debate, she had rebuttal time but chose not to use it. Instead, the room melted from her, and she spent every joule from that last Tom Collins to stay stoic as his evil stare penetrated her.

Melvin waited his turn and, after an acceptable pause, made his final move. "No response? Look, I'm an empathetic guy. I know I'm being a dick. I want to make it up to ya, Vassar. Here's a hundred bucks." He threw five twenties at her feet. "Take that for not taking your clothes off. Head home with a nice tip, and take the night off on me, Gypsy Lee."

Millicent didn't budge. The bills lay scattered. One partially covered the pinky toe on her right open stiletto.

"Fuck. Here's another hundred. Use it to take a typing course. Get yourself an employable skill, Vassar, because, let's face it, this is not your future." The little man gave a self-satisfied chortle and let the moment breathe. "Well now that we know our girlfriends, let the games begin."

Millicent looked at the others, who fanned out into the room as they'd been instructed. Two-and-a-half hours, each of them to receive two fifteen-minute breaks, and then they were free agents, off the clock and free to depart or stay and renegotiate. Millicent successfully fought back tears. She kept her head high, stared into the eyes of her tormentor, and headed back towards the door.

"Nah, nah. Vassar, sweetheart. I was fucking joking. Stay. It's my nature, just joking. You're still hot."

"Vassar! Hold on," pleaded Vamp. If she left, they'd all be chafed and sore in the morning.

"Tell Vince to go fuck himself. I quit."

The little crag man followed her out the door, down the hall towards the elevator, cutting the corner as the hallway turned, and brushing her unintentionally aside as he cut off her walking lane. "Look. I'm sorry. Come back, doll. I didn't mean anything by it. I'm just an asshole."

Millicent didn't say anything. She kept her head high and entered the elevator, turning her head away from the man as he tried to engage, apologizing, rationalizing. He continued to try to dissuade her from leaving all the way down to the lobby and until she got into a yellow cab just dropping off from the airport. She never said a word, but as the cab drove away, she took one last glimpse through the cab window into the narrow gray eyes of Melvin Horgan before averting once more, to gaze up Connecticut Avenue towards the solitude of home.

Chapter 24:
That Magic Feeling

By the time Melvin retreated from his viewing cave, the solo was half over. He remembered the name: Vassar. That strange alias for the aging petulant stripper at that party in D.C. He looked out at the twenty thousand souls, all on their feet, chanting in rhythm, and her perpetual adroit aloofness seemed inconsequential. He remembered what he said about the typewriter course, and thought to himself, *Man, that was a good one.*

He crawled out from his peephole back onto the stage, and once again, everything blurred in front of him. He took his tambourine in hand and started a jig in beat with the guitar. *Two hundred dollars for a typing course! It wasn't gang-raping Courtney the Hole, but it was pretty damned funny.* On stage, he hit the tambourine and hopped two steps in rhythm with the beat on the right and then leaned back on the left for a beat. Then leaning forward towards the right for a couple of beats, then back to the left. It was his transformative frolic, from a gargoyle to a Christmas elf, from an angry garden gnome to the motherfucking Lucky Charms leprechaun.

And as he cavorted on stage, basking in equal measures in the satisfaction of his conquest that night of Vassar, and of their mutual obsession, he noticed his heart pounding. Love. All these years without, and now, finally, even Melvin "the Troll" Horgan was experiencing sweaty palms, shallow breathing, lightheaded, heart pounding and racing—love. Somehow he'd fallen in love with Vassar, and based upon her coy pursuit, he was pretty sure she felt the same way.

Love, love, love. If he could play the damned guitar, he would do the first song of the encore as an homage, "Girl from Mars" or "A Girl Like

You." But just on the tambourine, and with his shitty voice, they'd laugh him offstage. He couldn't just out and confess to twenty thousand strangers, and maybe just maybe one Vassar, in the audience. He had to own up vocally, and the more his heart thumped, the more saturated in love he felt, and the more determined he was to share his elation. He wanted to scream out "Vassar" like Benjamin Braddock in the eaves, hoping his elusive paramour was furtively cloaked in the throng. But then he was conflicted, because if she was in the crowd, her life was at some risk, if only one in twenty thousand. As he considered this, he realized his heart was pounding harder, and he briefly considered stopping the song on her account, but on the huge stage, he suddenly felt powerless to fall back to Tiny or stage right to Goat.

The light show of the flourish started, and the sequences of strobes interwoven with streams of red, white, yellow, and blue blinded him, and through the haze, he saw her face, at first distant and high as if in the cheap seats to his left, and then in the middle section on the right. Finally, she seemed to migrate out of the crowd, floating towards him, not in the harlot's garb of the hotel room, but in a lovely yellow sundress, hair styled simply and elegantly in strawberry-blond bangs, freckles illuminated. Freckles on her face, freckles on the top of her bosom, exposed by the sundress. Just a hint, a sixteenth, of a double chin. Gone were the trampy hoops he remembered from the night she left his bed, to be usurped by that singing cunt, replaced by simple small gold hoops, and he half imagined, no, knew that he'd bought them and presented them himself as an anniversary present.

As she approached with a huge grin, he wanted to tell her she had won, but the music was too loud, the pounding in his heart too intense. But the song had to end soon, and all would be revealed. Before he knew it, he was on his knees, in preparation for subjugation to love. All the crappy, sappy love songs he detested, trite blech from Air Supply, 10cc, Boyz II Men, Lionel Richie, Foreigner, WHAM, NSYNC, darted through his head, somehow louder and louder than the boys beside him, and suddenly they seemed meaningful.

But just as he started gasping for air, the figure turned and floated and faded away into the smoke drifting up into the rafters of the Garden, and somehow, he understood that she was gone, never had been real, and he would never see her again. Whatever this was, love or otherwise, was unrequited, but he somehow still felt more uplifted than he ever had been before.

If there was any realization by the end that he was dying and that somehow Millicent had enacted some form of spectral revenge, you wouldn't have known by the massive grin on his mug as he lay prostate behind a large speaker and faded into his everlasting oblivion.

The End

Acknowledgments

The author would like to thank Chris White for editorial assistance, especially in correcting an especially egregious error in musical attribution.

www.ingramcontent.com/pod-product-compliance
Lightning Source LLC
Chambersburg PA
CBHW021722310125
21212CB00017B/133/J